# ADVENTURES IN LOGRES

IAN CLEARY

D1737986

# DEDICATION

This book is dedicated to my loving parents who

have provided so much support along the way.

# ACKNOWLEDGMENTS

I'd like to acknowledge all the scholars who have contributed to Arthurian literature to make the genre the living entity that it is today. I would also like to thank the sources that helped to make this book a possibility. The scholar and critical thinker Rachel Bromwich was indispensable for her countless contributions to the genre. Additionally, I'd like to thank the scribes who wrote the *Prose Vulgate & Post Vulgate*, the *High Book of the Grail*, *Wace's Brut*, *Taliesin*, *The Chetrien de Troyes* romances, Malory and Geoffrey of Monmouth. These authors were absolutely critical for my research. The second part of this book is highly indebted to Norris Lacy's translations of the cycle. Also, many compliments for the redaction materials that Nigel Bryant's translation of Perceforest and the Grail Continuations provided.

"The king established all the knights and gave them riches and lands — and charged them never to do outrageous things, and always to flee treason, and to give mercy unto he who asks mercy, upon pain of forfeiture; and always to do right by ladies, damsels, and women and widows so that no harm is done to them. also, that no man should take up arms in a wrongful quarrel, not for love or for the goods of the world."

-Sir *Thomas Malory*

# PART 1: 1 Marigart the Red at Raguidel Castle

Hector of the Fens was a most powerful knight among the many of King Arthur's court. It goes without saying that he could do so many deeds of prowess that he often left alone in search of adventure. Knight's often embarked on quests to attain greater renown and that was just what Hector did one hot summer day as he rode through the forest seeking adventure. A good knight was both an arbiter of equity and establisher of law. By his sword he governed in places that were lawless, as there were many who lived wickedly at this time. Here now about the dispossessed lady who was saved by the valiant Hector and why chivalry was so essential to establishing law in a land of treachery and oppression.

When he trotted along the road, in pleasant spirits, a dwarf on a mule waved him down and said: "Knight, go no farther. You will surely meet your death." Hector replied: "Whatever do you mean?" Though the dwarf only said: "I can't say anything more. You've been warned!"

A brave knight like Hector was not disturbed by a mere warning from a twisted dwarf. He kept going until he reached a large stone slab in the middle of the road. On the stone was etched an inscription: "DO NOT GO BEYOND THIS POINT WITHOUT EXPECTING SHAME AND DEFEAT." Again, Hector did not heed the warning for there was simply no reason to. He continued at a trot until two young women approached him and said: "I am very sad to see you come this way." And Hector replied: "How do you mean?" They said: "You seem most handsome and courteous but since you have come this way you will die and that is a great shame."

Hector said no more but commended them to God and continued on his way. Now he came to a strong, wide river with deep black water and tall banks. There was a bridge of stone ten yards wide that went over it. Near the bridge there was an elm tree with a lady sitting beneath it who said: "Since you have come this way you will surely drown." He replied: "Whatever do you mean?" The lady said: "The knight on the other side of the river, do you see him?" He nodded that he did, for there was a big knight in full armor on the other side of the bridge, seemingly fixed upon him. "He is the best knight in all the land. He will joust with you and put you with all the others who have been defeated. By God, every knight he defeats he hurls into the rapid river below, along with their horse. I would advise you take another path to avoid him." Hector observed the situation and replied: "You seem to think so highly of him. I'll challenge him head on and you can watch if he is as good as you say."

Hector said adieu to the fair lady and rode up to the bridge. He found a lance leaning on a tree and he grabbed it, securing it in his fist. Then he tucked his shield into his shoulder tightly so that he was well protected. In this way he rode onto the bridge and the knight on the opposite side told him to watch out because he was going to attack him. Hector said that he would do all he could to defend himself, and the other said he would do the same.

Without any more delay, the two knights galloped towards each other so they met in a terrible clash. Their lances were leveled and collided into one another's shields so that they splintered into tiny fragments. Neither knight was unhorsed. So they rallied back around with swords drawn and Hector gave the knight such a heavy blow on the right side of his head that he fell from his horse into the water. Luckily, he held tightly to the pillar that supported the bridge, otherwise he would have surely drowned by the weight of his armor. Hector glanced back at the lady by the elm tree who had warned him about the knight. She was astonished. He cordially bowed to her and spurred off towards the castle.

Right before he was about to enter the gate it slammed shut in front of his face. "What gives?" he attested. The gate keeper poked his head up from behind the walls and said: "Before you enter you must pledge that you will rid the castle of a wicked custom." Hector replied: "If there is an evil custom here I will do all in my power to vanquish it." When this was settled, he opened the gate for him. Hector was eager to learn about these evil customs. The people came around him and said: "We will surely tell you all about it. The knight who is lord of this castle is evil and treacherous. Yet, because he is so good at fighting he does what he pleases, killing all who come this way. Every knight he defeats he does so through guile and then shames them by dragging them through the streets, naked. So, since you are a foreign knight, I would beware! Oh, if that was all he did we'd hardly implore you. Every month he takes one of our daughters that is a virgin and rapes her. After he is finished with her he gives her to his servants as their concubine. He has done this with over forty maidens. Anyone who stands up to him is put to death, you must help us!"

Hector was really incensed about this, because he had never heard of such evil deeds before. It was truly a lawless land and, being a pillar of chivalry, it was his duty to help the people who were so unjustly oppressed. So Hector asked them: "Where can I find this knight?" They willingly took him to a garden that was hedged in all around by rose bushes and brambles. It was a very beautiful place. In the middle of the garden there was a large field about a square acre and it was surrounded by sharp stakes. Nearby there was a pine tree with an ivory horn hung from it. They told him that if he blew the horn the knight would come. So he gave the horn a loud blow and, sure enough, a knight emerged from a nearby tower.

He was armed except for his helmet, which he held in his hands. He was on a swift white charger and his arms were completely red, as was his shield. He had flaming red hair and freckles too. He was quite handsome except for the evil look he had on his face. You could tell by his countenance he was a violent man up to no good. He said: "Be on your guard, knight. For I will do my utmost to hurt you." Hector replied: "You look to your own safety, for I have never hated a knight more."

So their horses rode into the open field and charged into one another, creating a thunderous din. The charging hooves were swifter than lightning and tore up the grass in a flurry. The violent collision was head to head, body to body and horse to horse. It sent them both flying from their mounts and tumbling to the ground. Their lances were shattered to bits and either knight was stunned by the forceful impact. Then an even more violent sword fight ensued after they leapt up from the ground. They delivered mighty blows so that sparks flew, shields shattered and hauberks tore at the shoulder and waist. Blood spurted all over the grass and they ran about hacking and hewing one another senselessly. Both knights were strong and able so that they were exhausted from all the fighting.

Then Hector felt a renewal of strength and began pounding the red knight with such forceful blows that they penetrated to the flesh many times. Often, the knight who has right on his side, is given divine strength over his enemy. In this way was Hector refreshed by the Holy Spirit. The red knight could do little but put his shield over his head to protect himself from the flurry of blows. Hector continued the assault, blow after blow, until he broke through his armor and tore away the flesh from his arm. The red knight dropped his sword and cried out in anguish. Then Hector tackled him and threw him to the ground. He ripped the helm from his head and hit him in the head with the pommel of his sword so forcefully that blood came gushing out. Then he threatened to cut off his head. That wicked red knight refused to admit defeat so Hector chopped his head off so that it was severed from the body and flew through the air. The spectators all wondered at this for it was a marvel to them.

Just then Hector, quite pleased with himself, asked the people: "Is there anything else to be done?" They replied: "Yes! The lady of the castle is held captive. She is imprisoned in a cave below that is guarded by two lions." Hector said: "Whatever is she doing down there?" Then he realized it didn't matter at the moment and bade them lead him on towards the cave so he could free her.

So they went under the tower to the cave, telling him that the lady was held therein. Hector, brave as he was, made the sign of the cross on his face and went into the perilous cave, where two treacherous lions guarded the lady. Fortunately, he could see clearly in the cave because the light coming through the cracks at the top. The lions were massive and attached to iron chains. They each guarded a side of the path so that no one could easily en-

8

ter without being ravaged. Hector drew his sword and held his shield close so that it covered his face and chest. The lions seemed quite hungry for they roared mightily and clawed at the dirt, eagerly awaiting his approach.

Hector assailed the one on the left first, for it was closest to him. When the lion lunged at him he cut off its two front legs. Then, when it wallowed about, he struck him a blow upon the head that cleft the skull in two. It goes without saying that he died!

Then Hector went after the other lion, who was chained on the right side of the path. This lion attacked with his sharp claws and seized his shield. It ran at him so forcefully that it took away his shield and knocked him over. Just then, the lion's claws became stuck in the shield, that was very strong and sturdy. Hector got back up and pushed on the shield, forcing the lion back. Then he struck the lion on the face so that his lower jaw was detached. Then, with a mighty blow, he sliced off the lion's head, who was unable to do anything because the shield was stuck in his claws. When the lion was dead, Hector removed the claws from his shield and put it back over his shoulder by the leather strap.

Hector saw the lady and cut the iron shackles that bound her. It goes without saying that the lady welcomed him very cordially. He commended her to God and took her from the cave, where all the people were extremely joyful. The first thing they all did was gather at the church to thank God for the blessings they had received and the freeing of the lady.

Afterwards everyone in the town put on their finest raiments and celebrated. They greeted one another joyfully, dancing and caroling throughout the streets and playing games. They called Hector the "flower of all knights" which was a unique honor to be bestowed. Then Hector was led to the great hall which was splendidly arrayed in fine silk cloths and drapery. The hall was strewn about with fresh grass that smelled very sweet. He was unarmed by the people and given a silk mantle to wear.

Then the lady and Hector sat at the table and talked. Hector was eager to know her name, so he asked her. "I am Angale of Raguidel, which is the name of this castle. Is it true that you have slain Marigart the Red?"

"My lady, who is that?"

"The one who was lord of this castle."

"Then it is true, he is dead, that vile creature."

"How did he die?"

"With the edge of my blade I lopped off his head. You may have the body if you'd like."

"You are a most blessed man to have done such a good deed! Let me tell you why. It was one day that I learned he loved me. He begged me to love him in return but I knew that he was a wicked and incontinent man so I resisted him. He sent his brother as a messenger to my chamber almost every day, repeating his words of love. I told his brother never to return, but, he was so angry at my reply that he said some terrible things in front of my family to me. My cousin heard what he had said and was so offended by it that he killed him. Then Marigart the Red heard what had happened and planned his revenge. He came to my castle in the night and killed those who didn't surrender to him, including my cousin. Then he came to my chamber and raped me. He refused to take me as his wife afterwards but imprisoned me in that cave as you saw. He refused to free me and said that I could only be freed if a knight of prowess came and saved me. I remained a prisoner in the cave with the lions for twelve years, eating just bread and water brought to me by the towns people from a secret path. I am so happy to be free of that place and avenged. Blessed be your name!"

She asked all about him and learned that he was a knight of King Arthur, which only redounded on their honor. Then Hector, who was very sorrowful for the lady, asked her more about her family. She explained "I was born from a line of great nobility but my father and mother died before I was six months old, forcing me to abandon my title. Alas, I was sorely dispossessed." Hector swore that he would forever be her knight, and then he got on his knees and swore an oath that he would always protect her, and other maidens like her, from harms way. The people of the castle were very joyful and they celebrated all through the night.

10

The tale of the dispossessed lady is a reminder to all that tragedy can befall those who are oppressed by tyrants. In the absence of law justice must be sought through the might of a good and chivalrous knight, who, in this instance, was able to, by the power of God, avenge this lady on her wicked captor. Although she could never get back those twelve years she was imprisoned she could experience the joy of freedom and make the most of her future years.

# 2 THE SIEGE ON NEUF CHASTEL

What is told in the following story is truly a wonder that shows the extent of God's miracles. I'll tell you that the great knight Perceval of King Arthur's court was out seeking the holy grail. At the time that Perceval was doing this he came to a place called Neuf Chastel where Goranant, his lady Blanchleflore's uncle, was in residence. Goranant was the first teacher that Perceval had and taught him all he knew about being a knight. As his first master he taught him much about courtesy, chivalry and largesse. Moreover, he had him practice on the quintain tilting his lance so that he became an expert jouster; then he also taught him how to use a sword. It was no wonder Perceval was such an achieved knight for he had a just and wise master.

When Perceval arrived at the Neuf Chastel, which, mind you, was a very beautiful castle, well fortified and situated on a hill overlooking the sea, he was more than glad to be reunited with Goranant. The red and white towers of the stronghold brought back memories of his early days as a knight. Better yet, it reminded him of his vow to Blachleflore: that he would marry her as soon as he could for the love he had for her.

Perceval reflected on all of this as he entered through the gate and was joyfully met by Goranant. He had four sons who were with him that day. They were assembled in the great hall and armed to the teeth. You could tell they were battle weary by the gashes in their armor, wholes in their shields and the blood on their blades.

Whereas Perceval was hardly recognizable to them, for he had travelled many days in the forest without proper lodging. His face was covered with dirt-he had been wandering the forest for months after all- and a bushy beard that gave him little resemblance to his younger days. Goranant was very hospitable and, sought to give the good knight comfort. He was a strong believer in the patron saint Julian the Hospitaller who ardently attested that a weary traveler should never go without lodging from a stranger.

Thus, when Perceval was disarmed and given a comfortable mantle to wear, the group of knights sat in the hall around a table of remarkable beauty that was gilded with gold; each pillar was inlaid with the finest gems from all over the land. The table had trestles of fine silver and a board of bejeweled gold. The hall itself was decorated with precious samite and cloths of rich hues. The walls were adorned with gold mosaics that glimmered from the light of the torches for it was dusk.

Certainly, when Goranant learned that the traveling knight was Perceval, he was very pleased to see his companion and embraced him all the more warmly. He bellowed out "My, how you have grown since your days here!" Perceval replied: "I have gone very far and achieved a number of adventures. Yet, by the looks of your sons so heavily armed, it seems I am needed here!"

Indeed, a great tragedy had occurred in that place Goranant had been very distraught of late over this wicked custom which had come to the land. The knights all gazed down, unable to continue speaking. So Perceval said again: "By Saint Livinus, it appears you have become quite pale since I've seen you last. In fact, by the looks of the wounds I see on your sons it seems a great ill has befallen you. Are you sieged by a baron or a foreign invader? Tell me how I can help and, if it is in my power, I will certainly avenge you."

Goranant, who tried to smile and be as hospitable as a friend should, responded: "You have perceived rightly, my dear friend. Though I hope this has not taken from you're evening's lodging. It would be a very sad thing if I couldn't lodge a traveler well, despite the circumstance! It is true that a wicked custom from the devil has come to this land and I shall tell you all about it. But first, eat and be merry!" They sat down together at the table and a meal was prepared for Perceval. He was grateful for this but ate only a little, eager to learn more about his friend's plight.

After the meal, Goranant and his sons seemed very sad and pensive. The eldest was sorely wounded in the arm that it was a great effort to stop the bleeding; two maidens waited upon him the whole evening. One of the sons was full of tears that burst forth; he was too distraught to do anything but stare at the stone floor and sob. Then Goranant told the truth about the plight they were in: "Indeed, a terrible demon armed in black comes to the castle, everyday, with forty of his men. They are no ordinary knights but wicked demons. Day after day my sons and I leave out the front gate to battle them. When we slay them they always come back to life the next day, strong as ever. It has been months, and, by some strange magic, the same forty knights come back every time to torment us. No matter how many we kill or what we do it is always the same. This has gone on for so long that my sons are now with terrible wounds. It is without doubt that, if they come again tomorrow, we will surely perish. The main gate has not been fully repaired and if they wanted they could come into the castle willingly, storming it by force. The men are so exhausted they would almost gladly hand over the keys. We simply can't bear another assault."

When Perceval heard all that the good Goranant said he was filled with anger. He swore to avenge them tomorrow on the sward outside the main gate. "In the morning you will let down the main gate and I will pounce on your foes like a hungry lion. I have little doubt they can withstand my blows, for God is on our side." The sons were in despair for they knew that it would be hopeless because the knights could be resurrected by some strange magic. Still, they grew in courage at the sight of the honorable Perceval. Our hero spent the evening keeping vigil at the chapel, praying fervently that he could abolish the terrible custom. He also thought of the lovely Blanchleflore and how, when he returned, he would joyfully marry her. These two things were sure to bring justice and harmony to those he loved and keep him from sin. For by marriage he was doing a noble thing; he was giving himself to one woman rather than risking his flesh and soul to be burned by the fires of temptation. He reflected on all this a great deal.

Before dawn he readied his ash wood lance, put on his mighty hauberk, laced his silver helm that had a marvelous crest of blue feathers, and put his shield around his neck. His shield was trimmed with gules and sported a gold lion made of ermine. It was the finest shield one

14

could bear; yet he was to be rewarded an even better one at another time. Mind you, Perceval wasn't only a knight of prowess but one of the spirit; he could achieve great deeds and was one of the few who achieved the quest of the most Holy Grail.

Though, let's get back to the story. As he stood fully armed in the chamber a beautiful woman appeared before him. She appeared so suddenly that it seemed she came out of thin air; she was clearly some kind of spirit or fairy. In fact, it must have come from the Holy Ghost for a great radiant light glowed all around her as she floated in the air. Around her neck she had a wondrously handsome shield that was all white with a red cross on it. She offered it to Perceval willingly. Though, take a moment to hear where this shield came from.

On the cross there was a piece of holy wood from Jerusalem, upon which the flesh of Jesus Christ was so unjustly tortured to fulfill the scripture. This shield, because of it's wondrous origins, contained magical powers. Foremost, no knight could bear it unless he was pure, chaste and confessed of all his sins. If he were not shriven and pure, he would instantly perish when he touched it by a hail of one thousand stones. Second, any who wore it would not perish in battle for the power of Jesus Christ was on their side. Perceval heard the lady talk of the powers of the shield and was very happy to hear that he would receive it: "For it is clear that the devil and his followers fear nothing so much as the sign of the holy cross. Any knight who bears the cross and calls upon the name of Christ in battle will never be destroyed." Perceval, much enlivened by the Holy Spirit and the mighty shield went to take it from her and gave her his other shield; for he had replaced a shield of this world for one that was divine. For anyone who bears the armor of God in battle does not fear death. It made sense that he was given such a holy gift for he battled with terrible demons of the world that no human power could defeat. No matter how might or rich the evil spirits were able to make all their slaves unless a man, in the flesh, called for divine aid. Only then could he defeat the evil spirits of the world.

So ends the sermon and the diving gifting of the most holy shield. Perceval went out from the chamber and met with the other knights before the main gate in the morning. They were astonished to see the remarkable shield he carried and wondered at him; for his face was radiant with the light of the Holy Spirit. His eyes were like flaming lanterns and his gold girdle shined brightly in the sunlight. A rainbow of color swathed his head like a beautiful cloud. He bid all of them, for the sake of Jesus Christ, to say a prayer before battle. When this was done they had the gatekeeper lower the drawbridge.

The six knights spurred there destriers and launched themselves full tilt into the thickest press. Those demons were eagerly waiting for them on the outside. In the sward past the gate the forty demon knights were huddled about, they bellowed and had black smoke coming from their bodies. The stench was intolerable and some of them had shackles around their arms and ankles. They had clearly broken out from hell! Perceval had his pennoned lance leveled so that the first demon he struck on the body perished to dust by the forceful impact. The body tumbled into the ground and knocked over several other demon's. The brothers were so enlivened by his prowess and did the same to there enemies, toppling them to the ground with mighty force. In this way a multitude of demon's had been quickly toppled over.

When the demons witnessed their fellows in such disarray they began to swarm around the knights, hoping to outnumber them in combat. They were unafraid; the shield of the red cross radiated so much light from it so that many of the demons were blinded as he hewed apart their limbs. They were terrified of it and dared not get too close.

Also, Perceval was an excellent swordsman and used this well to his advantage. He went about chopping off limbs swiftly. He proceeded in a flurry raining down blows. Then he went about battering armor, smashing helms and clearing shields. So fierce was the combat that the demon knights lost twenty of their knights by Perceval alone. Goranant was no amateur in combat either. Though he was aged his sword was sharper than a sickle and had harvested many heads. Indeed, his sons spurred their steeds into combat too; they hewed straps from mail collars and slashed laces from their helms. Heads toppled to the ground by the might of our noble knights.

Then Perceval took his sword that cloves heads to the teeth and struck at his enemies in full force so that blood flowed on the green grass making it red. Though they weren't to leave the battle without wounds of their own. The brothers had received so many wounds that they could hardly continue. The brothers were greatly outnumbered and fought by faith alone; it was a great miracle no one perished in the battle. The demon's snarled at them but they redoubled their efforts, refreshing their advance and fixing their shields firmly on their shoulders to keep up a valiant defense. Knight's in utter despair are even more emboldened to fight, for they fear death all the more.

Two of the demon knights made the most ruckus. The one they called the bold ugly knight and the other the fair bad knight. These two were brothers and one was very ugly but good natured while the other was fair but wicked. They dealt a grievous wound to one of the brothers so that he was unsaddled from his horse. They lopped off the head of the horse and proceeded to hack away at the brother so that the straps of his helm were loosened and his hauberk was torn the shreds. He bled profusely from his wounds for he had lost a great deal of flesh from his left side. Luckily they could staunch the bleeding. Meanwhile, Perceval quickly came to the rescue. He grabbed a lance leaning on a tree nearby and dashed forth towards the wounded knight. The two demon's saw him and, when the light shined from the holy shield, they trembled in fear. He delivered a might blow with the lance so that it plunged into the chest of the one. He was hurled from his seat and into the ground, dead. Then he took his sword and gave a hammering blow to the other demon who was cut in two from the shoulder to the waist.

His aim was true and precise, he neither flinched in combat or shirked from the thick of the press. His sword, guiding by God, struck with such a fiery vengeance that these knights, who were undoubtedly strong and full of the devil's wickedness, were easily vanquished. So it was

17

that by the end of the day the six knights had been victorious over forty demons. Not a single demon remained and the entire sward was littered with corpses, limbs, and heads. It was a disgusting sight.

Yet Goranant fell into a swoon of despair at the sight of his wounded boys. He pleaded to the heavens, looking up to God in his pitiful plight: "It is no use! Even though we have slain them I have no doubt that they will appear again tomorrow in full strength against us. Now that we are so weary from battle and my sons are horribly wounded it is surely true that we will perish! Oh, Perceval, it is no use to contend with such wicked forces. Let us return to the castle and await certain death."

Perceval was not in the least bit worried and his calm deportment brought the men comfort. He looked towards Goranant and responded, "My dear friend, say no more. Go into the castle and rest with your sons. Make sure their wounds are tended to. I will remain here to find out how they can be revived and put an end to it." Perceval fixed his armor that had been somewhat displaced during the combat, then he tied his horse to a nearby tree and remained in the forest, behind a rock, well past dark to witness the great marvel. Meanwhile, his companions retired into the castle in great despair and anguish, for they were sorely wounded and certain of death. It was such an occurrence that showed the dark magic in the forest at the time. Fortunately there were good enough knights to protect against the perilous demon's who roamed the forest, stirring up mischief.

The good knight remained on the battlefield until the full moon raised into the sky. It shed enough light for him to see plainly what was about to occur. Out of the woods marched an old crone who was twisted, haggard and very wicked looking. She had a long, crooked nose and was dressed in black robes; she seemed to have an affliction that made her shake and shiver too. As she walked it was clear that she had a terrible limp and she was speaking in strange tongues of the devil. These incantations were most disturbing. Not to mention the foul smell of sulfur and the black smoke throughout the air; whether it was from the demonic corpses or her it didn't matter, it was terrible!

She held in each hand a cask and they were the most beautiful casks anyone could imagine. The casks were made of ivory and had gold handles. They were lined with sardonyx emeralds, chalcedony, sapphires, diamonds and topaz; it was a sheer wonder to behold them. Furthermore, the hoops and collarbones were completely inlaid with gold. Perceval watched intently as the casks twinkled and shined in the moonlight.

When the crone saw the once sortie band of forty demon knights completely slain she realized her work was cut out for her. She came upon one of the bodies and took from the cask an ointment. When she set it upon the dead demon's lips he was suddenly revived, as fresh as ever! Perceval marveled as she did this to four of the other corpses reviving them one after another, to his astonishment. One of the demons had lost his head but, once he had taken some of the potion, he got up and walked over to his head, which rolled around on the ground helplessly.

When Perceval saw this treachery he confronted the old crone directly: "Stop reviving these cruel men. It is not going to go any further. I've come here to kill you and these knights so that they never return. You have caused Goranant, my dear master, much suffering. I know that you are very clearly a spirit of the devil. So tell me, in the name of the one that holds power over you, why your master has done this?" When the old lady realized she was caught red handed she quickly thought up an escape plan.

She responded: "I knew you would come. It has been told to me in a vision that Perceval would take the casks. If anyone could kill me it would be you; you are the only one that I fear. I will answer you plainly. These demon knights were sent here by the devil. They were hoping to kill your master and torment him because he was a good teacher to you, the most holy knight who seeks to achieve the grail. One thousand curses on you, Perceval! Know that you will never achieve the grail, not for a million years!"

Perceval was full of wrath that the devil spoke to him about the grail, for he had spent many years in search of it and had suffered much because of it. Then the old lady applied the ointment to another one of the corpses. She had now revived five knights. He was amazed to see the magic and was very curious about it.

Perceval implored her to tell him about the casks and she said: "These have the power to revive even the most wicked of men. This ointment was the same that was given to Christ at the sepulcher. Though it was a misfortune for God that it has come to such good use by these demons. Surely it has the power to heal any wound and raise the dead back to life."

At this Perceval was greatly angered because she used a holy relic for evil. He drew his sword and ran towards her in a fury. "Repent of your evil deeds and I will spare you." She replied: "There is nothing that will make me do it." What more can I say? He lopped off her head and sent it flying over the castle wall and into the keep.

The five demons who had been revived ferociously ran at him with swords raised. Perceval battered them senselessly and crushed their might. He sent one to the ground with a crippling blow, another he smacked so hard with the pommel of his sword that his chest burst open. Then he spun around and dealt ferocious blows that knocked of an arm, another a leg, and so forth until all five of the demons were once again dead. Though they wouldn't have the option to come back to life this time, for now the good knight was in possession of the holy relic.

Now it was almost daylight. Perceval took the two holy casks and went to the castle gate, yelling out: "Open the gate, it is Perceval who has returned from the dead!" The gatekeeper marveled at this and ran to tell his master to wake, delivering the hope filled message. When they heard Perceval had survived the night they were astonished. They were quite certain that their departure from him the previous evening was to be the last time they would see him. The gates were flung open and Perceval entered boisterously and in a very joyous state. He had a smile brimming from ear to ear. In his hands the beautiful ivory casks, bejeweled and glimmering in the light of the morning, were a marvel to look at and behold. The brothers gathered around him and cheered to their amazement that the demon knights had been vanquished for good.

They asked him a thousand questions about what had happened and he answered every one truthfully. He told the story, from start to finish, just as you've heard it. Perceval took the ointment from the casks and gave it to each brother, who, being near death, were instantly healed by it's holy powers.

After they spoke at length they prepared a feast, for they were all very happy. Perceval was adorned in rich robes of samite and squirrel fur. They set the table and everyone sat down at table after hearing a beautifully sung mass. The dinner was exquisite and the highlight was a pressed fawn, which was the most luxurious dish at the time. They also served rabbit and had their fill of spiced wine.

The joyful knights had overcome a great evil; they shared battle stories and marveled at the wonders of the two holy relics before them: namely the cask and the shield. They were all convinced that the power of the Holy Spirit was working in Perceval.

"Indeed, it is a providence that brought you here to relieve the land of this wicked custom. God is good and gracious!" Said the deeply grateful Goranant. He who was glad to have been master to such a noble knight, implored Perceval: "There is still one quest you've yet to accomplish. It is something that, as a master, I beg of you." Perceval replied: "Ask and I will willingly grant it if it is in my power to do so." So he said: "You have promised to marry my niece, Blanchleflore. Yet it has been several years and she still waits patiently for you to return. I swear to you there is no more devout and faithful lover than her. She prays daily for your return. It is a sin that you have sworn such an oath to her and have left in unfulfilled." Perceval smiled and said: "You speak rightly and your counsel is good. I will gladly go to her and marry her for your sake. It is a sin that has weighed heavily on me. If I marry her I will have fulfilled my vow and can live more gloriously before God."

The next day they set out towards the castle where the maiden they spoke of lived, which was two leagues away. When they came near a messenger blew into a loud horn to let everybody know they were coming. I will not tell much of the wedding but know that, when she learned of Perceval's arrival, Blancheflore came running from the keep out into the meadow to embrace him. She was not in the least ashamed of her love for him, for he was such a proud and noble knight.

Tears came from her eyes as she gratefully held Perceval in her arms. Now she was graceful and full of beauty; no other compared to her in the whole kingdom. They were disarmed and led into a splendid hall that was adorned with gold embroidered samite which was green and red. The place smelled sweet and had freshly strewn grass laid all around, for it was a hot summer day.

She gave Perceval remarkable gifts; one a mantle of rich silk trimmed with squirrel fur and another a mighty Gascon steed that was swifter than an eagle. Know that they were happily married in a splendid ceremony. Bells clanged and minstrels plaid the hurdy gurdy into the late hours. During the feast a lady came to the hall who was wearing a green hood over her face. She said: "It is a very happy thing that you two are finally joined together. The fairies of the forest are happy that Perceval has sworn to protect the lands from the evil spirits. Go to your chamber and you will find my wedding gift, which I know you'll enjoy!" She suddenly disappeared and, full of excitement, they ran to the chamber to discover a marvelous bed that hadn't been there before!

This bed had a special quality that no one who slept in it could suffer madness or despair. Moreover, all the bishops in the land came to that bed and blessed it with both cross and fire. On the wedding night, when they retired to bed, they embraced and kissed one another fervently. As their naked bodies met they pondered the course of actions before them. Yet they were not, like the multitude, filled with the fires of lust. They did not so quickly indulge in that which turns one away from God. No, in fact, they swore to remain chaste and true. I will tell you why they chose this: For the young that throw themselves away in sex and delights tarnish their souls for but a brief moment of worldly pleasure. Those who are chaste and virgins seek to do charitable acts and are glorified by all. So that is why it is ever so important to refrain from sin, and, if you do to confess and purify yourself right away.

Now Blancheflore was a comely girl and full of beauty; yet she also had great wisdom and feared God. She said to her husband out of love: "Let us keep from the snares and wickedness of the devil. Let's not fall into sin by indulging too much in the ways of the flesh; if we can love one another and remain chaste, saving only for the necessity of procreation, we will honor God greatly."

Perceval agreed and felt sure he could not have asked for a better wife. That evening they lay naked, side by side, and did no more than embrace and kiss one another. For they truly feared God and desired nothing that would dishonor or shame them. They kneeled by the bed in prayer in the twilight hours, swearing to do that which was right by God and holy church. Know that God smiled upon them and gave them four beautiful children who would later rule all of Logres but the story does not tell of it here. It is a great thing when men and women choose to be chaste and give glory to God. If one is both chaste and a virgin his is doubly crowned in the kingdom of heaven.

# 3 LEANDER AND THE FLOWER OF BEAUTY

At this time in Logres there was a prince named Leander who lived near Mount Coriney which is rightly known as Cornwall. It was in the springtime beauty that the woods and field were once more donning their green mantles spangled with white, red and yellow. Leander spent this fine May morning jousting in the fields outside his castle with his blue shield blazoned with the head of a white stag. Men from the northlands of Orkney under King Lot came to joust with him constantly. He was known for his prowess and was ceaselessly challenged out of envy.

There was a custom in these lands that gave credence to his prowess. On the top of Mount Coriney there was a pillar twenty feet high. There was an ivory horn hung from the pillar that, when sounded by a challenger, summoned forth Leander to match him in a joust. Surrounding this pillar were a number of pinewood lances with the steel lance head facing down; they were sharp headed lances with strong, stout shafts. So there was no shortage of materials for jousting. Every morning after Leander said his prayers he ventured to the top of the mount and jousted with any opponent who challenged him.

One day a strong young knight came to joust with him. On his red shield there was emblazoned a white lion. He fixed his hauberk over a haqueton of cotton and silk. Then he laced his ventail and girded his sharp sword over his surcoat. He rode up the hill saying to himself: "Leander thinks he is so full of prowess and that no knight can match him. Ha! We will see about that. He wouldn't dare joust me, a foreign knight, who can level him flat on his butt at my desire!"

He took the horn and blew it liberally. Then he took one of the good lances on the ground, for it was better than his own. A clamor of bells sounded in the castle, suggesting that there was a commotion. Leander came forth, without fail, to the top of the hill. The knight fixed his spurs and aimed his lance towards his opponent, who

24

road up the hill in the highest spirits. In a great flurry both knights spurred their steeds and set off in a full gallop towards one another. Leander's horse was a strong destrier and sprang forward faster than a hound unleashed after a hare. It was little surprise that Leander tore through shield and hauberk, driving his lance clean through the bowels of his enemy. The man fell from the saddle and his horse, stumbling upon a ditch, tumbled to the ground with him.

Yet he was quick to rise holding his sword in his right hand and keeping his innards in with his left. Leander could not believe that the knight was still willing to do battle with his entrails falling out. "Come on, give it up! You haven't got long to live unless you see to getting that wound staunched and sowed up. I know a hermit who could do this for you." The other knight, ignorant and abundantly youthful, replied: "Let's keep the fight going you haven't won yet!"

Then the two entered a pitiful and fearsome combat. The steel blades came down like lightning bolts, making flares and sparks shoot up into the air. Armor was useless against the might of both knights. Both were wounded so that blood spurted out from a number of wounds. Everyone watching became quiet as the thunderous din of the two men yelling and the clanging of arms was all that was heard. Leander's hauberk was torn apart, along with his shield, by his furious opponent. The young knight was so badly wounded that his intestines were coming out and he was in shock after being unhorsed so traumatically.

The knight's smashed one another, body to body, and sent mail rings flying from their hauberks, their helmets now stove in. The good prince was too powerful and grew stronger as time went on. One fatal blow knocked the knight down and broke his arm so that the bone showed outwardly. He groveled on the ground. Leander saw his opponent weakening and flinching at fresh blows and called out: "You have fought bravely. Surrender to me and I will be merciful. God is on my side and you can't win now." The knight spoke softly as he coughed up blood: "I will never surrender to a traitor like you. You killed my brother through wickedness." Leander said: "Alas, I have never killed a man wickedly. Though it may be true I killed your brother, know that it was done honorably in combat when he challenged me on the mount. It is never treason for a noble knight to defend himself against a challenger."

Suddenly, out of the forest came a maiden riding on a white horse; she wore a spangled green gown of samite that sparkled with diamonds in the light. She had been searching for the knight on top of the mount and when she saw the two in combat she dismounted and ran over hastily. It was clear that the perilously wounded knight was her lover and companion; for when she saw him so battered and bloodied tears overwhelmed her. She got on her knees and begged Leander to forgive him: "Fair knight, let my lover go! He is too stubborn to realize that his life will be gone if he doesn't surrender to you. Know that I am with child." She showed herself to Leander and he saw that her belly was full with child. "You wouldn't kill this man, who is to become a father, would you?" Leander was full of pity for the man and spoke wisely: "Knight, take care of your family. There is no need to avenge yourself any further. If it is true that I killed your brother in battle I am ready to make amends in any way you feel it necessary."

The knight was very stubborn but eventually his lover persuaded him to yield after much argument. In this way the knight left the hill, full of shame and dishonor. He was lucky enough to have his lady take him to a hermitage where his wound was healed after several weeks of treatment. The good Leander was true and just. He made amends to that knight by gifting him many fine jewels, which were sent to him at the hermitage by his squire. The man was grateful for this and bestowed them on his new wife who was delighted. He never harbored anymore hatred to Leander and was always ready to serve him. So the combat was finished. Though, for Leander, this was one of many. It had been this way for many years that, in the morning, a great clammer from the bell on the church in town would sound after the ivory horn had been blown. Then, Leander, in all his armor, would ride to the top of the mount while the morning mist was still present. He had jousted over two hundred knights and never lost a single combat.

One evening the mighty prince that was so well renown rode on his horse into the forest until he came to a lovely glade at the edge of a dell; therein he found a garden enclosed by budding roses and eglantine. This was surely a most remarkable place to let his horse graze, take off his armor and rest! In the garden there was a calming pond which he sat near, taking ample time to drink from the spring was a pleasure. When he drank from it he found that he was immediately healed of all his wounds from combat. Being restored to his full health was a great marvel which he wondered at.

Moreover, he began to see a wisp of the wind, or some strange spirit, swirling in the air in colors of red, yellow and violet. It was an incredible sight to behold; the magic was surely the work of some fairy. The colorful spirits seemed to be leading him on. So he followed after it through the garden until he came upon a most astonishing sight. A stone figure of a women was stationed in the garden. She was more lovely to behold than his eyes could bare. The stone figure was so comely and fair that he was quite certain he would marry her if she was a real person.

Leander gazed on this stone statue for some time. The woman had long hair and seemed to be wearing a loose gown of silk with embroidered flowers on it. She seemed a girl of no more than eighteen and was standing with her hands clasped, somewhat in shock and sorrowful. In her hands there was a budding red rose, it seemed more perfect than any rose he had seen. Beneath the statue an inscription read: "HERE RESTS THE FLOWER OF BEAUTY, ONLY TO BE RELEASED BY THE TOUCH OF THE FLOWER OF PROWESS. KNOW THAT HE CARRIES A BLUE SHIELD EMBLAZONED WITH A WHITE STAG."

Leander studied the inscription and recognized that his coat of arms was described exactly. He was amazed by this most absurd magic that was holding a lady of such profound beauty captive within a stone statue. He was filled with pity when he recognized that, as according to the inscription, there was a soul trapped in the stone! This must be a horrific prison, he thought to himself. Not sure what to do, he put his hand upon her cheek. When he did this, to his amazement, the lady began to become full of color and life. The cold stone turned to warm flesh. The stone crumbled all around as if she was a baby chick breaking free from an egg shell. Her eyes were a lovely green and her face was whiter than a dove with rosy red cheeks that were flushed with excitement.

Indeed, she was as full as life as any youth in her prime! Her blonde tresses went all the way to her waist and were softer than the finest silk. Her features were perfect in every way and, suffice it say, that she was a more beautiful maiden than Leander had ever set eyes on. I know not how to describe it but that the stone statue was alive! He beheld the lady in wonder and awe. Leander was a knight of prowess but never before had he seen a spell of such magnitude. Leander was a fierce knight in combat but knew not how to speak to a lady, especially one as noble as she seemed.

When the lady was fully awake she set her gaze upon the noble Leander. He was very handsome and the girl delighted to see him. She fell in love with him when she looked into his eyes for there is the window to the soul. She knew that she had been freed by the Flower of Prowess. So she put her long and slender arms around Leander and warmly embraced him. Blood rushed throughout his body when she did this, for he was hot and a nervous wreck with her. She sang these words as she held him dearly, "It's been a long time since I've felt the air on my skin, and felt a strong man in my arms! What an absolute joy! You must be the very knight of prowess i've been looking for."

"My lady," stuttered Leander, "I've never been known as the Flower of Prowess, I can assure you. Though I do have the shield this inscription tells of."

"You are too humble, fair Leander. You have always been the Flower of Prowess. Don't you know that no one in all Cornwall has defeated two hundred knights in combat? Every knight cowers at your name and none commit injustice to your king the father because of you. Indeed, if you left this place, it is little doubt the whole kingdom would crumble; for foreign invaders would catch wind of it and set ablaze the lands, looting the churches and killing the kind people. Since you are so well renown, for now and all time, you are to be considered the Flower of Prowess." Leander marveled that she knew so much about him and his family.

She giggled and pretended to give him the accolade in the style of the knighting ceremony by placing an imaginary hilt on his shoulder. Leander laughed at this new name of his and shrewdly responded: "If I am the Flower of Prowess, does that make me a thorn bush to my enemies? Or better yet, am I a seasonal warrior that is well pollinated?" The lady smiled and said: "You are the rose, my lord. And as a rose many thorns are on your vines that can prick your foes who wonder about too rashly. As a rose you are the perfect ideal of manhood and chivalry."

Leander brushed this flattery off and responded: "Enough. You are so fair that I can barely control my mind which is aflame with desire for you. I have never taken a wife or ever felt the urge to until now. I want to know how you became a stone figure and what magic this is. It is self-evident why you are called the Flower of Beauty. Yet, you still need to tell me how I can have you. My father is king of all this country and I can make you a Queen one day."

The lady smiled and blushed when she heard this, for she loved Leander dearly. "Fair Leander, I will tell you all that you wish to know. When I was a girl I wandered through these gardens. An evil sorceress used to come here and, one day, she saw me here. I was young and full of mischief, disregarding that someone may be watching me. Foolishly, I plucked one of the roses because I thought it would look lovely on my mother's kitchen counter. When I did this the old crone cursed me so that I would remain a stone statue until the Flower of Prowess saved me. So I turned to stone and have been since. I am human now, as you can see, but listen well for I will only be so for another few moments."

Her voice began to sound frightened and she hurried her speech, "If you wish to set me free I will gladly be yours. There is something you must do. Go to the distant isle and slay the golden-haired giant. He lives on an island far from Britain but often comes here to terrorize the peo-

29

ple and eat the men. If you do this I will truly be set free. God keep you and may my love guide you onward!"

Before Leander could promise her he would do this or even ask her where the giant lived she changed back into her stone form, unable to talk any more. Leander tried to bring her back by touching her cheek but it didn't work. He was struck by love like a hammer in the skull. So enamored, he couldn't move from his spot in the garden for many hours as he gazed upon the features of the statue. He kissed her all over and worshipped her on his knees. Indeed, anyone watching would have thought him mad to be so intimate with stonework, unless he loved the mason who had made it!

Then he realized he had no choice but to go after the golden-haired giant, wherever he was. Then Leander set off at a brisk pace to his castle where he summoned his squire, Marmadon. He told him the story from start to finish. He was amazed by the stone figure and the quest that he was to embark on. Leander swore that he would set out immediately and that he should prepare provisions; he swore he wouldn't sleep more than a single night in any lodging until he accomplished the task before him. Leander and Marmadon left the castle as soon as there was sunlight the following day.

They headed for the coast and purchased a ship to take them to the isle. The biggest problem for them was that they had no idea where they were going. Indeed, they spent two years at sea wandering from isle to isle. Everywhere they went Leander asked: "Have you seen the giant they say has golden hair on his head? Have you seen the gnarly one with the fine locks?" It was with despair and sadness that they journeyed for so long without finding him. Whenever Leander was feeling hopeless Marmadon encouraged him: "You should never have fallen in love. Look at the torture you have put yourself through because of it! Two years of life, gone! Wasted time spent in the seas to slay a creature that may not even exist is truly a dishonor to us all. When will you return home and become king? It is a great folly to love someone desperately and, as the old adage goes: folly's better shunned than practiced."

Despite all the noble knight kept up his courage and did many feats of prowess in those two years. One day, they took shelter on an island where a terrible serpent attacked them. The mariners all said that this serpent had killed many before. He hacked off its head and threw it into the ocean. However, before the head could sink to the bottom, a great eagle came down and picked it up, flying away into the distance. These serpent was strange and extraordinarily large. On its neck was glimmering color that showed marvelous visions to the beholder, distracting him as it launched in attack, devouring all. Though Leander saw plainly that this evil beast was deceptive so he just cut off its head and that was the end of it. I couldn't tell you who that eagle was or why it flew away with the head.

Leander also produced a number of miracles, which reinforced his firm faith in God. He had a fishing net from Cornwall which he used frequently over the side of the boat. Whenever they were hungry he put the net down and, saying a prayer to God, pulled up the net with the help of Marmadon. Every time they did this there were more fish in the net than could be carried on the boat without it sinking! In this way God blessed their journey so that they were always fed abundantly.

One morning a great wind arose. This was God's doing too, for they were blown in the direction of the distant isle they were looking for. They hung on for dear life as the boat, at the mercy of the wide ocean, beached them upon the sands. When they realized the storm had abated and they had made it in one peace they crossed themselves in amazement, thanking the Lord for such swift guidance.

Leander disembarked, bringing his trusty horse with him. This was surely the isle he was looking for because he saw the bones of the men that had been eaten by the giant on the beach. They were stacked up in a big pile. Marmadon pointed out that all over the beach there were helmets, swords and hauberks littered about. They journeyed through the sand until they came to a grassy valley. A bow shot ahead they spotted a well fortified castle which stood upon a hill overlooking the sea. The island wasn't unexpectedly large but there were multitudes of sheep and cattle grazing about the land. The wall and fortified towers were all wrought with finely hewn sandstone. Great big towers that were well rounded went all along the perimeter.

They didn't dare enter the main gate but found a secret postern. Marmadon suggested: "Let us infiltrate the castle and see what the situation is before we get too hasty." So they made there way through the streets amongst the people and eventually climbed the steps to the great hall. Therein, they saw a great many shields hung upon the windows and battlements, displaying the numerous knights who had been slain there. "Maybe that lady of stone has sent others this way, for it seems over a hundred shields are hung up in this wall, some of them I recognize from Cornwall, too!" He was sad when he saw that golden haired giant had defeated so many knights.

They left the hall, for the giant wasn't there. They observed the grounds and found a spectacular garden, full of rose bushes and brambles. Suddenly, as they walked through the garden, they heard the sounds of a girl singing. Then, when they investigated, they saw that there was a patio where a young girl came out from behind a tall glass door, beckoning them.

This little girl was not so little. She was a giant and roughly the size of Leander at the age of fourteen. She was very beautiful and nearly naked but for a shift she wore. She led them in and wondered at their small size. When Leander saw her he hoped he could learn where to find the giant with the golden hair. The girl told him it was her father. Yet, she hated him terribly because he wanted to lay with her and make her his wife, which she thought strange and Leander agreed! She also told him that he had raped many of the women in the town and killed them because he was too big for them to bear. This made Leander ferocious and he now, more than ever, desired vengeance on the fowl beast. The girl directed him to the great hall where Leander was able to await the golden-haired giant. For he was out hunting when they arrived. While he waited in the hall, Marmadon thought about something completely different. For he had taken a fancy to the young girl, whose name was Nina. They began to play and banter. One thing led to another and they ended up laying together.

By the time Nina's father returned to the hall they had already done the deed and Nina had been summoned to the hall. The giant saw Nina there and boisterously called out: "You are looking fine, daughter. I can't wait to have you as my wife!" Yet Nina replied: "Oh, father. I've already found a lover of my own." When the giant heard this he was full of rage. "What? Has your mother been hiding boys in your room? I dare say, show me to them. I will tear apart their limbs!" Suddenly, Leander came out from behind a pillar in the hall and challenged the giant, who was eager to fight. "You have greatly wronged your little girl through your sins. Moreover, the people of this castle despise you for raping their daughters, wives and friends."

The giant was surprised to see that Leander did not fear him. Know that the giant was incredibly huge, about the size of ten men. He carried a club that he whirled around as lightly as if it was a stick. Yet any full grown man of strength would have had a hard time even lifting it. So he sported about in front of him, and said: "Let's play, though you won't be able to take my life!" Leander responded: "Enough games, giant. I challenge you. Are you going to arm yourself?" The giant replied: "I don't need armor to crush a puny thing like you. After I kill you I will boil you in a broth and suck on your bones!" He motioned to the ground and drew a circle with his cudgel, then he called out: "You will fight with me and not leave this circle. If you leave the circle, consider yourself defeated." Leander agreed to the terms. He fastened his hauberk and unsheathed his sword, remarking to himself that he was completely prepared for combat. That was good because he who is prepared has little to fear.

The giant was terrible to gaze at. He eyes were wide, bulgy and red with rage. His stumpy nose and big head made him look dumb. He moved with great agile and power, for he seemed to have the capacity to send Leander flying forty feet into the air with a single blow. His bulky body and arms made him look like a larger than life gorilla. Then he wailed wildly and swung his club at Leander so violently that the blow could have knocked down a stone wall. If the club had hit him he would have surely died instantly but Leander quickly dodged it.

Then he sliced the giant with his sword so that it took a handful of flesh from his thigh and blood spurted out. "You seemed to have wounded me! You will suffer for that." The giant flung around his club and sent another terrifying blow in the direction of Leander. This time Leander dodged it again, just in time. The cudgel smashed deep into the ground, breaking up the stone foundation in the hall. As the giant attempted to pull it up again Leander dealt him a blow on his side that was fatal. The sword came down mightily and cut off his arm from his right shoulder. By shear might alone the steel blade traveled down further taking off a huge chunk of flesh from the giant's side so that his bowels were showing plainly. Blood gushed out from the wound and all over the floor so that the giant could barely stand as he was slipping on his own blood.

The giant became desperate, "This is madness, come here so that I can eat you!" With wavering strength he raised the club a third time but the he had become so weakened the he fell to the ground in a swoon. Leander marveled at the giant. When he fell the whole earth shook and the roof of the hall seemed like it was going to cave in.

Then Leander aimed his true blade and, with a crushing blow, hewed off the giant's left hand completely. Now, with so much loss of blood and limb, the giant slid helplessly around in his own blood, unable to stand. In moments he perished and his soul left his body.

The whole castle rejoiced. They watched in astonishment as Leander climbed on the giant's neck and, using his sword, cut away at the golden tresses. He took the gold hair and stored it in his saddle. Then he removed the giants head and attached it to his saddlebow even though it was half the size of his horse!

Meanwhile, Marmadon, who had slept with Nina, pleaded with his lord: "Make me a knight and let me govern here. I will take Nina as my wife and protect these lands in the name of your father, the king." Leander was glad for him and made him lord over the giant's domain.

34

Without further ado he gave his squire the accolade, making him a knight. He provided a good sermon before letting him go and here is what he said: "You are a knight today by this ceremony but always remember the important deeds you must carry out. It is by deeds that you will be known and remembered. Your words and thoughts are little unless rightly manifested. Always strive for the good and do service to God and Holy church. Your sharp steel blade should always strike with the might of justice and never fear enemies. If you fall into sin, be sure to rise anew and confess of your sins. Once you are shriven go out and continue your journey. He who does wicked deeds and is not repentant will lose his soul. Take care that you do right by maidens and always treat them with kindness and charity."

After the good man was heard Marmadon smiled and thanked him graciously. Leander girded his sword and it was done. They all celebrated and, during the celebration, Marmadon married Nina for he loved her dearly. The irony was that Marmadon, who had mocked love so arduously, had fallen into love's snare so easily. Such is the power of love that it cunningly strikes those unaware, like an innocent roebuck in the forest is pounced upon by a lion or struck down by a good hunter's well placed arrow. Marmadon, now that he had become a knight, ruled graciously and fathered on Nina five boys who all became remarkable knights.

After the knighting ceremony and the wedding Leander headed home, grieved that he was leaving Marmadon. "You will surely need to come back to Cornwall when summoned, for i'll be hard pressed to find a squire of such worth!" Leander went on his ship and a swift wind took him, by the grace of God, home in a week.

His father and the whole court was happy to see him for they thought he might have been dead. There was great rejoicing throughout the kingdom when he returned. He recounted all that had happened and they were astonished by his adventure. He showed them the humungous giant head and the gold hair all to their surprise. These deeds were recorded for they were of great worth and a marvel for all the inhabitants of Cornwall.

That is why, when great adventure occurs, scribes record it so that it could be retold again and again. Lineages, bloodlines and heroic deeds are never forgotten, as long as there are people willing to learn of them.

Anyway, back to the story. Word traveled fast and when Cornwall discovered that Leander had slain the giant with the golden hair everyone was filled with joy. He became known as the true Flower of Chivalry from that day forward for his deeds were mighty.

Leander didn't forget to take his pleasure of that stone statue who had been so unjustly imprisoned when she explored the crone's garden. He went to her and brought that bloody head and golden hair along with him. He laid it before her and, unsure what to do next, rose and touched her stone cold cheek as he did before.

That which was cold and lifeless suddenly became full of life, warm and soft in the embrace of his hand. His touch was such that it awakened the soul inside. What is more mighty than saving one's soul? The two lovers embraced and, when she saw the head, realized she had been fully freed! She cried for joy and thanked Leander a thousand times over. "You have surely won my love for you have done what no other knight could do." Then they saw the rose in her hand that was still more perfect than any and as if it were plucked moments ago. He said: "That is an old rose, probably the oldest in the world!" She said, "Indeed it is, and I'm the oldest women you know, for I was imprisoned for over one hundred years, and I don't look a day over eighteen!" He roared with laughter and he took her on his horse back to the castle.

Leander made the Flower of Beauty his wife and he was in a hurry to do it, for he was eager to consummate their marriage. When Leander's father passed away the kingdom went into his hands and he ruled it in peace for forty years. The Flower of Beauty, who was no more than eighteen by appearance, never aged a day in her life. In this way was the pain of her imprisonment was balanced by the joy of her pleasure in marriage to the prince. Indeed, she was so full of vigor that Leander was always full of energy for love of her. She was a good and loyal wife, which is a rare treasure! They had three boys who also went on to be great leaders like their father. The lady of stone continued to live for many years after that. She never fell in love again but waded her time in nature, learning enchantments and magic. She befriended the Lady of the Lake, who was Lancelot's mother, and spent many years having her fun with her. The Lady of the Lake was known well for her knowledge of the stars and her ability to prophecy events in the future. So now you have heard the story of how the Flower of Chivalry became so widely known and the loving romance he had with his wife, who was known as the Lady of the Stone or the Flower of Beauty.

# 4 THE WOOD OF CLARADEURE

Deep in a wood four leagues in either direction there was a place that was so expelled from the good court of Arthur that it was full of the most cruel villains who lurked and prowled about. They were of a specific sort: enchanters of magic who deceived knights of prowess and led them to their death through spells. This was a most wicked custom that befell the lands. It wasn't just because they knew magic that they were hated; they were full of wickedness and sought to do evil by there spells. Wherever there was evil Arthur sent knights to the land to pacify it, for he was a good, just and generous king.

He learned of the conflict in this wood by a lady who came to the court. She had ridden far and you could tell by her emaciated face, wide eyes and tattered raiment that she had been attacked, seemingly by the most vile creatures of the forests. She came to the court and, just preparing for dinner, everyone stopped. They were filled with pity and urged the lady to bring the pressing matter to the King. So the court was assembled and they heard her. "My king, you rule the land of Britain and all the boundaries therein. You are the sovereign. As the sovereign you must take care of the people when evil spirits attack them and do wicked things. Us ladies are being forced into submission by the vile enchanters of the forest. They call themselves Darnisians. They have raped many of my friends and attacked our towns, burning them to the ground with vile magic."

Arthur heard all this and was so incensed he didn't know what to do. He took counsel and said: "Well, you have fought perilously and we will ensure that those enchanters are killed. For they are frauds and villains! I will send five of my best knights to escort you back to this wood. They will surely avenge you." The lady thanked him and those five good knights set out to the forest, directed by the maiden.

In the forest the band of thieves, murderers, and bandits lived together. It was their custom that they would have maidens who did their bidding through deception. So the maiden entreated all the knights: "Here is the forest before you. I advise that you each take a separate path until you discover where they are situated!"

So the good knights separated and went along the paths, many of which were compiled of dense thickets and bestrewn with so many weeds that they had a hard time of it. I will tell you what happened to the first knight. The first knight made his way boldly into the thickets until he came upon a lady. She was on the ground in feigned anguish, but it seemed real. She tore her hair, wept and beat at her chest: "Alas, good knight, you must help me! Two knights set off just now who raped me. See that I am avenged for my maidenhood is long lost!" The knight was totally buying it and the snare was laid before him. "What happened? Is he gone from here? Alas, I will chase him down and avenge you. By my honor that is why I came here from King Arthur's court." The lady entreated him: "Follow me this way."

She led him off the path into a dense thicket. They came to a muddy mire and stopped before a big pit that was dug as a trap. Since it was dusk the knight couldn't see that there was a big pit before him. The lady stopped and said: "Just over there is a house. You can see the candles burning now. That is where they live. Take care that you avenge me!" The knight puffed up his chest and said: "I will surely do so my lady. I will make them hurt for what they've done!" With that, he spurred his charger that set off right into that big pit. It fell head first and toppled over the knight who was severely wounded from the fall. Then a bunch of bandits came out and started hitting him with shovels. When he could endure no more they bound him up and put him in their prison. Alas, deceit is not honorable nor is it chivalrous. In this way four of the knights were led into a foul mire so that both horse and rider had little choice but to yield. They were all swarmed and imprisoned seemingly without hope of escape.

The fifth knight, however, had enough wit to take greater care when he approached the damsel in distress. He was a very perceptive man and was not blurred by the shimmering appeals of court life. In that sense he was very practical and down to earth. He came across this actress who feigned and lamented in her dramatic state so realistically it was little doubt that every man would see to it that she was avenged.

Yet, our good knight, named Guillame, refused to be so fooled. He looked at the woman, astute and full of surprise. He gazed all around and because he was more worldly than the rest he could perceive the ruse. He noticed no bruise or mark upon her. Her nails were clean and it was quite clear she had bathed that morning for she smelled fresher than a rose. By the looks of it this lady had just had a nice lunch in the meadow before gently resting beside the road. The most of her exertions were in her splendid acting!

Her tears were not real but just drops of water. Her hair was hardly torn, and her shift was neatly on her and completely clean! Now because Guillame was clever feigned to the actress, killing her with her very own poison! I waded about, astonished and angered, as if he couldn't bare to see the lady in such distress. "Horrible! How could they! Vile treason. I will put this blade so deep in his belly that, oh, he won't live another minute! No more, lady, no more. Take me to him. He will suffer." The lady was eager to take him along the path: "Follow this way, I will take you to him that I may be avenged."

Without further ado they road along the path until they neared the foul mire that had so treacherously trapped the other four companions. Guillame realized it was a trap, for he began to watch the maiden attentively as she stopped before the mire. "Good knight, the stronghold you seek is just over the ridge, you can see the candlelight where the villains are. Follow the path, I will go no further out of shear terror!" Guillame was quite for a moment and then responded: "My lady, take the road first and I will follow you. My horse will be guided by you, for it is getting dark and I can't see much. Take courage, I will not fail to avenge you!"

The woman brooded and refused to go further. Alas, Guillame saw that it was a ruse and he plainly told her: "You lie! If I go further it is surely a trap. Ride ahead and prove it. You and your friends plague the forest seeking knights to rob and harm. Show me to your lair so I can smote the whole lot of you for your treachery."

When the woman realized she had been discovered she yelled out loudly. Five of her companions, all of them vile murders, came running to her aid. Guillame took out his sword and assailed the men, slicing one's hand off and another he beat to the ground and cut him about the shoulder three finger lengths deep. They were stupid to attack him unarmed.

The lady tried to cast her magic on Guillame. She controlled the vines from the tree which began to come upon him, trapping him. But Guillame had something else to protect him. He was married to a beautiful lady who had gifted him a most precious ring. Since she had descended from fairies the ring had been imbued with magical powers and gifted to her. Her mother told her to give it to her husband and it would protect him from all enchantment. Alas, it was no wonder he could see right through their wicked plans!

So, because Guillame had on the stone ring with the emerald that was given to him by his lady, he was impenetrable to magic. Now, the enchantress tried her spell, giving it all her might. She was really frustrated! First, he realized she was acting and now she couldn't do any magic. Twice her plans were twice disrupted. She felt so powerless and, grabbing an axe leaning on the tree, ran towards the knight, exclaiming: "You will be killed one way or another!" As she ran towards him Guillame unsheathed his sword and sliced off both her hands. So much blood came from her that she screamed and ran away in fright. Later she died from this wound.

The rest of the vile bandits, who were armed, came from the castle when they heard the screams. They assailed the knight, charging at him with sharp, stout ashwood lances. They were unhorsed one after another. Their wood lances shattered and splintered along his blue shield emblazoned with white hart antlers.

He spurred his horse and thrust his lance through one of them so that it was plainly seen from the other side of his back. Then he removed it and charged at another, this time renting both shield and hauberk; the lance plunged into his chest and broke inside, killing him immediately. The other three men continued attacking him at

41

once, hacking away at his shield and hauberk. Guillame drew his sword and began dealing out blows on his opponents with fury. He doled out a blow to the helm of one man that was delivered with such might that the blade cut through the helm and went from the top of the head to the teeth. Another was quick to have his head split in two all the way down to the shoulders. The other two murderers attacked with sharp steel blades, ripping his ventail and cutting the laces from his gold veined helm so that it went flying into the trees.

Then Guillame, deeply enraged, yelled out: "Take care how you dole out your blows for they will be returned with interest! I always clear my debts as soon as they are due." Then, with a mighty flourish he struck one of them on the head, taking off a hand full of flesh from his cheek. The man, sorely afflicted, fell to the ground in a swoon. After witnessing this horror the remaining fighter was so terrified that he ran back to the stronghold across the bridge. Guillame quickly pursued him and, thrusting this spurs, used his keen-edged blade to slice the man's head clean from the body before he could escape.

Guillame was delighted that he had been victorious over the five murderers. Moreover, they had so cordially directed him to the stronghold! Guillame's pennon was stained red and his lance broken in half. He had recovered his helm and laced it on, then he fixed his hauberk, tightened his saddle and slung his shield over his neck before spurring onward to the stronghold across the drawbridge that was left undefended and open.

He found himself a beautiful courtyard hedged in by rose bushes. He tethered his horse and walked up the steps to a great hall. The hall was wide and spacious. He found therein three more treacherous villains who, unprepared, ran towards him with random weapons they found about the castle. One had an axe, and the other two swords.

Guillame said: "What? You didn't here your kin dying for the last twenty minutes outside? You must have been napping or fornicating!" He plunged his blade into the first man that came to him so that his bowels fell out. Then he hacked and hewed at the other two, who had little

42

armor to protect them, making them easy to kill. Indeed,
they fell into pools of their own blood and saw before
them their limbs separated from their bodies. They were so
beaten by the good knight that they could do nothing but
wallow in their own blood until their souls left their bodies.

When he had justly dealt with the robbers and
villains he searched through the entire castle. It was then
that he found his four companions who had set out with
him from Camelot. What joy he felt when he saw them all
together. They returned the feeling for they were completely grateful for being saved. He thrust his blade into
the gate so that it opened and they were happily freed.

The valorous knights rejoiced and ate all the food
in the hall. Then they raised the place to the ground, setting fire to the hall. It was such that all the knights that
came with Guillame were newer knights who had just recently been given the accolade by Arthur. It was later when
they journeyed home that they came across a wise hermit
who instructed them. He who is worldly and has endured
many trials has gained much by experience to defend himself from those that are wicked and deceive.

So before the knights returned to court they
stopped at a hermitage to rest. The holy man joyfully welcomed them and opened the wicket gate so that they could
enter. He sang a delightful service and all the knights
watched in rapt delight.

Guillame had a few wounds and it so happened
that a monk there was well advised in healing matters; he
attended to the wounds, patching them up nicely. The
priest served them with what little he had; they were fed
barley bread, nuts, berries and drank cold water from a
nearby spring.

After this, the hermit spoke to each one. Some
confessed of their sins and others sought advice. When he
had heard their fervent confessions and given absolution
he spoke to the whole group: "From a good woman there
are many blessings to be had but from a wicked one none
but ill and shame comes. A man who seeks ill will surely
find it. If he follows the good he will surely find it. What
does the good book say? Ask and it shall be given. Knock
and the door shall be opened. Take heed, all adventuring

knights, not to be deceived by the wicked who want to bring you shame and dishonor. There will be many strangers and women who you will encounter. Take care that you are not drawn in by the allure of worldly pleasures. For this will give you little in return and will leave you in despair. A knight should only pray for God's will and the power to carry it out. He need only grow in virtue, shunning worldly riches and delights. To follow them is ruin and folly. Vices plague the rich, so why ask for anything but the grace of God? The wicked are like a wolf who devours a fawn or baby calf. Don't be naive! Solomon and Samson were both deceived by women despite their strength and wisdom. That is proof enough that God alone can restore one to sanity and relieve his grievous afflictions. Indeed, the power of man can do little against the devil. Follow the good, trust in God, and pray fervently that he will bring you victory. For no knight who fervently prays to God will come to grief and despair. Pray that you can endure hardship patiently. The rewards are great to he who rebukes sin by confession and calls on God to protect him in battle."

Thus the knights were invigorated by the wise counsel. The young four who were pitifully captured and imprisoned by a lying lady never were fooled again, for by experience they learned to know better. As for Guillame, well, he was very grateful for the stone ring his lady had gifted him!

## 5 LA TERRE SAUVAIGE

Dear friends, let me relate to you another story that is of the utmost importance to the one who has ever been faced with evil, for it is a tale of overcoming evil.One of the most fair knights of the court found himself in a waste land nearing the brink of destruction and only the power of God could saved him. This was a land filled with horrors; the blackness of night brought the horsemen of bewilderment upon the people, wreaking havoc, confounding good souls and imprisoning them in the fires of hell. In this land, people were plagued by temptations and did wicked things to one another so that they were pitiful souls in the eyes of God. They had sinned so greatly and gone so low that only the power of God, in all his mercy, could help them. For humanity is a fragile thing, the will crumbles like bread crumbs if it is not taken proper care of.

Indeed, I will tell you of dark nights where the full moon turned bloody in the sky; for nothing good comes when darkness comes, except sleep! In the enchanted forest and waste land there are headless men and women who walk and fly in the forest; evil spirits plague the good people. Demons with blue smoke and flame belching from their chainmail wonder around, seeking flesh to eat. You may ask, was the devil ever disguised as a Sore Pucele? Indeed, he prowls about like a voracious leopard; for that is what we call a wondrously beautiful and golden-haired maiden who does evil by men. Yet, how much suffering comes before you see the stranger in the night isn't a maiden, she's a temptress seeking only to dig a grave for you! In such a way did the good knight Mardur, for that was the knights name, go in search of adventure at this terrible time in Cambria when the lands were truly wasted and possessed.

Mardur was a brave soul; he went to the holy service in that place they call La Terre Sauvaige or the Wild Lands. When he confessed of himself to the most holy hermit he was fairly warned of the treachery that awaited him in the depths of the wood. No knight going to battle doesn't first make sure he is shriven and his soul is pure.

That way, if he died in battle, he would be given entry to heaven.

So they sat in the church, Mardur pounding on his chest, telling the priest all. He was tearless but honest. The holy man said to him: "You have made a full confession of your wrongs, holding nothing back and you are truly penitent, for I see it in your tears. You have done very well to come here before going to the wood, for know that a different kind of enemy will be waiting to fight you there. He doesn't come with honor or respect, nor does he bring lance or blade. This enemy comes inflicting the mind with poison and setting man against himself, filling him with contempt and despair. For the disease of the mind affects all the limbs. Take care that you do only good from here on and not fail in the least. Easy is the trap of temptation set and, like a squirrel to the snake, you could fall prey to it. So, good knight, now that you are shriven, grow stronger in God's light. When you see wickedness call on God and cross yourself in the name of the Father, Son and Holy Ghost. Do this, and you will be freed of your temptations. For only true love of God can lift you from your foul sins and into the light of God. Your strength will double if you only resist temptation and continue to fight against evil. I swear that you will face many temptations in the forest because when the Devil sees that you have rebuked him he will double his efforts to bewilder you. For he is cunning; but if you trust in God you will always foil his wicked plans! So go forth, have no fear, for God is with you!"

Hearing these things enlivened Mardur's heart and prepared him for the quest he was about to undertake. He prepared to enter the dark forest to face the evil that awaited him; for he had a deep aversion to all base thoughts and deeds. Mardur crossed himself as he knelt before the tabernacle and then he exited the church, wishing the hermit farewell. He fixed his saddle and spurs. He donned a hauberk of pure gold that was inlaid with beautiful flowers. His saddle was worth an entire land for it was gold, embossed with patterns of beautiful birds and leaves. Then he laced his helm which had red peacock feathers that came from the crest of the helm all the way to the tail of his horse. His mount was a good strong destrier of the purest white. It was worth one thousand pounds and he wouldn't trade it for a whole kingdom! Then he took his stout and sharp pinewood lance from a nearby tree. It had a most handsome pennon of red silk on it. He girded his silver sword that was bejeweled round the hilt. He put his silver shield over his neck and rested it on his shoulder; the shield had a most intricate design of three blue fleurs-de-lis emblazoned on it. At last, he was ready to ride off down the path to hell. Lighting struck and his horse reared wildly. The hermit gazed in wonder and said: "Go with God!" Then he spurred his swift steed; his mount careened forward with the quickness of a chariot mastered by the devil.

The hermitage bells rang with an ominous clamor as he left into the forest; then the spirits of the night set upon him a most terrible storm. Thunder and lightning, wind and rain, hail and mist was all summoned to delude him. The forest branches were hewed by heavy winds; pouring rain, hail and thunder set upon Mardur; his vicious enemy the elements were controlled by the devil. The sky bellowed like a bull and a thunderous din sounded as in Gomorrah before its judgement.

I'll say it again: every kind of foul thing came from the skies: hail, thunder, lightning and rain. It pounded upon our pitied knight relentlessly. Mardur prayed and put his shield above him to protect himself from the skies terrible onslaught. These were the signs that the devil was upon him. Alas, a knight in black armor came riding from the forest so quickly and it was dark so that he could hardly be seen. He came upon Mardur, lance lowered, striking him square on the shield. The lance was shattered, knocking Mardur from his fine horse. Before Mardur could get up the knight was gone into the elm wood forest with his horse. Mardur was in a real fix, for he had lost his steed and been unhorsed so suddenly. He barely even saw the knight before he vanished.

He looked around and the blood orange moon shed enough light for him to see that he was in the very bowels of hell. The elm wood forest surrounded him. He saw dead knights hanging from the elm wood branches;

their arms were hung in the branches beside them showing that they had truly been slain by the evil spirits. He didn't count them but know that there were three thousand dead corpses hung in that forest upon the elm branches, many of them once incredibly valiant knights.

Then, as Mardur looked on in horror, the evil spirits surrounded the knight. The storm's violence increased and a whirlwind came from the sky that looked like three heads of a beast with the tongues of a demon. The gusts of wind and thunderous din would be terrifying to any knight who lacked faith. Among the demons that came out to attack him several were headless, others fowl and ghoulish. They had scabs on their skin and were covered in plumes of black smoke. And do you know what else? They desired nothing more than to eat his flesh and take his soul! How pitiful was Mardur's situation? When they had surrounded the unhorsed knight they came upon him with a mighty horde.

The brave Mardur gave out a roar like a lion and raised his sword, running into the thickest of the press: for their we're a good twenty demons that surrounded him. He brought his keen-edged blade out and began lopping off heads, arms, limbs and shedding much blood. He clove heads all the way to the shoulder with his heavy steel blade. He cut through mailhoods, battered the hoops, littered rings of mail from hauberks and ventails and shattered gems from helms. One demon came at him and, with a mighty flourish he struck him on the helm, splitting it to the nasal. He crushed them with his might, bringing his sword down on one so that it split him in two from the top of his head to his chest. He stuck his blade through another so that it went through his mouth and out the backend of his skull. He was surely dead from that blow. Then he swirled about, defending himself on all sides. He used the elm tree to protect his back, even though he could hardly bare to look at the dead corpse looming above him, swinging about the branch. He hurled his sword into the foe with all his might, plunging it into one's chest and another was beheaded swiftly thereafter.

What more is there to know? He was victorious over the enemy. His blows battered and hacked away demons so that bowels and brains flew everywhere. His agility and swift strength was such that no display of combat could compare. When he had felled ten demons in this way, he saw the other ten coming towards him; though he was little afraid, but rather crossed himself in the name of the Father, Son and Holy spirit. When he did this the remaining ten howled in fear and turned to dust. Such was the power of God that they feared his holy sign greatly.

Make no doubt that Mardur smashed helms from heads, shields from necks and knights from saddles that day. Even when he had lost his horse it was made clear that no opponent could strike him without paying dearly with fatal, mighty blows. Yet, the power of God was the ultimate defense against these cruel creatures.

When the smoke from the demons cleared he saw a beautiful horse whinnying in the forest. He ran towards it; yet the old destrier baulked and reared when he tried to mount it. It started pounding his hooves terribly. Nonetheless, Mardur was a skilled rider and managed to mount the horse.

Yet, when he finally mounted, he realized it was no horse, but a demon! It heeded him not one bit despite the spur but careened off towards the cliff at the edge of the forest. Mardur was sure it would run off the cliff with him on it! So, utterly helpless, he crossed himself and put his life into the hands of God. Then, a great gust of wind removed him from the saddle. Then Mardur watched in astonishment as the demonic horse galloped right off the cliff and fell amongst the rocks and river below, perishing.

Mardur was exhausted, for he had done combat with demons, been knocked from his horse unexpectedly, and almost been killed by a demonic horse! He rested on an elm tree, starring at the disfigured bodies which loomed above him as they rotted. A great horror was in these lands for truly it was full of wickedness and sin.

Though, despite all of this, he felt safer than any noble in the finest castle for he had the power of God with him. He walked about a league and it was still night when he arrived at a wide and deep river; he saw it by the light of the blood orange moon. He was thirsty so he kneeled to take a drink. Then, as he rested on the bank, he saw a curious light in the distance.

A boat came to the shore and it was covered in silk sheets checkered with indigo and green so that it was a beautiful marvel to gaze at. Squires came running unto the bank and pulled up the boat too; they hurried to land bringing with them a great many candles, torches and equipment. They set up a splendid pavilion of the finest red and put therein an exquisite bed of with blankets of samite.

Mardur was happy to see the active company for it seemed they were in high spirits. Just then, a beautiful maiden stepped from the boat. Her eyes were set upon Mardur and she came right for him. She had a lovely mantle of tyrian cloth lined with ermine. Her hair was golden and the color of a bright broom. Her skin was fairer than a white dove. Need I say more? She was very beautiful and was a familiar face to our knight. "Greetings, my love. I came seeking your company!"

He took a long look at the woman. Then, suddenly, he realized it was his lover whom he was planning to marry within the month, the beautiful Esmeraude! "My love! It is a strange thing seeing you here, in the forest of the waste land. Whatever are you doing?" Could he see through this deceit? Did he realize it was only a demon disguised as the one he loved, attempting to lead him into temptation? How cruel was his fate that night!

Through magic and deception she seemed in every way, by features and comeliness, to be the man's beloved Esmeraude. Indeed, he began kissing her and embracing her. Then she had a table on trestles set up in the pavilion. A great array of food was served and he ate heartily. He was well protected from the storm by the warmth of the squirrel lined mantle that she put on him. The nice fire they made and the marvelous feast that was prepared was all a luxury to distract him from the truth.

He ate and drank much, for he had gone through such distress that day without food or drink. After, he talked with this lovely woman and she said to him: "My Mardur, I came here seeking you, to bring you home! But why wait until the marriage? I want nothing more than to lay with you right now in this wondrous bed my men have prepared for us. I was so worried when I heard you took up the quest of the wasteland. I thought you would need my love to support you." He replied: "Well, I have survived. And, I am more pleased than anything that you are here." Flushed with wine, Mardur agreed to go to bed with her, for he was quite out of his wits by then; and who wouldn't be so eager to be with his lover after such torment?

They both got into the bed and, when he felt her naked body upon him he almost fell for it! Though something came to his mind that the good hermit said: that he should be vigilant of the evil-doer who comes in many forms. So he crossed himself in the name of the Father, Son and Holy spirit. When he did this, the whole pavilion, including the feigned Esmeraude, vanished into smoke. Alas, God had vanquished the demon who sought to make him sin mortally. The storm then abated, for it was God's will that it did. Mardur lay upon the river bank, in tears of wonder and shame. "Oh God, why hast thou forsaken me?" Then, slowly, the sun began to rise for it was a new day dawning. The light of day vanquishes any evil that boiled in the darkness and illuminates the heavens so that all can see God's beauty more clearly.

Another boat came to him, and know that it was the holy man from the hermitage. He was gracious in meeting him for truly the soul fights hard to be admitted into heaven. Then he spoke to him, calling out from the boat as he saw the pitiful man groveling on the shore: "Mardur, come aboard and I will give you great comfort. You have prevailed against the wicked devil and he will be smarting from your rebukes for some time! Know that he has been utterly confounded by your grace, patience and will to persevere. Know that God is always with you to bring you strength in tribulation; he has sent me here to heal you of your wounds and provide counsel."

With that Mardur, who was exhausted, came aboard the holy man's ship. He was well taken care of and many provisions were provided for him. At last, he was returned to the castle, never forgetting his horrible escapade in La Terre Sauvaige. When he recounted the tale at

51

court it was written down by the King's scribes so that we still know of it today.

# 6 THE ABDUCTION

Sagremor the unruly fell madly in love with a damsel from Arthur's court. They were so infatuated with one another that they set out into the forest, seeking adventure together for they could not be separated. At this time King Arthur was searching for his noble nephew Sir Gawain. Sagremor and the maiden, whose name was Blanche, set up a splendid pavilion of red silk; they positioned it in a fine meadow land of lush, green grass hoping to spot Gawain. The pavilion had a gold eagle on top of the beam, and could be seen clearly from the forest.

One day, Sagremor was out hunting. It wasn't long before the mighty Gawain came that way. He dismounted and entered the pavilion after tying his horse to an oak tree nearby. When he entered he found the maiden laying on a wondrous bed of samite; she was quite ready to greet him. "Welcome, good knight. What brings you to these parts?" And Gawain, after realizing she was alone, sat upon the bed beside her and said: "Well, my lady. I have come seeking adventure. I am a knight of King Arthur's court and swear to do right by all maidens. Tell me, do you have a lover?" As they talked in this way Gawain learned that she was betrothed to Sagremor. He replied: "I know him well; he is courteous and admirable. You have chosen wisely!"

Blanche was a fine host and very polite; she called to her girls to disarm Gawain. They placed on him a comfortable mantle of silk lined with squirrel fur that was peacock blue. It was a most beautiful mantle. When he was disarmed and his horse was given plenty of oats he became relaxed. They continued to talk for some time before a great villain arrived at the pavilion. A man in black arms came careening into the meadow and, seeing the lovely maiden Blanche, swore to take her: "By the Holy Ghost i've never seen such a gorgeous maiden, I will have her for myself!"

Then, before Gawain could get up, he rode before her and swooped her up unto his horse's neck. Then, like a hart in fright, galloped off into the woods. Gawain was enraged. "How could he take my friend's lady so ruthlessly! What shame, she is certainly not going to willingly. All maidens should be conducted in a way that gives leave only unto the things they willingly desire."

Gawain, so deeply incensed, without even arming, jumped on his horse; he quickly grabbed his lance, shield and girded on his sword, putting it in its scabbard. He spurred his horse and charged forth at an incredible speed. The hooves pounded with a thunderous din as he came upon the captive maiden and her abductor. He road through the forest until he came to a valley where the knight had slowed down.

When he saw Gawain coming for him unarmed he roared with laughter. Gawain called out to him: "Stop there! Give me back that maiden right now. I challenge you, and, come what may, you will suffer for your wrong!" The knight in black armor said nothing but set the maiden down on the grass and spurred his horse towards the knight.

With lances lowered they braced themselves in their stirrups until they stretched the straps. The black knight lowered his lance and struck Gawain's shield, shattering it into many pieces. Though Gawain was not moved. He returned the favor with interest, striking such a mighty blow that the knight toppled into a heap. Indeed, the lance struck him in the left side beneath the hauberk and rent his shield in two. When he fell his helm set with gems flew from his head and crashed into a tree, shattering the gems. Then he lay still on the ground, in shock at the blow.

Gawain dismounted, took his sword from its scabbard and ran towards the knight. He had no need to unlace his helm for it had already been removed in the blow he had given him; he put the keen-edged blade to the man's neck and spoke to him: "You are finished, surrender and become my prisoner!" Yet, there was no response. He realized the man was quite out of his wits so he waited for him to regain consciousness.

When he finally came to and realized that there was a sword on his neck, he pleaded as a men in the grips of death does: "Please have mercy, kind knight. Forgive me, I will be your servant and do anything you wish!" Gawain was unmoved: "Well, you ought to give yourself to the maiden here." The black knight replied: "Oh please, anything but that. If she takes me she will surely put me to death for my shame. Anything but that!" Gawain said: "Fine. You will go to the court of King Arthur and make yourself his prisoner." The black knight was happy with this and he rode off to court immediately. Gawain said: "Tell the good King that you are sent by Gawain and that I will return to court, God willing, by Pentecost."

Gawain put the maiden upon the neck of his horse and rode back to the red pavilion at a brisk pace. When they arrived Sagremor had just returned from the hunt. He saw the two approaching and was disturbed to see his maiden riding alongside another knight: "Who is he riding with my maiden? This is a grave offense and he will suffer for it!"

Yet, before he could get too labored with jealousy the servant girls explained to him the whole story about how Blanche was hastily kidnapped and Gawain rode after them without any armor. "And it appears he won over the black knight, for hear he comes riding with our lady!" When Sagremor learned that it was Gawain who had freed Blanche he was overcome with joy. When they saw each other they embraced and kissed most fervently, for it had been a long time since they had seen one another.

They spent time talking about Arthur's court and all the successes of the knights: "So many adventures have happened that our knights are renown throughout the whole world. There is little doubt that we have vanquished evil from the land of Logres. King Arthur would love you to return to court and celebrate your good deeds. Can you come with me at first light tomorrow?" Gawain said to him: "I can't return yet for there is still adventure I have sworn to complete. If I divert from it I will be much shamed. God willing, I will return by the feast of Pentecost, for it would be a great dishonor to miss his summons by then." Sagremor was happy to hear it and swore to bring his message to the king; they spoke only of joyous things and had a large meal prepared. After they had eaten and drank heartily, a large bed was prepared for Gawain in a separate pavilion and he slept deeply for it had been a long time since he felt the comfort of a bed.

55

# 7 BEAUREPAIRE

Before Gawain could arise a maiden rode into the pavilion at a swift pace. She saw Gawain there and sent for him directly. Gawain, half asleep, scratched his head and rose from the bed in a hurry; for it was clear by her demeanor that she had an important message. When he was prepared to receive her he had the ladies send for him. "Gawain, I bring word from your lover Cassandre. She is in much distress and pleads that you accept this call to arms. A wicked knight named Thoas has, thinking you dead, laid siege Beaurepaire. It won't be long before he takes it; if you don't hurry your lover will surely be lost! Don't let her loose her maidenhood to such a vile creature that does it by force; come to her rescue, for she is rightfully yours. I can take you there now if you mount and arm; but be quick about it for the castle is two leagues away and they are already under attack."

Gawain needed little else for he was already fully enraged. The thought of his lovely maiden being attacked forcefully made him completely mad. "It is absurd," he said, "no good knight who has taken the accolade, searing under oath to protect kingdom and do right by God, would ever, in his right mind, lay siege to a lady and demand her love by force! It is cruel, no, wicked! By God, such an act will be avenged." Completely overcome with anger and quite inconsolable the noble Gawain armed himself. Sagremor watched in delight and pity. Delight was on his side because he knew Gawain would make Thoas pay and pity because he saw how forlorn Gawain was by the message. The two bold knights embraced and kissed as they bid farewell. Gawain and the lovely maiden galloped off along the most straight road in a hurry towards Beaurepaire.

The castle two leagues away but they arrived by nones. When Gawain rode up to the castle wall, the fair Cassandre spotted him from the tower. It was a magnificent castle that was situated around meadows, vineyards and cornfields. Though Gawain came from the back end where the fortress wall was cornered by the sea on one half and the gloomy forest, which Gawain came from, on the other. When he entered through the gate and came into the courtyard Cassandre, dressed in the most magnificent indigo silk garment, ran towards him with her arms out. She embraced him and they exchanged many kisses, for it had been a long time since they saw one another. He was taken into a splendid hall where a feast was prepared; they opened the gold chest and had an ermine lined mantle brought to him that was made of precious scarlet. Gawain expressed to her his desire to avenge the wrong done to her by Thoas. He further mentioned: "On my way through the forest I saw that villainous knight encamped with about forty men at arms. They wouldn't dare attack me or the castle at the sight of me." Cassandre, over joyed at his arrival-for she had been on the brink of despair-had Gawain well taken care of. They ate a wondrous meal and spent the afternoon discussing the best course of action. Gawain said: "I will ride out and meet him at first light, trusting in God to protect me. It will be a challenge that, if I win, he will be forced to flee and never bother you again. For I truly love you, my dear. I will always be disposed to your will whenever you call." In this way they talked a great deal about love. Over the months since he had been gone Cassandre, who was well disposed to the arts, had a lay created. They called it the lay of love and it had been spread throughout Logres. Little did he know it was about him! After the meal a minstrel came to the court and played it so fluently that they both were overcome with tears. They really did love one another, and may you hear it sung now:

*Gracious lover out there,*
*I weave this lay for you,*
*That you may hear me sing,*
*Of a love that is new,*
*I told it to the birds,*
*They spread it far and wide,*
*That you may hear me sing,*
*From atop branches high,*
*The nightingale will sing,*
*Bringing my Love fresh news,*
*When you are so weary,*

57

*Hear this lay from the birds,*
*And you will be stronger,*
*Knowing your lover true,*
*I will never fail you,*
*I have just one request:*
*Come home! Bring me kisses!*
*That is little to ask,*
*You are battle weary,*
*Find rest and love at home.*

Gawain was completely overjoyed at the lay she had made for him. Indeed, he had heard it sung before amongst the birds while he was in the woods but never realized it had been made from him. In the thick of battle he had heard it from the highest branches; many knights had heard it, bringing them solace. That is how the fair Cassandre was made famous by this beautiful lay which had been carried across Logres by the birds. For she had been in such despair that her lover was gone she knew no other way to tell him how she felt. Gawain promised that he would return her love ten fold. He slept well that night in a separate chamber in a magnificent bed. For who doesn't sleep well when they have made their way home after many tribulations and much travel? Girls came to undress him, lighting candles for his pleasure by the bedside. When he rose in the morning he found his armor neatly laid on the table for him so that he could quickly put it on. He girded his keen-edged blade and put on his gold hauberk. He went outside to find his horse already saddled and well fed. Cassandre met with him in the courtyard and bid him come to mass. They celebrated mass in the morning; it was a glorious service and they were well graced by the presence of the holy spirit.

Just as the mass was ending a boy came rushing into the building, yelling: "The wicked betrayer Thoas has laid siege to the castle! He is out front with his men and demands a challenger or he will storm the castle by force, taking our lady as his own." At this Gawain was further incensed; he waited no longer but mounted and rode for the gate. When the gate was opened he went out into the field with little fear for he knew that God was by his side.

He crossed himself and shouted: "You think force can get you what you want? It does little when you are full of wickedness and deceit. My maiden has summoned me to do you harm and rightly so. Prepare to suffer for your transgression here. It is shameful to siege a castle with a helpless maiden inside. Shameful!" Thoas was not in the least bit disturbed but did recognize that it was Gawain who challenged him. He reeled with rage and it wasn't long before he had his men make way for the challenger and an accord was made: "If I win I will storm the castle and have the Lady. If you win I will leave these lands and never return to harm the maiden. Given you are of King Arthur's court, I will make myself his prisoner on your behalf if I am defeated." When it was settled they spoke no more, for they didn't like one another very much.

Thus they made ready to joust on the meadow out front of the castle. Both had stout, sharp lances of ash wood. They lowered them and spurred on in a gallop. The two horses collided head to head so that they both tumbled to the ground in a daze. Both knight's shattered their lances against shields, breaking both lance and shield apart. The knights rose quickly and drew their swords from their scabbards. I will not belabor the subject, the two fought and gave one another many wounds. Cassandre tried to watch from the tower but was so beside herself with fear and torment that she cried unceasingly, keeping her head in her arms. She was quite unable to watch for fear that she brought Gawain any harm for summoning him but she prayed fervently to God that he would be delivered. What an honorable woman she was! Maybe it was her prayers that gave him victory. For Gawain dealt a blow to Thoas that was so powerful it tore through hauberk and flesh and went to the bone. The man's shoulder was completely rent in two and he fell to the ground in a swoon of pain. Unable to rise, Gawain unlaced his gem studded helm and threatened to kill him. For all his fancy equipment he was surely humbled by that fierce blow! Just as the accord had been made, the man duly cried: "Oh knight, I have clearly been vanquished. I will leave these lands and never return, you have fought honorably." Gawain agreed to this. Thoas's men were all very bitter about seeing their master so easily defeated and shamed. They rode away in a dismal state while Gwain called out: "If you return be sure that I will be here to greet you. No doubt, any payment you make here will be returned with interest!"

Alas, Gawain was victorious. He returned to the castle and Cassandre gave him so many kisses that he was quite overwhelmed with it. They spent the night in the big, spacious hall with so many happy guests and delicious food. They were deeply in love and said much about their hopes for the future. Gawain managed to practice his talents and composed a lay of his own for the maiden. When it was done he had it presented to her in her chamber by one of the minstrels. Thanks to that good man of the silver harp we have it still recorded today, for he shared it with the scribes. Know that many knights heard this lay and found it useful with their own ladies: may it also point you in the right direction! Thus, King Arthur's nephew had a lay of love that went like this:

*My sweet, my love, my joy,*
*In combat my heart thumps,*
*For our souls are entwined,*
*I think of you always,*
*In darkness your with me,*
*A light that guides me through,*
*Love abides patiently,*
*In the midst of trials,*
*I dare to win you over,*
*Take my love and my heart,*
*Do with it as thou wilt,*
*Great delights we will share,*
*When the enemy dies!*

Since the noble Gawain was no poet this was a marvelous feat. Minstrels played it in courts far and wide so that it was heard many times over. When valiant knights heard it they repeated it and it became widely known. For every minstrel was sure to mention that it was sung by the nephew of King Arthur when he was in the very throes of love! Cassandre was elated to have such a great lover. When Gawain said it was time for him to leave she protested. After much debate she agreed to let him go, but not willingly. Before he left she gifted him a ring of stone that had in it the most eloquent ruby. "Take this, my love. You will see that this ruby has magical powers. It can ward off any wickedness or deception. If you are attacked by an enchantress you need only have it on your finger to see the truth and the way. For it, quite plainly, dispels all evil enchantments and magic. May the Lord bless you and keep you from harm. Return to me soon so that we can finally marry, I can't wait any longer you know!" With that Gawain rode from the castle at first light, leaving behind him the most beautiful maiden imaginable. Yet he still had more marvelous feats to accomplish before returning and marrying her.

# 8 THE FLOOD

I'll now tell you of a marvelous adventure that concluded with the making of what we today call Ireland. Indeed, there was a land in the seas where a wicked ruler and false prophet sought to control the people there. He was an enchanter of the magical arts and ruled the lands with the power of illusion. This king, named Ghenon, thought himself all powerful before the people. So great was his pride that he truly thought himself a God. He constructed a large stone tower and from it conducted a great many marvels of the dark arts that so happened to captivate the people of the land. His black magic projected to the people marvelous visions of him on a golden thrown next to his wife, the Queen. It seemed as if they were all omnipotent but it was no more than smoke and mirrors. He did not believe in the one true God and the trinity; his dark arts were wicked and he never aided the people. He used his power to bolster his own image rather than helping others. This was his greatest downfall for he would come to be destroyed by a true christian knight of valor.

Gadifer, at the time, who was the son of the King of Scotland, was just the right kind of knight for the job. The Queen's daughter, Flamine, was tired of Ghenon's ruse. She was eager to find help for her father was getting out of control. He even lusted after his own daughter and planned to marry her. This was a cruel wickedness for that man was set upon by the devil; if he was not destroyed he would continue his wickedness. So Flamine set messengers to far away lands in secret, hoping to find a knight to defeat her father.

So, as a mentioned, Gadifer was the right flavor of knight. The call to arms was answered by Gadifer who came to that isle to dispel the sorcery that so many feared. Know that he wore arms of vermillion and carried the blazon and pennon of the good King Arthur. He was a knight of the Round Table and took counsel among the twelve peers. He was well known for his deeds of prowess which is why he was able to assail all evil.

To tell you briefly, there were only three tables made in the likeness of the round: the first by Jesus at the last supper, the second by Josephus when they came to Britain and the last by Uther Pendragon, Arthur's father. This one became the Table Round when it was gifted to him when he married his daughter, Gwen. All of these tables were important for their own reasons. They all demonstrated the unity of the twelve peers, or apostles, and were intertwined in the miracles of the Holy Spirit. For Jesus broke the bread and gave it to his disciples. Josephus multiplied fish and bread by the power of God, giving it to his five thousand followers, and Arthur witnessed the presence of the Holy Spirit and the mystery of the grail at the round table. Also, at the round table, the miracle of the perilous seat-which you will hear more of later-occurred.

Let's get back to the story. The whole island believed in this hollow man's illusions for they seemed like holy visions because he disguised them so well with magic. Though they were not from the true God but from the devil; just as the devil was proud he produced things that attempted to rival God's power before he was struck down by his might; for the devil was imprisoned by his schemes which were foiled by the true master.

Know that Gadifer wore a ring which could detect all magic and enchantment; this ring had been gifted to him by his lover, a fairy. There were many rings of power. This one was most useful in a number of adventures. This ring proved very helpful when he discovered his friends imprisoned in the invisible castle; for he was the only one who could see the entrance and leapt to save them just before their execution. It also proved worthy in this test!

When they reached the island it was nearing night fall. Hear how he was able to find Flamine: The mariner had him hid in a package of silks and goods for the castle. These were, by God's grace, delivered directly to her room. So that, as he heard her weeping over her situation, he called out to her from the box: "Do not worry lady, I am a knight of King Arthur, descended from a king myself, and I have been summoned by your messenger to destroy your father the false prophet."

Flamine was terrified that the box in the room had a voice and thought it was a spell afoot. Though he repeatedly assured her he was good and true. Finally, she worked up the courage to open the box and was pleased to find a beautiful knight who was tall and handsome. Then she was quite relieved and made him comfortable. She told him "every night my father does a show with his powers at the tower. I will take you there so you can stop it."

At night time she took him to the tower to see the visions from Ghenon. At this time people from all over the land went to see these visions. Yet, as the illusions began to captivate the divers sorts of people Gadifer was unmoved. He saw nothing but a stone tower, for, as you may recall, his ring dispelled all kinds of magic. How foolish he thought the people they're worshiping this man!

He set off with helmet laced, sword girded and shield around neck towards the entrance of the tower. Flamine was terribly frightened for she saw something quite different. Here is what appeared in the vision: There were a great number of knights, fully armed, in procession around her father. Then there was a throne of gold with Ghenon upon it, with the Queen at his right hand.

A splendidly arrayed table with all kinds of food was laid out. One hundred trumpeters were making an extravagant display, with horns blaring. All sights and sounds were heard that delighted the people. These were all illusions, of course, and how the dark arts so impressed the multitude was truly astonishing. They craved to worship him.

Meanwhile, as this was going on, Gadifer meant business. He broke into the tower and climbed to the top of the spiral staircase until he reached a circular hall. It was a wide, circular hall that had large glass windows making the lands below fully visible. In that room sat Ghenon casting spells. A great many vials were littered throughout the room; at the center there was a stone that glowed with as many colors as the rainbow. The stone had many panels of glass surrounding it; the light reflected off of the glass so that when the glass turned by Ghenon's direction is projected different visions to awe the people.

Gadifer spoke to the man, saying: "How dare you lead these people into false worship. You are not a God but a false prophet and deserve to suffer for your transgression. In what world is it right to capture people with false promises and lead them unto blindness?

A shepherd that is blind does no good with the sheep, his followers! You are guided by yourself alone. For what you show them is fake and hollow; it is worth no more than a false oath. Then you claim to take your daughter as your wife? This is an even worse sin. If you think you are a God I will let you taste my steel blade and we can determine if your flesh is the same as mine."

Gadifer took his sword from his scabbard and began smashing all the vials and potions that were used. Ghenon attempted to cast two spells on him. The first was meant to paralyze him, though it had no effect because of the stone ring he wore. The second spell summoned a massive army of demons who were the most vile creatures anyone has seen. They bellowed loudly and were surrounded by black smoke and blue flames, for they had been summoned from Hell. Gadifer was assailed on all sides but the power of the ring protected him, for they could come no closer than nine feet.

When Ghenon saw his power was useless he called on the devil who quickly carried him away into the air on a swift chariot. Gadifer did not leave without destroying the tower and all that was inside it. When it was consumed in flames he exited, delighted. The people outside were aghast when they saw their beloved visions crumble before them. They thought that something terrible had happened to this fake God and suspected treachery. So they armed themselves and surrounded the tower, attempting to protect Ghenon, who they believed was still in the tower, from attack. Though little did they know he fled from them. In this way the people sinned greatly; even after the illusion was destroyed they continued to blindly worship.

Gadifer slipped out the back door and met with Flamine who was eagerly awaiting him. They took off in a hurry towards the shore and found the mariner waiting on the shore. When they made it to see they saw a terrible storm arise from the island. They watched with amazement as a terrible thing happened.

The winds became rough, smoke surrounded the island and great balls of fire hurled to the ground. Then a bright light was seen in the skies above. A white knight, carried on a bier by four men and surrounded by candles, soared through the air. Then he arose from the bier, and, drawing his sword, began attacking the demons that came from the island.

A tremendous battle ensued where the white knight delivered many fatal blows to the demon horde summoned by King Ghenon. The fight between the demons and this white knight lasted for some time; everyone on the boat watched in astonishment. Eventually, when all the demons were slain, the entire island erupted in flames and was then consumed by the sea. It sank into the deep ocean, nowhere to be seen. It was no doubt that this had been an act of God, purging away the wickedness of the people.

The next morning, at first light, they could see from the ship that, off in the distance, a new land had formed where Ghenon had been previously. This land was lush, green and nice. The skies were blue and the land appeared very fertile. The pastures and valley's had been tilled and it seemed like the whole place was perfect for humans.

They sailed towards the island to get a better look at it. When they came to the sandy shore Flamine was afraid to step ashore. So Gadifer let his horse go and, when he set his hooves on the hard ground he whinnied and reared with delight. Gadifer followed after him, mounted and galloped around, enjoying every moment.

He explored the land and the many sights. It was a very remarkable place, green and fertile, and was truly blessed by God. That island, so fair, was to be called Ireland. Gadifer found, in the center of the island, a marvelous stone tomb that was a great wonder to behold. It was entirely made of stone and had many precious jewels about it. On it read an inscription. It was the Queen, Flamine's mother, who was to be buried there. Fortunately, the mariner, while drifting near the shore, spotted her body floating in the sea. They brought it on a bier and buried her on the island. When she was put into the stone tomb it immediately closed so that no one could open it again.

After burying her mother they set sail for Britain. On the way back another terrible storm arose. It was a sign that evil was afoot and Gadifer unsheathed his sword and said: "Be on your guard for the evil spirits are lurking nearby."

Suddenly, Demons from the skies came down upon the boat, striking the sailors. They broke the masthead and tore the sail. The boat was completely destroyed but was still able to float around, aimlessly. All the sailors were killed by these terrible beasts who had sharp talons that ripped apart their helpless bodies; many of them were carried into the air and dropped into the ocean, drowning perilously.

Gadifer stood on the deck, attacking them wherever he could, splitting open their heads and cutting off their limbs. He was so incensed that his face blazed and his eyes burned in his head like candle flames. The demons saw him and scurried away, for they feared him greatly. From a distance they shouted: "We have come from Ghenon and ask for his daughter. His only wish is to have her with him in Hell where he dwells."

Gadifer heard the demon but didn't replay, at least with words. He replied with deeds. He took his lance from below deck and hurled it a great distance, it plunged into the demon's heart and he fell in a swoon the ocean, dead.

Then he yelled out to the other evil spirits: "Your master is in Hell where he belongs. That is what he gets for leading his people astray. He is eternally humbled, like Satan, for his wickedness. I know that the Holy Spirit wanted to destroy you treacherous beasts. Now a beautiful land has been replaced by the one you ruined. Take care never to return, for you shall never have Flamine or any earthly joy again! If you come back here, know I will be waiting to return blow for blow!" Then the demons wept as they soared into the air, leaving the ship in the ocean.

Thus Flamine and Gadifer remained in the boat that wandered aimlessly through the ocean. Though, by the grace of God, the wind guided it to the shores of England where they were met with delight by the King, who had many servants along the shore anxiously awaiting any sign of them. That is how they returned safely and the story of the founding of Ireland was recorded. Flamine fell in love with Gadifer and they were wedded. May the Holy Spirit continue to bless those lands that were founded by the righteous.

# 9 THE MYSTERY OF THE GOLDEN CART

There was a magnificent castle near a meadow and some rich mills that stood upon a hillside. Indeed, this was a place of excitement and marvels that demands we tell of it without expense; should you fail to hear it the misfortune would be yours! Like I said it was a good land: on one side there were corn fields, another lush green valleys and in front an open meadow with a mighty river that flowed around it. The castle was incredibly well fortified and provisioned with a wide, deep moat surrounding it.

At this time the king of that place was eager to marry off his daughter. He called for all his barons and had them assembled in court. A great train of man, adorned in samite and fine silk robes, came to the court with an array of squires, horses and friends. When they were all gathered the king said: "I'm growing old. It is high time my daughter finds a wife because she is going to have to provide me with an heir! I don't want the child to, well, be a child when I die." The barons agreed that this was very true. So, they arranged for a tournament in the meadow before the castle. They said: "Let the winner of the tournament have the prize, for he would surely be the best knight in all the land that is most deserving of your lands after you've gone." The king though this was a splendid idea and sent messages all across the land to come to his castle on the day of Pentecost where a marvelous tournament would be held.

Knights of prowess heeded the call, desirous to test their metal in the tourney lists. The messages said: "Two spectacular prizes will be awarded to the victor: the king is giving his beautiful sparrow hawk. The second, his beautiful daughter!" What a prize that was, for four hundred knights gathered on the day of the tournament to win the maiden's royal hand.

They came from foreign parts on big armored destriers with shields on necks and lances leveled. Some had vermillion arms and it was a wonder to behold the nobility. Each carried their arms and heraldry proudly, some carrying a pennon of their arms on their steel lance head. One thing was common: They were all very eager to do battle. Surely the promise of a noble maiden and great riches further motivated them.

There was one tiny detail of misfortune: lady who was to be given-the kings daughter-who was named Minerve, already had a lover! Such was the trouble of the time that father's went about arranging things, having their plans foiled by desire, passion and love! Love! That cruel entity that poisoned the hearts of many unto their destruction.

Minerve's lover, however, was a man of the utmost prowess and honor. He had left the castle years before, never to be seen again. His last words to his beloved were: "I am not worthy of your love. Alas, let me go about and do some great deed. Then, when I have won much honor, your father will approve of me." Miverve replied: "Oh, I can't bare it: you being gone. Please remember me by this ring." She gently placed a stone ring upon his finger. It had a bright ruby in it that shined as radiantly as the lady's face when she beheld her lover. She blushed deeply and kissed him on the cheek, a kiss that he would never forget.

Ah, how valiant and noble he was, for he went about seven years accomplishing a great many adventures. He sent over two hundred prisoners to the king, but the king knew him only as the knight of the serpent and not by any other name. He was easily recognized by his arms; he carried a blue shield emblazoned with a green serpent upon it. I will tell you that his name was Melian de Lis.

Meanwhile, Minerve, when she caught wind of the coming tournament, struggled with the prospect that she may be forced to wed someone that was not her lover. Minverve hoped and prayed that Melian was out there and returned in time for the tournament; for now was his chance to wed her! She, who had been his lover since before he could wield a sword.

Let us see what Melian was up to at this time. It wasn't easy being a knight on the road. He travelled aimlessly through the forest of marvels, seeking adventure. He had been riding for several days without any food or lodging when he came across a most peculiar adventure. Melian was trotting along when he came to a tent near a spring. A dwarf was outside the pavilion and yelled out: "Whatever are you doing in these parts? This is my lord's land." Then the dwarf, being very ungracious, took out a rod and started hitting Melian's horse on the head! Melian replied: "Stop that or I'll run you down!" So Melian spurred his horse so that the dwarf was hurled to the ground by the impact of his horse's chest.

Then, in all the commotion, a knight poked his head out of the tent. He had fiery red hair and an evil countenance. When he saw the knight he quickly donned his arms while saying: "Wait right there, I'm getting armed! How dare you strike my dwarf!"

"He was a very wicked dwarf that deserved to be struck."

"However you feel it is very shameful to attack someone so much smaller than you."

"You haven't taught your dwarf any manners, which means you have none yourself!"

Then the knight, tired of banter, came out of the pavilion fully armed. He carried a silver shield with a red fox upon it. He mounted a swift black charger and, charged faster than merlin's. The two knights spurred their steeds and, with lances leveled, hurled at each other, exchanging fierce blows. The serpent knight thrust his lance into the knight's shield, smashing it to pieces whilst splintering his spear; he bore the opposing knight to the ground in a heap.

The wounded knight, quite ashamed, was completely stunned. Melian dismounted and strode over to him with his sword drawn. When the other knight rose a sword fight began. They assailed one another exchanging perilous blows on the helm, chest and arms. Blood spurted out and they were both severely wounded. Though Melian was the better knight; he dealt him a staggering blow on the arm that cut into the flesh. The knight could do little but fall to the ground in a swoon.

When the battle was decisively over, the knight of the fox didn't try to continue the fight. This knight was known to be very wicked and an evil enchanter. So, listen closely to how he deceived Melian with his silver tongue.

He pleaded for his life so fervently: "Oh, great knight, I am lost. You have defeated me utterly, how ashamed I am. I swear to be your prisoner from here on out and will only do your will."

Just when Melian de Lis yielded to his pleas and turned his back the knight of fox enchanted him with a wicked spell. This spell put him into a deep sleep. He laid down near an oak tree and didn't wake up. Indeed, the magic was so forceful that he was unable to rise. This was a grave misfortune for the day of the tournament was fast approaching!

So the elated knight of the fox took the sleeping knight from that place and imprisoned him in his castle. He was kept there without food and tortured severely. Melian awoke in the prison and was deeply distressed; he kneeled down and prayed for safety. An amazing miracle occurred because of Melian's faith in God. He who prays is always answered: since God came to him in the form of an angel in the night. Smoke arose and a great light shined in the dark cell. The angel radiated with beauty and had in his hands an exquisite grail of silver and gems. He presented the grail before Melian and he looked inside. When he looked he was immediately filled with the Holy Spirit and was fed with heavenly food. In this way he didn't go hungry and lacked nothing, for that angel came to him daily.

While Melian De Lis endured imprisonment the knight of the fox pondered what to do with him. He decided it would be most prudent to behead him since he had been so shamed. Moreover, since he was loved much by the king, take the head to him as a present. So he sent word to his guards who aggressively pulled Melian from the cell and into the courtyard where they were sharpening an axe. They were just getting ready to do the deed when, suddenly, a loud horn blast was heard three times from outside the castle.

The knight of the fox went to the tower to see who it was and, to his dismay, he saw the last person he wanted to see. It was one of the most beautiful maidens in the world and she was flanked by two knights and followed by three beautiful maidens and each had a knight as escort. They rode to the front gate of the castle and the squire

with them blew the ivory horn so loud that it made the
castle hall and surrounding forest quake.

The knight of the fox was beside himself with
rage because he knew the fun was over. That lady was no
other than the Queen of the forest of marvels and her
majesty was unrivaled. Everyone in the forest did as she
commanded, for if they didn't they would face ruin. The
Queen saw the knight of the fox peeking from the fortified tower and she yelled out: "The knight you have imprisoned against his will must be freed. You have done a
great wrong and, if you don't release him immediately, you
can be sure that I will make you suffer for it." The knight
of the fox had no choice but to yield his prisoner or lose
his life. "Fair Queen, I humbly ask for your grace and do
not be angered with me. It was by a fair fight this knight
became my prisoners. Although, since you ask, I will willingly hand him over." Though, all he said was but lies and
folly, but the fox was clever enough to negotiate his own
freedom.

The Queen took Melian away to the forest where
she healed him of his wounds. Melian de Lis remained in a
daze and trance for some time but realized he had been
rescued. He had visions of a beautiful spring in the forest
where a number of physicians nursed him back to health.
The Queen knew much of the forest and the art of healing herbs. All his torment at the prison was rightly amended. The Queen's lodgings in the forest were hidden by all
but to those who were allowed to see them. The palace
was marvelous and was supported by big, marble columns.
They had lavish banquets and celebrated his good health.
He spent time in good spirits dancing, caroling and playing
games. When it came near to Pentecost Melian described
to the Queen his predicament and she said: "I have a plan,
don't worry in the least. I promise that you will be at the
tournament in time."

Back at the Castle Minerve was very worried, for
she had received no word of her knight. Knight's had arrived from all over and set up their tents around the castle.
The servants made a splendid stand beneath a bower from
which the spectators could watch the tournament without
being in the oppressive heat. The evening before the tour-

nament all the knights gathered to display their arms as was the custom at the time. They jousted with one another, showing off their prowess. This was known as the turpinoy and was a prelude to the actual tournament.

On the day the tournament began there was no holding back. A great din arose and horses ran full tilt at one another; there was a massive splintering of lances. Knights hurled their opponents to the ground in a heap and the clashing of swords sounded like God's terrible wrath at Gomorra. It was a splendid tournament. Hundreds of maidens watched from the castle wall and stands as the knight's battled, pointing out the ones who did the best deeds of prowess.

Lord's from the nearby castles came to watch the joust with great pleasure, some even participating in it. Everyone else came from the town along with the heralds who were yelling out, recounting the deeds of all the knights that day. The excitement filled the air and the crackling sound of splintered lances and the clashing of arms was a wondrous sight to behold.

On the first day of the tournament Minerve was worried because she didn't see Melian de Lis, no matter where she looked. Yet there was a mighty red knight who had trumped everyone during the jousting that day. He unhorsed five knights without breaking his lance. He bore one man to the ground so that he was completely stunned. He broke another mans arm with a sword blow, leaving the man unhorsed and in a perilous state. All the heralds shouted out: "The fair red knight! He's our man. See how gallant he is and he has already unhorsed so many!" They claimed he was the best and had earned all praise, though he was so arrogant that the maidens all brushed him off. "I will win the lady and there is nothing anyone can do about it. I can't wait to have her love, fie on you all!"

He seemed a wicked man and more was known to that story. He had killed his last wife, hanging her treacherously for no apparent reason. That is the real reason why, when Minverve imagined herself wed to such a man, she trembled with fear. "Oh Melian, wherever you are, know that I'm in real trouble!" Everyone pitied her as they saw the treacherous red knight unseating all the opponents and even the foreign knights. The heralds gave him all the acclaim and, at the days end, they sounded the horns for the tournament's end. A large table was brought out and there was a great feast. The king returned to the hall with his daughter where they brought the noble's back for a celebration. The great hall was bestrewn with fresh, sweet smelling grass because it was very hot outside.

On the second day the tournament resumed. A mighty clash of arms rung through the valley, some were brought honor and others shame. There were battered shields, shattered lances, smashed helms, and broken swords littered all over the field. The red knight was terribly fierce and brought another ten knights tumbling to the earth with his lance. Then he took out his sword and went into the thickest press of the skirmish. He unhorsed even more and delivered blows with his sharp sword that made everyone who opposed him deeply regret it.

The battling went on and it seemed the red knight was carrying away all the honor, once again. Though the maiden's all rebuked him a second time for his arrogance, praying that the serpent knight would come and avenge them. Just as things were going bad to worse and the maiden was faced with the reality of marrying the red knight, a great marvel happened.

Suddenly, to the ladies bemusement, a handsome wagon emerged with gold cloth all around it; it steered itself without horse or man into the center of the field so that everyone stopped to stare at it. Then, two maidens appeared from the forest, one held a horse by the reins and the other bore a gold shield emblazoned with a blue serpent and a stout, sharp lance. They went to the wagon, throwing off the gold cloth to reveal a magnificently armored knight who glimmered in the sun. The good knight, who, have no doubt, was the great Melian de Lis, rose up from the wagon, mounting his horse and taking both shield and lance from the maiden. "Thank you, my lady. You have restored my health and brought me safely to the tournament!"

He commended the Queen of the forest to God and set out on his charger towards the tournament. He was very eager for battle and now that he was armed. He spurred off in a gallop, straight towards the red knight. The two knights came flying at each other more quickly than a merlin or swallow coming down in a swoop. They struck one another with such force that their lances chattered, flying into the air.

Melian de Lis, who had great strength and might, had managed to leave the red knight impaled with his lance. The blow left the red knight crashing from his horse and bleeding from the chest where it had broken through the hauberk. He was sent flying from his horse and was borne so painfully to the earth that he came close to breaking his neck. He did mange to break his arm in two places, and what a terrible fall it was! All the crowd rejoiced that the red knight they hated was so utterly shamed.

Then Melian de Lis yelled out, "To helms!" Know that this was Arthur's battle cry. And, spurting blood out of his mouth, he grabbed a fresh lance off the ground that was stout and sharp and began charging furiously at the other knights on the field, unseating four before shattering his lance.

The knights were terribly afflicted by this mighty warrior. No one dared challenge him for they thought him crazed and possessed. Though he came at them like a lion and those that kept up the fight were sorely dishonored. He raised his sword and struck his enemy, one took a blow full on the helm that smashed clean through to the skull. Another was borne to the ground by a hammering blow over his head, making his shield a pitiful defense. The knight could do nothing but cover himself with his shield and hope for the best. Yet, this did not help, for the sharp steel hammered through his shield and came down on his body, slicing it from the shoulder to the waistline.

Just as I tell you it happened. Melian de Lis carried away all the honor at the tournament and the red knight was utterly shamed. The heralds shouted: "The knight of the gold cart is storming the field. My lady, he has the serpent on his shield! It is the knight of the serpent, the lady's one, true amorous lover!"

When the battle had ceased all the knights were exhausted and weary. The heralds sounded their horns calling the tournament to a halt. The heralds were sure to

76

announce the victor and the king invited all the partici-
pants to a great feast afterwards. The tables were set and
many servants brought forth all kinds of dishes. Melian de
Lis came to the courtyard and servants helped him dismount and led his horse to a magnificent stable. The horse
was provided with an abundance of oats and was well tak-
en care of. They hastily unarmed him and gave him a scarlet mantle that was embroidered with little gold birds. He
was adorned in exquisite robes and the people made sure
that nothing was lacking.

He happily entered the spacious hall and was
amazed to find the chamber entirely wrought with gold.
Large windows led to a garden behind the keep that was
full of magnificent flowers and plants. I will spare you the
explanation of the feast. Know that they had every kind of
dish. Also, he marveled at the well built galleries and great
hall. This king was, no doubt, very wealth and it had been
since he was a boy that he had seen the place.

At the table Melian de Lis found himself sitting
across from his lady, who was amazed to find that he had
worn both the shield of the serpent and the emerald ring.
She knew indeed that he was the lover she had lost for so
long. "It is great to see you again, I thought you were lost.
For many reported you had gone completely mad in the
forest, having a taste only for animal flesh, violence and
slaying all those who came after you." The knight, who was
very nervous, replied: "Alas, my lady. Ask the king. I have
sent him several hundred prisoners. I only stayed away so
that I could achieve enough prowess to be worthy of your
love."

In this way Melian explained to them how he had
become mad with love and then went off to do adventures, delivering hundreds of prisoners to the king under
the name of the serpent knight. "You are the knight of the
serpent?" pondered the king. The king was taken back and,
for all his astonishment, was very happy to receive him as
his son in law for he had well proven his prowess through
many good deeds.

Then Melian recounted in detail how he had become imprisoned through sorcery and swore that he would
take vengeance on the knight of the fox as soon as he

could. "I almost missed the tournament from that wicked enchanter. I hereby swear an oath that I will not rest a single night in the same place until I destroy all enchanters in this land!"

Suddenly, while they were at the boards eating, the earth began to quake and the hall seemed to be moving about. The windows shook and trembled. People fell from their chairs and nearly choked while eating. Everyone was amazed and full of fright. A white dove flew in through the window and into a bed chamber. Then, a series of apparitions appeared in the hall following after the white dove. Ghostly figures loomed about the place. A gorgeous damsel dressed in a white silk gown came across the chamber holding two magnificent silver platters; attached to them was a candelabra with twelve candles on it, six on each side. Then came a youth who bore a lance that bled drops of blood from the tip. The lance was held upside down so that the blood went into a gold vessel carried by two servants that held it beneath the lance.

Do you need ask what marvels these were? Melian de Lis had been graced with the presence of the most Holy Grail. It was no other than the grail that Joseph had held while he was in prison, keeping him nourished for forty years while the Jews unjustly imprisoned him. That grail was only shown to those who were worthy; and Melian was a very worthy man with a pure spirit.

Then, after the spirits had walked with the grail through the hall, a loud voice thundered throughout the chamber, though it addressed Melian: "Know that this is the grail that kept you fed while you were imprisoned by the knight of the red fox. Now you see that the Holy Ghost has delivered you from your enemies and brought you the woman who you were destined to marry. Praise its glory and be grateful! It is said that you will bring a child into this world. By your marriage there will come forth a child that will be called the Flower of Prowess. He will be the most legendary king in all Logres as long as you continue to grow in faith and worship the lord. And from your line will be the one who will achieve the quest of the grail and heal the maimed king, bringing all the lands from ruin to salvation."

78

After the voice had finished a great light filled the hall and everyone became completely confounded. Some spoke in foreign languages, others made strange movements with their hands while others had terrific visions. All began to marvel at this. When these things subsided, Melian swore he wouldn't rest until he fathered the child that was professed and discovered the mystery of the grail. Though it would be many years before he could learn of it. Here ends the story of Melian de Lis who was cordially married to the lady Minerve and given many good lands throughout the kingdom.

# 10 THE MIRROR

In the deep forest's of Logres there was a beautiful meadow surrounded by trees. Next to it there was a cool spring and, two knights, who were very content in the world, set up their pavilion before it. The two knights stayed there for many days because of a great marvel which I will tell you of.

In the nearby meadow they had found a mirror, it had glass like crystal and it was wrapped in a fine gold frame that was designed so exquisitely it seemed it came from heaven. Not only was it a beautiful object to gaze at it held a property of enchantment that allowed the beholder to view the thing he most desired. For some this was knowledge of an event in the future, for others it was a lover. Some, being a touch on the dark side, had deep obsessions that the mirror portrayed to them openly.

In this way the mirror was found and the two knights worshipped it regularly. The mirror was powerful and, when the two knights looked into it, they saw what they desired most. What did they desire most? When the blue knight looked he saw a beautiful maiden beckoning him. She smiled and talked with him, exchanging many glances, some subtle and others not, of love. The red knight saw a lady of his own liking, who adored him.

They would spend the whole day sharing time at the mirror where they could behold their lovers. At this time two knights from Arthur's court trotted along the road until they came to this very meadow. They saw the two knights in front of the mirror and marveled: "Sagremor, tell me why this knight bows before the mirror? It is most strange. Also, he seems to be conversing with it." Then he replied, "It is a marvel indeed, do you think he is mad?" Gawain said: "I'm not sure, let's go find out but it would be a shame to harm someone who has been driven mad."

They went right up to the knights, who were so enraptured by the mirror that they failed to notice them. The two knights nudged up to them so close that they could feel the breath of their horse's on them and said: "Hail Arthur! We have ridden through the lands seeking adventure, God be with you!" The two knights, one in red arms and the other in blue, suddenly realized them and looked up, very concerted that they had been interrupted from the mirror. The blue knight was very handsome and had curly blonde hair that went down to his shoulders. The red knight was also very handsome, but a bit older, and he had jet black hair and freckles on his fair skinned face. "Blessed be God."

"I must ask, why do you stare so intently at that mirror?"

"It is the mirror of desires. All those who gaze at it see what they most desire."

"I'd like to try it!"

"Back up, knight, for we found it first!"

"I will challenge you for it."

"Don't get the idea, for you'll be sore about it later."

Then there arose so much animosity that they could not avoid a vicious joust. The red and blue knight ran back to their tent to get their helmets on and mounted, since they already had all their armor on. Sagremor said to his fellow: "Let me take the joust, and if they can beat me then you come to my aid." Gawain agreed to this.

Sagremor launched his charger forward and thrust his spear so deep into the blue knight's side that he was deeply wounded and hurled into the air the length of a lance before hitting the ground, stunned. The red knight, angered by the sight of his wounded friend, renewed the combat. Sagremor took a fresh lance leaning against a tree near the pavilion and they jousted. They collided head to head, body to body and horse to horse. The impact was so forceful that both knights flew from their horse's and splintered their lances.

The red knight was stunned but got up just in time, for Sagremor was already up and running towards him with his sword out. They started hacking at one another with their steel blades. Sagremor delivered a blow that cut through his shield. Then he gave him another that knocked him over. He tried to get up but Sagremor hit him with the pommel of his sword, smashing his helm, which had been staved in completely. Then he ripped it off his head and threatened to behead him if he didn't surrender.

81

The fight was up. Sagremor had defeated both the knights of the mirror. Then he said: "Since you are now our prisoners you must do as we say."

The red knight, lamenting his situation and seeing no other choice but to obey, said: "That is true for we have no choice." Sagremor said: "Than, by God, take that mirror to King Arthur's court. Tell him on our behalf that we wish to make a present of it." Both the red and blue knight's agreed with this.

Sagremor gazed at the wondrous mirror and then bid Gawain to look into it. When he did, he saw something most strange. He saw himself but, behind him, there was a treacherous murderer who had a knife in his hand. He look as if he was going to kill him. Terrified, he ducked as the enemy lunged at him. Then he looked away, realizing it was only a phantom in the mirror.

"This is what I most desire? To be murdered by an invisible ghost?"

The blue knight replied: "It shows what you most desire, which, in this case, is knowledge of an event in the future, though you wouldn't have known of it otherwise. It can foresee things, in order to protect you. It seems like you may have someone who wants to kill you. I suggest you be on your guard."

In this way they marveled at the mirror. So it was true that, when they returned to court, Gawain was attacked by a man with a dagger, who hated him. They were all in court when, suddenly, the man charged at him from behind. Gawain's fellow blocked the attack and stuck a blade into his stomach so that his guts spilled out all over the great hall. Apparently, this man had lost his brother in a joust to Gawain. This attempt at vengeance was thwarted since the mirror had foretold it and Gawain had men around him at all times to protect him. Everyone wondered at this and Gawain said: "It is the mirror that saved me. For it foretold of this many months ago."

Meanwhile, Arthur became extremely intrigued by the mirror. He locked it away in the treasury, where it was hid for many ages, only used by the leaders of the world in most dire situations. They coveted it and used it sparingly because it was a dangerous thing to alter fortune. Also, there was an evil side to the mirror. It corrupted people to power and created obsessions so severe that they were crippling. If it was used moderately it could be beneficial but, if used wrongly, it would create tyrants. Arthur used it sparingly in his campaign against the Saxons, and it even foretold his death by Mordred at the battle of Salisbury plain. Then again, even prophecy cannot save one from his inevitable death, for fate is a powerful thing: no one can truly cheat his fate no matter how much magic they have!

# 11 THE LAY OF THE ROSE

*Remember all the fruitful lovers dear,*
*Most truthful to their loves and full of cheer,*
*Fidelity is like a fresh pure rose,*
*With each year its beauty increases more,*
*Steadfast in trusting the almighty one,*
*More fruit is yielded as our grace abounds!*
*The spinner doubted and he is cast out,*
*With spindle and distaff he gets to work,*
*Wishing he never doubted God's true love!*

The Lay of the Rose was recorded many years ago and shows that true fidelity puts the envious doubters to shame! A strapping and mighty knight came to the court of the round table seeking a position of servitude. He was a poor knight but great in deeds of prowess. He had married a woman far above in station and with many riches; the father of this girl was weary and disapproving of their marriage. So he banished the knight, whose name was Margon. Margon left the Marches in search of riches through his deeds of prowess, hoping to provide for his new wife. The lady was the most beautiful and abiding woman you could imagine. There was no one who could question her fidelity to her husband.

He came to court, just as I said: "Hail, Arthur! I want to be in your service. For no knight who joins your service doesn't accomplish great feats of prowess." Arthur was very grateful to have such a noble man in his court. He let him join the Round Table and in no time he was doing many deeds of prowess and acts of chivalry.

I should tell you that before Margon was to be away for so long he worried his lady would find another love. She reassured him in a most clever way. She gifted him a small ivory box. Inside of it was a little pouch with the freshest, sweet scented rose than any could gaze upon. It bloomed in the first day of February, which was quite unordinary. No matter how much time passed, it remained fresh as if plucked the day before. Such was the magic of this rose that it would remain forever fresh as long as the lady remained faithful to Margon.

When Margon was at court he found himself continuously stealing away secretly to chambers and opening the little box to see the rose. Many in the court wondered why he left so often and thought he may meant some kind of treachery. The barons talked about it: "If he is going around secretly he can't be trusted. What if he is plotting to kill the king?" In this way they all agreed that they would confront him about the disappearances.

One day, the king saw him depart to another chamber and he followed him, demanding he know what he was up to. Margon was very reluctant to tell of the ivory box given him by his lady; for love kept secret is kept safe. Though, when the king persisted, he told him all that you have learned. So Margon du Gorre's secret love and her oath of fidelity was told throughout the court.

The king was elated that Margon wasn't a murderer and really just was deeply in love. He honored the knight all the more for knowing this. Yet jealously has a way of making problems. There were two knights at court, once made prisoners by the noble Lancelot, who had come from the forest and had descended from a line of evil enchanters. Since their ancestors had been deposed by Arthur they always harbored a secret hatred to him.

They remained in the lands only because Arthur was generous and pitied them and gave them lands because of it. These two knights, Dorrus and Borrus, found themselves very envious of Margon because the king held him in such high esteem. These two wished to shame him and plotted against him. The one said: "There is no doubt that women are fickle and easily led astray by false lovers." The other retorted: "Give me one week and I will surely turn his good and faithful lady from him. For she will be unable to resist my looks and charm!" These two knights were full of pride, which was their downfall. In this way they plotted.

So Dorrus and Borrus came to the court at the feast of St. John when all the barons were present. They said to Margon, in front of everyone: "We will prove your wife unfaithful and watch that rose of yours wither and die." Margon was very incensed and rose up from the table immediately. If he had a sword he would have attacked them. With a threatening voice bellowed out: "I will not take this disrespect any longer. How long has it been since you have scurried about the dark corners of the castle, profaning my lady, who is good and faithful, with poisonous slander. I challenge you to combat!"

Then Dorrus cleverly said: "I have another idea. Put your ladies faithfulness to the test. I will go to her and, if I can persuade her to be my lover, you will be shamed. If I win her you will have no choice but to wear a shield emblazoned with a knight on his knees and a lady riding his back! If she remains faithful, I will give you all our lands which we hold by the grace of the king." So the agreement was made that if the lady proved unfaithful he would wear the shameful shield. Dorrus and Borrus hoped they could win the king's favor by this rouse but they were wicked rogues and there was little they could do but increase their shame.

Dorrus set out into the country towards the house of Margon's wife, whose name was Verumes, which stands for truth in latin. When Dorrus arrived he was greeted warmly and with the best hospitality, for Verumes was a very gracious and courteous host; she held nothing back and only wished people well.

Dorrus told her that he had come from court to bring good tidings of Margon and that he was achieving much. An array of food was provided and they talked of Margon. She said: "I am so happy to hear that he is doing well and look forward to his return after his many adventures!" When Verumes had been taken with wine later into the evening, Dorrus made his first move: "Are you not lonely here, with your husband being so far off?"

"I miss him but know that he is out achieving deeds of prowess so that we may be better supported. He was never a knight of means but I loved him all the more for it. Since my father the king has disowned us we have to do the best we can."

"Well, my lady, know that I hold a great many lands and would be happy to give you my love if you would receive it." She really appalled his advances. Her only reply was that she was very happy her husband had been well received at court.

Dorrus remained in the castle for three days. At last he became desperate to woo her for he realized she was a person of great virtue. He went to her chamber and professed: "My lady, I completely and utterly love you. Please take me as your lover, Margon will never know of it!" The lady abruptly refused his advances, thinking them a joke, and pleaded he speak no more of it.

When he continued to bother her with these advances she told him plainly: "Later, I want you to come to this chamber deep in the castle and wait for me. At nightfall I shall come to you." Delighted, Dorrus went his way to a spacious chamber with an exquisite bed. He waited there for many hours and, dismayed, found himself sleeping well into the morning the next day without any word from Verumes.

By late morning the next day he realized he had been fooled, for he tried to leave the chamber and found the doors locked up. An inscription etched into the stone wall read: "Anyone who makes base advances on the lady of the house will be imprisoned here for one year and forced to spin thread if he wants to eat."

Then a window opened and a voice rang out: "If you have read the inscription you know now that you have been imprisoned for your base advances on my lady. If you want to eat, you better spin!" Dorrus looked down and noticed there was a spindle and distaff on the stony ground. Dorrus was of noble birth and considered spinning far below his station. Sure enough, after a day, he became so desperate for food that he took to spinning gratefully. This went on for some time and Dorrus became quite an expert, producing fine bundles of yarn. I'd consider the lady did him a favor and it may even have been his vocational calling all along for he had done little else but prattle and gossip in the courts before then!

When Borrus saw no sign of his brother for several months he started to worry. So he set out without delay for the house in the country. When he reached the place he was joyfully welcomed by Verumes, who gave him great hospitality. He tried to woo her but in a different way. He said: "My lady, I bring tidings from court. Your husband has found a lover and has become so taken with her that he has renounced you publicly. All the revelry of court life has highly corrupted his values and, if you desire his love, I suggest you return the favor and find a lover of your own!"

In this way he tried to stir up jealously in her. But Verumes was unmoved by the knight's plea. "I dare not believe you, for my fair husband would never do such a thing." When this failed he resorted to other means. He followed her about in the garden, making a fool of himself with base flattery.

Eventually, when all else failed, Borrus professed his love plainly to Verumes. She looked at him pleasantly and said: "If you wait in this chamber deep in the halls I will come to you this very night." Borrus, delighted, suspected no plot against him and blindly went into the chamber.

Yet, to his amazement, instead of finding a lovely damsel, he met with his brother who was eagerly spinning away. Dorrus told him: "Oh, you've really done well for yourself! Why would you come here, of all places? You were better off at court. Now we are both shamed. Well, since you've come here, you better get to spinning. For if you don't spin you don't eat!" Borrus was confounded and replied: "A fig for thee! I would never do servant work no matter how hungry I am." In this way he brooded his fate. His brother reminded him: "Read the wall: if you don't spin you don't eat!"

Then a maiden came to the window and shouted: "Dorrus, how well you have done today! For you there will be beef and beer. Has Borrus started yet?" Dorrus replied: "He still refusing to take to spinning." The lady laughed: "Ah, he must still have a full belly. He will surely take to it when he gets hungry enough! Has he read the inscription?"
"He has, my lady. Only he still refuses." Sure enough, the next day, Borrus eagerly took to spinning even more hurriedly than his brother Dorrus, often haranguing him for being too slow!

Such was the fate of those proud men who sought to dishonor a most devout wife that they were imprisoned, forced into hard labor to atone. Eventually, Margon wondered what all the fuss was about, for it had been many weeks since he saw either Borrus or Dorrus. He took leave of the king and set off for the forest.

He worried that he would find the two men there with his wife taking their pleasure of her. In his own anxieties he began to doubt the power of the rose and, stopping near a meadow, took to cursing his fate and the whole idea of marriage: "My life used to be so simple. I slept when I wanted and ate when I wanted. Now I have to go to court to earn honor and deal with treacherous people full of jealousy and treason. What more could I need in life? It is but undue stress to be constantly opposed by these wicked folks!" As he lamented beneath a chestnut tree in the shade near a meadow there were a group of knights on the other side of a thicket who could hear him plainly. Margon fell asleep but when he awoke he found the knights had come out of the thicket and were looking right at him.

They were no other than the most noble knights of the court. One of them, who was a very honorable knight, said to him: "Good knight, did I hear you lamenting the prospect of marriage so? All of us knights here were recently wed and we are profoundly happy in the accord. Have faith that your wife is still true to you, for the rose is still fresher than one that hadn't been plucked! With patience, a mustard seed becomes a great, sprawling tree! It is so with marriage. Those good trees bear abundant fruit while the bad branches are shriven, for they produce nothing good!"

Margon was encouraged by them; so they all set out together for his house in the country. When Verumes saw them arrive she was so happy that she could barely contain herself. She greeted her loving husband with open arms, recognizing him immediately. When she had heard from the knights his doubt she was saddened but reassured him with her appeals and loving eyes. "I have no doubt," said Margon, "now that I behold you, your love has been faithful and true."

Then she told him: "Let me show you something." She took them to the chamber where Borrus and Dorrus were imprisoned. They opened the window and looked inside to see that they were both busy spinning away with distaff and spindle, eager to get the job done! When the knights of the court entered the chamber they roared with laughter at the two arrogant prisoners. Indeed, this was the end of the line for them: for they were so shamed they hardly knew what to do.

It was then determined that Margon had won the bargain and that he should have all their lands. "Oh, we have been so deeply shamed that we hereby relinquish our lands to you. We will go far away from here to a place where no one knows us. Also, my lady, let us leave this prison for your point has been made! There is nothing more we have to lose and the joke is up." Then they pleaded in this way until she agreed that they could leave but offered them a meal before they did so. Yet they were in a hurry to get out of there and declined anything further. They quickly set out for a land where no one would ever recognize them!

In this way did the good Margon and his loyal wife Verumes receive many lands in Logres. Such is the fate of those that are true and noble in action; they are always able to multiply their fortune and remain in good graces. Verumes's father was later reconciled with the wedded couple, for he realized Margon was a noble knight, especially after he had won the respect of King Arthur. Margon swore to be a vassal to both kings and fought in the war against the Saxons. He defeated many knights and proved his worth in combat, you may have no doubt of it. This story was such a joy and delight at court that it was told many times over. It was later called the Lay of the Rose and was told afar in many kingdoms as a story of true love and fidelity.

# 12 CHEVALIER AVENTUREUX

After the Saxons had destroyed the lands entirely, there was little else for the Britons to do but mourn those who had died. Indeed, a maiden in Roevant, or I should say the ruins of Roevant, recounted the scene after the battle: "The thousands lay dead throughout the valley. The green grass was red. Our good knights were tended to with the utmost care by their wives, who had an enchantment on them which was such that they felt no emotion but were stimulated to help in any way they could. The good king had pieces of sword hacked flesh hanging from every part of him. He couldn't speak for his jaw was dislocated and his eyes drooped down as bloody tears came from them.

His cup bearer was equally misconstrued, he had twelve wounds on the head so that his brain was almost spilling out; so butchered was he that his arm was left on the field and his guts were spilling from his belly. He called for his son who came to him. He pressed his cheek against him so that the blood from his wounds went all over his son. That is why is son was called thereafter Sanguine for he was last seen by his father with that crimson face. God-frey was all but lost too. His skull laid bare and broken open to the brain in four places.

When these knights died the land was completely wasted, bereft of all hope and deliverance. They had killed all the Saxons but were equally defeated. It remained so for some time. Foul things occurred in Logres from then on. Tempests arose, lurking creatures of the night prowled and the joyful cities were in ruins, desolate. The King's wife took off with her retinue for Avalon. The royal line knew, from much study of the stars, that events were to come, but could not be avoided, for such was God's will. They believed the kingdom was crushed because of their sins. Some remained in the city but lived obscure lives amongst the ruins.

At this time a terrible serpent with a gaping maw came through the city devouring anyone who came out at night. He had terrible fangs that seeped poison from them. His green scales were like armor and glistened in the moonlight. His body was thirty yards long and he even had the legs and feet of a griffon with great talons for striking. All the people who remained in the cities feared him greatly. Such was the fact that, after the destruction of Logres, foul beasts prowled about seeking the ruin of souls."

It was at this time the lady of the house of Roevant, whom you have just heard recount the events after the battle, fell asleep and had a marvelous dream. She envisioned a mighty bear with claws in the sky. He pulled the stars down and charged ferociously towards the gates of heaven. Suddenly, a battalion of white knights came riding forth from the gate. Loud trumpets blared from the angels on high behind the gates, then the angel knights went to battle. These angels rebuked the bear for attacking the gate, but realized he meant no harm for he was only warning them.

He led them down a path until they reached a mighty dragon who was sleeping by a pond. The bear told them that he had come from the depths of hell. He was so foul and evil that he was terrible to look at. The dragon awoke at the sight of the angels and charged at them. He breathed fire and scorched many of those noble white knights. The dragon yelped so loud that he summoned an army of demons who were also from hell.

Then a great battle began, where demons and knights began fighting in the skies. Suddenly, the bear went after the dragon and seeped his teeth into his neck. It bled everywhere and retreated back to earth. The company of white knights chased the dragon and found him laying on the ground near a spring, wounded. Then they bound him up and imprisoned him in the deep caverns of earth, locking him away for all time. They made sure he was tightly locked away inside a mountain in the deepest cavern they could find. No light came there ever. They built an iron prison with four hundred men. They shackled the dragon in there and cast a spell on him so he slept for all time. Then the bear returned to earth and the land began to prosper once again. The Lady awoke and was astonished by her dream, though she had little clue what it meant.

Such was the situation when the Knight of the Bear, a descendent of the most royal line of Britain, came from Rome seeking his parents. For his father had been taken away at a very young age as a curiosity in Rome by the messengers traveling their at the time. Yet his father had become a highly renown man in Rome, for he fought in the perilous Indian wars, slaying King Porrus with his own hands.

The senators of Rome adored him and gave him land and riches. He had twelve sons, all of noble stock in the city of Rome. Then one day the Knight of the Bear, one of his twelve sons, vowed to find his family in Britain. When he was of age he set off without delay until he came to the isle of Britain.

He arrived in Roevant in this way, much to his astonishment he found the land completely wasted. To the amazement of the broken people they beheld, for the first time in what seemed forever, a knight of noble stock! Now they had not seen a knight for many years so it came as a great surprise.

The Knight of the Bear went through the streets of the ruined city mounted on a mighty black destrier. He had a stout lance of pine with a black pennon of the bear. In his hand he had a black shield with a yellow bear head emblazoned on it. These were his family arms that had been carried over from Britain. His glimmering hauberk, helm and ventail were all marvelously gold. His helm was strong. He had a bejeweled sword which he kept inside his scabbard; then he sported a golden girdle that was also a marvel to look at. His saddle was the finest one you can imagine and had been gifted to him by the emperor on behalf of his father; it was embroidered with marvelous gold flowers and stars and made of silver.

Now, as he went through the streets he was doing what a good knight should: making sure that no maiden was left unaided. There happened to be a woman, the same woman that gave us the earlier account, in Roevant who was very distraught, for her husband had been terribly slain in the battle with the Saxons. When she saw the bear emblazoned on his shield she recalled her dream and was filled with excitement in the hope he was the one she had dreamed of.

Suddenly, after so much pain and woe, she experienced a glimmer of hope: "Maybe the lands aren't completely ruined. Maybe there is a chance that Britain could be restored to its former glory by a knight of prowess." The Knight of the Bear was raised a Roman but, make no doubt, he was descended from a long line of Britons; though he didn't know it! The lady waved to him and came from her tiny home that was built upon a stone foundation and half in ruins from the siege. Indeed, there were simply no men in that region to rebuild the city that had fallen.

The lady spoke to him in this way: "It is a great honor to behold a knight like you; I feared there would never be one such as yourself in these parts again. Tell me, what business to you have here?" The knight replied: "Hail, demoiselle! I come from the city of Rome where my father is well known by the emperor for his accomplishments in India. I come here because I seek to know my lineage and ancestors; it is possible that some of them live yet in these lands. Tell me, do you know of the King of this land? All my father told me is that I descended from a royal line of these parts."

The lady was enamored by his fine speech and words. "If anyone were to know of the royal ancestors it would be the hermits at the temple in the Forest of Marvels. To get to them you will have to get through the Stony Pass which is heavily guarded by a host peasant villeins. Yes, make no doubt those hermits would know it if anyone did. It is told that the ancestors you seek weren't killed in the battle but, foreseeing the events, fled to the isle of life and will remain there until the coming of Christ.

In fact, after the terrible war, the dead royal knights were carried away by the fairy's in large biers. Those fairies definitely healed them, or if they didn't, are keeping them alive until the vessels that Christ's followers bring with them along with the word do that miracle. To find the isle of life is a perilous journey, although if you are meant to find it than it will be made easy. It seems you are meant for great honor and will become the great Chevalier Aventureux that we hoped for. Restoring the lands will be a perilous quest full of mystery and astonishment. Though, seeing a knight as strong as yourself, I have little doubt you could achieve the impossible!"

He commended her to God for her kind words. The two went into the house and she took off his armor with care and kindness. The knight took a bow that was on the floor and, after disarming, went into the forests to hunt. He brought back a fine stag and gave it to the lady to prepare, who hadn't tasted venison in years. She introduced him her sons, who she had kept hidden in the ruins for fear of the serpent. Out of the back of the house came three young boys. Two were armed and were of just of age. The other was but a small boy. All were very noble and courteous despite the hardships they had endured in childhood. They had fair golden tresses and wore green tunics. "These are my boys, two of which would gladly be knighted, for they long to bear arms as their father did. They desire little else than to avenge the lands that were so utterly betrayed by the raiding Saxons."

The Knight of the Bear, or Ursa, as they called him, was a jolly knight and replied: "I will gladly make them knights. For this land truly needs good men of prowess to repopulate the lands. Yet, what deeds have you accomplished to receive the accolade? For, young boys, a knight is only given that honor upon his deeds. For a good knight is most upright and holy, he is a defender of Church and also an advocate for justice. He should also take care of the poor and rebuke the wicked."

The children swore they would set out and achieve deeds worthy of knighthood. They told him of a great marvel. They explained that the land was plagued by a terrible serpent who fed upon the remaining people there. They told him that everyone lived in fear and nothing would be accomplished unless he were slain. They entreated The Knight of the Bear to kill it and, they would prove themselves by leading him there and helping in the battle. They all agreed on this and, should they help kill the serpent, he would make them knights.

That night they went out into the dormant city that was so desolate it would have been a very sad thing to behold. It was as if the plague had swept it of all life; for war is very much like a plague, bringing tragedy to places that once held much joy. As in this place: In the absence of law great monsters rule the lands, exacting heavy tolls on the people and doing violent deeds whenever they please. The Knight of the Bear was a true relief to the people of Britain, for he came, donned in marvelous armor, reminding the people of a chivalric past.

Led by the two boys he rode on towards the serpent, who was most active at night; when they found him lurking in the usual place the full moon made his scales glimmer so that he was seen plainly. The boy said: "Just passed this alleyway is where his den is, he comes out at night to eat people." Ursa nobly advanced into the dark alleyway until he beheld the strange creature. As they approached a great storm arose. The clouds were dark and all the light left. Thunder and rain hurled upon them with ferocity. Ursa gazed upon the large beast and crossed himself in amazement, for he had never seen such a demon.

He heard a voice aloud: "Careful to go further, proud knight. The serpent here has a horrible spirit in him that swears to never allow chivalry to return to these lands." Then, smoke of the foulest kind gushed from the serpent; a terrible sulphur smell emanated from him. He smelled like the pit of sin where he came from; for one could make no mistake that the beast came from the very depths of hell where Satan, being cast down from heaven, dwelled in eternal torment.

When the serpent saw that he had a challenger he darted at him faster than a flying hawk at his prey. The knight spurred his steed and leveled his sharp lance so that it grazed the side of the serpent but the scaly armor didn't allow it to go through. Meanwhile, the serpent went straight for the horse. His sharp fangs tore through the champron that protected his horse's neck and went into the flesh. Blood spurted everywhere. It was done so easily that it seemed the metal protecting his neck was but scraps of parchment. The blow delivered was so powerful that it knocked both horse and rider down and they came crashing to the ground. The horse didn't live after that and the serpent thoroughly enjoyed ripping off his head and flinging Ursa to the ground.

The Knight of the Bear was still undeterred. He roared like a lion and began charging forward on foot with his keen sword. The serpent struck him with his sharp talons only to shatter his shield completely. Yet, the claws were stuck in the shield. The serpent began desperately lunging at him but his sight was blocked by the shield which was latched into his claws.

Then, Ursa cleverly ducked so that the serpent overshot him. While he was underneath the large serpent he delivered a fatal blow in the belly, where the armor was least and skin the softest, so that it began spilling his guts all over. The serpent howled in anguish at this. He slashed into him so that his sword plunged in all the way to the hilt. His black blood covered Ursa, who began drinking it with delight and roaring with laughter.

Suddenly a black plume of smoke arose around the serpent's body; the foulest stench ever could be smelled throughout the city. The serpent shook violently and everyone became blinded by the smokey plume. Then, when it had cleared up, one could see plainly a man with a red face who had a black robe and hood on. He had sharp yellow eyes and walked around the snake, cursing it.

Then a voice cried out: "That is the demon who was inside the serpent. Before its too late and he changes shapes again, invoke the power of St. David or he will never leave us!" Ursa trusted the voice and did just as it said. So the knight raised his shield and called upon God almighty. "By St. David, hear me! Let this demon terrorize the people no more!"

The demon with the red face, or the rousse couane, as they called him, was struck down by a bolt of lightning that hurled from the sky. He fell to the ground, realizing that the one who had banished him was exuding his wrath on him again. When the red faced demon fell down a light came forth from the sky and, in the clouds, a group of brown eagles flew over the city. They dropped garlands of flowers from their talons and adorned the streets with them. The smell of the flowers lifted the foul stench of the demon and made everyone feel joy. All around light began to shine wherever the flowers went and the vicious storm that had arisen before the battle abated.

When they went to look at the red faced man they realized he had vanished. Then a voice said: "He has been put into the iron prison where he will stay for eternity. When the eagle came everyone came out from hiding and rejoiced, praising the Knight of the Bear for his good deeds.

When Ursa saw the eagle he was astonished, for it was a great miracle. When the bird saw that all was safe and that the demon was gone he began the ascent back to heaven, saluting the earthy inhabitants very graciously. A voice called out: "See how he called on the Lord and we were delivered. This is a good sign. Spread the word that Britain will be restored!" Everyone who had been hiding in the city from the serpent saw the light emanating from the sky and the rose garlands. They realized the storm was over and that they had been saved. They gathered around the knight and cheered for him. Though he was quiet and humble, as a good warrior should be. He asked for no more honor than the next man. Then Ursa gave the two boys the accolade, for they had been very brave before the mighty serpent. Know that the two boys were the sons of that lady whose name was Gaudine. She was sister to the King of Scotland before he was killed in the battle with the Saxons. So her sons were most noble and the honor of knighthood befitted them. So the Knight of the Bear took to passionately giving them the accolade in front of a large crowd of people. They were happy to see knights return to Logres, for they feared the adventures had ended forever.

Afterwards, the kingdom was restored. Knight's rose up everywhere and people, finding that they had a sovereign lord, rebuilt the towns and castles. Great tournaments and jousts were held once again, and all the people returned to their former ways of life. They never forgot the day they were freed of that vile serpent.

# 13 THE VICTORY AT LOUGH DERG

Now I will tell you about something much different. One of the good knights of the court found himself embarking on a spectacular adventure to an isle in Ireland. Galopin was his name, and he was a knight that could play the harp so well that he always made a din in the courts so that the windows shook and the foundations trembled with delight at the sounds of the crowd stamping their feet to the melody; truthfully, his melodious voice was sweeter than spring flowers and carried with it the wonder of the Holy Spirit so that everyone that heard him was the better for it.

At this time, the minstrel knight Galopin rode fully armed through the forest of Landone, unperturbed. It was quite suddenly that something astonishing happened, as it is known to happen in the forest of marvels. He was overcome with a sweet smell, it made overcome him and made him feel drowsy. He dismounted to rest his head upon his shield and lay down, for the spell was powerful. In this way he fell into a deep sleep.

As he slept a great storm arose that was terrible and frightening. The wind howled and the rain pummeled him. Branches broke off trees and hail began to descend upon him. Disturbed, he awoke to a most displeasing sight: He smelled the foulest smells and then, from the sky, a host of evil spirits, black as the night and covered by a large mass of smoke belching from their bodies, surrounded him. They jeered and yelled at him. "You made a big mistake coming to the forest of enchantments and will pay for it dearly."

Galopin saw the demons and mounted his horse, hoping to fight them off. He took out his sword from his scabbard and charged at them but it was no use, for no mortal power could hurt them. As he horse road towards one of the evil spirits, who seemed to be a knight, the multitude lifted him up and bore him away into the sky, to his terror.

Then he heard voices calling out: "We can't take him any further. His guardian won't let us. Oh, this knight is full of virtue, his soul isn't for us!" Everything got blurry until he awoke and found himself on an island. This island was surrounded by a massive lake. A river ran through the middle of the island, separating the two bodies of land from one another.

Galopin viewed all this from an elevated position and scratched his head in wonder for he clearly saw that he was stuck on top of a chestnut tree. It seemed that he was dropped from the sky and landed there, much to his amusement. His hauberk was intertwined with the branches and he was uncomfortably entangled; he was barely able to grab his shield which was stuck atop another branch. Twigs and thistles poked his limbs and it was an unnerving pain.

Eventually he situated himself and managed to descend from the tree. When he got his feet on the ground he realized a great combat ensued on that island. There were two castles, one on each side of the river. Both of the castles were surrounded by thick moats and well fortified. A large procession of knights came forth from both sides. They met at a stone bridge which connected the two places.

The one isle had a great array of men-at-arms, knights and bowmen. All of which donned white raiment and arms. The other isle wore black. Knights were jousting and doing much damage to one another with the sword. These two forces collided with one another creating a great din and the combat was fierce. Indeed, this was no display of arms in a tournament but a combat to the death; gaping wounds were seen and limbs were stuck off by spears and lance thrusts; body parts were scattered about and a great many wounded were left crying in anguish on the battlefield.

The knight's in white bore the holy cross upon their shields. The knights in black had a yellow dragon emblazoned on theirs. It seemed from all this that they were the very forces of light and dark, trapped in an endless battle. In this way a huge battle took place while Galopin had finally overcome his struggle to remove himself from the chestnut tree.

As he saw all this a knight in black galloped towards him and, giving him a charger he had just won, called out: "What ever were you doing in that tree? Nonetheless, you seem to be a traitor. Though, I wouldn't dare wound you while I am mounted and you are on foot for that would be a great shame! Take this charger and, see there upon the tree that ash wood lance? Take it, it seems to be sharp and stout enough. It has the banderole of the Holy Ghost upon it. Fie on God! Fie on all that is good! Come, challenge me! For I am the knight of the dragon, sworn to protect the demonic laws and help contrive sin in your life. There you go, take this horse and away with you! Let's do combat and see who is of greater might!"

He was amazed. The knight was in all black and had blazing yellow eyes that could be seen plainly from inside his helm. He had great horns upon his head that came out from the helmet too. Fire surrounded him and seemed to be emanating from his body. Then Galopin, incensed by the knight's challenge, took the charger and mounted it. He took the reins and whirled himself around towards the good lance in the tree. The two separated about a bow shot length and then, charging full tilt into action, collided with one another.

Their lances and horses collided and they came crashing to the ground, shattering and tearing apart shields. Galopin's shield was torn apart and the lance went through his hauberk, grievously wounding him on the left side. He remained mounted long enough to see his spear plunged into the demon's heart.

Then he took another lance and went after a knight nearby. They swiftly charged into one another but Galopin had aimed his lance too high; it bored into the knight's ventail just below the chin and proceeded through his neck and out the other side! Blood spurted everywhere and he was well mangled. The knight was killed immediately as he tumbled from his horse.

The lance he had picked up had the most exquisite pennon of white that was marked with the holy cross upon it and nailed to the lance with golden nails. It was once the purest white but was now completely drenched in red blood. When these two black knights perished a cloud of smoke surrounded them and a demonic beast with wings flew from their bodies and attempted to flee. But their wings were clipped and they were shackled with iron bands. In this way these spirits were lead off by an angelic host into a nearby cave. Those were the souls of the devils that were now captured, being vanquished. Each was to be judged according to his sins.

Galopin continued to look around the island in astonishment. Then, the battle calmed and he recognized that the white knights were gathering around a chapel on their side of the island. Bells rang and a priest in the Lord's armor began singing the service. All the army in white delighted at this.

The evil spirits cowered when they heard the clanging bells and crept across the bridge back to their land, defeated. The black knights were all distraught and had there heads down as they went away, shamed. A vile tempest arose on that side of the island so that dark clouds covered it from sight. They were swathed in darkness all around and stayed on that side of the island.

When Galopin pondered what he heard a loud voice: "That side of the isle is full of evil spirits. They carry the banner of the dragon, who is the serpentine Devil. They live in torment for they serve the demonic lord and all their efforts are towards evil. On this other side you can clearly see the holiness of the people; they are angels from heaven who are dedicated to fighting the evil spirits every day. They keep them from escaping the isle, where they are imprisoned; if they escaped they would go to the world and do much evil upon mankind, corrupting the good with mortal sin. So these holy knights protect all humanity and fight valiantly.

In an attempt to escape the dark forces make a fresh assault upon the fortress to attempt to assail the army in white every day; if successful great peril would befall everyone. Fortunately the knights of God have held firm against the wicked, and we all might praise the Lord for that! This river, as you see, divides the forces of good and evil.

You, being sinless and a good knight, have done well by slaying two black knights, who are know captives of the lord. The one you first slew was a very evil spirit. Indeed, he was the very one who raped the Prince's wife at

102

the garden of delight when she tried to take a rose petal from the bush. The evil ones will be smarting from the blow you so ruthlessly delivered!"

Galopin was pleased to learn about the isle and walked towards the chapel. They invited him to join in. Cherubim's unarmed him and gave him a silk mantle of white embroidered with gold flowers and song birds. Galopin was delighted by all the dancing and celebrations after the mass, for they held a great feast in his honor.

Just then, a beautiful maiden approached him who was more stunning than any he had ever seen. She said: "Take heart, good knight. Your deeds are very noble. When you slew the black knight you were quite fearless! Listen to this: We are called the Castle of Maidens because we women protect our maidenhood, saving it for God alone! That is why were are full of purity. The men here are all angels and they worship the Lord with the same devotion and chastity. You will see that on the other side of the river they are the Castle of Ladies; for the women there are full of lust and wantonness. You can even see now how they are all frolicking with one another, passing the time fulfilling their carnal aspirations. Surely they are not protective of the body, which is a very vessel and temple of God. It is to be worshiped! But see how they commit carnal sins as they please?"

Then Galopin looked across the bridge and saw the demon knights on the banks of the river. Many of them were carousing and consorting with strange concubines. They weren't ladies but had tails like lions and heads like snakes. They were fornicating and swearing and raising all kinds of hell. Galopin didn't know what to think, other than that he was pleased to be safely in the castle: "God be with you, my lady."

Galopin retired form the feast and the ladies in the castle led him into another chamber where there was a group of elderly knights standing around a table. They were wise, sober and had long flowing beards. They were all still in their armor but had removed their helms so that you could see their faces clearly. Their shields were slung along their backs by a leather strap, for they had little use of them in the chamber. They had eyes like balls of fire

103

and their whole face radiated with holy light, for they were imbued with the power of the Holy Spirit. Their armor was gold throughout and they were a great marvel to behold. Anyone who looked directly at these angels was shocked and immediately felt the presence of the Lord upon him and throughout his body. For they were so radiant and full of joy that no one could help confessing their sins and repenting at the sight of them.

It is an important detail that they all bore the red cross on their gold shields. And it was a red cross because it was His blood that was sacrificed for mankind. In fact, Jesus, when he first went to heaven, took his own blood and put it on every shield that was there. For these knights were part of his most devout angelic host.

Galopin wondered at them for they were all so strong and mighty. They invited him to the table, which was just like the round table but had twelve seats for the twelve peers and counselors. One of them embraced Galopin and said: "Have a seat good knight. You fought well today. Your blow to the black knight made them cower in fear. Tomorrow, if you choose to ride with us, we plan to storm their keep and take prisoners! We have found that a direct charge across the bridge will leave them in utter despair, as long as it is done when the sun is at its highest zenith. For the lady of the castle, who has studied the stars and heavens, informed us that if we strike then we will be able to send those spirits back to hell and imprison them for all time! She mentioned that this light, being so bright at this hour, would blind them and shine to light all their sins. Will you take part in the fighting?"

Galopin was astonished and responded: "If we can banish these wicked spirits for all time then you have my full participation for I would like nothing more!" After this all the men around the table cheered and were merry. They went back into the splendid hall where the feasting was. The good knights, who were twelve in number, were helped by many maidens with their arms and were given scarlet mantles and robes of silk to where comfortably around the castle. Each of them began dancing and taking part in the festivities which continued thereafter.

Galopin himself was attended by two of the most graceful maidens imaginable. Know that he had not a care in the world. They tended to his wounds and were very eager to please him. He was blooding in one area and they staunched the bleeding. He was given an ointment that was most holy and restored him to strength. He never felt stronger! When he was ready to retire they took him to a magnificent chamber that had a bed that was more comfortable than any you have ever seen. It was the most comfortable and splendid bed in the world. The maidens stayed with him and watched over him until he fell asleep.

In the morning, when he awoke, he donned his armor and was invited to mass. They went to mass outside the keep in the splendid chapel at first light. Afterwards, they broke their fast and prepared to do battle. The black knights were already outside cavorting on the grass, plotting ill for the good and holy knights. Although, when the battle began, they were stunned. Galopin was the first across the bridge. He thrust his spear into a demon so violently that it cut through his chest leaving a gaping whole, killing him instantly. Then he saw another enemy on his right side and delivered a blow with his lance that went through both shield and hauberk; the lance burst through his chest and out the other side. This knight also died instantly. He removed the lance and turned his horse around, charging at another. He thrust it into another knight, penetrating shield and hauberk and going through the shoulder. Once inside the knight's shoulder the lance snapped and the sharp point was left lodged inside his body.

When his spear shattered, Galopin drew a gem enriched blade from his scabbard and began assailing his enemies on all sides. He rained blows upon his enemies dealing with them violently. One demon drove a spear into his horse and the charger came crashing to the ground.

Galopin was deeply angered that he had lost his horse but he got up almost immediately. He jumped into the air and struck that mounted knight; the steel hammered on his head and clove him to the shoulder.

When he was avenged he took the swift charger and advanced again upon the enemy. He continued to deliver blows with his bejeweled blade that were so fierce that all knights that went before him were slain. He split heads from the top of the skull to the waist. He tore apart limbs and lashed open bellies so that intestines fell onto the field.

Once again the demons turned to dust and were bound in iron shackles by the angelic hosts and led off to the cave of judgement. The white knights all admired his strength and prowess. One could plainly see the field littered with mail hood rings, helms which went flying from heads without the laces, and shattered shields. A great trail of destruction followed Galopin who was the very fount of holiness that day as he exuded staunch righteousness against the forces of evil. Know that the angelic knights were also fighting bravely. They followed his example and were deeply honored by his efforts.

When the day reached the point where the sun was at its highest zenith the holy knights sounded a golden trumpet which blared loudly, making the whole island quake. The castle's trembled and the demon's shook with fright. The knight yelled: "Come, let us advance across the bridge while the sun is at its highest zenith." Just then, the sun's light became divine light. It burned the demon flesh and blinded them so they were completely defenseless.

The sunlight emanated from God. Indeed, all things emanate from him, so praise him! The angelic host road across the bridge, spurring their mighty steeds directly into the demon's army. They routed them so successfully and killed them in large numbers. It was soon that the dark forces were completely overrun.

When the field was won the holy knight's charged into the fortress. "Come, let us uproot them, half measures do not avail!" They stormed the keep, going chamber to chamber, slaying many and taking captive those who begged for mercy. All who surrendered were forced to attest that God was the true governor of all. At the days end, four hundred evil spirits were slain; they also took fifty captives. These captives were imprisoned in the rock on the isle along with the unfortunate spirits that were to be judged accordingly.

The holy knight's were so pleased and thanked Galopin for his efforts. "You have helped us free the isle of the evil spirits, God bless you!" They all were full of joy and celebrated.

Before long they realized that the dark side of the isle was not hospitable. They simply could not remain in that place, for the power of the devil still was there. A foul stench remained and the dark clouds still pervaded. All the knights who tried to stay there could not last more than a day before perishing. The very air was corrupted. To this day that isle of darkness is still corrupted; despite any efforts to purify it. Anyone who tries to stay there more than a fortnight is killed or disappears. Meanwhile, the demon army was vanquished and such was the fate of those souls who chose to dwell in the demon land, serving him fruitlessly. The holy host made sure to make sure they would never rebel again.

He bid all his friends, for they were the best of friends after the battle they had shared, farewell. A great eagle flew from the sky and invited him to mount. He mounted it and it took him back to the land of Logres where he found his old charger right where he left him in the meadow. When he realized that he was back in the forest of Landone he was happy indeed; for he saw the clear meadows and the peaceful land and recalled that he had vanquished the forces of darkness.

He thought to himself: "It is surely true that God is in all things and all the beauty of Logres comes from him." When he finally returned to court and recounted his adventure everyone marveled at him. The King said: "I couldn't believe such a place exists! You'll have to contrive a marvelous lay that will put the event to life for us, for I'm having a difficult time imagining this." Galopin enjoyed this reply full heartily since he was not only a knight of prowess but a minstrel by craft. Everything was recorded in detail about his adventures. So he spun together this lay and played it on his golden harp:

*"I rode along the path steeped in my own troubles,*
*Then a host of evil spirits bore me away,*
*To an island divided by a river wide,*
*I fell from the sky into a chestnut tree,*
*Where I was in the midst of a great battle,*

Angels battled dragons and the combat was fierce,
I took a lance and thrust it into a demon,
His eyes bulged from his head and his neck tore open,
The ghoul howled like a ravaging wolf and then died,
Black smoke and his nasty spirit were foul smelling,
I left that rotted corpse and it returned to hell,
They were taken in shackles to the depths below,
I delighted in Christ who had given me strength,
The next day when the sun was highest we attacked,
We stormed the keep killing them and taking captives,
The devil was so frightened he flew from the isle!"

# 14 THE RED SWORD

In the wild marches of Scotland there was a forest ridden with enchantments and many wicked snares. Maidens there devised a plan to entrap the noble lineage of that region by tempting them to lust. These ladies knew that they could elude them through the carnal passions and delights. They had a stunning palace in the forest where the Goddess Venus reigned quite freely. She was the one that steered young men away to treachery. Unabated lusts flamed like a fire and, as it is said, going near the fire creates warmth while getting further away makes you colder.

The maidens used their magic to put in the forest a stone pillar. On it hung a golden hook with a bright red sword, as red as a rose. On the pillar there was an inscription: "HE WHO BEARS THE SWORD MOST COME FROM THE ROYAL LINE OF SCOTLAND." While on the sword it said: "REMAIN FAITHFUL TO YOUR TRUE LOVE AND DON'T LET THE SWORD TURN BLACK." Everyone heard about this quest and said that, surely, the one who achieved it would restore the land and rid it of all evil enchantments. Word got around that such a miraculous pillar had been erected. The nobles of Scotland were sure that this would be an adventure worth trying, and so they all gathered together.

Indeed, there were four sons from that line, most noble and full of prowess. They were named Gadifer, Gullier, Guntiem and Gallifer. All of them were strong knights, bold and most respected. It was prophesied in the stars that the strongest of them would bear a son who would restore Britain to its former glory and that was clearly why those wicked maidens were so eager to have them all in bed!

So they went about there business until Gadifer, the first brother, took the red sword from the hook. When he did this he rode into a meadow where a splendid pavilion was erected. He let his horse graze and he entered the pavilion. Inside he found a beautiful bed that was magnificently arrayed with fine furs; the aroma from the pavilion was equally appealing. A sumptuous spread of food and spiced drinks were there on the table next to the bed. He took freely of these delights and, what struck the youth more than anything was that, in the bed, lay a woman of fare skin, with red cheeks and long flowing hair.

She turned towards him and when he saw her naked body and pert breasts he was hot with lust. Gadifer was afflicted and the power of Venus came over him. He went to bed with her and, its safe to say, she was as delighted as he was. In the morning Gadifer armed and left that place in a hurry, for he was eager to continue the quest. Though, to his great dismay, he found that the red sword had turned black as ink! Alas, he had failed the quest completely. An old man came from the woods who was shrouded in a black hood. He exclaimed: "That sword is not yours to keep, you have acted dishonorably. Give it back!" The next day it was seen hung on the stone pillar just as before.

Gadifer was full of shame and dared not recount what had happened to his brothers. Though, to grave misfortune, similar things happened to Gullier and Gunriem. For they had no true love to be faithful to, and pleasantly gave in to their lustful appetites when it was presented. They so happened to be easily deceived by the ladies of Venus's palace. They each bore a son to those tricksters!

Alas, the royal line was under assault! They had been wickedly ensnared by the wiles and enchantments of the maidens. The girls thought they had it easy, for they had achieved success so easily. Many months had passed and still no one could achieve the adventure. Many were concerned the land would never be restored to its former glory and the enchantments would keep many imprisoned and the land laid waste.

Gadifer, the last of the brothers, was a very virtuous knight. He believed in God and dared not flee from the challenge of the red sword. He even said: "It says I must be faithful to true love. Well, I'll tell you, my love is God. He created all, and will confound anyone who says otherwise." So, crossing himself and asking for St. David's intercession, took the red sword and proceeded into the forest.

When he rode that day he came across a spring in the forest. He let his horse drink and sat by it to rest. To his surprise he saw four maidens bathing and talking on the other side of the wood. They were steeped in the hot water and were naked. Three of which were pleasantly showing off that they were with child while the fourth, a most beautiful youth, was envious of it! The ladies spoke: "Who would have thought that we would be so lucky. Fortune has smiled on us. We have three children from the noble line of Scotland! We need only give our sister to Gadifer to ensure that the one who is told to be the restorer of Britain will come from our family. When he arrives, be sure to woo him in every way you can. As soon as he comes accept him most graciously and give him all he needs."

Alas, when Gadifer heard this he was confused. He desired to accomplish the quest of the red sword and saw that these ladies might have known something of what happened to his brothers. He truly wasn't sure of their aims but he was confident he'd get to the bottom of it. "As long as I remain faithful to my true love then I will be ok."

Gadifer's horse gave out a whinny and all the ladies ran over to see if he was the knight they so desired. They sent one of their servants over through the thicket to invite him over: "Good knight, I hear you are about the quest of the red sword. My lady is master of that quest and she is one who can help you accomplish it."

Although what the lady spoke was very different from the truth. In reality, she was hoping to deceive him to sleep with the young girl so that he lost the quest and all honor with it. For the victor of the quest had to remain faithful to his true love and not be tempted. So he replied: "I heard you speak of my brothers who have all failed this quest. I know that, in order to complete it, I must, as the inscription says, remain faithful to my Love. Know that my love is God alone, so that is easy enough said right away." The maiden went back to the ladies and told them that this was a man of God, and that he may not be so easily tempted as the others.

Still, she brought him back to the palace of Venus, which was a great marvel to behold. The marble pillars and spanning great hall was a remarkable sight. So the ladies prepared a sumptuous feast where all delicacies were pro-

111

vided. Gadifer disarmed and donned a beautiful mantle that was fit for a king. The sight's, sounds and smells were so permissible in that house that any man would surely have been struck with love in such an atmosphere.

The ladies were so abundantly beautiful that it was a shame to any man not to honor them the way nature commanded him to do so. They were also rife with love and desired nothing more than the man's noble seed. Yet, Gadifer was different. His love, both soul and flesh, was for God. His carnal instincts were shunned by his armor of faith. So the knight was tempted in many ways by the ladies to no avail.

On the first night they ran late into the evening talking of many things. He was flushed with wine and had eaten a good deal. The lady took him to a grassy glade that was lit well by the moon. She wore little more than a shift and was all too revealing of her desire. She plainly pleaded that he take her. She said: "In the name of the Goddess Venus you must have me, my flesh is aching for you, Gadifer!"

Though, being a strong knight he sat down in prayer, refusing to give her more than his protection. "Fair lady, though I wish you well, my love is for God alone." Thus they cast him from the house of pleasure and into the woods, where he was cold in the night. By morning he found his way to the spring again and that same maiden, who was servant to the sisters, approached him. She tried to flatter him with honey-dipped words to fool him into lust: "Dear knight, so well you preformed showing your loyalty to God that my lady is sure you are the one destined to win the quest of the red sword. For you are so loyal to your cause that she does not predict you will waver. She invites you again tonight to her house to take part in the celebration, for you are to win much renown."

Clouded by the guise of flattery, Gadifer graciously assented to go to the house a second time. Yet, when night fell, all kinds of wickedness emerged from that place. The youngest sister was serving him hand and foot. When he became flushed with wine she coxed him to a chamber where she undressed before him. She put her naked body on his and they, flesh to flesh, began to spark the flames

112

of lust. Just then, when Gadifer realized the situation, he crossed himself and asked for the Holy Spirit to help him, for he was in real trouble this time! Soon enough, light shined from above piercing the chamber of darkness. The naked girl flew from the bed to the floor, as if struck by the hand of righteousness, and Gadifer arose, arming himself. The ladies kicked him out of the house a second time, yelling: "You will never accomplish the quest of the red sword, coward!"

Gadifer thanked God for saving him from another near fall into mortal sin. So he rode from there and made his way back to the spring again. On the third day he was met by the servant girl who spoke to him cleverly: "Truly you deserve all honor and praise. For by denying the girl a second time you have accomplished all that the quest asks. We invite you to our home so that you may celebrate this marvelous achievement. For many good knights have failed to do what you have done."

Gadifer, enamored by her praise, was quick to be filled with excitement at his achievement. Little did he know it wasn't yet achieved! For the lady deceived him just as the devil does when he makes a good man aware of his good deeds so that he becomes filled with vain self-righteousness. Gadifer took the sword from his scabbard and realized that, despite everything, it still remained redder than ever.

So, with hope, he entered the palace a third time and was met by the girls who honored him in every way they could. Once again, a sumptuous feast was prepared. He went to the great hall and paid his respects to the ladies. When he went to greet the girls the eldest sister used wicked magic to deceive him. This time she wasn't playing fair. She cast such a spell that she concealed her face. At the sight of her, he truly thought that the hostess was Mary, the mother of God. She had used her magic to conceal her face. When he saw that he really thought she came from the one he so devoutly served.

So he kneeled before her in tears and praying: "My lady, your wish is my command! You have my body and soul to do with as thou wilt." The lady, who had deceived him yet again with her magic, entreated him in this way: "I

113

ask, in the name of the Lord, that you enjoy this feast and celebrate. You have achieved the quest and, as a reward, I ask that you marry this young girl here. She will be the one to bear your child who will become the most noble king of Britain and will through his prowess restore the lands."

When he saw the fake Mary entreat him in this way he could do nothing else but agree. They joined hands in marriage and were led into the bed chamber. Then Mary said: "Now you need to consummate the marriage, don't be lacking in any of those natural gifts God gave you!" He replied, "Surely, if it is as you say, there will be no shortage of abounding grace and love pouring out from me!"

They entered into the chamber and began kissing fervently. As he saw her undress he grew hot and Venus did all in her power to arouse them to love's call. Yet, in the midst of the rapture, he paused a moment and thought to himself: "The inscription said that I need exit the forest before achieving the quest. I have endured little hardship and it doesn't seem right that victory was so easily won! Alas, I'm betrayed! This was no marriage, for where was the priest to administer the most holy sacrament? Oh, fie on thee, ladies of the forest, who are full of wicked magic." With that he tore away from the young girl and ran from the palace, bewildered. They all cursed him and swore that he would loose the sword and his honor. He didn't care what they said. They had harassed him so much that he didn't know what to think.

He mounted and rode from that place until the brink of daylight. Just as he saw the exit of the forest he was met by four stout knights. They spurred their chargers directly at him and challenged him. He flashed with anger and went into combat. He took his lance and thrust it into a knight so that he sent him flying from his horse and tumbling to the ground.

Then he assailed the second knight who received a blow on the shoulder that sent him over his horse's rump and into the dirt, breaking his arm in the fall. His lance broke inside the man's body and so he took that mighty red sword, which still glowed redder than a ruby, and struck the other two knights with so many blows that they were bleeding everywhere. He struck one on the head with such force that he clove him through helm, flesh and bone. His sword was sharp and went straight from the top of the skull to the teeth. The final knight was very frightened but galloped towards him for fear of shame and with a deep desire to avenge his fellows. Gadifer struck him a mighty blow on the left shoulder that tore through shield, hauberk and flesh and went right to the bone. Blood spurted out and he fell to the ground in anguish.

Gadifer unlaced his helm and threatened to cut off his head if he didn't tell him who sent him. He told him all: "Don't kill me, I beg your mercy! The ladies from the forest sent us to kill you and take the red sword. For they had planned all of this from the beginning in hopes that you would fall from God's grace, loosing the quest and your honor with it. They wanted to keep the forest in their power by birthing the great king who would restore the lands. They were jealous that you had achieved the quest. Your brothers all failed when they slept with those ladies because they didn't follow the voice of God who told them to stay clear of lust. So, since you have done so well, spare my life in your grace!" Gadifer roared with laughter when he learned that he had bested the clever enchantresses of the forest. Indeed, he spared the knight's life at this good news.

Without further ado he rode out of the forest and was met by an old man with a flowing white beard that went all the way to his knees. He said to him: "Give me the sword, lusty knight, for you are clearly not honorable to have it girded on you." When Gadifer unsheathed it and the old man saw it glowing red, bright as ever, he was astonished and said: "Praise to God, you have come through the forest untainted and pure from all sin. Take the sword wherever you please, for it is yours for all time!" Then the old man commended him to God and vanished as quick as he came. Gadifer rejoiced and he girded the red sword about him, taking it wherever he went. That sword gave him eternal joy and comfort. It was able to assail opponents with ease for it was divinely crafted. The forest was rid of all enchantments and those ladies stayed in the forest, bitter at loosing Gadifer's love.

The noble knight was elated to have accomplished the test despite so many temptations. As he rode along a narrow pathway that was overburdened with wild rose-bushes, brambles and thorns he found an old man cloaked in a black hood who said: "You have done well, lad. Although, to win your lady's love completely there is still more for you to accomplish. You must make the red sword turn white! This is only done by vanquishing the evil spirits of the land."

The man suddenly vanished and Gadifer hadn't a clue how to achieve what he asked. Yet he was determined to win the lady's love at any cost, for the power of love is a remarkable thing. He went to the Chapel of Dreams, which was in that forest and prayed for guidance.

When he did this he fell into an entranced daze. He found himself in a luxurious hall full of gold ornaments and upon a throne sat the most beautiful woman he had ever seen with a gold circlet on her head. She gave him, as he knelt before her, a chaplet of roses and said: "You have done well in proving your loyalty. Now this is a call to action: The evil spirits of the forest are to reign no longer. You will cast them out with the New Law, that is, Christianity."

Then a squire stepped forward with a perfect shield of the purest white with a red cross upon it. "Take this shield," the lady said, "and you will be able to cast out the evil spirits. For no human will power can achieve this quest. All those who have gone before you have failed. It isn't will power but the source of God, and the ever abundant fount of holiness, that can have victory here. When you encounter the wicked ones simply call upon Christ and say: By the power of Christ I banish you forthright! They will have no choice but to flee and they will likely be terrified by your shield. Do not fear, but go with God. Your faith will carry away the victory. There is little else to say, but go forth and purge the land of it's wickedness!"

After this marvelous dream he awoke in the Chapel, where he had clearly been all night without realizing it. He was astonished to find both the chaplet of roses and the white shield with the red cross were in his possession. He left that most holy place and set off into the forest, realizing what he needed to accomplish. He met with a forester and he begged him tell where he could find the dwelling of the evil enchanter who plagued the lands and was the source of all wickedness in Britain. The old forester told him of two locations were they were known to be. He thanked the man and set off along the path, as directed.

The first place he came to was an open field in the forest where, at the center, there was a large stone tomb. It housed the body of the most wicked knight who had ruled the forest by evil deeds. He was the king enchanter. He had been the leader of all the evil spirits until he was killed by the good king. He loved to rape women and his followers did the same. Also, they had no sense of generosity nor did they follow the precepts of chivalry in the least! Since he had been buried, evil spirits under his command still inhabited the forest and terrorized the living.

At the tomb Gadifer found four knights who openly opposed him: "Are you a knight of Britain? If so, you must leave us here to our enchantments. This is a place only for those you deem evil." Yet the fearless Gadifer replied: "I have come to purge the land of wickedness. By the very power of Christ I forthright banish you!" The four knights were terrified when they heard the name of the one they truly hated; they, and the spirits in the forest, all shrieked in anguish. Suddenly a loud din arose and black smoke was everywhere. A host of evil spirits began flying into the stone tomb for fear. The black wisps created a loud noise and a great rush of turbulent wind that brought down branches from the surrounding trees.

Then the four knights, who were in despair at the hearing the name of Christ, charged at Gadifer. They were wild with rage, their white eyes spun to the back of their heads and their heads twisted in full circles as they rode towards him, cackling and grinding their teeth ceaselessly. One could say they were already dead for they were truly from the demonic hosts. Gadifer thrust his lance into the first one so that he was knocked far from his horse and went toppling to the ground over the rump.

Then he drew back around and rode over him with his charger, breaking his bones. He was quickly beset

117

by the others when he assailed them with his sword
valiantly, giving one such a mighty blow on the helm that it
cut through mail coif and flesh and directly to the brain.
The other two tried to attack him but the shield with the
red cross was so terrifying and it beamed forth holy light
that was blinding to them. So, in the midst of despair, they
felt compelled to flee!

Gadifer then went to the stone tomb and struck it
with his blade in such a forceful way that the sword penetrated all the way to the hilt. A loud din was heard
throughout the forest and light flashed from the heavens.
Suddenly, the stone tomb cracked and all the evil spirits
hiding inside were banished. They fled into the air, howling
desperately.

Gadifer was filled with excitement when he saw
the tomb crumble and realized that much of his sword had
turned white. He proceeded into the thick of the woods
until he came across another marvel. Two lances were dug
into the ground with the spear point facing the sky. Atop
the lances were two heads that were still fresh with blood
and looked like they'd only been put up the day before.
This was the second place that the evil spirit's inhabited.
These knights had been killed by the good king many years
ago when they were caught assaulting a woman. This was
left as a memorial to that wicked dead and was a place
where those evil being's inhabited, harassing the living!

Gadifer marveled at the heads, which seemed
alive, until darkness came. The crescent moon gave him
enough light to see a host of evil spirits surrounding the
bodiless heads fixed on the lances. Then two headless
knights rode towards him and demanded to joust. They
were black and purple and covered in smoke. The evil spirits realized that the holy shield was impenetrable to them.
So they devised a cunning scheme to get it away from him.
They argued and there horses reared about: "Prepare to be
challenged, for you have come too far along the path of
the dead, and you are of the living. Only, I implore you, do
away with that shield of yours and use one of ours, for
that is the custom of the land. Surely if you prove your
feats without the magic of that shield you will gain much

greater honor and renown. Also, if you win, you can be admitted into the land of paradise where our master lives."

In this way the demon coxed him to remove the shield. For it was by no human power he could achieve victory over the evil spirits, as had been testified by the many knights who had died trying before him, but only by the power of God. That shield was his protection again the spirits, cause it was not made of man.

So, it was because the evil spirits were so terrified of the strange sign on his shield that it made them unable to successfully attack him. Thus they resorted to many deeds to cleverly disarm him without the use of arms. Yet these silver tongued words were to no avail, for Gadifer realized their treachery.

Gadifer replied: "I will fight with none but my own shield. I'd also much prefer it if you had heads about you, too!" So the two knights took their heads from the lances and, as easy as could be, set them upon their bodies so that they reconnected. Then the noble Gadifer spurred off the distance of a bowshot before hurling back at a pace swifter than a crossbow bolt. He came to the battle dealing a flurry of deathly blows. His lance impaled one of the knights to a nearby tree as it went clean through his body and half way through the stump. Then he drew his sword and struck the other a mighty blow, cutting through shield and ventail and lopping off his head which had only just been returned to him!

When the great host of evil spirits, who had been spectators of the whole combat, saw that their two headless knights were so utterly defeated and shamed, they were full of terror. Then Gadifer took his lance from the tree, which had fixed the dead corpse into it, and roared like a lion: "In the name of Christ I hereby banish you from this land!" When he said this a great light came from the heavens and the evil spirits cowered, running to and fro without a care but to save themselves. When the din ceased Gadifer realized he had truly vanquished the lands of the evil enchantment before it.

He saw the sword turned fully white, and it was to his delight that a voice called out: "Rejoice, for you have truly accomplished the quest and restored the lands."

119

Then, much elated, he felt compelled to return home to his castle and to be with God and his lady love. For, by his merits, he had accomplished the quest and been given a most beautiful wife to wed and father the next King of Scotland.

# 15 THE SECRET BURIAL

What a spectacular miracle happened that I'm about to tell you of. Grab a chair and brace yourself to know more about the splendid marvel which occurred in the year of our Lord when King Arthur's lands were his own. Though let me wander a bit. Did you know that many believe he's yet to return? A good two cowherds in the valley who were tending to both bulls and cows saw him the other day! He was out hunting, and said he'd be back to court soon. So the good King is but a little way off now, and be sure that when he comes he will return Britain to its former glory!

Now hear something that is a wonder and could only happen in a time where adventures and magic were quite common. Two knights wandered through the Forest of Gloeven. They had been traveling for some time and been quite weary as a result. They came upon a broad and deep river. The water was black and the tide fierce. There seemed to be no way across. On the other side there was a well situated castle; it was both well provisioned and fortified. Battlements surrounded the castle in addition to a deep moat. The crenelated walls were tall and thick. On the one side it bordered the vast sea while it was equally surrounded by meadows, farmlands and grassy hills on the other sides.

These two knights were marveling at the beautiful castle when the drawbridge suddenly lowered. Out came three peasants, armed with battle axes, leading a poor damsel towards the river. She was completely naked but for her shift. It simply isn't right to leave a lady in such a plight! The wicked men were abusing and beating her all the way to the river. The damsel saw the knights on the other side and called out: "Help me from these cruel peasants. They mean to kill me for no good cause! Please, if you have any honor in you, save me from certain death!" The two knights, who, mind you, were cousins, were both extremely distraught at their predicament. They decided it was best to cross the river, even though there was no way to do so but by jumping straight in. They spurred their horses and, crossing themselves on the brow, dove into the wide river. Their horses were strong and, luckily, they made it to the other side despite the heavy armor weighing them down.

When they came across the first knight galloped towards a peasant and drove his lance clear through his body so that he died instantly. The other two were terrified and ran back towards the castle. The damsel was greatly pleased with this outcome, though she was still in fear: "There is a knight in the castle who will come for you. You have to save me or i'm dead!"

The good knight responded: "Worry not, damsel, I am bound by an oath to protect all maidens and damsels alike from harm." Just then, a knight galloped out from the keep in full armor. He rode quickly towards them, yelling: "Give me back that lady, she is mine by right! How dare you assault my servants who were only doing my bidding." With that the two knights spurred their steeds and went crashing into one another. Horse collided with horse and body with body. The good knight kept in his saddle while the other fell over his horse's rump and to the earth. The lance shattered on his shield but he was returned a piercing blow that went straight through the shoulder; once it was lodged in the body and through the hauberk the other lance snapped.

Without more ado the good knight dismounted and drew his keen edged sword. He ran ferociously towards the knight from the castle, who was quite out of his wits and stunned from the blow. Slowly, the dazed knight got up but was immediately assailed by his opponent. He came upon him like a leopard and struck a mighty blow on the helm that cut through to the skull. The knight tried to respond but only had strength enough to cover himself with his shield and hope for the best. Under so much pressure he collapsed. The good knight delivered blow after blow until the shield was completely torn to shreds and the hauberk was gone. Now he dealt blows directly on the flesh and the knight, without any more life in him, fell in a swoon. The good knight removed his helm by the laces and chopped off his head, rolling it into the river. He had no mercy for any knight who hurt a lady.

The damsel delighted at this and said: "Having no more to fear, I can only praise and honor you for saving me from certain death and avenging me so well!" The good knight said: "Tell me how this came about?" She replied: "I was out riding with my brother and we ventured to this castle. We found it so splendidly situated that we took a look around the gardens. When the Lord of the castle's brother saw me he was taken by my looks. He grabbed me off my horse and my brother, heartily dismayed, challenged him.

They fought a bitter battle until my brother slew the man. When the Lord of the castle saw this he was very bitter about it and, as vengeance, he summoned ten men at arms who took my brother captive and beheaded him! Alas, I was so distraught that I could do nothing but cry and lament. Then, suddenly, the Lord ordered his men to take me to this river and slay me. By fortune, you were here to save me from certain death! That is what happened until now."

The two cousins were so sad about her brother's death and consoled her in any way they could. He kept in his saddle a scarlet mantle which he wrapped around her to cover her naked body, for she was covered only by a light shift that was heavily torn up. When she warmed up a bit they took her back to the castle and the people, seeing their lord was dead, surrendered immediately.

The people all celebrated when they saw the two valiant knights in the courtyard. They told of how they didn't like the count for his wickedness and the fact that he had recently denounced christianity. "He kept from us all the things we toiled for, and punished those who kept what they harvested. He killed all the christians among us who wouldn't renounce our faith." Meanwhile, the servants and squires of the castle did everything imaginable to secure the two cousins. They let their horses graze about and wrapped them in splendid mantles of ermine. They graciously removed their arms, for they were no surely longer needing them!

The two knights climbed up the steps to a large and spacious hall where a splendid feast was prepared. The feast was sumptuous and it was followed by much caroling and dancing. The damsel, however, was so grieved for her brother that she ate very little and did not have much pleasure of the company.

The two knight's made an oath to her that they would do anything she needed, provided it was in their power, to make her more merry. The good knight suddenly had a good idea, so he said: "Bring me the elders of this castle, I wish to speak with them." Just as he said it was so.

The elders came to him in the midst of all the merry making. The cousin spoke to them: "My lady has lost her brother by the wicked hand of your former lord. I ask that you amend this situation with what you have at your disposal. Tell me, where is the most splendid tomb in all the land held? For I know that we may bury the good man in it."

The elders consoled with one another until they agreed this would be a good amends. The lead elder replied: "I will take you to a place within the castle. Beneath the chapel altar there is a tomb of the utmost beauty. For it was built neither of gold nor silver, but was rather crafted entirely of precious stones joined together so subtly that it appears no mortal man could have done it. The old king, a Saracen, had been buried there. Yet, when Joseph came and brought Christianity, they removed the king's body and threw it into the moat. Thus, the tomb has been enclosed since and no one has touched it." This was a great joy to the lady.

The next day the whole town went to hear mass at the chapel. After, they dug up the ground and found the magnificent tomb. They moved it to the hall and buried the brother. After much mourning and ceremony, the faithful knight was interred.

That same night, something terrible happened. A great storm arose and the wind swept through the castle making a great din like thunder. The cousin's both arose and donned their armor for they feared some evil was afoot. They heard loud voices yelling and raising all hell in the hall where they buried the brother of the damsel.

So they crept inside with shield around neck, sword in hand and helm on head. They found a great evil spirit, covered in black smoke, skulking over the tomb. It yelled out in anguish: "This knight has taken my tomb from me! I already suffer enough in Hell. Oh, the pain is so abundant I cannot bear it. And now this, a christian man takes my precious tomb, the most magnificent ever created."

He turned to the cousins, snarling with rage: "This is you're doing, defend yourselves!" The spirit hurled himself at them. He ran through one of the knights and out the other side, for he was incorporeal. A cold chill overwhelmed the knight and he fell to the ground, shocked.

When the good knight saw his cousin wounded he was filled with rage. He roared like a lion and charged at the demon, slicing his head off in a fatal blow. When he saw that the evil spirit, who was none other than the Saracen King, was beheaded he ran to comfort his cousin. He was pale and shivered. Thereafter he could eat only a little and became very thin. The evil spirit had cursed him wickedly. Indeed, he stayed that way for several months before being healed. He had seen something terrible in his visions and dreams too. At last, there was a great doctor in that place who was able to heal him with certain herbs from the forest. Though these only made him a little better until the priest came and heard his confession. Then the evil spirit could dwell in him no longer and was instantly cast out. Praise to the Lord for his deliverance! It was then that they made all the inhabitants christians and had them baptized, for the place was clearly needing it!

# 16 THE CASTLE OF MAIDENS

If marvels happened anywhere that were astonishing to all the people it was at the time when Logres was ruled by the glorious and magnanimous King Arthur. He governed so well that he conquered Europe and Italy and all of the Northlands. Since the beginning, when Brutus first brought the Trojans to the land of Britain, there were no human inhabitants in the land. Yet many giants ruled the land of Britain at this time. These were fierce creatures who were much larger than man. Yet they had no law or craft; they took to ruling the lands with great big clubs and loved eating human flesh. When Brutus came seeking lands he deemed the fair isle of Britain as his own and that is why it is called such.

He gave his three sons rule over it. Locrinus was made king of all Logres. Camber, his brother, was made lord over Cambria or Wales. Then Albanactus, a mighty Trojan, was given the lands to the North known as Albania or modern Scotland. They constructed a large city and called it Troiam Novam or "New Troy" after their homeland. For they were much aggrieved that Troy had been toppled by the wicked Greeks and hoped to reestablish themselves in honor through their ancient lineage of heroes. That is why the mighty Britains are so powerful for they come from that same marvelous line of heroes.

Troiam Novam was later named Caer Lud or Lud's City after Cassibellanus defended it so admirably against Caesar the tyrant invader. So powerful were the Britains in later years that they sent massive armies after the Romans and chased them all the way back to Rome, sacking it. Then they went as far as to demand tribute from them as they had so wickedly exacted it from us at the time of Caesar. Indeed, Caesar was harshly rebuked twice when he came to Britain by the good and noble Cassibellanus. Once he invaded by the river Thames. Since the Britains learned of the plan they planted a number of stakes in the river so that when he entered with his fleet half of it was completely destroyed, drowning the army.

When Brutus first came to the land it was wild, full of strange magic, and dumb giants inhabited the lands. So he and his valiant warriors inhabited the land of Britain by slaying these giants. It was not only the violent giants which opposed the first Britons. In the seas there were many perils. Indeed, near the shores of Britain there were mermaids who were also known as sirens. These creatures were capable of singing a song so beautiful that they could capture a man's soul for all his life. Josephus and his followers were only able to thwart them through much prayer and fasting. In a previous time, Ajax had his warriors plug their ears as they crossed through the channel to avoid the captivating song of these creatures. The alluring noises of the sirens often led great men, regardless of their strength to treachery; for the sweetness of the sin often turns to bitterness thereafter. Those captivated by the sirens were brought death when they answered the call; for Sirens feed on the flesh of man. In a similar way was Samson taken in by his lady despite his ferocity and strength of a lion.

Time progressed and the Britains rid themselves of the evil spirits in the land and Christianity purified it. When the Kingdom of Logres was established another marvelous castle was constructed. They called it the Castle of the Maidens. It was a brilliant fortress that overlooked a beautiful meadow and farmlands on one side and cornered the sea on the other. The cascading towers were red and white; the walls were thick, high and well fortified. It was indeed a well provisioned and positioned castle with a deep, wide moat and the walls were of the most exquisite marble. The lovely gate was so intricately designed that no more ornately crafted one was in all the land; it was composed entirely of ivory and was a source of wonder. This fortress rested on a hill and was a beautiful sight as one exited the nearby forest which was quite dark and gloomy.

In that land Perceval's father once ruled over the whole region. Yet, at the time Perceval was born, his father had lost the land to Hector of the Fens. Hector killed all the males of the family and frequently chastised the people there. Over the course of time he took all of the castles in the region and further chastised Perceval's mother. The women of the castle were torn by anguish and grief for

127

they had no one to protect them. Perceval's mother had told him when he was born that his name meant "the one who lost the vales". That was because Hector, evil as he was, had stripped the land of its rightful holder when all the males of the line went to their deaths, sadly.

Perceval would have avenged his family on Hector of the Fens had he known of the circumstance but he was quite busy with the Quest of the Grail; he was also wrapped up in that other mystery: the reconnecting of the broken sword. Both of which required a knight of prowess and dignity. When he returned to the Castle of the Maidens and his homeland, he had been sailing the oceans for several years. When he saw the lands barren and the castle besieged he suddenly realized how tormented his mother and sister were by Hector of the Fens.

On the day he returned one of the knights of the castle was out hunting. He was a good liege man. When he was in the forest, Hector's knights attacked him. Four knights came upon the lone man with ferocity and slew him, as shameful as it was those knights cared little, for they were vile murderers. The ladies saw it from the tower as the gazed below in astonishment at the dead body, which was cruelly left on the field. This tragedy was later recounted in the court so the whole house was grieving bitterly. Perceval's mother was terribly distraught. When she told Perceval he was filled with a desire to avenge his people. For when Perceval arrived through the postern, he was sorely grieved to see the whole place in despair.

The next day when it was bright, and just after hearing mass, Perceval rode out hunting to the forest. He made sure to don his armor completely before setting out. The excitement of the hunt led deep into the woods. He brought several companions along with him so that the chase was not dull. By the afternoon their hunt led them to a group of Hector's knights. They met at a ford so that ten knights were present in total. Perceval called out: "Are you with Hector of the Fens?" The one, who seemed to be the leader, said: "Indeed we are. In fact we rule these woods and do away with all traitorous knights, especially those from the Castle of Maidens. For the woman there is a most base creature as is her lineage that has all been killed by my lord." When Perceval heard this he grew full of rage and replied: "You have disturbed my mother for too long. It is not courteous nor a quality of a knight to insult a defenseless maiden. Your sin will bring you torment if I can help it. Taste the edge of my blade and be avenged for your wicked acts!" At this, Perceval and his companions charged forward.

The encounter was a dreadful sight for the knights clashed like thunder, making a din all throughout the forest. Perceval plunged his lance into the knight so that it broke inside his chest. His heart burst as he came tumbling from his horse. The other companions were routed in the same way. When Perceval had so effortlessly killed his opponent the others were much encouraged; they also brought their opponents to the ground, unhorsing them. Then a great battle with swords ensued. The clash was loud and fierce. Perceval delivered many blows, tearing shields from necks, helms from heads and drawing blood the whole time. Six of the knights were slain in the bitter struggle, and those which remained which were captured by the other knights.

Perceval brought the four captured knights back to his mother. Their treason was fully realized and they were imprisoned. Not long after Hector heard of all this. He was terribly angry and decided to go after Perceval. He ventured into the forest with a large entourage. They were so close to the Castle of Maidens that they could be seen from the rampart. Perceval was hearing mass when he heard the sound of hooves and the shouts of men. A squire ran into the chapel and told him that the enemy was near. Perceval crossed himself at the brow and armed himself. Before leaving his mother blessed him in the name of the father, son and holy spirit. His sister gave him a scarlet sash and he put it on his arm, adorning it in battle.

The drawbridge was lowered and Perceval rode out at a brisk pace. He was so valiant that those who saw him cowered in fear. His shield was checkered green and white and he had the holy cross on his tabard which came over his hauberk. He bounded towards the enemy and leveled his lance. The first knight to see him was struck dead. The lance plunged through his shield, hauberk and chest so that it stuck out the other side, renting him from his saddle and through the air. Others rode after him but were quickly unhorsed by the strength of Perceval and the might of his sharp, stout lance. They fell in ah heap and one became sorely bruised as he went crashing from his saddle into the moat, drowning by the weight of his armor. A vicious combat ensued between Hector's knights and Perceval. Swords clashed and many limbs were lost. Perceval dodged many attacks from the comfort of his horse and struck blows that cleft arms, legs and spilled guts. When the Maiden's saw him in distress the squire blew an ivory horn and ten knights, fully armed and mounted, sallied forth from the keep. They brought aid and the combat continued for many hours.

Perceval's achievements were beyond measure. No one could remove him from his horse and that is why his horse was called Llamrei or "swift one". The clash of arms could be heard throughout the valley. The men from the castle all had God with them and they could not be defeated. He drove the keen blade into knights so mercilessly that those who opposed him were killed immediately.

Perceval then saw Hector of the Fens in the distance near a copse of trees. Hector watched the battle in horror as many of his good knights perished seemingly without much effort. When Perceval saw him he was filled with eagerness to assault him. One of his fellow knights said: "There is Hector of the Fens. Go after him and we can end this battle right away." So Perceval took another lance from the ground, for his had broken, and he charged towards Hector.

This clash of arms was brief for Perceval was far too skilled in combat. Indeed, the lance struck Hector in the side so that he became wounded. The two horses collided, but Perceval was unmoved from the saddle. Hector had received such a blow that he crumbled and the harness broke as he went tumbling to the ground. Hector got up and drew his sword, charging at Perceval. Perceval dismounted and approached the knight. Hector struck at him but the blow was easily dodged. Then, with a powerful stroke, Hector lost his right arm. The sword came down like a hammer, breaking the bone and flesh completely.

130

The blade was powerful and cleft his arm from the shoulder. He bled profusely and fell to the ground in a swoon.

As Hector swooned on the ground Perceval tore the laces from his helm and threw his helm into the forest. He was dazed but could understand when the fierce knight shouted: "You are to be prisoner and should be shamed for your treachery against my mother. Alas, surrender now or I will behead you!" Hector could do nothing else but nod in agreement for he had nearly broke his windpipe in the fall.

The good knights took Hector prisoner and carried him on a litter back to the Castle of the Maidens. Some spent their time chasing the stragglers of his army. That very day the siege was lifted and the knights returned to the keep, victorious. They took that man to the gallows and imprisoned him until they figured out what to do.

When they returned to the castle a number of maidens and servants came to help them. They took their horses and disarmed them. Then they placed scarlet mantles on them so that they were quite comfortable. They sate down at a great feast were there was much caroling, singing and dancing. There was joy and celebration for they had captured the evil tyrant who had brought so much grief to them!

Perceval told his mother and the counsel: "This knight has brought evil on us. He has murdered innocent men in acts of treachery. There was no chivalry when he killed the outnumbered knights of the maiden. Since he has so willingly betrayed God's commandment and defiled the land, we have no choice but to kill him." So the counsel decided that he should be killed.

The dead knights from the field were drained of all their blood and that blood was released into a large vat and boiled in the great hall. Then Hector was tied to a rope that was attached to the upper beam of the hall; he was upside down and lowered, head first, into the vat of blood which boiled vigorously. When his head was completely submerged in the blood his body flailed about in agony for he was both burned and drowned.

When his flailing body ceased to move they recognized that he was dead and the people of the town, all

131

spectating with illuminated eyes, rejoiced. They buried him with the rest of his men in a burial ground behind the castle. Perceval and his sister then poured the blood into the river so that it ran red. At this time all of the castles that Hector had taken from Perceval's mother were restored to her out of fear of Perceval.

# 17 THE TWO BROTHERS

At this time there was an uproar in the kingdom because Bellius and Benoic, two brothers, were greedily fighting over the kingdom. They had amassed equally large armies and jeered at one another; it wasn't before long that a massive pitched battle ensued. This news brought extreme grief to their mother, who saw no reason that two brothers should do anything but love one another. She went to the battlefield and called for her sons. She found Bellius and said to him: "How could you kill your own brother? This would be a tremendous sin that you would suffer for all your life. The kingdom is big enough for the both of you. You both loved each other so fervently, what has changed? If you do this God will banish you and the lands will be wasted. Do not suffer such violence. I am your mother. I gave birth to both of you. In this way I can make peace between you both." Bellius had tears in his eyes at his mothers words.

So the two brothers, who once bore each other ill will, met in the field to be reconciled. The two armies were extremely happy for no blood was shed. The civil war would have brought grief for many families and the kingdom would have been in ruin. When the brothers were reconciled they suddenly realized they had a large force and this led them to take on another adventure. While they knew that further combat between one another could very well bring them grief they decided to go into France because the people there were heathens. They sought to bring the law of Christians to these lands and set sail across the channel.

This was decided and announced before the two massive armies, where much rejoicing was had at the prospect of taking lands from the heathens. The wind was in their favor and brought their fleet of ships swiftly to the shore of Gaul. The army unloaded at a castle called the Iron Tower. It was called this because it was made entirely of iron. This castle had much to do with iron for they had a large deposit of it in the fields overlooking the castle. The inhabitants were evil because they took little care for the people, often starving and overworking them. The leaders worshipped a strange law and did violence to many chivalrous knights who passed by. So Bellius commanded his force to the gates and they laid siege to it. When they came near, archers gathered on the walls and let fly arrows.

Bellius rode ahead, for he was a fearless leader, and stormed into the keep. His man, much convinced of his divinity, ran after. They smashed through the doors and met the forces ferociously. When they entered the keep, four large statues of iron came alive and attacked him. They were each the size of three men, and they were incredibly strong with the iron spears they wielded. Bellius was brave and he assailed them on either side, making circles around them with his horse as he gave them heavy blows. His blade was fierce and it sank into the limbs of those statues so that they instantly shattered. When the four statues had been slain the castle immediately forfeited for they realized resistance was futile. The army infiltrated the towers like a swarm of bees to a hive and took many prisoners.

The Britons rejoiced at this victory and proceeded to convert the people in the Iron Tower to the new law. The king of that place had a brother who was terribly inflicted; he had been dealt a wound to the head. It was such a bad wound that his skull was fractured and his brains were plainly visible. When Bellius saw this he felt a great deal of pity, and asked the king: "If I could restore him to life would you be evinced that the God of christianity is the one true God? The king was sure that he would, for he believed no divine thing could possibly heal his brother: "I have already prayed to the Gods without any avail, but if you do it and are successful I will be sure to praise the Lord of the new law. So Bellius got down on his knees, right in the middle of the hall, and prayed fervently: "Lord, Father in heaven, through your greatness all things come into existence. I hereby ask you to relieve this man of his wound, not for my own glory but to show these people that you are the one true God." When he said this he stood up and, suddenly, a great light came from the heavens and shot through the king's brother like an arrow. When this happened he was relieved of his wound, and everyone was amazed.

They were baptized and Bellius, following the ways of Josephus, had disciples rule over the people and the word of God quickly flourished in that land. He also balked at the strength Bellius had when he slew the iron statues, which were constructed in a way that no man could defeat them. When he had seen this he looked at his counselors in terror and said: "The word of God must be true for no knight could possibly defeat the iron statues single handedly unless he was invulnerable. Those creatures were designed to be powerless against any man."

It was also so that one of the king's sons had been slain during the battle. This loss was extremely sorrowful for the king. So Bellius felt pity for them and said: "If the rest of your people convert to the new law and you spread it accordingly throughout the lands I will happily bring him back to life by the power of the omnipotent God." The king laughed at this and replied: "There is no God that can do such a thing regardless of how much prayer. Indeed, if you can make it happen, we will have no choice but to worship your Lord." So Bellius got on his knees and said this prayer: "Dear Lord, bring this youth back to life so that, by this miracle, these people can see your truth and begin to follow you." In this way the miracle was completed and the king's son arose from the dead. A great light came into the dark hall and everyone was shocked by it. When the light faded, everyone realized a wondrous miracle had occurred. The son, now alive, fell to Bellius' knees, kissed his feet and thanked him most tenderly. The king was equally thankful for he thought he would never see his son again.

The Britons were extremely happy with the defeat of the Iron Tower. A hermit in these lands came to them when he saw the Iron Tower fall. He told them: "This place has been the dwelling of a vicious demon for many centuries. The people here would never have been converted had not the great warrior Bellius shown the might of God." As soon as the miracles were performed the demon was banished, for it feared the light that came from heaven it scurried off into the forest. Bellius had converted thousands through the two miracles he preformed that day. So there was great rejoicing in that land for the people were very happy at their new found joy.

Bellius set out from the Iron Tower and met with his brother Benoic. Together they rode throughout all France, conquering it. The two brothers came upon another castle which was well situated in a valley. However, it was much impoverished for the walls were not maintained and the wooden doors were completely rotted. It seemed more like a bunch of ruins than a well fortified keep. When the brothers entered the castle the conditions were appalling. They found dead corpses by the road and starving people everywhere. Those living were hungry and full of despair. There was no one there who seemed happy for all were in misery. The poverty was clearly discernible to the brothers and they realized a wicked custom must have made them this way. Many of the peasants shouted: "Don't come near, strong knights, for you will meet your death here!" Many of them yelled out that they should turn back and fear for their lives. Yet the two brothers were hardly afraid and continued onward.

They dismounted in a courtyard and climbed up a series of steps to a hall that resembled one of the old style. In there they found the lord of that place, who was richly adorned. The hall was sharply contrasted with the poverty in the streets. For the man was donned in exquisite garments and there was a sumptuous feast laid on the table. There were many opulent men in the court, running around the pillars playing all kinds of games with the ladies.

The Lord greeted them and offered all the hospitality he could, for he seemed to horde all his wealth in that hall of his. Besides those few among the court that lived in the main hall, all of the others, even though they were very noble in appearance and demeanor, were in garments that were rent and tattered. They had little to eat but a few crumbs of bread. So why was there only so much wealth in the hall? The two brothers greeted the king and said: "My Lord, it seems a great feast is prepared here. Though everyone in your land is living in abject poverty and suffers greatly, what gives?"

136

The fearful Lord greeted them but strictly forbade them to touch any of the food on the table. He told the brothers: "Alas, you have made it to the Poor Castle, we are unjustly abused by a knight in these lands that takes everything from us. This feast is prepared for him alone! He comes when he desires and takes his fill. We all toil and labour for him. The nobles you see playing games are his henchmen who guard the place. Indeed, be careful, for they will likely report to their master about your arrival! He takes all and we toil for him in all things. For the rich often bully the poor and make them miserable. The only way that we can be free is if someone challenges the knight who has opposed us for so long. For his barons and henchmen, as you see, have taken all of our treasure away and they squander it in games and revelry while we long only to have food again to feed our citizens." He pointed out of the window to a hill that had a strong pine tree at the top of it, next to the tree were five wooden crosses in the ground. Somberly, he pointed to this and, with his face cast downward, said: "Just last night he took from us four of my bravest warriors. They were valiant but too weakened to fight anymore and so they gave up the ghost. So the Dragon Knight, as they call him, came here and slew them in combat." He started to lament bitterly and all in the court did the same.

When the henchmen saw the meeting and heard the cries they perked their ears and strode over to that side of the hall. Three of them refused to stop the revelry to investigate and were largely over weight. Plainly, they had lived quite opulently as oppressors of the kind country folk. Among their company was a stout dwarf who was hunchbacked, twisted and all black. He carried a stick and rode around on a mule. He began hitting the poor people in the hall who were only trying to offer him water.

Benoic couldn't stand it any longer. His face was red with rage and he went over to the dwarf and delivered such a strong kick that he was sent flying from his mule into the fire pit. He tried to move but was enrapt in flames and burned alive. The henchmen all saw this and fled the court, very afraid. "We will tell our master what you've done, he will not have pity on you for this! All of you will be punished!"

The brothers were full of pity and wished to avenge the poor king. They knew that the people there were good and unjustly oppressed. Benoic agreed to enter the forest and challenge the Dragon Knight. The Lord of Poor Castle said to him: "Know that the knight you wish to do combat with is no ordinary knight. He is descended from giants and is incredibly powerful. If you fight him know that none have won against him before. He carries a dragon with him who breathes fire. This is how he can be so terrible and people fear him. If you fight him you must slay the dragon on his shield before anything, for it will otherwise burn you." Benoic said he would do so and was not afraid. Like his brother, Benoic also had strong faith in God.

In the morning they heard mass and Benoic donned his armor. He rode a splendid white charger and carried a silver shield with a blue swan on it. He rode from the castle into the forest, awaiting the messenger of the Dragon Knight. A squire led him to a path where he met a company of men. One messenger shouted: "If you wish to challenge the Dragon Knight you must follow me along the path." So they set rode all day until they reached a lake. His castle was on an isle off the coast. So Benoic took a boat that was already waiting for him.

When the Dragon Knight saw the lone challenger approaching he laughed. For he had slain so many that he had little fear of errant knights. So the Dragon Knight came from his castle and, summoned to combat, charged towards Benoic. He rode a huge black charger and was in armor that was all black. He was terrible to gaze at. His shield had a dragon head emblazoned on it that was living and flew all around breathing fire.

Benoic's horse leapt from the boat onto the shore. He seized his reigns and spurred forth in a full gallop. He careened over a hill and spurted off. The two collided and the impact made the whole earth shake. Those who watched from the castle wall were amazed. One maiden, who was imprisoned, saw that the knight who opposed her Lord was very valiant. This gave her hope: "Just maybe he

138

can defeat the Dragon Knight and free me. For my father , who is now known as the Poor Lord, longs to see me once again!"

The two knights collided and, when their horses met they both tumbled out of their saddles. The impact sounded like a great redwood tree falling to the earth. The lances shattered against the shields and Benoic's was split to the boss. Benoic arose first, drew his sword and attacked the Dragon Knight. The Dragon Knight unsheathed a flaming sword that was frightening to behold. Yet his vicious stroke was blocked by Benoic, who bore a sacred shield. Know that he carried the shield that was brought into battle against Tholomer and blessed with sacred blood. That shield, since it was made by Josephus on his death bead, was invulnerable against evil and did harm to the wicked. Know too that the valiant Benoic was the first to successfully block the Dragon Knight's attacks.

While the knight was astonished to see someone oppose his might, the dragon was summoned from the shield to breath fire; it reared its ugly head and spat out vicious flames directly unto Benoic. Yet God protected Benoic so that the fire turned on the dragon who breathed it. It was as if a mirror came back around towards the enemy, striking him with his own weapon. In this way the dragon burned himself with the fire that he had killed many with before. When the knight saw his dragon perish by his own flames and his shield burn up, he grew full of rage and ran at Benoic, flailing about. Though Benoic was crafty and realized the Dragon Knight was out of his wits with animosity. So he quickly dodged the flaming sword and stuck his blade beneath the knight's hauberk so that it lodged into his stomach. For he had no shield or defense as he ran into him, full of rage. The blood boiled and exuded from his stomach when the blade went through his body and out the other side.

When the Dragon Knight realized he had been pitifully slain, he grew full of fear. Blood spurted everywhere and his intestines came out. He was full of grief for all the wrong he had done and slowly died in agony. Benoic did not pity the man at all and beheaded him. He attached the head to his saddle and went into the castle.

The nobles and ladies all welcomed him graciously; many were relieved at having been freed of the villainous Dragon Knight. No one really liked him for he was so wicked. Benoic had carts prepared and they hauled all the gold that was left in the keep, stolen by the Dragon Knight, unto the carts. Then, as he prepared to leave, he got to talking with the maiden, who was none other than the daughter of the Poor Lord. She begged the good knight to escort her home. Benoic graciously accepted. He put her on the neck of his horse and set out without delay, followed by the cast of gold.

When Benoic returned with the king's daughter the people of the town could not have been happier. Men were sent off to help with the carts and they were amazed at all the recovered treasure that had been stolen. The robbers were so afraid when they saw their lord dead that they fled from the land, fearing the good knight. In this way the Poor Castle became a rich one, thanks to God and Benoic who opposed the wicked.

The two brothers bid the people farewell even though they begged them to stay: "All that I have is yours since you have saved me from my greatest enemy and returned to me my captive daughter. All honor is truly yours!" They were very grateful to have helped but had urgent matters to take care of, and the army was awaiting further commands. So they left the castle rather quickly. There were many other adventures but this book does not tell of it. One may find that old French book tells more about the adventures of Bellius and Benoic. Know that after taking all of France, the brothers came upon Rome. The romans feared them so much that they surrendered immediately without a battle. The Britons thus had conquered much of Europe due to their mother's good advice.

They were able to unify with one another rather than create an internal feud that would have brought the lands to ruin. In this way they were rewarded by conquering many lands and bringing the new law to far off places. When Bellius destroyed the Iron Tower statues he had purged that place of a wicked custom and demonic spirit. Similarly, when Benoic defeated the Dragon Knight he was able to restore an impoverished land to its former glory. In

140

this way they brought the love of God to many places and were rewarded abundantly.

# 18 PETER IN IRELAND

At the time in Ireland a marvel occurred that I will now speak of. Peter was his name and he had been both saintly and a warrior of esteem and prowess. Who would have known that one sole act of treachery gave him such a terrible wound that who would never forget. For he had several brothers who were full of folly and sin. The brothers conspired: "Our brother has done many good deeds. He has slain the monsters of the land and brought peace to people. It is no doubt that they will want him to be king, but that is not how it will be. Come, brothers, let us conspire and devise a plan that will rid him of the land so that we can rule in his stead." So they wickedly tried to kill him for he was good and saintly: that is because jealousy is an ugly feature. One day, when he entered the court to give counsel, his brothers surrounded him and assailed him on all sides. He was left with a wound that had venomous poison. Thinking it fatal, he was fearful for his life. He wandered the lands and sought counsel with several healers. None of which could successfully revive him, for they knew not that the blade which wounded him had been poisoned.

Trusting in God, Peter had his men take him in a litter to the coast. There he found a boat which was among the rocks. So he set out, alone, on the boat, hoping that God would take him to a land where his wound could be remedied. His great faith brought him further into the deep ocean for many days. He ate sparingly and put his trust completely in the winds. After much traveling the boat reached a coast. Know that this was the coast of Ireland. By the time Peter reached land he was very close to death. He grew thin from lack of food and was very weary.

The king of that land had a most beautiful daughter named Menlya. That day she happened to be on the beach going for a walk. When she saw Peter she realized that he was in great need. For he was almost naked for his clothes had been torn after many days in the sea. His body was very weak from lack of food. Though she saw from his visage and demeanor that he was of a noble line. Menlya awakened Peter and asked him where he had come from. Peter told her: "I am a Christian who has been wounded. I am seeking someone to heal this wound. I come from the land of Wales over the sea and have traveled under God's protection with the hope that someone can heal me." Menlya saw the terrible wound in the side of his naked body. It bled and smelled most foul. She cringed and told him: "My father the king has a prisoner in his castle who is a Christian. If there is any man that can heal you it will be him." So Peter, relieved at this news, implored the damsel to help him. Driven by pity and realizing Peter was a noble person, she agreed to help him. Besides, should could not help but deny the flare and sparks of love in the air at the sight of him.

The Princess's maidens removed Peter to the castle secretly, so that no one saw him. There they found a room for him where he could be left alone and was given rest. The king was not aware that he harbored another Christian, for this would have incensed him greatly. Though Peter was in the very throws of death and if the maiden had waited another day it was plausible that he would have died. That evening, when the guards were asleep, she freed the prisoner and brought the two together. Menlya told the man: "If you can heal this wound then I will give you your freedom and send you on your way." So the man got to work and, in a month's time, managed to heal Peter completely. For he was a very good healer and recognized that the wound had poison in it. He removed the poison and completely healed Peter, to everyone's amazement.

Peter was happy and healthy; he began walking and his strength returned. He was able to don his armor and had grown back to his original size. At this time the king, named Orcant, had a feast. He invited Marahad, the king of Ireland. Marahad was the fiercest warrior in the land. He brought with him his son, who was very strong and full of prowess. During the feast, the wicked wine steward poisoned Marahad's son. Through treachery and without any other counsel this deed made Orcant seem like the culprit. Marahad was enraged and felt that this was surely an act of murder on behalf King Orcant, even though he had little knowledge that the steward had done

143

it. He brought the issue to London and all the court heard of it. Marahad challenged Orcant to combat to prove him guilty. Know that Marahad was surely the best fighter in the land so Orcant grew worried. If he didn't find someone to help him he would surely be in trouble. Orcant was given forty days of respite in which he could find a challenger to fight in his stead, for such was the custom of the land.

Orcant was eager to determine who was the bravest fighter in his lands. He gathered twelve of the best knights from his realm and told them: "A foreign knight has come here to challenge us. I will not let him leave without being well met in combat. Go to the circling pines tomorrow and meet him there. Show him that we are strong warriors in this land." Since the twelve were the best fighters in the land he felt sure he could determine the right person to take up the challenge against Marahad.

On the morrow the king secretly armed himself and left for the circling pines. He painted his shield green so no one recognized him. He prepared to fight the challengers. Though, when the twelve arrived, Orcant was deeply dismayed. For a series of jousts ensued where all twelve of those knights were easily unhorsed by the "foreigner". He made them all his prisoner and said: "You must return to King Orcant and pledge your lives to him."

Much aggrieved the king realized he was in a very sorry plight, for his best knights weren't worth much. So he issued another challenge and had his messengers spread the news to all the lands. He told the people that whoever could defeat the knight of the circling pines would be rewarded great treasures and wealth. So, everyday, he set out to the circling pines to find a knight more powerful than him, in hopes of finding one to defeat Marahad.

At this time Peter had grown strong and mighty. Menlya saw how courageous he was and felt sure he was a knight of prowess. Peter was pensive and sad for he felt that he had been left alone too long. Menlya asked him: "What makes you so sad? It is truly clear you have been brought back to health, ask what else you can of me and I will grant it." She was very fond of Peter. Peter replied to her: "I am a knight and, because I have not been given leave to go joust, I am sad. I wish to challenge the knight of the circling pines, and, come what may, find victory in these lands." Menlya realized that Peter was a very strong knight for he was abundantly confident. She provided him with a good horse and a strong ash wood lance; she also gave him her glove, saying: "Take my gauge, good Lord. For I feel you are the right man to carry it. Do so with honor and swear you will return to me when I ask." Peter, who loved her deeply, agreed to this. In this way he set out for the circling pines to joust with King Orcant.

That very day he reached the circling pines and Orcant was delighted to find a challenger for he had waited a long time without seeing any combat; it had been so long that the day set to face Marahad was fast approaching. What more can I say? The two knights met at the hill of the circling pines; they met in a clash, giving a marvelous display of arms that the noblest ladies in the land would have watched with great excitement. Sparks flew and helms flew from heads. Both knights were very chivalrous and full of might. Yet Peter was able to knock the king to the ground with a well positioned lance. The king was sorely wounded as he had been hit in the left side. Though the battle was not finished.

The king and Peter began to fight with their swords. Both drew blood and had many wounds. The king was valiant but not as strong as Peter. For Peter was so good in combat that he brought the king to his knees with many decisive blows. He unlaced his helmet and asked him to surrender. Orcant told him: "All earthly kings would be forever shamed if I surrendered to you." When Peter realized that the knight was a king he was startled. He gave him his sword and begged him on his knees for mercy. When this was granted he then asked: "What king are you, for I may be sorely mistaken for entering combat with you." When he learned that it was Orcant he pleaded for forgiveness for striking him, for he felt he had shamed the one whose gauge he wore by hurting her father.

Then, in tears, he said: "Gracious king, I have received much from your daughter who restored me to health from a terrible wound. In return, I dare not ever hurt you but swear to serve you in any way." The king was

145

very happy when he heard this and asked that Peter fight Marahad for him. Peter agreed almost immediately. When this accord was made the two embraced. For it was clear that Peter was willing to save Orcant just as his daughter had saved him.

The two returned to the castle together and a great feast was prepared. They were very happy to have met one another and talked of many things, including his daughter. When they were fully healed they set out for London to see Marahad.

They arrived with a great company of knights, nobles and maidens. When he came from the shore to the castle a great crowd was already gathered in the field where the combat was to be. On the day of the combat heralds blew horns and stands were erected in the field to view the battle. It was a clear day and the sun showed brightly.

Peter through his gauntlet down and Marahad did the same, signifying the challenge was set. Relics were brought out and each swore to fight for honor, until resolution was had. Without further ado the two knights separated the length of a bow shot and then, in a thunderous din, came charging towards one another. The fight was ferocious for both knights were very powerful. Everyone felt sure Marahad would be the victor, but when Peter charged forth in a furious blaze they saw how passionate he was and felt otherwise. He dealt such heavy blows that everyone marveled at his unrelenting strength.

After an hour Marahad was left with many wounds so that he flinched at the blows he was delivered. The sword strokes were mighty and the two knights hacked and hewed with might and force. Marahad lunged forward, missing Peter and then received a blow that cut his hand off completely. He lost a lot of blood and it spurted everywhere. In a swoon he fell to the ground, for this wound was very painful. He had already received so many wounds that he was spitting blood from his mouth. When he tried to stand up Peter hit him with the hilt of his blade upon the nose-guard so that blood spurted from his nose and ran all down his face. His body was uncontrollable and weakened. It shivered and he cowered on the ground. Peter unlaced his helm and threatened him with death. He saw that Marahad had no fight left in him.

"I have come here to protect the honor of the good King Orcant, who did not conspire to kill your son and is innocent of the charge. I hereby demand you retract that claim and pay Orcant the respect he deserves." Though Marahad was a stubborn man and he refused to admit even this much. But when Peter raised his sword on high as if he was to take off his head the King whimpered and swore he would surrender under the conditions. So the challenge was well met and Orcant was free from all charges of treason before all the kings and the barons of the land.

There was a marvelous celebration back in Ireland for Orcant had been freed of the charges of murder. Orcant was eager to reward Peter for everything he had done. Peter told him he wanted just one thing. "I ask that you and your people abandon your pagan ways and become Christians." The king readily agreed to this and all his people were baptized. They took Christian names. Menlya was named Clemance. The king was very happy and said to Peter: "I have done as you wished and all my people are now Christian. Yet there is still one thing I ask of you. Take my gracious daughter, Clemance, as your wife. Also, rule these lands when I perish from the earth, for I have not long to live and my daughter needs a Lord! You are by far a warrior of great prowess and you would make a good leader." Peter was thankful for this and agreed. The marriage was celebrated and, since Clemance had been so kind to Peter, they were deeply in love. They lived happily together all their days. Know that Peter brought the line of Josephus directly into the kingdom of Britain, for he was descended from that noble and most holy line. For from him later came Lot, Morgan, Gawain, Aggravain and his other brothers.

# 19 THE DISTANT ISLE

At this time in the Kingdom of Logres King
Arthur's realm was in the utmost peril. Heathens attacked
him from both sides and he was hard pressed to find heroes to protect the land. The court often argued of the
best course of action and Brein of the Isle's, who was one
of the people Arthur trusted most, was really a traitor.
When counselors ill advise their masters the whole nation
suffers. For a sick sovereign lends itself to a nation in turmoil! Brein, who the king trusted greatly, had once been
defeated in an uprising but now, pleading that he had been
reformed, gave only bad advice to the king. Such was the
state of the court when the kingdom was in jeopardy.

At this time Lancelot was on a quest from a
damsel who secretly hated him. She wished him ill and her
greatest wish was that he would die in the quest. This
maiden had arrived one day and a great marvel occurred;
moments before she entered the hall a golden crossbow
bolt whizzed past the King and went into a post. It had
flown so swiftly and with such precision it seemed a great
feat of magic. Everyone curiously examined the bolt and
saw a piece of parchment attached to it that read: "He
who can pull out the bolt must take the adventure." Many
tried but only Lancelot succeeded.

The maiden entered thereafter, recognizing that
Lancelot had pulled out the bolt. She told him: "Since you
have taken the bolt from the post it is right that you help
in the adventure set before you. The knight Meligias is very
ill. You know that he had fought alongside Arthur against
Brien during the uprising and is a loyal liegeman. But there
is only one way to heal the knight: go to the perilous
chapel, one of the most dangerous places in Logres, and
obtain the sword and bloody cloth from the tomb of the
dead knight there."

Lancelot was a very proud knight and replied:
"Maiden, if it is you wish that I go there I will gladly do so,
especially if it is to heal Meligias." So they set out together
as the damsel was eager to show him the way. Arthur

grieved bitterly, for he had lost his best knight on a perilous journey.

Know that this was a very dangerous adventure that would easily cost him his life had not the maiden who was master over the perilous chapel and who controlled the demon army not utterly loved Lancelot. So did every maiden love Lancelot dearly for his prowess. For when he arrived at that chapel he was able to enter without harm, remove the tomb and see the dead knight. He smelled of many perfumes and his flesh was completely intact as if he was buried only yesterday. Beside him was both the sword and the bloody cloth, which was the same cloth that Jesus used to wipe his face before he was crucified.

When he had what he needed he didn't stay long, for that place was creepy and it was already night. Though, as he left, a large din arose in the forest. An army of demonic knights, who bellowed and howled like the evil spirits they were, surrounded him. The jeered and threatened him. It was no wonder no knight who came there ever survived. Though, the master was a lady who loved Lancelot greatly. She said to him: "Oh Lancelot, put down those trinkets from the tomb and stay a while. I have prepared a place for you at my castle where you would never lack anything." Yet Lancelot was loyal only to the king and his love for the queen. He replied: "Dear lady, I thank you for that honor. Though my heart is saved for another, despite the circumstance and even though I face certain death, I can't grant you my love." His sin for the love of the king's wife cursed him so that he could never open his heart to any dear maiden. This was the greatest tragedy that led to his miserable end. Though, these honorable words coaxed the lady otherwise, for she let him path through the cemetery without attack from the perilous demon knights.

When Lancelot was off on the quest just told of a warlord from a far away land attacked the borders of King Arthur's realm. His name was King Denover and he was a wicked pagan. He besieged Avalon and brought the people there to ruin. With his host of evil men they pillaged the lands, set towns to fire, and killed many good Christians. This man was very treacherous and cared little for the

149

preservation of life. He was merciless and lusted for the blood of innocents. When he raided the towns he killed many innocent women and children and set towns ablaze. He converted people to the pagan law and abolished Christianity. Those who would not abandon the faith were executed. Know that, when Arthur had word of this, he was very grieved and filled with rage. For this lord came from Ireland and was the same knight who carried the shield full of beards. It was his custom that every king he conquered would have to give him his beard as homage. So he had a shield with thirty beards from all the kings who paid him homage. His messenger came to Arthur, saying: "You who claim to be such a good king are full of air! Though, my lord, what an incredible and full red beard you have. Give it to my lord and thus pay him homage so that you may keep your land in peace. Otherwise, know that he will truly conquer all this land and burn it to the ground." Lord Arthur found this request appalling and refused it to the utmost. He sent messengers in search of Lancelot to help the people of Avalon, who were in dire need of him.

It was clear that Lancelot was the only man that Denover would fear. That was made clear when Brein of the Isles had been sent the first time to resist the war lord but was easily defeated. Brien was a traitor and he was a half-hearted knight that cared little for the good of King Arthur. Indeed, it was a shame the king relied on such a man.

However, everyone was surprised to see that Lancelot eventually accomplished the quest of the golden crossbow bolt. He returned to the castle and, as a result, brought the sword and cloth to Meligias who was healed by its power. He touched the cloth and put it to his face, being healed almost instantly. Such was the power of God's love! They placed the sword in Arthur's treasury, marveling at its beauty and the bejeweled hilt upon it. It was the same blade that struck the knight during the first revolt against Arthur, which was why having it returned to that place restored his wound completely.

Lancelot was delighted to be back at the court. He heard from Arthur and the knights all about how King Denover had demanded homage from Arthur, as you have heard shortly ago. He was utterly astonished and felt that this was a very wicked band of men to do innocent people such harm. Meanwhile, messengers from the borderlands flocked to court, pleading that Lancelot come to their rescue. They even wished to grant him kingship over the land because his prowess had made him so worthy. Lancelot set out without delay, taking with him sixty knights from Arthur's court. Each was a fine knight of the table round.

Up until this time Denover had achieved much success and taken several castles. He laid siege to Avalon and it was a terrible sight, for many of the inhabitants were starved for food. He went through the entire land completely unopposed, burning everything at every chance. However, he was unprepared for Lancelot and the knights of the table round.

Lancelot arrived and encamped near the shore. He sent out scouts who quickly returned; they reported that the King had a fleet of ships hidden in a bay on the coast. So he did something very clever: he brought ten knights out to the coast where the ships were. In the dark night they set fire to the ships. When Denover realized this he was very weary and full of despair. His entire fleet of ships had been destroyed and sent to the bottom of the sea in flames. By dawn, the army was circling the forest seeking the men who had destroyed their fleet. Then Lancelot divided his knights into three companies and attacked the enemy head on. Each knight was worth a hundred of Denover's warriors. For they were wild men and many were not properly armed. Arthur's knights were all skilled in combat.

The battle was fierce and many were killed that day. Lancelot killed one hundred men all by himself. He assailed foes with his sword and brought havoc on the enemy. Slashing off arms, breaking bones, cutting into flesh so deep that blood poured out like rivers. He lopped of so many heads that it seemed the forest was full of talking heads many years after. He was unmatched in power and might. He drove his horse into the thickest press and refused to leave the middle of the battle. No matter how many surrounded him no one found a way to penetrate his trusty hauberk. His eyes were ablaze and he yelled out: "To

151

arms! For the Queen!" All his knights rallied around him. They drove their lances into the foremost rank. Blood spurted out as the sharp lances went through the body and out the other side. When Denover saw the mighty din and combat that arose he was terrified of Lancelot.

Lancelot fought so brilliantly that his entire visage gave forth a light that blinded his enemies. All who opposed him eventually fled in terror. He was a lion charging forth into a herd of deer. He was a boar against unarmed men. He brought his might to the forefront of the battle while his comrades followed his example. He struck terrible blows with his steel blade that cleft heads and limbs from their bodies. Blood flowed like a river through the marshy fields of Avalon. Denover's forces cowered at the sight of such powerful knights. For each knight from Arthur's court was worth fifty men. Though Denover greatly outnumbered Lancelot he gave little resistance.

In fact, Lancelot drove into the center of the enemy forces. They confused their opponent by striking so efficiently and driving the line, like a dagger, into the heart of the enemy. The mounted knights came upon Denover and his men and broke the line completely. The core of the army was engulfed. At this time Lancelot could clearly see Denover, rallied around his elite guard. He lopped of a man's head, and when he slew him he took his spear. He lifted it and launched it with such accuracy that it flew into the heart of Denover's cup bearer who was in the saddle next to the frightened king. When he saw that his cup bearer was killed, the cowardly Denover turned to flee as his whole army watched in amazement and followed him. Arthur's knight's pursued and gathered up a mass of dead bodies. He yelled out: "Coward! You ask my King for his beard, and then flee when you are challenged? I find it laughable. Go back to Ireland. Oh, wait, where are your ships? Lost in a bit of flames? Never come back to Britain or you will be slain outright!"

In this way they went after the broken army and made a trail of blood all the way to the sea. Many preferred drowning to getting cut down from behind. Denover did not fight but, in his cowardice, showed his back. Lancelot grabbed him by the helmet and pulled him from the saddle so that he tumbled to the ground. "Give up your battle and surrender to Arthur, maybe give him your beard too!" Though the stubborn Denover refused to say a word but only spit in Lancelot's face. Greatly incensed, Lancelot chopped his head off, without any other exchange of words.

When Lancelot and his knights defeated the forces and captured Denover they were greatly pleased. Lancelot and his knights sought lodging in the town after the battle. They spent much time there to rest from their wounds. It was during this time that they found the wreckage from Denover's conquest. In the town, churches were destroyed. People were starved in the streets. Pits were dug and filled full of dead bodies. Many of the dead were women and innocent children. Such was the law of those heathens who came to Avalon. The dead were killed just because they refused to abandon their faith. Blessed are those who were martyred!

Since the devastation had been so great Lancelot spent many months in Avalon helping those people rebuild. They continued to route the remnants of Denover's forces and attacked them in the forests. They rebuilt the churches and brought food and coin from Arthur's coffers too. Then Lancelot took Denover's head and, sticking it on a lance, paraded it through the city. They buried the lance in the ground outside the city so that all could see what happens to those who commit treachery.

After his victory Lancelot reestablished the new law and reformed the people there. People began to believe in the good of the world again for the heathens had been destroyed. They sent messengers to King Arthur's court, bearing the head of his enemy. The people of Avalon had begged him to stay and protect them, for they feared a renewal of attacks. They implored Lancelot to become their king and remain there. Yet Lancelot was a most loyal knight in these affairs; so he left them with these words: "Lord Arthur is your king and has summoned me here to protect you in his name. If trouble comes again I will be here."

So Lancelot left the people there and celebrated the victory over Denover at King Arthur's court. Yet, after

153

he left, word was spread that the conqueror of Avalon had been defeated and shamed. Denover's brother, who was also in Ireland, was full of anger about the death of his brother. So he gathered a large army and sailed towards Avalon to avenge him.

Know that Denover's brother was named Demnon. He was also a very lusty pagan who sought to pillage Arthur's lands. He sailed a very long way from his home to get to Avalon. When they arrived, they set fire to the lands a second time. He brought so much grief to the people of Avalon, who had only recently been restored to good health, that many were in complete despair. For Demnon was even more cruel than his brother.

When Arthur heard about this there arose in the court a great lamentation; maidens and men alike all took to weeping for those suffering in the borderlands. Then they summoned Lancelot a second time. Fortunately, this time, he was ready. He was summoned to court that very day.

King Arthur, who was very pensive and sad, stood up and said: "Fair Lancelot, I would be ill advised to speak anything against you. For you are the greatest knight of my lands and have brought me more glory than any other. My enemies fear me and know that, with your protection, I cannot be defeated. It brings me immense grief to learn that Avalon is under attack again. I would gladly send another to the task but know that no other will be able to defeat Demnon as decisively as you could. For he is so cruel, much crueler than his brother, that it is entirely necessary that you go there. He has turned our people from the new law and seeks to destroy good Christian people. Not for me but for the love of God and Kingdom, avenge us on this man!"

Lancelot stood up in the court and pounded his chest, saying: "Do not say more. Give me leave and I will bring you his head!" The men of the round table pounded their fists on the table and chanted in agreement. It was said that the sound of their lamentations could be heard all the way in Avalon which was a great many leagues away. The men blew the ivory horns and the battle gear was readied. The good knights of the court donned their armor and prepared for a mighty battle.

The warriors in Arthur's hall were the most respected fighters in all the world. They were also good Christians and to hear that Avalon was persecuted in this way a second time brought all of them to anger. They had little choice but to avenge their people. For even though Avalon was far away it was still Arthur's kingdom. Indeed, they were most eager to do battle: every man in that hall stood up to volunteer to fight.

So Lancelot left Camelot with a full host of five hundred knights of the round table. Each of these knights had been fully armed, well equipped and renown for prowess. It was a great shame that so many wished to do evil to King Arthur's court and God. For Denover's brother had gathered a terrible host; thousands of wild men were gathered to take over Britain with sheer numbers. Though it was by God's power that those good knights were able and willing to protect the land from harm. Such are the miracles of God. So Lancelot and his band rode tirelessly towards Avalon until they arrived. It rained on the day they arrived, and they were not in the least bit weary from the travel. They figured that every day they took in delay was another day where the demon hordes killed hundreds of women and children.

At that time Demnon had just taken a castle near Avalon, one of its neighbor forts. Demnon ordered the people in that place killed for they were Christians and refused to revert to the old law. The whole city was raised and set to flames. The thousands of men gathered in the castle and took to raping the women there. Lancelot was tireless and full of rage when he came to that place and heard the reports. It was nearing dusk when he arrived. He saw the castle and heard the screams of good Christians who were being slaughtered within. He became mad like a vicious boar and charged at full gallop towards the gate. His man blew a horn that startled the enemy, for they knew that God's vengeance was upon them for their wickedness. In his might Lancelot broke through the gate and his men followed him, screaming at the tops of their lungs with wild eyes. Demnon, who had only just retired from battle, was completely taken by surprise at the assault.

The knights galloped through the gates and knocked down handfuls of men, plunging their lances deep into hearts. They took out their keen edged, blades and hacked away limbs. Battle resumed on all sides until the castle was stormed by King Arthur's bold knights. They held their shields, emblazoned with so many colors, high upon their necks and sliced with sharp steel through the enemy ranks. The wild men assailed them on all sides but had little good armor.

When enough blood had been shed to make the wicked King baulk, he yelled out: "I challenge Lancelot Du Lac to combat. Whoever wins can have the victory. If you defeat me I will leave the land. But if I win you must yield the whole land and remain as my prisoner!" When Demnon said this Lancelot heard report of it and made his way to the front ranks. The combat was suspended. It was clear that Arthur's knights had done so much damage that much of his force was wounded or scattered. This challenge was a desperate attempt to save the invasion.

Lancelot and Demnon, who was also a very bold knight, met in the courtyard. They did away with pleasantries and, since both had their horses killed from under them, they resumed combat on foot. Demnon had a terrible battle axe that he wielded about mightily. He flung it towards Lancelot and dealt heavy, ferocious strokes. Though Lancelot blocked these with his shield and returned the favor, with interest. He delivered blows that sent sparks flying on his helm. Indeed, he tore his helm from his head and cut the hauberk in so many places that he bleed abundantly. Demnon, in desperation, hurled his axe at him but Lancelot ducked so that it hit a stone pillar and shattered. When he lost his weapon, Lancelot came at him and dropped his sword upon him so that his arm fell off from the shoulder. Then he had no fight in him, for he was whimpering on the ground. Lancelot made him give up the fight. His army was disbanded, though some, fearing certain death, took to fleeing. Demnon had lost so much blood that he later died a most pitiful death.

Meanwhile, the rest of the knights of the round table went through the castle killing all those that refused to surrender. Arthur's men encircled them and slaughtered the ones who resisted. By nightfall there were only a handful of the three thousand men Demnon had brought with him. They were trapped in the keep, barring the doors for fear that they would be killed. Lancelot and his men tied lances together and devised a makeshift battering ram. In this way they broke down the door and slaughtered every one of the wild men that resisted. After that there was a long, deep silence. The enemy was scattered across the castle grounds, lying in their own blood dead or in the grips of death. The wild men had so much blood on their hands and were full of sins for what they did to the people of the castle. Lancelot wept as he saw the naked women in the houses who had been taken by force and then murdered. He made sure that, by defeating Demnon, no man ever returned to Logres to do it harm.

After Demnon was beheaded in the courtyard of the castle, the knights sent a report to Arthur, recounting all that had occurred. When the people saw that Lancelot had freed them a second time, those who were still alive wept for joy. The people of Avalon turned back to God and the new law. Lancelot had holy men come to that land. They built a marvelous church in Avalon that had the first bell ever erected in a church in that land. Every day, before mass at matins, the bell sounded like sweet music to the ears of the townsfolk. They always cherished that place and the lord for he had brought them protection in a time of great peril. That land was safe from harm for many years because of the good works of Lancelot. It was only later when the Saxons came that they faced peril again, but this story wont talk of that at this time.

# 20 THE BRIDGE OF SWORDS

At this time the land of Logres had one knight who, once a naive boy, became a marvelous hero throughout the land. He lived deep in the country of Wales and knew little of combat. Though, he came from a noble line of warriors who had died fighting for the land. He didn't know what knight was because he mother sheltered him, fearing that if he knew a thing about chivalry he would surely meet the same fate as his brothers and father. Eventually, when he went about hunting in the countryside with his javelins, he came across a group of knights. The fantastic display of their armor and weaponry made him want nothing more but to become one. So he set off without delay to do exactly that, killing his mother who was full of grief at the sight of it!

Know that his name was Perceval and the old French book speaks much of him. At this time there was a good king who was wise and his name was Meliot. The trouble was that he had a son that was full of treachery. One day, after he had become a knight and achieved many good honors at King Arthur's court, Perceval arrived at the castle after defeating a wicked giant in the badlands. Meliot's son was at court when he returned. His name was Dracmore and he was very jealous seeing Perceval, who paraded the giant's head around while many knights fervently praised him. Through his folly he went to the king and said: "Father, why do you honor a man like Perceval who is full of villainy? I would challenge him to battle and make him suffer for it!" The king was grieved that his son said such a thing in public, for he knew that if he challenged Perceval he would easily be defeated and shamed throughout the land for his jealousy.

Yet, when Perceval got word of it, he remained kind and forgiving, as it suited the code of chivalry greatly. Even though Dracmore continuously said such evil things Perceval was a merciful man and refused to do combat with him. He knew that his father was a good man and left it at that.

One day, Perceval went to mass and afterwards, dined and donned his armor. He asked for leave to go to the forest. Yet Dracmore, yet again, was in the hall then and he spoke to his friends with vile words saying that he wished to challenge Perceval to combat. "That Perceval is just a naive boy. He didn't accomplish anything that they said he did. I could easily defeat him if I was given the chance." The prince was a jealous prince and loathed those who took attention from him. Though, again, Perceval did not wish to do combat with the knight out of respect for the king. So the challenge was deferred and Perceval left the lands. This was clearly not for shame but out of respect for Meliot. Yet, that day Dracmore had thrown his gauntlet down and many had seen this. So he went through the lands and spread the word far that Perceval was a coward and many believed him.

After a span of time which Perceval sought other adventures, Dracmore did something devilish to irritate him further. Know that Perceval lived with his beloved wife Blanchleflor at the castle they called Joyous Guard. This was a place that had been freed from demons by Perceval. Indeed, before that time a great many demons took the castle and Perceval slew them for he was so valiant. When he did so he took Blanchleflor as his wife for she was the maiden of that castle and she owed everything to him. Perceval and Blanchleflor loved each other deeply and many often attended mass there just to see the couple together.

So Dracmore plotted something very evil. He took his friends to the Joyous Guard and, in the night, they kidnapped Blanchleflor. Perceval was away in the forest hunting when this happened and didn't learn of the abduction until later. When he returned from the forest a great many lamented and were sobbing in the streets publicly. When he heard that Dracmore took his beloved he grew full of rage. That very day he remounted and set out for Meliot's castle.

At this time Meliot had a bridge that blocked all intruders. It was known as the Bridge of Swords. It was impassible for no knight had made way across it before. The bridge was small and only approachable by one who could endure much pain. All along its surface were sharp points of blades so that if anyone tried to cross they would surely bleed to death or fall when they felt the sharp pain of the swords cutting their skin. When the king heard that Perceval came after him he became very scared. So he cursed his son Dracmore for his wickedness. Yet he loved his son and so he protected him, as any father would. He removed the drawbridge and made it so that Perceval could only enter by the perilous Bridge of Swords.

Even as he approached the bridge he was challenged by ten different knights, all coming from the castle of Meliot. They were unhorsed individually by the good knight, who bore his lance proudly, plunging it into the knights and hurling them from their chargers. The last of the ten was dragged all the way to the river by his horse that took off in fright after the joust while his left leg was stuck in the stirrup. Everyone in the castle saw how all ten jousters were defeated and they were distraught because Dracmore was sure to be in trouble. The king was so disturbed that his son would do something as stupid as kidnapping Perceval's lover, so he bitterly lamented his fortune. Meliot made sure that Blancheflore was well taken care of and not a thing was lacking; he kept her safe from Dracmore, who wanted nothing else than to have his way with her. It seemed the lusty fellow was quite blinded.

Perceval, after defeating the ten jousters, went to the bridge of swords. He dismounted and approached the bridge. His armor was heavy so he removed it and threw it to the other side of the bridge. Since the bridge was very thin he had to balance himself carefully. Yet, surely, since he was so valiant, he made his way across. The swords cut at his feet so that a long trail of blood was left across the bridge. He also bled from the hands for he used those for greater balance. Perceval had endured many combats and could tolerate more pain than any other knight. His feet bled profusely as they went against the blades but he did not cry out once. From the highest tower Meliot watched as Perceval bravely did what no man had done before. When he crossed the bridge completely Meliot crossed himself in amazement. He knew that his son would be forced to face Perceval in combat.

Meliot decided to send for Perceval immediately. He went to the bridge and saw the knight arming himself.

160

Meliot welcomed him graciously and said: "Fair knight, we wish to give you lodging and fair hospitality. You have achieved a marvelous wonder by crossing the perilous bridge that no other dare cross." Perceval was not in the mood for pleasantry. He responded: "Meliot, I do not wish to hear your good tidings. Your son has committed an act of treason. He has willingly taken my beloved wife. I challenge him to combat and will take his head for this." When Meliot realized that he could do little to appease the situation he became very sad and pensive.

Meliot begged Blancheflore, who he had kept safe her whole stay at the castle, for a favor. She agreed that Meliot had treated her well and protected her, so she agreed. "At any time, if I call on you for a favor, I ask that you grant it, provided it is within your power to do so." It was agreed upon and they went forth from the castle.

In a desperate effort he wished to delay the impending combat: "Well, if it must happen, let it happen tomorrow. For you are wounded and it is nearing dusk. Tonight I will lodge you in the castle and give you everything you need." Perceval willingly agreed to this and was lodged for the night. Perceval was given a splendid room and cared for. In the evening after this was done Meliot went to his son and begged him: "Son, give back the man's wife or he will surely kill you. Your pride has gone too far in this matter. I would not have this kingdom bereft of its heir for such a folly." Yet Dracmore was a stubborn prince and refused his father's wishes. He spent the knight in revelry with his friends and mocked Perceval.

In the morning Perceval donned his armor and prepared for the combat between them. Perceval said his prayers, crossed himself and armed. The two met on a field outside the castle walls. No amount of pleaded from the king could stop the battle from happening, for his son had greatly dishonored the good knight. Meliot brought Blanchleflor with him to the stands so that Perceval could see her. Dracmore mocked him and he was greatly shamed for it. When Perceval saw his beloved tears came to his eyes. He yelled out: "Swear that she has not been violated or I will surely behead you!" The king, hearing this, pleaded to him: "Know that your wife has been safe in my pro-

161

tection this whole time. No man has touched her or dealt with her vilely." Perceval was comforted by the king's words but still enraged.

Without further ado an unsettling combat began. In a fury Perceval careened his horse into a swift gallop. He went hurling towards Dracmore and pounced upon him like a lion, for he was a cowardly knight. He leveled his lance and drove it through shield and hauberk. The lance pounded into Dracmore's chest and sent him flying ten feet back and into the nearby thicket. He was given a thorny welcome and had a hard enough time getting out of the rose bush.

Meanwhile, Dracmore's lance broke against Perceval's shield which was very sturdy. Indeed, Perceval's shield had the cross of Jesus Christ on it which protected him from all evil. It was known that, when he faced the demons at Joyous Gaurde, many perished by the sight of his shield alone. For it was the very presence of Christ that made the demons flee in terror. Know that this shield was also the same given by Josephus to battle against Tholomer when the Britons first came to the land by the power of God.

After the joust had been settled Perceval dismounted and went over to the struggling Dracmore. He pounded on him with his sword with a fiery vengeance. He was not playing games with the boy, who tried valiantly to fight in return. And, indeed, he would be a valiant knight, if he wasn't so filled with treachery and baseness. The combat sent sparks flying. Perceval gave him a deathly blow that sent his helm flying into the bushes. He couldn't stand any longer and went tumbling to the ground. When he rose, Perceval gave him a blow on the shoulder that cut right through the shield and came down into the flesh about the width of the finger. When the blade broke through to his skin he cried out in anguish.

The king was bewildered when he saw his son being made a laughing stock. He pleaded to Blancheflore: "My lady, you told me you would give me a boon if I asked it. Well, plainly, I ask of you the life of my son, who is sure to perish if you don't tell your lover to leave him be." Then he called out to the knight: "Perceval, you can see my son

162

is shamed. Let him live and I will surely reward you." Perceval realized that the foolish prince was weak. When he heard the king's words, and saw that his wife pleaded intently as well, he chose to be merciful. "I will let him live if you swear to give back my love." The king willingly assented to this and the agreement was made.

Perceval left that place and Meliot gave him many riches so that he would never avenge himself on Dracmore again. In this way was the foolish prince was saved by the wisdom of his father. That is the story of how Perceval crossed the perilous Bridge of Swords to avenge his beautiful wife. So Perceval should be remembered for his chivalry. For no knight of courtesy would defile or steal a maiden for the sake of jealousy. Perceval always upheld maidens and did what was right by those who were treated ill.

# 21 THE POOR MAIDEN'S CASTLE

At this time in Logres there was a castle run by a group of ladies and it was entirely bereft of all things good. The land was wasted; no crops grew nor did the sun shine in that place. The wells were dried up, the birds and animals were not found in the forest nor were the flowers blooming; trees were barren and there was no rain to be had. Violent storms often arose but they were just evil spirits whipping around, creating trouble, rather than any life returning to the land.

There lived a maiden in these parts, whose name was Ronawan, who was left with a lofty inheritance; the castle and many lands surrounding it had been left to her by her father. That was why it was called the Poor Maiden's Castle. When her father the king had died he gave it to her because she was a good daughter. Indeed, she loved him as much as a daughter should but never lied or flattered him. Yet, the eldest sister, in jealousy, sought to take those lands from her. So the eldest sister gathered a large force together and enlisted the help of her uncle, whose name was Bernald. Bernald was a powerful duke who held many other lands. So it was quite easy for him to gather a large force and harass the younger sister, because he was an already mighty lord. Though he did wrong to attack his niece, for it was a great sin to betray family like this. He mostly desired the gold in her coffers that the king had left behind. There was much gold in that place.

So at the time Ronawan was harassed by a large force. Her castle had been destroyed through many months of siege. She had fifty knights but had lost all but ten in the battles. They had no food remaining because the land had been ravaged and burned. The people in the castle were lost from God and distraught. So abundant was their despair that there was little hope in their minds.

It was at this time that Perceval came riding through the forest, searching for adventure as he always did. Perceval was a valiant knight who never let a damsel go without help. He found an old man beside the road and asked him where he could find lodging. The man told him: "Just down the road the Castle of the Poor Maiden can be found. She will give what little she has and will lodge you." Perceval asked the man: "Why is she so poor?" The old man recounted the story just as I have told you. Perceval was shocked that a maiden could be treated so poorly, especially by her own family. He was full of anger and became determined to help the maiden. One attribute Perceval didn't lack was empathy, and that was one of the greatest hallmarks of chivalry. That, and the will and might to defeat those who did wicked deeds.

He rode to the castle and saw how distraught the people were. Many of them were starving for food and there eyes were sunken in their skulls. Garments were rent and, i'll tell you plainly, there was very little "milk and honey". The entire town lay in ruins. If you were there you would think it was an old haunt rather than a place people actually lived. The perimeter of the castle was completely undefended and the stakes were torn down. The moat was dried up and the ramparts were battered.

Everyone was centralized in the main keep for they had been resigned to the fact that they would soon be defeated by the lady's uncle. Wicked fortune, see how you gave this girl the whole world and then took it away through jealousy and strife! She was never meant to be a general but a benevolent leader who gave to her people generously sharing with all the great gifts of prosperity.

When Perceval arrived the people felt a glimmer of hope, for he was armed with the shield of the holy cross and had girded upon him a bejeweled blade that sparkled and dazzled all the spectators. He was cordially welcomed by the beautiful maiden, and given the best hospitality that a poor maiden could give. Ronawan was clearly worn out from too much fasting and little sleep. She was thin and stern after loosing her nobility and receiving such grief. It was as if she was mourning a great loss.

Yet she was still very beautiful and Perceval saw that plainly. She also knew how to welcome someone and was very elegant. The whole court followed her lead in welcoming the valiant knight who was clearly a man of great prowess. They wondered at his big destrier, shining arms and heraldry. He was healthy and at his strongest when he arrived at the Castle of the Poor Maiden. She

165

gave him a beautiful scarlet mantle and the servants helped him unarm; they climbed the steps to the hall where bread and cold spring water was prepared.

What they did share they did with the utmost care and consideration. After dinner the maiden sat with Perceval for a long time. She was very sad and pensive. The maiden then related to Perceval everything that had happened. She told him about how her wicked uncle was attacking her and that her eldest sister had plotted to take her life. She told him how this was the last castle left to her by her father and she would likely lose it the next day, for the siege had been endured already for so long.

Perceval was astonished by all this and told her: "Fair maiden, I swear to you that I will avenge you on your enemies. You have very little to fear from them now that I am here." They talked in this way late into the night. They shared the same bed and caressed and kissed one another very fervently. For the two were intertwined in love's grasp and knew it from the start. That whole night they spent lying in each others arms.

When the hour of prime arrived Perceval eagerly arose from the bed. He put on his armor, crossed himself and said his prayers. Then he went to the chapel to hear mass sung. After he had received the body of our Lord Jesus Christ he gathered all his strength and prepared for combat. He mounted his black destrier and rode out of the castle and into the field. Bernald was already out front of the castle preparing to lay siege to it. He had figured there would be little resistance yet had a full force of armed knights with him.

Perceval was very bold when he rode out to meet the enemy. He threw his gage into the field and challenged any knight who dared to do combat with him. "I am here to defend the noble maiden's honor. She is, by right, the heir to this whole kingdom. All those who oppose this then let them come forward and do combat with me." Ten knights mounted and attacked him. They were not courteous enough to joust individually but set upon him all together, eager to dash the maiden's hopes of keeping the realm.

166

Though Perceval, who was beyond his years in courage, unhorsed each one. He tore through their hauberks with ease and knocked the knights from their horses swiftly. Indeed, he never needed to dismount and draw his sword for any of those ten knights he defeated. They were all completely shamed, one even broke his neck in the fall; another died when the lance broke inside his chest, renting his heart in two.

Then, after an extraordinary victory, Perceval's lance broke. He began to assail his opponents with his sword. The first man who came upon him was beheaded. His head rolled down the field to the amazement of his fellows. The second was struck in the neck, just above the ventail, and the steel spurted out blood, as if spraying from a fount. His sharp steel blade cut through hauberk and bone, making things difficult for the assailants. Blood flowed unto the green grass so abundantly that the spectators were both happy to see the knight winning them honor but horrified at the graphic violence. It was a bloody spring day and it was in this combat that the restoration of the lands could be hoped for.

When Bernald saw that his army was in fear of a single combatant he challenged Perceval to fight with him. This challenge came abruptly when he yelled out: "Enough. You have shown your skill. I challenge you to combat, as you say. We will go, lance to lance, let God decide who is the victor." The skirmish stopped and the spurred off towards each other, eager to unhorse one another. The lance thrusts and horses collided making a terrible shattering noise. Bernald was caught in the shoulder with the pine wood lance, the tip breaking as it stuck inside him. Perceval came through unscathed, despite a close encounter that resulted in the top corner of his shield snapping off. Bernald fell to the ground in pain when he received the terrible blow, but he wasn't one to resign his fate. He arose and drew his sword from its scabbard, yelling: "Come knight, you must take me in battle for I am ready to win honor. Sometimes the worst of knights win over the best, whether by fortune or chance!"

Perceval dismounted and charged with his bejeweled sword glimmering in the sunlight. They were both

167

very skilled with the sword. Bernald lunged at him and was met with heavy resistance. Perceval returned a blow that cut deep into his arm, and the blood went everywhere. Bernald, in a rage, began assailing Perceval with mighty strokes. He delivered blows left and right, until he was completely exhausted from attacking. Perceval was a clever fighter and defended himself well, bringing his shield over his head. When Bernald was too tired to continue, he went on the attack, reigning mighty blows on the weakened Bernald.

He caught him beneath the hauberk, tearing a chunk of flesh from he left thigh. Unable to walk, Bernald clamored to the ground in despair. Then Perceval struck him again and cleft his arm from his shoulder completely. This was a definitive stroke that left Bernald in great anguish. It was certain that he had little life left in him.

Perceval unlaced his helmet and threatened to behead him if he did not surrender. He was greatly shamed and begged for mercy. Perceval said: "I may grant you mercy if you give yourself to the Poor Maiden who you have so wickedly harassed. Give her all the lands you've taken and swear never to attack her again."

Bernald replied: "I'll leave here and do as you say, but don't give me as a prisoner to my niece, she will surely kill me!" So Perceval said: "Withdraw your forces and give back the lands you stole. Then go to Camelot to be Arthur's prisoner. Let them decide what to do with you." To this Bernald readily agreed. He had the best doctors of the time staunch the bleeding from his wound. He didn't recover for two months and, when he did, was left without an arm! Due to extraordinary medical care, however, he was healed. Know that the physicians who treated him were none other than his niece's, so he would be smart to thank her at any point for doing so! For she was always full of generosity and mercy. Still, everywhere Bernald went his missing arm showed plainly his sin and misdeed.

When the knights who besieged the Castle of the Poor Maiden were defeated Perceval returned to the keep. He was welcomed splendidly by the maiden of the castle. The maiden went directly to him and embraced him, giving him many kisses. She was very grateful for the marvelous

168

display of arms he had preformed. By the grace of God, that very day a merchant ship full of goods arrived at the shore near the castle. When the ship was spotted Perceval and his fellow knights rode out to meet it. When they saw that the ship was loaded with goods including meat, cheese, wine and bread they gave abundantly of their gold for it. For the Maiden had much gold in her coffers; it was only food they lacked! When the people realized they were saved they rejoiced. They ate and drank heartily.

In the midst of the excitement Perceval and Ronawan exclaimed their love for one another. That very week they were married. They brought forth a child into the world who would be of the line of Joseph de Arimathea and a very strong knight. This book will not tell more about that child at this time. Know that Perceval was very gracious, noble and generous. He made sure that Bernald gave back all the land that she was owed. Meanwhile, Ronawan decided to give her sister a castle rather than imprisoning her, which was another way in which she showed her generous spirit.

## 22 CRADOC'S FIGHT AGAINST THE SAXONS

Arthur's court was full of revelry because he was so powerful, victorious, noble and generous. He had taken lands far and wide and many swore fealty to him, doing him homage and bringing many fine gifts. He ventured to the far reaches of Britain, conquering the men of Orkney and the Picts. Then he went to Denmark, Ireland and across the sea to Iceland. So large was his kingdom that everyone feared him. So they paid him homage in the form of gold, horses and other fineries. It wasn't long before the great king took France and defeated the emperor Lucias of Rome. This story is told in great detail in the histories.

There was no court more luxurious or splendid than that of Arthur's. He sat on a marvelous gold throne and the hall was great and wide so that he could sit a mighty throng of nobles, warriors, and lovely ladies. At this time there was a remarkable warrior who was loyal to Arthur. His name was Cradoc and he was a powerful Briton who was lord in the land of Kent. His castle rested near the ocean and kept watch over the kingdom. That was because many invaders entered the land through Kent which is why he was constantly harassed by enemies. This made his warriors the fiercest and they protected Briton well.

When Arthur left for France with that great host of knights many thought that his homeland would be vulnerable to attack. While Mordred conspired against him, for that was a most wicked sin, messengers spread the news about the king's absence. Foreign armies gathered on the shores to try and plunder the land which they hoped would be so vulnerable. The Saxon's landed their fleet on the beach and stepped out, armed to the teeth with blades. They were in no other place but the land of Kent, where Lord Cradoc resided.

Cradoc was eager to test his prowess in arms; when he heard the Saxon's had arrived he brought together his counselors in the hall. A scout from Cradoc's castle reported that they were many in number. The beach was near the castle and just past the forest. The scout had ridden quickly to court and after seeing them along the coast. One of the elders, who was very wise, spoke first: "It seems the best course of action is a surprise attack, let us rush upon them immediately, giving them little chance to get comfortable." Everyone agreed that this was the best course of action. He had three ivory horns in the hall that they blew loudly so that all the knights in the castle heard them. They hastily armed and came as a mighty throng to the hall. Meanwhile, messengers were sent out through the region, bringing knights both noble and bold. The message was heard throughout the land so that three thousand noble warriors gathered in Kent by the next morning.

At first light they began the advance to the beachhead where they sought to slaughter the enemy invaders. Cradoc and his brother Rhun were both clever leaders. Since they didn't want to lose all of their forces it was logical that Rhun was left in the castle with one thousand men in order to protect it from harm should they need to. The other two thousand prepared to go to beaches with Cradoc.

Before they left the castle they all said a great many prayers for they were good Christian knights. They confessed of their sins to one another and took blades of grass between their hands and ate it, for such was the custom for warriors in that time.

When they were ready they set out at a swift pace, some on horseback and others running. While they were so many in number they were silent. The Saxon's had only arrived the night before. Many of them were still sleeping for it was hardly first light. They advanced about four bow shots from the castle until they arrived at the beached head behind a mass thicket and the forest line, which kept them well concealed.

In this way the two thousand knights boldly rode into the forest to meet the Saxons. Messengers road ahead to witness the enemy horde. One returned and brought word that the enemy was encamped on the beach. Some were eating while others were still asleep. They had barely pitched even a few tents. This news greatly excited Cradoc who endeavored to take his enemy by surprise. So the

171

knights fixed their spurs, drew their swords and crossed themselves; For they were hidden by the forest but not twenty yards from their enemy. Cradoc observed his men and saw they were ready for battle. Then he spoke to them: "Brave warriors, let us make these invaders suffer, for they transgress by coming here, to the land of the Britons! Your prowess was seen when you killed Hengist for Arthur. Make known your bravery once more as we ride against the raiders on our shore, who come to plunder and destroy our land, taking our wives as their own! Prove your worth so that Arthur and all his court honors us as the protectors of the land." Everyone was full of passion and ready for a great battle after Cradoc spoke so nobly.

Then the entire company of two thousand knights rode at a full gallop towards the beaches. When they came out from the tree line it was shocking to the enemy, for they were completely unaware of the situation. The Britons leapt into battle like fierce lions upon a deer and the Saxons knew not what peril they were in. The Saxons were like the peaceful deer who drink from the river expecting no predator.

At first the sound of the hooves sounded like a great earthquake. Then, suddenly, out of the forest appeared a massive horde of armed knights; the tree line was near the beach and made them only visible once they were far too close for the Saxons to prepare for battle. The whole tree line was full of warriors. In desperation some of the Saxons tried to arm themselves. Some were lucky enough to grab a spear to brace the galloping charge. Others fled into the ocean and drowned themselves.

Cradoc rode at the front of his men, for such was his nature that he would lead by example. He broke his lance on the first man he saw, piercing him through the chest and killing him instantly. Then he drew his blade which was called Coreuseuse, which meant wrathful. His blade was wicked, sharp and bejeweled at the hilt. It took heads, limbs, and cut through bones. His other knights followed his lead, killing many. The fight was ruthless. The Saxons had over six thousand men on the beach. They circled together in a desperate attempt to defend themselves. The clash of arms was loud and spectacular. Blood

172

made the beach sand and ocean tide red. Limbs were torn apart and many suffered awful torment. When the Saxons huddled together on the beach Cradoc split his force into two divisions. The first attacked them in the front while the second came upon the flanks, dealing pressure in a way that chocked the Saxon line and gave them nowhere to flee to. This made it very difficult for them to go anywhere but into the ocean to drown.

The Saxons had the worst of the battle because Cradoc was so fierce. He hacked and hewed his way through the ranks, delivering blows on heads that cut to the teeth. Bodies were strewn throughout the sandy beach and wounds were grievous. Many of the Saxon's had been unarmed making the attack all the more fatal. Alas, it was a slaughter. They were just swine going to the butcher. Bewildered, some sought the comfort of their ships and set sail. Others fought on the beach or drowned. Of the six thousand only one thousand survived the attacks. Some broke through the line and managed to flee to the forest. Though Cradoc took a division of men and pursued them hotly, cutting many fleeing men to the ground. Others were taken prisoner, fled in the ships, or were grievously wounded. All of the Saxons felt heavy despair when this happened for they were utterly destroyed.

The Saxon leader managed to sail away with a small number of men in one of the ships. Though Cradoc had archers positioned on the rocky reef that let loose a hail of arrows at them the whole time, killing those on the ships.

What more can I say? A tragedy was turned into a victory. Cradoc returned to Rhun and, to his delight, they were still as strong in number as when they left; they recounted how many they killed and this was an astonishing number! They prepared a feast in the hall and all the men who had been summoned were invited. It was a splendid feast and everyone put on special garments. The men wore red tunics with golden belt buckles. Some wore purple capes made of the finest silk; others had adorned scarlet mantles or mantles of ermine. The ladies were also splendidly arrayed in gowns with bejeweled circlets. The noble knights who had fought that day were given rose chaplets and they graciously donned them on their heads, to the delight of the ladies who were given much pleasure by this. The delight was so great that many lovers were joined that night. In the midst of the sumptuous feast of venison, capon and every kind of flavored dish you could think of, there was caroling and dancing to everyones contentment.

Cradoc wore his red gold crown over his plenteous head of blonde hair; it had at the top a diadem of emeralds. Cradoc's wife walked through the court followed by a train of maidens and servants so that the whole party gazed at her in amazement. She wore a crown of white gold and had three white doves on her shoulder. Her gown was of green silk with gold embroidered on it. Mass was sung wonderfully for those who stayed awake into the next day and many came just to gaze at the beautiful queen. Afterwards, the whole court listened to beautiful music from the minstrels who played from morning until night in the midst of all the celebration. Then a bard prepared a special lay, recounting the battle.

When Arthur received word that Cradoc had so boldly conquered the Saxon invaders he rejoiced. When he returned from conquering France he went to Cradoc's castle and brought him wondrous gifts from the French country. Also, he gave him even more land for being so loyal. They celebrated together and the king joyfully heard the entire story just as you've been told from the minstrel. That is how Cradoc, who was a very loyal warrior, managed to protect the land from enemy invaders.

After greeting Cradoc, Arthur went to the site of the battle and marveled at the place, for he felt it was full of magic. He had a monument constructed there in honor of Cradoc and his noble defense against the Saxons. Next to it he put a tall watchtower. The watchtower was so high that any man could see into the distant sea from it; this helped protect against invaders; for from that day on there was always a guard in it to keep watch.

As for the monument, it was crafted out of purple marble. It was Cradoc on his black destrier, with Coreuseuse in his hand, pointing fiercely into the seas, forbidding any challenger to come that way. It was inscribed: "Here rests the guardian of Briton, and leave it as a fair

174

warning to any who wishes to storm the land by force, you will be defeated!" This monument, so richly displayed and inlaid with gold, was said to have the power to protect the land from any foreign invaders.

One time, a great horde of Saxons set out to Briton to plunder. It was not fifty years later that they came to the beaches of Kent. When they saw the monument, they cowered in fear, for in the dawn they could see the statue moving its limbs of marble. It came alive, watching them with vengeful eyes. As they drew closer to the beach, they could clearly see his horse rearing and even heard it whinny too! Then they saw him draw Coreuseuse and point it directly at them! Oh, they were terrified. When they saw the beach so well guarded they feared to go there and set sail immediately.

# 23 LAMOIT A MARVIEILLES

Now comes a tale for lovers. Hence the title: The love of marvels. I will now tell you of Gawain, who was a most worthy knight in King Arthur's court; he was also Arthur's nephew which gave him a great amount of honor. You ought to know that those who fought him met cruel resistance. Though to be defeated by such a knight brought little shame for he was so marvelous. Gawain took many adventures. When Arthur set out to besiege Donidel's lands in the North, for he was the one king of Britain who refused him homage, Gawain was right at the frontline taking part in the battle. For it was in his nature always to do the bidding of the King.

In that pitched battle there was a great clash of arms. Gawain unhorsed many foes and used his blade to carve out his legacy. For the spirits of the ones he killed , along with the living families, would forever remember him with a bitter taste. His sword was swathed in blood and brain by the days end. Yet this battle lasted for many years for the fortress was completely impenetrable despite the many siege weapons brought forth by Arthur. In fact, no matter how long the skirmishes ran the siege continued ceaselessly, for the defenders were so well fortified Arthur could do very little.

However, after four years Donidel's people were beginning to starve. They had not eaten for two days when they devised a clever plan. One evening, Donidel sent his men out in secret to Arthur's camps. As they slept, Donidel set upon them in a way that was very clever. Rather than attacking them head on in an act of desperation, he ransacked food, baggage and other goods from the camp. He put them on packhorses and led the train away in the night.

Gawain awoke at the sound of the hooves; when he saw this he was outraged. He awoke just in time to see the baggage train leaving the camp. So he quickly mounted and rode after Donidel, who led the train. He galloped straight for him, without donning any armor. He only had time enough to grab his shield and lance before mounting. Gawain, flushed with anger that they had been fooled- and not excited about enduring the siege another two years-galloped after Donidel. When the King realized he was challenged he turned around and spurred his stead into him. The two met in a loud calamitous crash that wounded both grievously. Donidel was pierced by the lance beneath the hauberk and fell from his saddle. Gawain was hit square in the chest so that the lance went through the other side. Oh, it was a terrible wound! He was full of pain and fell from his horse. How frail he was when the lance penetrated him. Since he had no armor on this wound put him in perilous danger, everyone feared greatly for his life.

Donidel, not realizing who it was, hastily remounted and brought the supplies into the castle. They were fortunate to hold out for another two years as a result. Though Gawain found himself terribly wounded. His chest was full of blood and he lay unconscious. The best physicians went to work on him; they realized they could remove the lance, though with great difficulty. Before doing this they made sure that Gawain was confessed of all his sins should he die. Gawain, in the worst pain, was completely shriven and crossed himself on the brow, saying: "Do what you will, if I die for the King's honor, then so be it." He prayed to God that he would live through the wound. Fortunately the royal physicians from King Arthur were the best. They staunched the bleeding and pulled the lance from his shoulder. He was made to rest and didn't heal for three months time.

During this time the siege continued. After three months Gawain found that he could ride again as his health was returning. He called for his armor and a squire brought it to him, fearing to go against such a noble knight. In this way he armed and mounted, beginning to ride around the camp. Then, gaining some confidence, he ventured out into the meadow nearby. King Arthur was given word that Gawain was out of bed. He was worried because he feared for his dear nephew's life. He said: "Nephew, do not go seeking battle just yet for your wounds are still tender. It would be a tragedy if you were killed in battle before you were healed." Gawain replied: "Yes, Uncle, I am aware. I just felt better today and wanted to go for a ride. I only armed myself to see how I was far-

177

ing and if I could bare arms." King Arthur, assured by this, had him swear he would return before nones.

So Gawain set out on horseback through the meadow, seeking adventure. It was May and the lush fields were full of green grass and many new flowers blooming. There was a creek that trickled cool water through the valley and it was a very pleasant sight. Gawain's horse happily drank from this creek as he viewed the blooming countryside. The birds sang gracefully as ever and the sun shined brightly. Gawain was overjoyed for he had been inside the pavilion resting for far too long. Then he went off in a gallop down a path. He felt more strength and vigor than ever before.

He rode past this meadow to a distant copse. Then there was an open glade and he discovered, in the distance, a pavilion. It was a rich blue color and had gold posts with an eagle standard on the top. It was richly adorned and it seemed that whoever dwelled there was very noble. He though he would say hello.

Gawain rode there and hung his shield on an oak tree nearby. Then he dismounted and entered. Inside he found an exquisite bed with rich samite spread across it. On the bed was a beautiful maiden who curiously poked her head out from the ermine covers when she saw him approaching. Gawain, seeing the maiden, called out: "Greetings, fair maiden, I wish to bring you joy!" The maiden didn't respond so Gawain spoke again: "Greetings, damsel, I wish you happiness!" Then the lady spoke: "I also wish you safe travels and much joy, Gawain!" Gawain was startled that he heard his name before telling her and replied: "Why have you addressed me as Gawain?" The lady responded: "I call my brother and father by the name Gawain, so that when they enter they may aspire to his strength, prowess, courage and nobility. For I have heard much of him and know that he is the strongest and most virtuous knight of all. It is my deepest wish that my brother and father can be more like him!"

Gawain was taken back by the beautiful damsel's words, that played so well with his delicate heart strings. So he bowed and said: "Sweet maiden, that is very wise of you. Though know that I have never hidden my name

178

from anyone. I am the one you speak of so often; I am Gawain!" When the maiden heard this she jumped out of bed, full of joy and wearing nothing more than a small white shift that was see through. Gawain was startled by her overwhelmingly beautiful appearance; he was aroused and blushed, growing hot with lust for her.

The lady then looked closely at him and said: "If you are Gawain, take off your armor so that I may see your body and visage more clearly. Only then I can determine if you are he." Gawain quickly undressed so that his whole form was before her. She found him very attractive in both body and form; she gazed at him for some time. Very excited, the maiden ran off into the other room that was enclosed by purple samite covered with ofrey. In the other room there was an Arabic woman that was once a servant in King Arthur's court. She had painted a portrait of Gawain that was so realistic that it was almost exact in appearance. Indeed, there was very little difference between the two. So the maiden looked at the man in front of her and then stole away to the other room and compared him with the portrait. Much to her happiness she at once knew that it was Gawain.

So the maiden, full of excitement, ran into the room where Gawain was waiting. She screamed out: "Surely you are he! I am very happy to know it! Take me to bed for I swore to give myself entirely to you should you ever come here." Then she took off her shift so that she was entirely naked. Her skin was fair and white. Her hair was a fiery red and her eyes more green than the May grass. Her breasts were so perfectly rounded and softer than peaches. The rest of her body was full and delightful so that it was a great treasure to explore.

I will say nothing else about it but know that there was no dove more beautiful in all the world. When Gawain set his eyes upon her naked body he was completely enraptured. He crossed himself in amazement. The woman leapt into his arms and they went to the bed kissing and caressing. Know that, as much as Gawain resisted, the two lovers were completely drawn together so that there souls converged. It can be said that, after the day's events, the maiden was no longer a maiden. Indeed, they slept togeth-

179

er and made vigorous love throughout the day and into the evening.

Afterwards they sat in silence for sometime as they were truly amazed at what had occurred. Then, having explored one another so fantastically, they stayed up talking about courtly love. For this lady was named Deserey, and she was of noble blood.

When Gawain had noticed much time had passed he bid the lady adieu and left. She was very sad because of this for she had given her maidenhood to him completely. "Where are you going? Surely it isn't honorable to leave a damsel in such a state!" He replied, "My lady, you are surely my love and will be always. I have promised the King I would return to the siege, and it is almost the next day. He is surely worried that I may be dead or wounded." She replied: "You will be dead or wounded if you don't return to this bed and tell me you love me and swear upon relics that you are to marry me." Though Gawain was stubborn and left in a hurry, donning his armor and putting his shield on his neck and grabbing his lance, which was leaning on a nearby pine.

She wept and lamented a great deal; something told her that his seed was inside her and she would be with child. Several hours had passed before Goshaut, the maiden's father, came to the pavilion. He entered and saw his daughter crying. "What is wrong my sweet maiden?" And she replied: "I am no longer a maiden, the Lord Gawain was here and he took me as his own!" When her father heard this he was so overwhelmed with rage that his eyes were bursting from his head. He trembled and said not a word more but grabbed his weapons and mounted his horse, for he was already armed to the teeth and ready for battle. He rode swiftly in the tracks of Gawain. He rode fast enough so that he caught up with him after a short time, for Gawain was trotting along, quite bedazzled with the love he had received from Deseray. When Goshaut came upon him he yelled out: "How could you so selfishly steal my daughters maidenhood and leave her in despair! You will suffer for this."

Gawain was unsure how to answer the knight; for it was completely true that he had committed such a sin despite his many prayers to avoid it. When he saw the big man hurling towards him in a full gallop, full of rage, he realized his sin. Nonetheless, he leveled his lance and rode into the fray. Yet his wound was not fully healed and all the exertion opened it back up so that he bled everywhere. They met paths and collided fiercely. Goshaut was terribly wounded beneath the hauberk his left side, for Gawain placed the lance just passed the shield with a great amount of force. He fell from his horse and tumbled to the ground in a daze; the force of the fall hurt him greatly so that he broke his leg, for he was a very big man. Goshaut towered over his opponent. He leapt up, unfazed by the broken bone, and ran after Gawain. Gawain dismounted for it was very discourteous to fight a knight on horseback when he was on foot.

The clash of blades sent sparks flying in every direction. The two were both matched in might and strength. The blades came down creating a furious din. Gawain was flushed from all the combat and his wounds were not alleviated, in fact they festered from the exertion. After two hours they were completely exhausted from all the blows. Each had laid on heavy strokes. Goshaut was still unwounded but Gawain's old wound had completely reopened from all the combat. He began to bleed profusely and feared for his life. So Gawain, in his eagerness to get out of there, reasoned with Goshaut. "Let us put off this fight for I am weary. I will give you my honor and swear to wed your daughter, since I have shamefully taken her maidenhood. Indeed my cause is not righteous. In marriage I can make rightful amends to her."

The father realized this was a gratuitous offer and assented. So they put off the challenge and Gawain promised to marry the girl. Thus Gawain returned to King Arthur's camp where he was sorely missed. When they saw him riding forth in such a state they were very concerned. Fortunately the physicians of the king's court healed him but it took six months before he could walk. They put him in Arthur's nearby castle until he was fully healed.

During this time Gawain recalled his oath to Goshaut and sent for him. Goshaut, Deseray and her brother Ukrin all came to the castle. When they were

181

summoned to the castle a great train of nobles accompanied them for they were all of noble stock. Then a marvelous wedding ceremony began; for Gawain kept his word and married the lady, despite the fact he could barely walk during the ceremony. In this way he and the damsel were married and Arthur was elated to have such a beautiful damsel joining the family. Since she was with child, they rejoiced at the new life and seed that came forth too. Everyone was seemingly satisfied at the arrangement, all thanks to Goshaut and his noble attack on Gawain.

Eventually the siege was lifted after six years of carnage. It is known that Gawain, in full health, was the first to ride through the gate, carrying the Lord of the Castle's head on the tip of his lance. He spurred into combat like a demon, plunging into the thick of the press. He dealt so many fatal wounds that he immediately repaid them with interest for the time he spent injured.

Indeed, he laid on such a violent storm that a thunderous din came down upon them as if God was set against them. Black smoke arose around him and the heat of battle created so much of it that he was nearly invisible; except he continued to reign blows that hacked away limbs and lopped off heads. Each blow was dealt with precision and wrath that made the castle defenders weary and wish they never were born.

When the siege was lifted and the Lord defeated Arthur gave Gawain that castle; the first thing he did was give it to Goshaut, for his valiant opposition against him that day in the meadow. Gawain said: "I'm so thankful you defeated me, for now I have the most beautiful wife in the world! And this castle shall be hers to do as she pleases!"

# 24 DAME DE ROHESTOC ET LE FORTE BATAILLE

Now follows a story about a marvelous battle and the Lady of Roestec who was in great peril but freed by King Arthur's knights. At this time the Saxons were pillaging the land of Logres far and wide. Their numbers were great; they were evil and proud. It had long been professed, for the stars told of it, that they would come from the North, wreaking havoc on the good people of Logres.

At the behest of King Arthur, King Lot set out with his four sons to deliver an important message to the kings of the northlands; Lot knew the rebel princes well enough to coax them to fight for Lord Arthur. For the Saxons were invading and the internal divide and strife amongst the Briton kings had to be amended if they were to withstand the attacks. They wanted to unify so that, bound together, they could drive the Saxons from the land. So King Lot was on his way to the northlands to entice the other kings to join Lord Arthur. With him were his four sons Gawain, Guerrehet, Gaheriet and Agravain. All of whom were mighty warriors and strong in battle.

Along the way they talked of many things. The brothers often played games, sang and brawled with one another; for they were brothers who both loved and hated one another with the kind of spirit brothers shared. The first castle they came upon was well positioned on a hill overlooking a beautiful meadow and spring. The Lord there, named Eliezer, had been under extreme duress since the Saxons began attacking. His army was nearly lost in the battle and they had received no help despite sending messengers. They were greatly outnumbered too. In this way did that King lament his fate bitterly: "Alas, they have seized us so long it is unlikely my men can resist any longer! It is for God to decide if I will perish, what misfortune!"

King Lot led his train of knights until they reached the hill by following the path from the forest. Eliezer was in front of a series of brightly colored pavilions that stood before the castle rampart. His knights had been summoned by blaring horns to do combat in the valley below. He was perturbed and in much duress because the battle had been unsuccessful; the man felt sure he would soon lose his lands. Lot spoke to him: "Great King Eliezer, we bring you good tidings. Lord Arthur wishes to bring us all together to slay the Saxon hordes." Eliezer was delighted to hear this and said: "Fair king, I appreciate the sentiment and greatly await his protection. The Saxons have harassed my lands for many days now and I don't know how much longer I can hold out. In fact, I'm quite sure I will lose my keep to them this very day!"

Just as Eliezer spoke the clash of arms echoed throughout the valley. Then his forces were seen fleeing from the Saxons back up the hill to the castle. They chased them and slaughtered many good Christians. Eliezer, whose face was somber and covered in dirt from much battle, looked down in shame. "My men flee before my eyes. They will likely be routed for the last time. For I once had a good two hundred knights and now I have no more than thirty." King Lot, grieved at his situation, placed his hand on his shoulder, reassuring him: "Do not fear, give us lodging tonight; my sons and I will help you."

The five companions fixed their spurs and swung their shields around their necks, leveled their lances and spurred off down the hill. The Saxons were chasing after the defeated Briton knights when, suddenly, they saw the five valiant knights charging in the opposite direction. They were shocked at such a challenge when they saw that the five had tilted their lances for combat.

The fleeing knights were encouraged as they saw the emblazoned shields of King Arthur's court. Pennons unfurled in the wind displaying a wonderful array of colors while their armor gleamed. They turned to face the enemy and began assailing them on all sides. Then the five made contact, knocking men from their saddles. They unhorsed five who were very bitter, but the blows were so fierce that they were left in a daze, loosing both seat and helm.

The next round of opponents were equally well met, being unhorsed in such a way that they dared not return to combat. The men flew from the saddle and howled in anguish and defeat. When the good lances splintered

184

and shattered against the hard shields and hauberks they drew their swords and began to assail the enemy company. The battle became bloody then as the brothers hacked and hewed limbs apart without mercy. Much blood, flesh and limbs were littered on the field that day. Each of the brothers felled handfuls of Saxons.

Aggravain delivered a blow so powerful it cut through helm and head all the way to the shoulder. Two other's had their skull was split to the teeth while Gawain lopped off a few heads himself. So many heads littered the field that the villagers later proclaimed they saw them talking amongst themselves, years later. Those men were felled because of the prowess of Arthur's men, who were so skilled in combat that the enemy had little chance to resist. They were so skilled in arms that they could easily rout four hundred against five, for such was the circumstance; know that the Saxon army was four hundred strong.

So they persisted in the heat of combat. Gawain delivered so many terrible blows that a black smoke surrounded him, as if the steam of combat had created an aura around him making it more difficult to see him. Blood was steaming and gushing everywhere around him, for he was quick to hammer his opponents to the ground so they could not return to battle.

Gawain was riding on Gringalet. This was the best of horses in all Logres; he came upon his foes like a raging bear, often running them through completely. His horse's chest knocked men down and they were helplessly crushed beneath the horse's hard gallop. He hacked and hewed on each side and rode foremost into the press. Indeed, his brothers saw him so far ahead, he was completely surrounded by Saxons; though he was never unhorsed and the enemy fled from him in terror. His sword was so sharp that it hewed through both shield and hauberk with ease. Arms, legs and bodiless heads littered the ground; blood and brain flowed unto the field in abundance.

In the midst of the fighting Agravain and Gaheriet were unhorsed by a group of Saxons who used their spears to drive them into their horse's chests. When they fell down, King Lot saw how his sons were in danger and yelled out: "Guerrehet, save your brothers for they are in

185

the midst of the enemy!" When Geurrehet heard this he turned and spurred his horse into a full gallop towards the enemy. He tilted his lance and knocked over five Saxon's, one after the other. He unhorsed them with terrible blows that shattered their shields and left them bleeding, unable to get up. Then he took out his sword and began hacking away. The knights tried to run but he assailed them hard, delivering blows that cut them down from behind. He beheaded one knight and then stabbed another in the stomach so that his intestines came out.

When that company was completely slaughtered he took two horses by the reins and delivered them to his brothers, who were marveling at his prowess. "Dear brother, you seem more like a ferocious boar than a nobleman." He replied: "Well, brother, we're a long ways off from the court. This is the wild!" Roaring with laughter they remounted and renewed the attack on the Saxon line. They came through the forest and rode hard into the rear of the enemy that was being assailed at the front by their companions.

This attack was fatal for they knocked about the men in the back; they were so rough with them that the whole company of Saxon's panicked and fled to the trees. Screams of pain were heard a league away, for sharp steel was clearly getting put to work. Each knight's keen edged blade was covered in blood, all the way to the hilt. King Lot marveled at the prowess of Geurrehet who proved himself so well that day. Guerrehet did even more marvels on the battlefield. His took the head of one man in a single stroke; then he drove his lance through a man's chest.

The knights pressed them so hard they were left with no choice but to flee. They had never seen such mighty warriors. Yet, the front ranks were so large in number that they continued to resist until King Eliezer, who was also at the front encouraging his knights, was unhorsed. When the Saxon's saw that a nobleman was on the ground they quickly wrestled him into submission and took him prisoner. He was taken prisoner by the four Saxon kings whose names were Moydas, Brandalis, Oriance and Dodalis.

When this happened King Lot immediately saw it and cried out: "Gawain, save Eliezer for he has been taken captive!" When Gawain heard this he drove the mighty Gringalet through the Saxon press to where he saw Eliezer. Then he took a lance from the ground and charged into the battle line. He plunged the sharp lance into the chest of Moydas whose heart burst when it reached him. Then he drew his sword and dealt heavy blows. The two kings, Brandalis and Oriance, came at him together, hoping to beat him down. Though they were weak minded and full of treachery; it is never chivalrous to assail a single knight with two. For where is the honor in that?

Gawain, however, merely saw this as an opportunity to double his prowess. He made quick work of them. He dodged the lance thrust and took the other on the shield; when the lance splintered he struck Brandalis in the side and it went straight through his hauberk. He bled out and died on the field after being unhorsed so fiercely. Then he hammered on Oriance and completely cleft his arm from his shoulder; it fell to the ground and blood went everywhere. Oriance was in such pain that he fainted. Gawain then leapt from his horse, took his sharp blade and, unlacing the king's helm, drove it into the man's neck, making the head roll to the ground. The other one was just about to die when he cried out: "Oh, my life was wasted, I should never have come here hoping to plunder the land. The Britons are so brave that I have been well met." When the Saxons saw how their kings had been slain they fled in terror; for they didn't want to have any more of the combat. Agravain and Gaheriet chased after them and began removing heads from bodies and felling enemies to the ground as they turned their backs.

Agravain drove his horse far from the battle in the chase until he reached deep into the forest where there was a fork in the road. In one direction he heard the screams of a man while in the other a maiden. The maiden exclaimed: "Mother Mary, save me from these wicked hounds before I am lost!" The maiden's frightened screams made him desire nothing more than to save her. He immediately went in that direction, hoping to get there before any dishonor was shown to her. Indeed, he muttered to himself: "Much more important it is to save a maiden in distress than a knight, who can well take care of himself if the Lord wills it." So he prayed that the man would be delivered and set off for the lady.

He followed the woman's screams until he came upon them. There were six knights who surrounded her, all of them were chastising her. One of the men dragged her by her golden tresses and hit her with a rod over the head so she bled from her forehead; she was very beautiful and the lustful men looked to shame her. That man tore her clothes and opened her legs being quite ready to do the wicked act before Agravain, greatly incensed, yelled out: "Remove your hands from that maiden! She does not deserve such horrible behavior. No woman should give of herself unless she is willing, now I challenge you for that right."

The man who was holding the lady said: "Will we have any trouble from you, then?" Agravain became bored with words and charged at them full tilt. He unhorsed two of the challengers and then went straight towards the man on top of the lady. Before he could raise his shield, which was hung on an oak tree in near the spring, he received his death wound: Aggravain's lance plunged into his chest and through to his back several feet before snapping. He opened his mouth in anguish and fell on top of the lady, dead. She was horrified but had enough strength to push him off of her and run behind the oak tree to await the combat's end.

Then, seeing the lady was now safe, Agravain unsheathed his sword and laid on them the most perilous blows you could imagine. They could do little but hold up their shields, hoping they wouldn't give under the pressure of his mighty strength. He beheaded one that came after him on horseback. Then he knocked another from his horse so that he tumbled over the rump. He dealt another heavy stroke that cut through shoulder, waist and saddle all the way to the horse's belly. Then another knight hit his head on a rock and died, for he was so harshly unhorsed that the fall killed him. His body trembled in shock as his head smacked a nearby rock, cracking the skull and sounding like a loud clap of thunder.

When they were all dead he sought the maiden. She said: "Where will you take me?" Agravain replied: "I won't take you anywhere you don't wish to go. Tell me, how did all this come about?" The maiden, who was very happy that she had been rescued, said: "I am the Lady of Roestec. I was riding through the forest that I own with my cousin and we were set upon by a band of men. They took me captive and my cousin fought them but he was unarmed. He killed one of them with his fists and was almost beaten to death by their men because of it. Maybe there is still time to save him." Agravain then remembered the groans of the man he heard in the other direction. "Alas, lady, I heard him struggling with them moments ago. Quick!" He grabbed her hand and gently placed her on the neck of his horse and spurred off in the direction of the knight he had heard earlier.

Fortunately, during the battle between Agravain and the lady's captors Gaheriet had followed his brother until he heard the groans of the knight who was being beaten to death. Taking the opposite path, he rode at a swift pace in the direction of the peril. Five knights surrounded the Lady of Roestec's cousin and were beating him to death. He was on the ground, near death, while the men kicked at him and hit him with the pommels of their swords. His face was full of gushing blood and he was so crippled that he couldn't walk. Gaheriet said not a word but galloped towards them, challenging them. He unhorsed three, one after the other. Then one of them wickedly killed his horse with a sword. So he assailed them on foot and a violent combat ensued. He dealt terrible blows that were never seen before. He cut a man across the face so that his skull split in to and his eyes bulged out. Then he hammered a man to the ground so forcefully that he broke his leg in the impact.

In the midst of the combat, Agravain arrived and, setting down the lady by a tree, he galloped fiercely at the other knights. He unhorsed one, splintering his lance to tiny pieces. Then he jumped on the other knight, wrestling him to the ground. He hit him with the hilt of his sword, crushing his helm and nose-guard so that he bled copiously from his nose and mouth. Then he unlaced his helm and

189

threw it far from him, threatening to behead him if he didn't surrender: "Give up the fight, all of your men are dead." The knight was utterly shamed, for he told him: "I will have no honor no matter what. We are defectors from the army. We were so afraid of the Saxon's that we fled in terror, chastising these innocent nobles." Agravain thought to himself for a moment and then replied: "Alas, your treason is double. You sought to dishonor a lady and committed treason to your king." So he said no more and gave him a mighty blow that lopped off the head, sending it flying into the thicket nearby.

They took the extra horses and Gaheriet thanked his brother: "Brother, I am so thankful that you made it." Then he looked over at the wounded knight, who was the lady's cousin, and was full of pity: "Is this man going to live?" The Dame de Roestec ran to her cousin, embracing him. She saw that he was sorely wounded and tried to bandage him with her garments and staunch the bleeding as best she could. They made a litter and attached it to the horses: "I suggest we take him back to the castle where the king has physicians who can heal him." They all agreed. So they mounted and had the litter carried back to the castle.

There was incredible rejoicing at the castle when they saw that the Saxon's fled. When the two knights returned with the lady and her cousin Eliezer marveled at it: "Indeed, those are my brother and sister's kids! You have done well, for if they had perished I would never have been forgiven." He took them away and made sure that a physician tended to the man, who was in a pitiful state. He was eventually healed, after several months.

That evening they celebrated in the castle. Servants unarmed the guests and gave them splendid mantles to adorn. A sumptuous feast was prepared and great dishes came in a number of splendid courses. After that a minstrel sang so wonderfully that he had all of the knight's sobbing for love and honor. "No knight, however bold, will fail to heed the call of love. Every true lover knows that his deeds of prowess are for the one he calls his own." After dinner and all the merry making they talked at great length about the forthcoming alliance between King Arthur and the rebel princes; they adjourned the meeting with high hopes that Logres would unite against their common enemy and, with the help of God, persevere.

# 25 THE GOOD KNIGHT AT THE BOIL-ING RIVER

At this time in Logres there was a wicked evil custom that befell one of the forests in the kingdom. For every wicked custom there is a good knight around to oppose it. I shall now tell of a knight who was mighty and earned himself the name "li Biaux, li Boens" which means the Fair Good knight. At this time an evil demon had possessed a knight of the court. Know that I wouldn't tell you his name to cause any further shame to him, for he was deeply afflicted by this evil spirit both night and day. In the land he was known as the Demon Knight, for he had little control over his limbs that so pitifully did only the bidding of the demon inside him. His armor was all black and he rode a ruddy destrier with a black shield that had a green serpent on it. At the top of his helmet there were red letters engraved, plainly showing the triple sixes which are the sign of the devil.

The Demon Knight was banished from the court for his wickedness and deceit. At one time he had been given to drunkenness and, to his dishonor, slept with one of the Queen's maidservants. Then he told lies about it and raped a maiden in the town one night.

Given to anger, he fled to the forest and made his home near a river, where he set up a pavilion and challenged all passersby. When he came there the river began to boil because he was so full of lust and wickedness. That was where the demon willed he be, defending the boiling river that signified his great treachery. Since he was a servant of the Devil he was considered an incubus like the one that fathered Merlin. Holy men in this forest forbade people to travel there because of this vile creature.

Later, he brought demonic women, wicked followers of the same serpent, to the pavilion to live with him. These women were possessed also and they committed many lustful acts. You see, they were all servants of the devil; though they appeared very beautiful they would wickedly betray any knight by luring him to the river. Then they would sleep with him on the river bank and, in the night, the Demon Knight would behead them, throwing their body into the boiling river to feed it. Know that this river was boiling hot, searing the flesh of any who went into it.

In this way the Demon Knight lived in his pavilion near the boiling river for many years. He spent that time fornicating with the other demons and killing knights who were lured there. Many good knights were captured and killed by the Demon Knight; so many that it would take too long to recount and I want to tell you how this evil custom was overcome by a single brave knight from Arthur's court.

Caliburn was his name and at this time he roamed the forest looking for adventure. He reached a hermitage in that same forest near the boiling river. The place was in a deep wood and when he got there a very gracious holy man came out, opening the wicket gate, and said: "Greetings, you must be seeking adventure for there is no castle for many leagues. Come, disarm and take solace here. Hear the mass and partake of this bread the lord has offered us."

Caliburn replied: "Holy man, I will listen to your mass and I appreciate your greetings. Tell me, is there any place where I can find adventure here?" The man responded: "Proud knight, I would venture no further into the forest. A wicked demon has possessed a knight there. The Devil has many disguises and will lure you to that place through lust. It wouldn't be hard for him to take your soul, for no source of human strength can resist him; God alone can deliver you from such a demon. Humble yourself before God and ask for his strength. Confess your sins with me and I will give you relief and grace to go on." Caliburn said: "If there is evil in these lands it is my wish to absolve it. Where there is sin I will shine the light of God and slay the evildoer." The hermit praised his words of bravery and spoke further: "Know that many knights have passed this way with the intention of slaying the Demon Knight. Every one of them has become so enflamed with lust that they were murdered treacherously. If you are truly holy and full of virtue than you may be able to defeat him. Whatever you choose, may you go with God!"

Caliburn stayed the night with the hermit. When he had sung mass and dined on bread and drank cold water from the spring, he laid strewn grass in one of the rooms that he slept on, for it was a very hot July night. In the morning, before leaving, he was sure he made a clean breast of his sins so that he rode off completely free and pure.

After the uplifting time with the hermit he took to riding at a brisk pace towards the pavilion. As he came near to the boiling river, for he could smell its foul stench from afar, he was greeted by a beautiful woman. Know that she was the most beautiful woman he had ever seen. Her bosom was coming out of her shirt and her skin was a golden hue. Her burnished hair glowed in the light beneath the oak tree she leaned against. She had many jewels and a beautiful circlet on her head. She was adorned in the finest garments and had rich perfumes on. Her lips were treachery to any good knight. I will speak no more on her beauty but must say that it was very deceiving; for inside this one was more wickedness and sin than any creature on earth. For she was no more than a servant of the Demon Knight!

The woman approached Caliburn and spoke to him: "Come with me, for you seem fair and strong. I will gladly give you lodging and rest. Take me as your lover, right here in the forest, and we can be together happily. For I feel love in my heart and cannot escape it." When Caliburn looked upon her his mind was enflamed with lust. The fires of lust seemed to be overcoming him right there in the forest. He prayed fervently to God and crossed himself. It took some time for him to speak. Then he said: "Cruel and wretched are you. For I know your ways. You have brought many valiant knights to their death. I know that you sleep with them and the Demon Knight, your lord, comes in the night to slay them. For God has told me your deeds. I call on God to banish you from the earth for this!" When he said this, the lady was unable to resist the summoning of God. She turned from a beautiful lady into a gnarly old hag. Her back was hunched and her face was twisted, her swarthy skin and clothes were wrinkled and rent. Such was the true nature of that evil spirit. The Caliburn yelled out: "Now, you who are unable to resist God's power, take me to the Demon Knight. I will fight him in broad daylight and avenge the ones he has killed."

The lady realized that she could not coax Caliburn. She took him by the hand and led him to the boiling river. Just then he saw the Demon Knight, who was kneeling over a stone bridge casting stones into the boiling river. He was four times the size of any man with arms strong and thick. His steel blade was massive so that it seemed like a razor sharp tree trunk. Caliburn saw beside him the dead body of another knight who had just been killed, as the blood was fresh and hot with steam. The man's head had already rolled into the river. His body was lifeless though it twitched about helplessly. Then the Demon Knight effortlessly tossed the dead corpse into the boiling river with a single hand. In this way Demon Knight killed all those who fell into temptation through his alluring concubines.

When the Demon Knight saw Caliburn approach he was senseless, with his eyes drawn to the river where the flesh of that dead man simmered. He numbly said: "Do you see that knight whose flesh now boils in the fires of hell? He slept with one of my girls. So I stole away in the darkness of the night and gutted him as he slept in lusty bliss. I ripped open his throat and intestines. What a joy and delight to take a soul and deliver it to my master! He is hungry and feeds on the soul of man, you know. My master is happy to take his soul for his was valiant and did many brave deeds before committing such a folly. The juicier the peach, the more noble the man, and the more noble the man the sweeter the soul! So it is with the downfall of all great men, their pride and lust make them give up the ghost so quickly."

Caliburn was astonished at this cruelty and replied: "Why do you tempt good men from the way of the light? Broad is the path of all sinners, must you make it wider? You bring men to destruction through guile and deceit; all of Logres loathes you for it. You will suffer by my hand, as God wills it. So be on your guard, for I chal-

195

lenge you! By the power of God, I demand that you are forthright banished from this place. Go back to hell!"

The Demon whirled about in anger when he heard the word God, how he so loathed that man who had imprisoned him on earth. The Holy Spirit then came down from the sky. An angel of God launched his lance through the Demon so that he fell to the ground. Caliburn saw this and set off in a full gallop towards the Demon Knight like a raging lion. The Demon Knight arose but was in great pain from the angel's wound. They met upon the stone bridge that crossed the boiling river. The impact created a thunderous din and could be heard several leagues in either direction. Caliburn's lance shattered as it hit the demon's black shield; he was unhurt. The demon then dealt him a stroke with his steel blade that he dodged but subsequently chopped his horse's head off, forcing Caliburn to the ground in a heap.

Caliburn tumbled from his destrier but arose quickly. He unsheathed his sword and the demon dismounted also. They ran at each other yelling mightily. Sparks flew in all directions as the two clashed. Caliburn gave him a fierce blow that made him bleed in his thigh. Then the demon ran towards him, tackling him to the ground. He then hammered down with his massive blade but Caliburn rolled away, just dodging the blow.

The fight was treacherous and the demon's concubines all watched with wide eyes; for they had never seen a knight challenge the demon with such vigor. Caliburn slashed and hacked away the knight's armor little by little. One blow went through his hauberk and took a chunk of flesh; for it was too powerful to be stopped by the black shield. The Demon Knight returned the favor and sliced Caliburn on the thigh so that he too lost flesh. Since his strength was of four men, each blow was exhausting to the mortal Caliburn.

When our good knight felt his strength waning he began to pray, for the Demon Knight hacked away at him and after an hour his armor was completely rent and his shield was useless. Blood ran down his face so that he was completely blinded. His flesh was stinging with pain and he felt sure that death approached. Though, as he prayed, he heard a voice call out from above: "Have ye so little faith?" Alas, he fell to his knees, exhausted, unsure what else to do. The Demon Knight grinned and felt sure it was time to take his soul. He prepared the final blow to behead him. The wicked ladies all laughed and scorned the good knight, who had fought so valiantly.

Yet, Caliburn did a wondrous thing. He closed his eyes and prayed a second time. Suddenly, something astonishing happened when he said: "St. David, the water drinker: I call upon you to purify the land as you once did. Through your blessedness vanquish this terrible demon! In the name of God and St. David, help me!" When he said this the Demon Knight was mid stroke and suddenly became paralyzed. His wretched lady servants all began to scream and whirl about.

Then a marvelous spirit came riding on a white horse. He was riding right over the boiling river. Make no confusion, it was no other than the mighty St. David, water drinker and savior of Wales. Know that no sight was more glorious, nor was there a man more holy in all of Britain. Light shined all around him and it blinded the Demon, who was howling in anguish at the sight of God's servant.

As I said, he horse galloped along the river water towards the demon. He was adorned in a robe, with a staff and a white dove resting on his shoulder. He smiled and pointed his staff at the demons; a powerful aura of light came forth from the staff and penetrated the demons. This transfiguration was a great miracle to behold, as it is reported by Caliburn who saw it plainly as day. The ladies' beautiful flesh burned from the light, they turned to wicked old hags like the other one; then, after giving up their true state, the flesh was completely burned to ashes by the holy light. St. David brought forth holy light that scorched the sinners.

All of those evil women were sent back to hell then and there. At the same time the Demon Knight couldn't move or speak; for he was completely suspended by the power of St. David. Then St. David came up to him and said: "Back, demon!" He pointed his staff at him so forcefully that rays of light struck the man in the chest. Then, suddenly, black smoke came out of the knight's

197

body. It came from his eyes, mouth ears and hands. When this happened the demon spoke many words but the language was undistinguishable; St. David muttered replies as Caliburn gazed in wonder. This black smoke was the demon who had been inside the knight's body; it was the very spirit within him. Finally, it left into the air completely so that the knight turned to his original form and fell to the ground in tears. So the demon was expelled from the knight's body and he was restored. St. David did still another marvel, as if that wasn't enough. He touched the water in the boiling river. When he did this it turned cool as a spring and ceased to boil.

Then he smiled and blessed Caliburn, saying: "This knight will return to God, take care that he is given all he needs. You will be richly rewarded for your bravery. Call on me anytime you need help. I will be there." Then St. David spurred his white steed, rode across the river and disappeared. Caliburn was completely amazed at the wonders he had seen. He later recounted them to King Arthur and the scribes so that they set it down in writing.

The knight who had been so possessed was whirling about on the ground in tears. It had been so long since he had felt his true self. He gave up his sword and begged Caliburn on his knees: "You have saved me. Please, I beg you, let me live. I will serve you for all time, for I was possessed for so long that I remember little of the wicked deeds I did." Caliburn replied: "I know that you were not as your true self. Much of your deeds will be forgiven. You must seek counsel with holy men to determine the next steps. I will bring you back to court gladly."

He was full of shame and tears. Caliburn comforted him. They sat near the spring and a voice called out: "This river is blessed for all time by St. David. Drink from it and your wounds will be healed!" So the two knights, full of pain from their many wounds, drank from the river and found themselves healed almost instantly. They returned to their former strength and vigor, crossing themselves in amazement.

Caliburn was so overcome with the holy spirit after that day that he used his inheritance to build a monastery in the name of St. David near that place. The former Demon Knight, no longer possessed, made himself a holy man to repent for his deeds. He later retired to this monastery and mended his ways; for the spirit that had been within him was languishing in hell. He was later called the "White Knight" for he had washed his sins away through many years of repentance.

Indeed, no evil could come near the monastery for it had been blessed and protected by the invocation of St. David. The court of King Arthur, when they heard of what happened, renamed the boiling river to the eternal river. Wounded knights went there to receive healing for many years. The monastery taught that the river boiled because it fed off of the lust of man; when Caliburn had turned away from lust he was able to defeat the evil one and purify the river. It was taught that the Demon Knight grew in strength when he took souls to the devil; but that he could only kill those who were tempted into lust. Later Caliburn was known all across Logres for his bravery and was called "li Biaux, li Boens" which means the Fair Good knight.

# 26 THE ROMANCE OF GUENIER AND IREL

Guenier, as they called him, was a fair knight of much prowess who had come from King Arthur's court. It is no surprise that his great deeds were chronicled in detail. Guenier had a horn made of ivory that he sounded whenever he was roused to combat. This horn was so loud that it made the forest shake and his enemies tremble; it had the power to eradicate evil and make his enemies tremble. It was a custom of his that he only fought battles that were righteous and he never feared an opponent. His shield was gold and it had emblazoned on it three blue lions. How he found his lover is a most enjoyable tale which I will tell of now. If you can hear it aloud that is the best way.

Geunier rode in the forest doing something he loved most: hunting. He set out early in the morning and, suddenly, from out of the thicket, he spotted a white hart. That was a most rare thing to see so, eager to find it, he galloped off ahead of the hunting party. He chased the hart far into the depth of the forest and, when it took to a spring to drink water, he found his horse couldn't bear it any longer. He let his horse graze and it rested beneath an oak tree in the shade of the meadow. He fell into a deep sleep, for he was very weary. It wasn't until several hours had passed that he awoke and went looking for his hound, who had disappeared.

Know that he was in a very remote part of Logres; there was no one near him except for a magical castle that was hidden. It was governed by fairies and would only reveal itself at the behest of those who lived there. The castle itself, though invisible, was well situated on a rocky knoll overlooking the forest; such were its natural defenses most troublesome for any invader. It also had a deep, wide moat encircling it along with well fortified walls.

It was a great wonder when Geunier, who was eager for proper lodging, had the castle revealed to him. He rode in with ease through a marvelous gateway and into a courtyard. Since no one was around he tethered his horse there and went inside. Little did he know that a Faery watched him plainly from a window, and led him on to an important task.

He climbed up the steps and into a glorious hall that was rich and full of gold. The pillars and floors were all constructed of fine marble; there were magnificent statues, and gold doors leading to an array of richly adorned chambers with large beds in them. Rich tapestries bestrewed the walls evoking the imagination. Scenes of hunting and battle were etched into them with such artistry and wonder it was a real treasure to behold. There were large windows in the hall on each side that allowed plenty of natural light in. He peeked through one of these windows, overviewing the surrounding, and found the most beautiful spring and garden. In the garden there were exquisite hedges and colorful flowers; in the bushes he saw rose petals in bloom of red, pink, white and yellow. He also saw, across from the garden, a number of pavilions next to the cool spring. Nearby, he saw a lion sleeping too. Geunier took all this in and thought it a great marvel. So he hurried down the steps from the hall and went outside to the garden. But as he neared the pavilions that treacherous lion awoke at the sound of his approach.

When the lion saw him he roared terribly loud and made way straight to him. He leapt through the air and tackled Geunier, tearing his shield apart with his sharp claws. Geunier unexpectedly took a tumble, bruising himself. Though as the lion showed his razor sharp teeth he dodged out of the way, drawing his sword from its scabbard. The lion leapt a second time but he maneuvered around him ever so swiftly, for he greatly feared for his life. Then he thrust his blade forward, gutting the lion at his third attack. It was furious and he could plainly see the white in his eyes. It leapt again and this time he cut him to the ground with a ferocious blow. When the lion fell to the ground he struck it again, this time he hit him on the neck so that the head detached from the body. Geunier, exhausted and covered in blood, walked around the meadow and quenched his thirst at the spring. He said to himself: "Sometimes, when you least expect it, a vicious lion lunges at you're, making a terrible fuss. What more can you do but stand your ground, hoping he doesn't kill you?"

201

Geunier rested, marveling at the massive lion body on the ground. Then he explored the rest of the meadow, and it was no wonder that he marveled at the richly adorned pavilions. He entered there and found an elaborate bed covered with the finest furs and silks. Next to it was a table full of meat pies, fresh wine and fruit. Geunier went to the table and began eating feverishly, for it had been some time since he had the pleasure. Yet there was a lady lying in the bed and when she heard the thunderous din the knight made at the table she awoke. It was plainly visible that he was covered in blood and this greatly terrified the maiden who yelled loudly. "What knight is this who is covered in wounds and so terrifying to behold?"

When the lady called out a knight came from the other pavilion; he was fully armed and seemed to have been napping until he had heard her call. When he saw Geunier covered in blood he was wroth: "What brought you here?" exclaimed the disgruntled knight. Geunier replied: "I was hoping to drink from the spring you have here. As I approached it that terrible lion attacked me and I slew it." Geunier was proud of the fact he had done so since the lion was very strong. "Alas," cried the knight, "that beast was a close companion of mine, you shall suffer for it!" In this way was Geunier, who barely had time to rest in between fights, was challenged. A company of squires made way and brought forth a bundle of sharp, stout lances. They also brought his horse, which had been in the courtyard. The meadow opened up to a plain that was a league wide and two leagues long. The horses pranced about on the grass and separated about a bow shot length to start the joust.

The knight called out: "Here is my gage." And he threw out his glove to the ground. "I challenge you on behalf of the lion, my friend, who you have treacherously murdered for no good reason." Geunier responded: "It was for a very good reason, he had me by the throat and was about to throttle me. Should I have let him do it? This is treachery and I gladly defend the claim that it was murder." He also threw is gage to the ground, furious at the challenge.

Without further ado the two knights spurred their steeds and collided, head to head, body to body, making a terrible sound. The two splintered their lances with such might force. Each shield was shattered into pieces and the knights tumbled to the ground in a heap! They arose quickly and drew their swords, eager to show off their prowess. By midday the clash of arms was loudly heard so that everyone in the castle was now watching from windows in the hall and from the lawn by the meadow. Sparks flew and armor was torn apart. The field was littered with pieces of lance, shield and hauberk. Blood began to flow freely.

Just then, when the combat grew thick and terrible, Geunier pulled out his horn of ivory and gave it a loud blow. The sound blared loudly and throughout the land. Many were drawn to tears at the sound of it. Meanwhile, sinners cringed and ran from it. Only the most noble and virtuous people could stand the might of the horn. His enemy, who was full of treachery, cowered and shook. After that Geunier became even more fierce, for he had stunned his enemy. He delivered a blow that was so mighty it cut him to the ground, taking out a chunk of flesh from his shoulder. Bloody and ill-tempered, he met his man on the field. When he got back up, Geunier gave him a second blow that was so powerful he flew into the meadow and was submerged in the water. His armor was heavy and he began to drown! Luckily his squires pulled him out, bidding him to retaliate and gain back his honor: "For God's sake-the ladies are watching!"

He glanced painfully at the tower and grew red with shame at being played with by the knight. He knew that the challenger had come from the fairy. He had, some months ago, trapped a fairy in the meadow. She was locked in the tower but still had magical powers. "It was she who must have brought this knight here to dishonor me!" Well, thought the fairy from the imprisoned tower: "You shouldn't capture a lady against her wishes, especially one with magical powers!"

Then Geunier and the knight assailed each other with many might sword strokes. The one hit the other, sometimes gaining ground and at other times losing it.

203

They fought this way for some time before Geunier, clearly the stronger, overpowered him with a painful blow on the head. This wound cut through the knight's helm and into the flesh. It was struck with such force that it stunned him completely and he fell down like a shriven tree. He was now on the ground in a swoon, crying out: "Alas, I am defeated, I swear to be your prisoner. Do what you will!" Geunier enjoyed this and responded: "Tell me your name, dear knight." The knight replied: "I am called Arbour of the woodlands. My unfortunate defeat will be known far and wide. It is no simple task to defeat me in battle. Be sure that you shall gain much renown for it. Tell me your name so I may know who has defeated me?" Geunier told him: "I will never hide my name from he who asks. I am called Geunier the fair; I am a knight of the Table Round and lord King Arthur. As my prisoner you are to go to him and give yourself to him by my name." When Arbour heard his name he was astonished and said: "It is no wonder. I have heard much of your valor and no longer feel as much shame for being defeated by such a remarkable knight."

That wasn't the end of it, however. Suddenly a voice called out, saying: "You must tell him about the fairy you have imprisoned, otherwise it wouldn't be a right and true amends!" Arbour was mystified by this and didn't know what to do, so in desperation he blurted out the story: "That's right, this castle is enchanted so that it is completely visible. You only found it because I did a wicked deed, which I now sorely repent of. I captured a fairy from the wood, and hoped to make her my wife. She refused and I imprisoned her in the tower. She let you in and, now that you defeated me, I have no choice but to disclose this."

Geunier replied: "Wouldn't it be right that you set her free? For it is sure that a man should never, if he cares to be chivalrous, do anything against a lady's wishes. If she wished to marry you, than it would make perfect sense. But, alas, you have wrongfully imprisoned her. So, by God and all who are here to witness, I demand you set her free to the wood." Arbour agreed to do this, for he felt great guilt at having imprisoned her against her will; he had tried many times to force himself upon her though she always eluded him with her enchantments. Now he was sure that if she could make the invisible castle visible she would, at one point or another, kill him if he did not free her.

Meanwhile, Arbour was very pleased to make himself Arthur's prisoner. Yet the day was far from over. They embraced and made peace and spent the day talking. Arbour called for tables to be set so they could eat. Bustling squires came from the castle laying out a large carpet of samite upon a wooden table; they carried it to the meadow. Many more tables were brought by a large multitude of squires. Each knight was carefully attended to and helped out of his armor and they were given marvelous scarlet mantles lined with vair. The rejoicing was great when the food arrived; it was a sumptuous feast with pressed fawn, one of the most luxurious dishes of the time. The lord of the land ate heartily and spoke many joyous words with Geunier. They passed that evening merrily. At evening time the squires slept along the grass in the cool July night while Geunier was allowed to sleep in the pavilion on the exquisite bed. The stars were very beautiful in the clear sky. The owls were heard hooting and the frogs croaking; these sounds lulled our fair adventurers to sleep.

Geunier arose at first light and was eager to continue his journey. He bid Arbour rise and he immediately did so. In the morning Arbour and his mistress did much to get ready to leave for King Arthur's court. They adorned themselves in the richest garments they had and mounted mighty steeds. The travelers set out, bidding the surrounding forest and the splendid castle of the meadow farewell. Arbour and his lady took a path to the left and Geunier went to the right. They said goodbye at this point. I tell no further of Arbour but that he gave himself to King Arthur and he was very grateful to have such a worthy knight in his court; for Abour became a knight of the round table and was very admirable. Meanwhile, Geunier continued his journey until he was even deeper into the wild forest.

The knight rode along a path that was hardly recognizable. Thorns and brambles covered it so that his horse's feet bleed from all the thorns. The forest was a dark place and inhospitable to those custom to court life. So thick were the branches covering the path that he had to cut away at them with his sword. His horse whinnied and resisted and a turbulent wind arose; that violent storm made gusts of wind and rain fall ceaselessly. There was little else to do but sit and wait for the storm to abate. He found a cave where he could rest, leaving his unfortunate horse just outside, tied to a pine tree. He made a fire and kept warm the whole night, marveling at the hard rain. In the morning he rose to continue his adventure. He said his prayers and rode at a fierce pace along the same path. For the storm had cut down many of the branches that had hindered his movement the night before.

Geunier went on for three days without finding man or beast. Indeed, he went without food for that time and was very weary because of it. In fact, he quite lost the path altogether. On the third day, at midday, he spotted a trail leading to a brook. Then, near the brook, he saw a wide open valley that was very green and beautiful. Then a sturdy wooden bridge took him over the brook and he came before a large, well positioned castle. It had well fortified ramparts and thick stone walls.

The place seemed uninhabited and completely empty. No bird sang or person walked around the place. Geunier tied his horse to a pine tree and walked towards the hall. The hall was very beautiful and well maintained. The doors of the keep were completely open, inviting him in. Inside the hall a massive table was set with all kinds of food; fish, fowl and game of every kind was set on the table. There was plenty of bread and wine too. Geunier eagerly ate and drank merrily all by himself for he had not done so for three days.

While he was eating a lady peaked through the door of the hall. Geunier noticed her and shouted: "Hello, lady, come in and tell me where you come from. I've seen no one at this place but the food is delicious. Did you prepare it?" The lady came through the door. She was beautiful but very weak for she seemed not to have been well nourished. Her gaunt looks and wide eyes were full of fright. She was also wearing the same tattered clothes that seemed to have been on her for months. They were ripped in every place and her naked body showed plainly. There wasn't much of her but bones for she was so very thin.

Geunier pitied her but saw great beauty in her eyes. Indeed, her impoverished clothing and worn face showed signs of incomprehensible suffering. The lady said to him: "I warn you not to eat any longer, but be on your guard! You are in the keep of a very powerful giant. No knight who has entered this place has escaped to tell of it. I would arm right away for he could be back at any minute. You may be able to escape if you leave now!"

Geunier gazed at the lady in wonder for she was very pretty despite her appearance. For Geunier could tell she was noble of heart and soul. He said: "I thank you, but I will not run away from a fight. When he comes here I will kill him for making you suffer so." Geunier, armed and eager, faced a broad window looking out towards the castle gate. Then footsteps sounded like thunder and the whole hall shook. The iron gate flung into the air as the giant passed that way. He had just returned from hunting and had three stags slung over his back.

The lady cried: "Here he comes; it is such a shame that a fair knight like you will be killed in such a foul way!" The giant ran towards the keep, smelling the human visitors. He was massive and held a big cudgel. When he saw Geunier's horse tied to the pine tree he hit it with his cudgel so that it split in half. When Geunier saw this he was completely enraged. He immediately drew his sword and rushed down the steps of the hall towards the giant, wishing to avenge his horse for this great wrong. He was absolutely furious that his noble steed had been killed: "That will be avenged, my lady. For that steed was very good and kind." He gave a mighty blow of his ivory horn, making the giant cower, for he had never heard such a noble sound. Then the good knight charged towards him, thrusting his sword into his leg with all his might.

The giant waved his massive cudgel about and tried to hit Geunier. Surely a single blow from it would be the last needed for there would be nothing left of him afterwards. Yet, Geunier was very agile and a cunning swordsman. The giant was slow and encumbered with the weight of the cudgel.

Geunier dodged the first attack and struck the giant a well calculated blow by the thrust of his sword. Although, he missed his desired target and, instead of grazing his body tore the flesh from his heel. This was very painful for the beast, who howled in anguish. He charged at Geunier and brought down a second mighty stroke upon him but Geunier dodged it again. This time, the cudgel hit the rocks and shattered into many pieces.

Relieved, Geunier countered his stroke with a mighty blow, he let his sword come down upon the giant so that it cut off his ear. Then it came down even more and cleft his arm from the body. At the last, a great deal of flesh was torn from his waist so that his ribs and liver showed plainly. The giant fell to the ground in a swoon when this happened. After he had completely fainted from the blood and pain, Geunier drove his blade into his chest. Then the giant died.

Geunier rejoiced at killing the evil beast. The lady had watched the whole thing from the window in the hall; she was quite astonished and felt all the more joy, for she had been freed. She ran out to the field and embraced Geunier. She bid him come back to the hall and he humbly agreed, for he was tired. She took off his armor gently and washed his wounds, staunching the bleeding where it was needed. Then she put on him a scarlet mantle that she retrieved from the hall. She waited on him, tending to his wounds and bringing him back to good health through the course of the night. They retired to the hall and went to eat. What surprised him was that she refused to eat beside him, as it had not been the custom of that place that she should eat more than a morsel, as a slave dog would be given by its master.

Geunier realized the lady was impoverished and used to intense servitude. He bid the lady to sit by him: "My dear, have no fear. Eat with me and enjoy the fruits of the castle. For what is here is now yours. I hereby make you queen of this whole place." The lady was very grateful to Geunier. They sat together, eating and drinking into the late hours of the night. When Geunier was finally exhausted from the day and his wounds he took to bed. She prepared a marvelous bed for him that was very comfortable and waiting for him to fall asleep before leaving.

In the morning he rose and found the lady waiting on him. She immediately dressed him in the same mantle and made him very comfortable. He was quite delighted and fond of the girl, for nothing was missing! He donned the garment and was so happy to have the lady's attention. Know that Geunier was a very noble man, and always returned a favor. He saw that the lady was beautiful despite the condition she was in. He asked, "What is your name?" and she replied, "They call me Irel." she responded. They looked into each others eyes and gazed for some time.

It seemed as if their spirits were intertwining at the sight of one another. Both Irel and Geunier were struck by the look of the other. It was as if they had consumed a great potion of love, like Isolde and Tristan, and could no longer be without one another. So powerful are the eyes when they lock with one another for they are truly the windows to the soul! Geunier took her by the hand and went to the spring behind the castle where he bid her to wash. She washed herself and became clean. Then he put an ermine mantle upon her naked, fair skin. She was comforted by this. For he took great care of her and worshiped her above all else but God.

When they returned from the spring, Geunier asked her: "That ugly giant killed my very noble steed. Do you know if there is another horse here?" The lady replied: "Indeed there is. In the cellar there are two beautiful horses. They are well fed. For the giant slew two knights who came here before and he kept the horses." Geunier and the lady went to the cellar and looked at the horses. They were black and marvelously healthy. Geunier said to her: "These are very powerful steeds. I'm much delighted. Let us take to the fields. There is something I will show you." So Geunier called upon the servants of the castle to saddle the horses. When everything was prepared they rode out through the castle gate and into the fields. They arrived at a village near the castle. This village had been destitute because the giant often pillaged it, taking all their wealth and even killing some of the people. Everything they had gained had been taken, so this people were full of grief.

When Geunier arrived with the lady the village people were shocked to see him, for he was a proud knight and he beamed with light as if God watched over him.

Geunier gathered all the people and spoke to them, saying: "The evil giant of these lands has been slain. Irel, such a beautiful lady that she is, will be your queen from this day forth. For she is more fit to rule and govern than any. Since it is now her lands, I bid all of you, by the power of King Arthur my lord, to diligently work for her. Each should work according to their craft. One shall work the land, tilling away, and provide crops to be stored. Another shall hunt in the forest and bring back game. Some shall sow wondrous garments. Others shall craft weapons to defend the land while others will become soldiers, learning the ways of battle. In this way we will grow strong. Know that this land will prosper because of Irel's wisdom. This place is but a mustard seed but it will become the great tree of life as it grows by your labour. Do not fear oppression, for each will be paid his due. The fruits of labour will readily come back to you if you but work hard and provide for others."

When Geunier had finished speaking the whole village yelled out, rejoicing. "All hail Irel, queen of the land!" Alas, they all celebrated and a feast was called. All the servants were summoned and they put together a sumptuous spread where everyone ate. Geunier had the squires set the table and serve the dishes. A single loaf of bread was multiplied to a hundred, a single fish by one hundred, and all who were there ate to their fulfillment; this was done because God had blessed Geunier, Irel and the people there. When everyone had eaten, they set to work, marveling at the many miracles they saw. Hunters went to the forest, sowers sowed, reapers reaped and the harvest was good that year. Never again would those villagers know hunger. For their lives had been wasted many years by the giant; he had kept them in poverty and never encouraged them to rise above their station. Indeed, under Irel's rule, the village prospered greatly. Geunier was sure to establish the Christian law in the land so that the people would derive much strength by their faith. This was done in accordance with the customs of the time and everyone was wondrously happy at the grace they found in God.

After Geunier established governance in the village they rested in the castle. Although there were very few days that they spent without labour. For Geunier helped the villagers plant seeds in the fields, hunt game and the like. One day a serf from the field came to the hall and spoke to Geunier, saying: "There is talk of a phantom white stag who has been in the forest. It is a great mystery and everyone is saying that this creature is from the otherworld. Indeed, if we could capture it that would be a great marvel. God grant you success in this adventure!"

Geunier was pensive for a while before speaking. He looked at the fair Irel and then spoke plainly: "My lady, do you wish to have the head of the white stag as a gift?" Irel was humbled. She had gone from being a lowly servant girl of a treacherous giant to a powerful queen. Know that the head of the white stag was the most prized possession that any maiden or lady could wish for; for it was a miracle and marvel to behold the white stag. She was much delighted and encouraged Geunier to pursue the white stag: "Take with you my dog who will help you find your mark. Indeed, if you bring me his head I will give you my love." Geunier was most eager above all else to have her love. He crossed himself and was delighted. Immediately, he sent for his horse and sword. Without bow or arrow he rode deep into the forest after the white stag.

Irel's dog had better hunting instincts than he did It wasn't long before he spotted the white stag and cornered it in a mountain pass. Geunier leapt from his horse and beheaded the stag so swiftly. Its red blood covered the white fur and Geunier's blade. When he had killed it a voice called out: "Take this treasure home to your lady, for she is very deserving of it. Know that, even though you found her a servant, she actually comes from a royal line. She has told you little, but her father was the Lord of that castle. He was the rightful king and she is the rightful heir. It was only when the giant seized the land that he killed her whole family and made her a slave. She would never tell you about it for she is forever shamed by that wicked giant. Though, it is ordained that you will go to her, marry her, and set forth a noble line to rule these lands."

Geunier was shocked by these words and tried to question the voice but it said no more. He took the head of the stag and attached it to his saddle, scaling down the treacherous mountain back to the castle. He was delighted with the kill and excited to share it with his love.

He prayed to God and gave thanks for such success. When he rode back to the castle and entered through the gate with the white stag head attached to his saddle a company of squires helped him unsaddle and removed his armor. When he arrived he sounded the ivory horn. The ground shook and Irel marveled at it. Her legs shook and the earth quaked so that she revealed her thighs to him. All the people in the land heard the horn and marveled at Geunier's strength too.

He had the head of the white stag laid on a golden grail and taken before his lady. She rejoiced and a great feast was prepared. The stag's head was sacred and many, astonished, prayed before it. It was considered a miracle that the white stag was found. At this time, since the people were so enamored, Geunier brought the love of Christ to the people. He did this not forcefully but with great charm and goodwill. For he was very generous and gave all he had to the people. They were all baptized in the name of the Holy Spirit, as was the custom then. He had a church constructed near a beautiful garden that they made. It was done right where the giant was killed. They put up a movement and etched an inscription that read: "The giant was killed here by the grace of God and the power of Geunier's ivory horn." The castle became full of the love of Christ for Geunier had preformed so many miracles.

It comes as little surprise that Irel and Geunier fell deeply in love. That same night when the stag head was brought to the castle they decided to marry. It was in due time that they both overflowed with passion for one another to the point where they couldn't hide it any longer. They both were boiling with infatuation so that they could do nothing but sing at the tops of their lungs the song of love.

Geunier was a great harpist. He bid a craftsman make him one of gold. When this was done he plucked at the strings for many hours and sang his song of love for the beautiful Irel. She often heard him from the other room and wept a stream of tears. For she felt that he would never truly love her until he knew her secret. For she adored him more than any man for freeing her from the treacherous giant. Little did she know that he already knew her secret! The voice had already told it to him when he killed the stag.

When the feast of the white stag had ended the two lovers retired to the same bed chamber. A rich silk blanket was laid for them. Irel was on the edge of the bed in tears. Her head was lowered and she cried. The sorrow felt by Geunier, to see his lover this way, was unimaginable. "Tell me what ails you my sweet. I will surely fix it. Not for a thousand evil deeds could your love be forsaken. Whatever it is, I forgive you." Irel responded: "I grant you my love willingly; but I'm not worthy of one so noble and courteous. I lived in this place my whole life. When I was sixteen, the giant came here. He killed the king of this castle, who was my father. He also killed my sister and brothers, who tried to fight him in combat. Since then the place has remained desolate and the people distraught. The giant has done wicked things to me; making me a terrible sinner. He has defiled me so that I am not a maiden any longer, he took the flower of my soul away! This horrible rape has scarred me. I am so grateful for you because you have saved my people. Though how could I love one so noble after what's been done to me?"

In this way Irel confessed all that had happened to her since the giant came to that place. When Geunier heard of it he was full of anger at the giant but happy he had made him suffer so much before killing him.

Geunier remarked that he had been told of her nobility by a voice on the mountain when he killed the white stag. He said that there was nothing to worry for he loved her all the more for her beauty and nobility. He had her crowned in an opulent ceremony that same month, on the saint's day. At her coronation the whole village came and celebrated. For they loved the queen dearly for all she

213

suffered. Know that she was freed of her sins by a holy man and, since Geunier loved her so, he married her. They had four children who grew up to be very strong knights. They all went to King Arthur and swore allegiance. From their line came the fiercest warriors of all Briton who did so many mighty deeds of prowess they are endless to recount.

That land grew so much in prosperity that King Arthur visited them and held the great feast of St. John there every year where he held counsel with all his barons. Such was the splendor of the castle and the prosperity of the people that sowed the lands. Alas, so beautiful was the tale of Geunier and Irel that it makes me have hope for the world. In their story is such magical love, creation and wonder. For evil is always rightly killed and the good rise again. Sick souls can repent and evil is rooted out like a weed from the garden. Geunier and Irel were given the kingdom of heaven and prospered one hundred fold for their good deeds. Since my heart is filled with the passion of the two lovers I will briefly recount a part of Geunier's song on the harp. It went like this:

*Fair Dame, where have you gone?*
*At night I hear weeping,*
*Tears falling as a stream,*
*Pour forth your heart's content,*
*Sing me you're suffering,*
*Wash in the spring your sin,*
*You are the swan vessel,*
*Prodding along a boat,*
*Carrying my soul far,*
*Into the misty sea,*
*Where do you take my heart?*
*Where you go I follow,*
*Even to certain death,*
*Greatly I weep for love,*
*What a faithless gamble,*
*A bleeding wound unhealed,*
*There is no remedy,*
*The harp is my comfort,*
*Console me with your warmth,*

*Let the horn sound, we fight!*
*I'll quickly don my arms,*
*You are safe my sweet love,*
*No harm will befall you,*
*I'll happily die now,*
*When you have become queen,*
*My love always endures,*
*For it is in my soul,*
*Crying out in worship,*
*My love is like a rock,*
*It is constant in rain,*
*Wind howls but it is still,*
*Nothing can dislodge it,*
*So I commend my heart,*
*Keep it from the devil,*
*Let it grow as a tree,*
*In loves marvelous land!*

# 27 CLADMANDU AND THE DWARF

At this time in Logres a knight from King Arthur's table round set out for adventure. He was a kind, strong and courteous knight that always upheld chivalry; though he made a very small mistake with grave consequences! A maiden on the side of the road was horribly distressed; her knight had been slain! Yet the foolish Cladmandu passed her in a full gallop without regarding her in the least. His pride led him to believe that he was seeking more perilous adventures of import.

The maiden was weeping for her dead lover, who had just had a lance lodged deep into his chest; it is no surprise she was in great need of relief! Cladmandu failed to stop to help the maiden who was clearly troubled and for this he suffered, which is the essence of this tale. For a knight should always avenge a maiden when the cause is just. This maiden who was so wrongly snapped by the proud knight was very powerful and had the ability to cast wild enchantments.

Make no doubt, she cursed Cladmandu for his wrong. Indeed, at this time in Logres, it was a great folly for a knight to pass a maiden without greeting her. The maiden yelled out to him: "Cursed are you, most faithless knight. May the first person you greet change shapes with you!" Cladmandu did not heed these words in the least and swiftly continued down the road, feeling he had many other busy things to accomplish. But no one likes a busybody who gets nothing done! Such was his state, that he pranced around like an exotic belly dancer, doing nothing but shimmer in his fancy arms.

Our faithless knight ventured deep into the forest until he came upon a damsel with her lover. They were just newly married and, make no doubt, were deeply in love. Yet there was something Cladmandu noticed that seemed disconcerting. The damsel was absolutely gorgeous with the fairest skin and most comely features; the knight with her, however, was a dwarf! His back was hunched over and his face all twisted. He had all his armor arranged to fit his little body and carried a lance that was four times his height. He snarled as Cladmandu past him. Cladmandu, recalling his former discourtesy was quick to greet them: "Greetings, may God protect you!" He shouted out. They were much comforted by his words, for a great marvel occurred then.

Cladmandu slowly began to shrink in size. His armor loosened so that he could barely fit into it. In no time he had become a dwarf! Though he was still as strong as ever an able to defeat knights; the damsel had had her sweet revenge. As for the dwarf who was with his lover, he was returned to his former state. Make no mistake, it was now known throughout the land why that lady had married a dwarf, for when the curse was lifted he turned into the most handsome fellow they had ever seen. He had long blonde hair and a fair, handsome face that any lady could love for all time!

It was really no wonder that lady had married him, for she knew that eventually he would return to the lovely, handsome man she once fell so deeply in love with. When the damsel saw that he was back to his former appearance she was incredibly excited and embraced her lover most dearly. Know that this dwarf was a valiant knight and the son of a king.

This happy exchange between the lovers was opposed by the grief felt by our unlucky Cladmandu. For he realized his plight and sorrow filled him full. "Blasted damsel! She cursed me and now I cannot return to court. I am an unlucky dwarf and will suffer greatly for it!" Cladmandu had become a dwarf, and he struggled in the saddle for he had been accustomed to a bit more height. He rode into the forest, shamed and dismayed: "How can I ever return to court again, looking like this? They will laugh at me!" He began to weep and anyone who might have seen him then would have felt great pity.

As he ventured into the forest a group of four knights were along the path and they happened to be beating up a poor, helpless maiden. The maiden was in tears and cried for help. Cladmandu was very sore to see this and had a deep desire to atone for his lack of courtesy before. He called out: "Let your hands off her for she doesn't deserve to be hit by you wicked men; you call yourself men of good conduct but shame is with you. You are

217

merely servants of the devil and if you take her maiden-hood it will be certain that hell will greet you, for there is no greater sin!"

When the knights realized he was a dwarf the roared with laughter: "Do you think you're going to do anything about it? And why are you on a charger with a great big lance? Shouldn't you have a mule and a rod? They berated Cladmandu in this way and continued: "Look, my friends, we have a dwarf after the maiden's heart. How would you save her? Your arms are but stubs; I could throw you from your saddle with ease." Cladmandu, who was still strong as ever, sorely rebuked these knights. He was so incensed by their remarks that he spurred towards them in a quick gallop.

He exchanged lance thrusts with the first knight and gave him a wicked blow that snared him under the ventail, ripping open his neck. The knight was helpless and fell to the ground, gushing out blood in the throes of death. Then he flung himself into combat with a great rage; like a wild boar he set off at a gallop plunging his lance into the chest of the other enemy. The lance went into the chest and out the other side, bursting his heart to pieces. The knights were all confounded, for Cladmandu fought with the strength of a knight but appeared as a dwarf. Then Cladmandu drew his sword and began hammering the most mighty strokes upon his enemies. He made one of them fly from his horse and into a nearby thicket. They saw his might and were terrified. One tried to oppose him but received a fatal wound: Cladmandu's sword hammered down and split his skull in two. The others fled into the forest, shocked at what they had seen.

Cladmandu had saved the maiden, who, though in great pain, arose to thank him. Cladmandu put her on the neck of his horse and rode with her to a nearby hermitage. She was healed of her wounds there. Cladmandu stayed the week at the place seeking counsel from the hermit; for he was quite certain he had been cursed for his sins. Then he confessed of all his sins, especially pride and promised that he would always help a maiden in distress even if he was preoccupied with another mission.

Meanwhile, the knight who had long been a dwarf was rejoicing at his change in fortune. He took his wife in his arms, for now he could fully embrace her the whole way round! They set off to King Arthur's court and celebrated. King Arthur, who had knighted the dwarf previously, did not recognize him in the least. The maiden had to do some serious explaining before her faithful lover could be properly received; for his first appearance at court resulted in Kay mocking him. To Sir Kay's shame, that same knight was more comely and handsome than any other. But Kay kept his mouth shut this time, for he saw plainly that he was a very handsome knight.

As I mentioned, Cladmandu stayed the week at the hermitage. He confessed of his sins and heard mass every morning. He greatly hoped that this would eradicate the curse upon him. After seeing the maiden fully healed and purifying his soul he set off into the forest. The maiden was sure to thank him and she set off for her father's castle, which was nearby.

When Cladmandu set out on the trail again all the forest creatures had to suffer his bitter lamentations: "Oh cruel fate! How you have turned the wheel of fortune. From the highest peaks of grace I was at the court of the valiant King Arthur. And now I am loathing existence in this perilous forest and i'm in a horrible condition. I rot in hell on earth. See how you made my excitement turn to anguish? I'm a dwarf! Look at how stubby my arms are. What if I met a lover, do you think she would have me like this? How could I ever return to my lord's court? I would be horribly shamed and laughed at. My enemies would destroy me. I need to be cured of this, but how could I? The fair maiden certainly did a number on me. I will be forever scarred. Who knew how important it was to be courteous to passing damsels? Who knew they had such power?"

At this time, Cladmandu was deep in the forest; in fact he was quite lost. The place he was at was in Logres and it was called the Darnant forest. It was full of magic and it was largely known that no man who ventured too far in would ever return. He kept riding and was seemingly transported by the evil spirits who lived there to many

219

places. No one really knows where he went. Some say Brittany and others that he stayed in Darnant forest. It is clear that he went mad and only recovered his wit long enough to defeat knights who mocked him. One day, as he rode aimlessly with tears streaming down his face, he called upon God to help him. He had long forgot God and recognized that his plea for help was an important step in the right direction.

At that time he heard a voice in the trees: "Greetings Cladmandu, do not be frightened! Maybe you would recognize who is speaking to you if we were in the court. For I long to be there and it seems, after being so long adrift, I have lost all common courtesy so that I may not be recognized. No matter, I have important news for you, and it may alleviate some of your, how should I say it delicately, growing pains." Cladmandu heard the voice but knew not where it came from. So he replied: "Where are you, man? Can you show yourself?" And the voice returned: "I cannot. For I have been imprisoned by my lady love in this strong tower that is invisible to man. I will forever be locked here. You are the last person to hear me. Don't you recognize my voice? Come on, I saved King Arthur many times and even arranged his birth. Hello?"

Than Cladmandu swore with all his life that this was the voice of Merlin. "Are you really Merlin? The king is worried sick about your absence. Please, counsel me so I can remove this horrible curse!" Merlin said that it was he. Then he went about telling him what needed to be done. "Tell the king that I will not be able to return; though you can send him my good graces. Know that all has been written and chronicled-both what has happened and what will come-by the good and honorable clerk Blaise. As for the curse upon you, know that it will be removed when you plead with the maiden. You need only return to the same place you found her who cursed you; when find her be sure to greet her this time!"

So Cladmandu set off towards that place, newly invigorated with hope. Merlin's grief and imprisonment by his lady love was disheartening but no one could do anything about it. He was the wisest man in Logres but a fool in the ways of love. Such was the irony! He told all his

220

magical enchantments to that lady who used them to imprison him for fear that he would one day ask for her love. An old man isn't wise to wed a young girl, for she will surely betray him at the first chance!

As I was saying, Cladmandu set off into the woods until he neared the place he had met the maiden that so openly cursed him. He kept his eyes wide and feared that all his musing was a distraction. His thoughts went adrift and at one point or another he thought he might have missed the maiden all together. Soon enough, he reached the same copse of trees where he had gone passed her in a hurry to nowhere.

Suddenly, behind an oak tree in the distance, he saw that same maiden and she was being attacked by a knight. The knight was wickedly upbraiding her and even hit her. Cladmandu galloped towards them, fully enraged. He thought that now was his chance to redeem himself. "You will suffer for that slap, worthless knight! To think you call yourself one of us when you treat a lady so!" Alas, little did he know that it was all a spectacle and he was being toyed with again. That damsel was very clever and had arranged this test with the knight to see what Cladmandu would do. She was clever and had the knight do her bidding.

The damsel cried out: "Help me, Cladmandu." Then she whispered into her fellows ear so that the other could not hear: "Enter into combat with this knight, but know that I will cast a spell on you so that you will not be hurt in the least." The maiden used her enchantment so that the knight could not be wounded and he willingly agreed to challenge the dwarf. Then the two galloped towards one another. Cladmandu sunk his spurs deep into his horse so that blood spurted out its sides. The horse was sweating and charing forward, giving all it had. So much force was behind him that he could have brought down a stone wall with the impact.

This clash of arms created a most thunderous din. Cladmandu sent his lance into the knights shield and he tumbled over his horse's rump and into the ground. Cladmandu dismounted and tied his horse to an oak before taking out his sword; a swift exchange of sword strokes then began. Both knights were admirable fighters. Now the knight was protected by magic and could not be wounded. Meanwhile, Cladmandu was getting hit on all sides and bled from a wound on the shoulder. The knight's sword went through his hauberk and sank into his flesh all the way to the bone. This made him full of rage. So Cladmandu started dealing out blows in a storm of anger. He knocked the knight to the ground and assailed him further, ripping off his helm and hitting him in the face with the hilt of his sword. Each stroke had the power to tear apart a horse but did no damage, to the knight's confusion. That enchantment kept the knight afloat who was utterly defeated.

Eventually he was so tired of fighting that he said: "Let me talk to you for a moment, knight." Cladmandu gladly accepted the pause in combat for he was bleeding all over the grass by now. "Tell me your name." Cladmandu responded: "I have never hid it from anyone who asks, not for shame or for pride, I am called Cladmandu. I am a knight of the Table Round. And who are you?" The knight shamefully responded: "I am no one of consequence. Indeed, the maiden sent me upon you to test your will. I am invulnerable by a spell she cast on me. Even so, you have still defeated me, for I am exhausted. Know that I will go and tell of your name and your fame will be spread through the land. The two knights made peace and embraced.

Eventually the maiden sauntered over to them, after the sparks had stopped flying, and she had a sly grin on her face when she said: "Cladmandu, do you repent of your offense and discourtesy to me? Don't you know that every maiden should be consoled by a knight even if he is in duress himself?"

Cladmandu got down on his knees and laid himself before the maiden, handing her his sword. Then he pleaded: "I am horribly shamed and give myself entirely to your will. Know that never again will I so helplessly ignore a maiden who is in distress. Forgive me and know that I am yours." So the maiden, happy at his words, responded: "Here is your oath so that you shall never commit this

222

wrong again: You are to swear by these relics that you will always suffer a maiden's call at any time. Also, you will see to it that all maidens are honored and held in the highest esteem. If you fail to do this I will turn you back into a dwarf for the rest of your life."

Cladmandu swore to do so on one condition. The condition was that, should a maiden be wicked, he would rightly not suffer her cause. The damsel agreed to this and, suddenly, he returned to his former state. When Cladmandu received his former limbs and body back he rejoiced. Alas, Cladmandu was a dwarf no longer. He bid the maiden farewell, returned to the court of King Arthur and recounted this tale leaving out no details. When the knights of the Table Round had heard the oath he was made to swear they all in turn took the same oath. For the knights of King Arthur's court all counted it as one of their key attributes of chivalry to always honor maidens. Indeed, for many years knights that were so worthy always upheld the good and righteous doing right to maidens everywhere.

# 28 THE ONE MAN SIEGE

I'll tell you now of two fierce knights that were so esteemed in feats of prowess that they singlehandedly besieged an entire fortress! This was never done before and considered a wondrous marvel. Our friendly knights were the very pillars of chivalry and went into combat with red roses emblazoned on their pure white shields. They were bounding in largesse and courtesy, truly the best of the romantic heroes of that age; for they were truly honorable and hoped only to serve holy God and church foremost and good maidens thereafter.

Hear how they achieved the impossible and be encouraged that you my take it upon yourself to attack your foes relentlessly. Never did two knights fear combat less. Know that our fair knights had been on adventure for some time in the forest; they were weary from extensive travel too. For they sought after the wicked men of the forest who did the King evil and were traitors. They stood for that which chivalry loathed; that is: debasement of women, lasciviousness, cruelty, deception, idolatry and a slew of other things that make the soul foul smelling.

It was a marvelous surprise to them when they came upon a well positioned fortress upon a glade; the battlement were of colored marble and there was a deep, wide moat around it. The handsome and the beautifully wrought castle was a fine example of a well founded fortress for it was also incredibly well provisioned with food and harbored a number of people. Yet, even then, the people of that place were full of evil, and it was no doubt that the place was long overlooked! The surrounding meadows and farmland were a marvel to look on, for their had never been a finer land. Meanwhile, the red and white towers loomed into the clouds as the bright daylight made the whole place sparkle as if it were bejeweled.

Tors and Ares, for those were the names of our two valiant knights, saw the black banner hung atop the tower and were dismayed. "Alas, it is the enemy. They have such a great castle, let is take it for the glory and honor of the King!" For at this time in the forest a great series of battles were taking place. The knights of the black flag had done a really bad deed: they took advantage of maidens and raped many of them; this had scourged the lands with sin and suffering. They were not knights but demons who were defiling the country.

Tors and Ares, as was right, set out to purify the place and were very eager to do so. Tors blew upon his ivory horn so that the whole forest thundered. They sounded the charge, making haste to defeat their foes. They ran upon the drawbridge in front of the castle, picking out three knights outside the rampart. As our brave knights went to combat they rode in a full gallop, feverish to draw bled from the enemy. And, make no doubt, they were well met. Three knights were outside the castle wall near the shepherd's lodge which was constructed in the Welsh manner with many interwoven branches.

When these knights saw the two approaching a great combat ensued. Tors tilted his lance and charged forward, launching the knight from his horse and into the moat so he drowned. Indeed, Tors was sitting upon a strong Gascon steed that was mighty and swift. The second knight was unhorsed in a similar way, he fell hard to the ground and his helmet flew into the trees. The knight took a perilous tumble and was so stunned he could hardly rise.

Tors came off his horse, drew his sword and sent his head flying right after the helmet! Ares plunged his lance into the other knight's hauberk and through the other side of him. The lance broke and he just barely stayed in his stirrups. The knight was sure to die but had enough wherewithal to turn his horse around and gallop back into the castle. When Ares realized the man fled for the castle he went hurling after him on his steed. Though, at the same time that Ares leapt in after the knight, the gate came crushing down behind him. Before Ares realized he was captured inside he delivered a blow to the fleeing knight that struck him to the ground and tore through his flesh so that the blood flowed copiously. Then, when he realized his predicament, he beheaded the dead knight and sent it flying through a window to the great hall; all the people inside shrieked in horror when this happened.

Ares was quickly surrounded by ten knights, fully armed. They came at him, angered that he had killed their friend. He resisted honorably for being so outnumbered. He put his back to the stone wall for protection and raised his shield high to protect himself from the flurry of blows that they delivered. They pounded him ceaselessly until he was weary and bruised. Though he struck back with great might, hacking and hewing off legs and arms. He killed four knights before finally yielding as their prisoner.

Tors watched in despair, with no way of getting in to save his best friend. "Don't worry, Ares, I won't leave here without you." He was very distraught that his fellow was captured inside the keep. Now the man who Tors had slain outside happened to have been the lord of that castle; his wife, the queen, was very saddened to hear he was dead.

She boiled with rage and desired vengeance. She planned to keep Ares in the courtyard so that he would freeze to death, so the angry knights surrounded him dealing blows so that he was badly bruised and wounded by the end of it. Fortunately, a maiden of hers, who had some power of persuasion, saved his life. She secretly hated the queen and thereby wished to use the knights to destroy her. She pleaded: "Rather than let him starve and freeze in the courtyard, wounded as he is, it would be right to give him lodging and good comfort; for his fellow is outside and we may learn more of his kin before slaying him." These arguments seemed reasonable to the queen and so the good Ares was imprisoned in the highest tower. The lady, whose name was Silva, sought to feed him and take care of him during that time. She was to become reliable and true to those knights, helping them storm the castle.

Meanwhile, the valiant Tors refused to leave the place until he had rescued his friend. Fortunately there was a shepherd in the area who had a great many sheep. He befriended this man and he, in turn, fed him; for that shepherd also hated the lord of the land and was very glad he had been killed. "The lord you killed was a very wicked man. He raped and held captive women from the town that he took to liking. He also shared very little of his wealth with the people." Such were the grievances against that man. So the shepherd helped Tors. Tors was delighted, he slew one of the sheep and had a great fire made in front of the castle. He camped out and roasted the big haunch and ate with contentment. As he feasted he yelled out to the inhabitants of the castle: "I won't leave without a fight. You can be sure that you are now besieged by a single man."

After he ate he gathered the lances of the dead knights and planted them into the ground so that he could have them at his will if needed. He set on the ground a large amount of hay for a bed and used the shepherd's lodge when he needed to keep himself safe from the weather. In this way he created a very nice house for himself to endure anything during the siege. Though he was to face many challenges.

The next day a messenger of the evil knight's of the forest came, hoping to summon the knight to battle. Yet, he was very unfortunate to come that way. For Tors came out from the shepherds house yelling all kinds of profanity: "Stop where you are, rider, let me get my hauberk on! You aren't coming any closer to the castle." He hustled out in full armor and took up a lance: "You will joust with me, also, tell me the message you have." The messenger was fully confounded by all this and refused to deliver any message at all. Tors galloped towards him and thrust his lance so that the rider went flying to the ground after going through the air a full ten feet! When he tried to get up Tor wrestled him to the ground, grabbed his sword, and plunged it into his chest, for this one was a bit squirmy. The Queen had watched all this from the safety of the tower and bitterly lamented her fate. She was sure no good would come of it.

Not realizing what had happened, many other knight's of the black banner tried to entreat the lord of the castle; for a great war was going on at this time and he had been summoned by his brother. Yet, all the messengers and groups of knights who went to the castle were killed by Tors! By the second week he had amassed a pile of bodies. Ten knights had come to that castle and were killed by Tors who, seeing them, would not let them pass into the keep. Whether they came in groups or alone, Tors refused them entry to the castle and did combat with them. The Queen grew more and more bitter, unsure what to do.

The Queen took counsel and devised a plan to kill Tors. She declared that they ought to ride out and fight him. She sent ten of her knights out to attack Sir Tors in the night when he was asleep. Though Tors wasn't so easily fooled. He slept in full armor and was very alert. He awoke easily when he heard the loud drawbridge and thunderous clanking of the ten knights in armor. He hurled his lance at the man in the front of the company so that he went straight through his helmet, eye and out through his head.

Then he mounted quickly and charged furiously into the thick of the press, knocking four of the men off the drawbridge into the moat with the chest of his charger. They fell a long ways before drowning in the water. When five had been killed so quickly, the others fled back into the castle. Though he didn't let them off so easily. He struck another two with his sword, hacking away an arm and beheading the other. Such was the prowess of Sir Tors. By this time his shield was torn to bits and his sword well bloodied; but he continued to fight for he greatly desired to free his kin. He could always use a shield from one of the dead he had slain. By now there was a great pile of dead bodies that he considered a badge of honor; he had them arranged in a way that every passerby wondered with terror.

The Queen was now completely beside herself. She decided that she would send a secret message to her brother in law so that he would come to lift the siege. For they were nearly starved by a single knight! There was an exit from the castle that was a secret; this postern in the back may have proven vital to the safety of the besieged. She had a boy equipped with a message and prepared to send him out of the postern.

Yet, before doing so, she asked her ever too trusted Silva to make sure that Tors was nowhere near. She feared that if he spotted the messenger word would never get out. "My Queen, let me go outside first and make sure the dreadful knight is nowhere nearby." Silva exited the postern and, instead of making sure Tors was not around, she called to him. Tors arose from his sleep and listened eagerly for word: "Hide near this postern, for very soon a messenger will come out of it. You must kill him or he will get the brother of the lord you slew and he will bring a large number of knights to kill you." Tors was relieved and incredibly grateful at this news and swore he would do as she bid. The messenger left the postern that same hour and, as he exited, Tors grabbed him by the neck and lopped off his head. He made a fire that evening outside the shepherds house and burned the message. It was done so quietly that the Queen was quite sure the message had been successfully sent out.

The next day yet another messenger came to the castle. When he approached the front gate Tors stopped him. When he demanded the letter and the messenger refused Tors hit him so hard with the back of his sword that his neck broke. He took the letter and read it, learning news that was most displeasing. The letter said that, in two days, the brother in law of the Queen would arrive with sixty knights. He was obviously coming because no summons from the court had been answered for several weeks. Since it had been so long without any communication they were very worried that ill had befallen the castle. How right they were!

Tors needed to act quickly or he would surely lose the siege and his companion Ares, who had now been imprisoned for some time. Fortunately, Silva had been taking good care of him. If not, he surely would not have lasted! So Tors contrived a most clever plan. That next morning he lay down in front of the castle as if completely dead. He was quite the actor and it truly seemed he was dead. The gatekeeper from the tower saw this and summoned the Queen: "My queen, it seems that the lone knight outside is dead!" The queen, suspecting a plot, was sure that he was not really dead. So she waited. Hours passed and the shepherd, seeing Tors on the ground in this way, wept. For he also felt sure that the knight was completely dead after such a glorious resistance. When the queen saw the shepherd weeping so, she realized he may actually have died. To be sure, she sent two of her best knights out to examine the body. The drawbridge was lowered and the two knights went out to inspect the feigning Tors, who deserved an award for his acting. The one man poked him with his lance three times, and know that Tors was in great pain because of it; yet he didn't show it! His only thought was that he would avenge that hurtful "tap".

Just as the knights agreed he was really dead and turned around, Tors leapt to his feet in a rage. He thrust his blade through the man's body and out the other side. Then, the other attempted to defended himself but he hammered him with a might blow that cut him from the top of the helm to the teeth. When he had beheaded the man who had poked him he felt a little better, but only a little. How gloriously was he avenged on him!

Tors dragged the senseless body from its horse and mounted it himself. Before the Queen could raise the drawbridge Tors galloped in through the gate and stormed the castle. It was the last thing she wanted: him running through the castle. He was a turbulent bull raising such a din with his mighty sword strokes and violence that everyone had no choice but to yield.

Tors made rounds through each tower and chamber, killing those who resisted. He killed a good fifteen knights that evening. He had black smoke rising around him. It was the very steam of battle. The stone of that castle was stained red all around by his fury. He rampaged about knocking men down and cutting off their limbs and sending sparks flying so that a fire of vengeance swirled around him. That is why he was called Le Tors, otherwise known as "the bull". The shepherd watched all this in wonder; he witnessed it all and later told it to the King. All he could hear were the bitter lamentations and screams from those he was killing as he made his way through the whole place.

The whole earth quaked as he stormed about in this way. It seemed as if this was Gomorrah being torn to bits by the fiery maelstrom the most omnipotent one devised of when they sinned so greatly. And the Sheppard was Lot, looking back on his former friends in horror, yet hoping to be saved himself!

When everyone was killed, including that bloody Queen, he freed Ares. "Many thanks, dear friend. I'm so well avenged too! Only, take pity on this lady, for she has

230

done well by me this whole time. I would probably be dead if she didn't do all she did." So he thanked Silva for saving his friend's life and, in turn, spared hers.

Ares and Tors, being courteous and full of the best things, made sure they had their shields repaired. Those white shields with red roses were the very center of the stage, so beautiful and amorous was the light that gleamed from them! Meanwhile, Tors was eager to introduce Ares to the shepherd, and share with him a few haunches of good meat! Suffice it to say they did another noble act before running from that place. They made sure everybody was converted to christianity.

Tors got up and shouted: "Now listen, you saw me kill a full twenty armed knights yesterday. Do you know how I did it? It wasn't by my own power, but by the power of God. So, you should take refuge in God. For if you do, miracles will happen in your life and, just as you saw me slay twenty evil spirits, so will you be able to do the impossible. Only by the grace of God can we achieve great miracles."

After that delightful speech a great celebration ensued. Everyone was pretty much miserable except for Silva, Tors and Ares. So they ate heartily and sang merrily into the late hours of the night. They sat in the great hall in the midst of a large table of brass. The pedestals were of copper and inlaid with Arcadian gold. In the hall there were many silken drapes of blue and violet embroidered with gold.

The chamber was paved with silver and lined with gilded panels. On top of the table there was beautiful silver grail. It served all the food the inhabitants could possibly desire. Everyone was completely satisfied. When the meal was finished, a light came forth from the grail. It had three flaming tongues on it and they were full of light. That grail was holy and held within it the great mystery of the trinity. Everyone was seemingly full of the Holy Spirit, rejoicing gladly and so grateful to be alive. It was a marvel to see all the people running about the castle, swearing they were full of some kind of indescribable joy that they only desired to share fervently with all.

After this great marvel, they explored about the castle for a while. Silva took them to another chamber in a separate wing of the castle. A multitude of damsels were congregated there. Many of the ladies there had toiled many hours to embroider the ermine drapes with gold. They had also done other garments and been the primary source of income for that evil Queen. They were sowing garments and seemed to be malnourished and overworked to the bone. To call them slaves would have been an understatement. The room was stuffy and they clearly slept right where the worked and that was the end of it.

When they saw the noble knights and learned the Queen was dead they were very happy. "That wicked crone has kept us trapped here, weaving garments, for far too many years. I haven't left this grimy chamber in a decade!" They gifted the knights with mantles of ermine that had little gold birds and flowers embroidered on them. It was truly the work of an artist, for they knew well how to make garments. This gift was a great delight to Ares, who found the mantles very beautiful. He said: "I'm afraid i'll be keeping that, thank you."

After they had dined the knights wondered at the mysteries in the castle. They were very relieved to have been completely healed of their wounds after the meal. They retired to another chamber with two rich beds covered with red samite and embroidered with golden flowers. They slept very well and found much comfort after all the excitement. The next day Tors and his fellow piled the bodies of the dead knights on a nearby mountain and set them on fire; to their delight they watched the evil spirits burn and fester. That fire continuously burned for forty years and was called the burning mountain thereafter. It burned for so long because it was a monument from the Holy Spirit that the evil spirits would always be punished in the flames of hell.

The next day when the large force of besiegers arrived they were distraught to find the large heap of bodies on burning mountain. The army of sixty knights thought there were many more than just two knights inside the castle for obvious reasons. They yelled out: "Come on, do combat with us now rather than endure a long siege.

You will be punished for killing our kin, however large your forces are your time is now up!"

Meanwhile, Tors and Ares had spent that whole morning in prayer, for they were completely unsure how to defeat such a large force. Know that God truly answered their pleas. For when they saw the great big force of sixty men outside the castle, they were confounded.

Yet, just as those knights set up camp next to the shepherds house in the meadow, an opposing force gathered near the forest about a bow shot length away. Know that these were all brethren of Tors and Ares, who had been searching the whole forest for them, now that they had been lost so long. In this way they were found by their fellows and their prayers to God were answered!

Thus a great battle ensued outside the castle. The knights charged into battle and a thunderous din arose on all sides. Sparks flew in different directions and lances splintered, littering the ground with pieces of shield and limbs. Blood spurted everywhere. So many were unhorsed in the fever of combat that Le Tor was getting jealous that he hadn't gotten any yet!

When Tors and Ares saw that their friends had arrived with about twenty knights. They were sorely outnumbered by the sixty attackers! They donned their armor and put those beautiful white shields with red roses around their necks. The drawbridge lowered with a great thud and the two knights galloped out into the thick of the press dealing fatal blows.

In this way Tors and Ares rode out from the gate to meet the enemy force. The enemy was bewildered by the attack from both sides. Tors thrust his lance through seven knights, unhorsing them and killing them, before taking out his sword. He did even more damage; for he decisively hammered away at the whole company so that they trembled in fear. He killed another five before taking a quick rest near a cool spring in the meadow. Ares unhorsed six with his lance, plunging it into hauberks and make the knight's fly into the air and tumble to the ground. He gathered a number of prisoners too, forcing them back into the castle after they gave up their swords. Then he assailed his opponents with his sword, lopping off heads, arms,

233

legs and making guts leak out of holes made with his sharp blade.

So powerful were these attacks that no enemy could withstand them, for they had God on their side. That was a day of great rejoicing. The women of the forest came there and proclaimed the message of good hope: "You have freed us from the evil tyrants of this forest. They were so wicked and cruel. Many times my sisters have been raped in the forest for they took advantage of us regularly. Such was their wicked disease of the flesh that they were many of them lepers. Now that we are free of them and their customs we wish you to be lord over all this land and do what thou wilt." In this way the castle was freed from all wicked customs and re-established by the good knights. They lamented bitterly for the maidens who had been treated so horribly by those evil knights.

When Tors and Ares did so much damage to the company they realized it was an ill fated battle from the start. The good knights assailed them on both sides, rolling up their line like a fine carpet. The final twenty evil spirits surrendered and were made prisoner.

They all rejoiced at the this marvelous victory. Tors freed the maidens that were servants in the chamber. Then he gave the castle to Silva and proclaimed that everyone was now free of any evil knight that did them harm. Everybody was happy and praised the good knights. They took the prisoners back to the King, who marveled greatly at the deeds of Le Tors, who was thereafter given the name the Mighty Bull.

# 29 THE KNIGHT OF THE TOMB

I will tell you now of a wondrous adventure that occurred around the same time. A lover may give a man great hope and security if she is good and true. The power of a woman can both curse a man to death or give him everlasting life if he is honorable. That is what this story largely surrounds, for the Knight of the Tomb was a man who's station was greatly enhanced for the love of a maiden.

There was once a knight in the forest who was very mighty. His name was Taules de Rougemont. He spent his whole life performing feats of valor and defeating those who challenged him. He was the very King of Jousters because no knight could unseat him from his swift charger. Yet, for all his valor in prowess, he one day disappeared and no one knew where he went. In fact, this story is only known because his brother found him after twenty years at the tomb where he stayed, where he recounted it all. When his true story was told it spread throughout the lands as a marvelous romance.

As I wrote, Taules de Rougemont had gained great renown in the lands. One day he rode in the forest seeking adventure. He was deep in the woods, letting his horse drink at a cool spring. In the nearby meadow he beheld the most beautiful maiden sitting on a rock. She was wearing the most exquisite ermine-lined silk gown that was both red and blue. This maiden was more beautiful than words can describe. She was whiter than a flower of hawthorn or sweet briar. Her face, body, hands and features were so comely that even the strictest monk would have seemingly thrown away his vows for but a moment with her.

When Taules saw this maiden he could do nothing but weep for joy. He went on his knees and humbly asked for the maiden's love. He did it in a way that she granted him her love for he was equally charming and valorous. "You are so lovely that I wish to quit my blundering and wandering through the forest entirely. Alas, all I've done till now has been complete folly. I see now that God has led me to you; to give you my love. Maiden, tell me how I can

235

have your love and I will gladly do what you ask, for I am your humble servant." The maiden quickly recognized that this knight was noble and chivalrous for she was very perceptive. She also saw his handsome features and broad shoulders. So she said this to him: "I will happily grant you the love you seek if you do my bidding completely. At anytime I ask anything of you it should be done." So Taules said: "My lady, I grant that willingly." So he embraced her. That was how they came together and from that day forth they were inseparable.

This lady was no ordinary maiden but a fairy well versed in the language of enchantment. She was capable of incredible feats of magic. Spending time in the forest with the other fairies helped her supersede all in these qualities; she could truly produce total marvels on a whim and without much effort at all. She could erect rivers where she pleased, build castles and smote her enemies by the sway of her hand. So the Maiden, with her lover as a witness, constructed there in the furthest reaches of the forest, an incredible castle. It had countless chambers, all perfectly decorated. The place was stocked well with provisions such as an abundance of fish, fowl, venison, bread and wine. It was very suddenly that this magical place was erected so I will tell you more about the details. It was situated on that very meadow and incredibly well positioned. It was not humble but a very marvelous castle to behold, even though the lady wished it so that it remained invisible to travelers! Squires and servants prepared meals and tended to the needs of the noble residents.

Indeed, this castle was so magnificent that no man or woman could possible wish for anything more, for everything was provided for. So, when the maiden had created this, she also made it so that it was completely invisible to anyone who came there. In this way the castle was only made visible to Taules, the company of ladies, squires and servants and of course the faery who was the creator of it all. They lived there very happily enjoying the world's gifts and making merry.

Taules, seeing the massive castle erected before his very eyes, fell in a swoon; for he was quite astonished by the ladies sorcery and not very accustomed to magic.

236

He was a knight, after all, who knew little more than the law of the sword.

The lady consoled and comforted him with these words: "Take heart, fair knight! For you have asked for my love, and I grant it willingly. You will be my lover and I will give you everything you need. Stay with me in the castle for all time and we will live happily. For we will lack nothing and enjoy our lives in this magnificent castle, newly erected in our honor. Although you must do one thing and never fail in this. Though this whole place is invisible I will construct a tomb in the front of the castle that can be seen by approaching knights. I want you to wait there in the day and challenge any knight who comes there. If he questions why you live in a tomb, scorn him all the more and prove your prowess in a joust. This way, you can keep jousting to your heart's content and never cease your prowess or have people say you grew soft in marriage." Taules willingly granted the girls wish and enjoyed testing his valor against traveling knights.

There was much talk at this time around who enjoyed more feats of prowess: the married or the bachelors. For the single were always the more eager to prove their might, especially if a lady happened to be watching nearby. Indeed, the married had already received love and the gifts that come with it, so what more did they need to prove? Alas, but they had more to protect, for their honor was always at stake. In this way the debate continued, but Taules was happy that he had a chance to continue feats of prowess, for he would feel depressed in the castle without any combat.

From that day forth Taules enjoyed the fruits of the castle and was quite enraptured with his lady love; for she was full of magical spells and there was never a dull moment. She would often bring exotic creatures to dinner and even had talking birds who could tell the secrets of the world. Taules marveled at this and became much more than a knight in his days there, for he learned much of wisdom and magic.

Each day he would go to the tomb before the invisible castle and knights would come there, saying: "Why do you tarry in that tiny tomb, knight? Are you grieving

237

the death of a loved one? It makes little sense for you to waste your days in the forest like this." Taules, enraged, would exit the tomb to fight. He would mount a mighty black charger and spurring towards the challenger, unseating him with a perilous thrust from his lance that would often leave the knight so thrashed and treacherously knocked from his saddle that he wanted to do little else but mourn his losses, right where he lay! From the very beginning and for all time Taules earned himself a name: he was called the Knight of the Tomb. He unhorsed so many that everyone in the land learned his name and stayed clear of the tomb for fear of being defeated. Though, real knights of courage, would seek him out, hoping to win him over.

At this time there was a fair and noble knight named Galuer. He was known as the red knight, for his arms were entirely red. He rode a white charger and had a red shield with a gold rose emblazoned on it. He was quite a marvelous knight to behold and he bedazzled all the ladies too. He was in court one day at Pentecost where a great feast was held. All the ladies were there and the Queen said: "Fair knights of the court, I want to know how much you love me. I ask that each of you make an oath, on these holy relics, according to the depths of your fidelity to me and the king. It will only win you honor to achieve what you swear!" All the knights, eager to do the Queen's bidding and flushed with wine, made many marvelous oaths. One knight swore "to kiss every maiden he saw with a knight, without question or remark". Another said he would: "Ride with one arm behind his back and only one foot in the stirrup, jousting with good knights until I was unhorsed or defeated." A third claimed he would "make ten knights prisoner, giving her the horse's and all their armor." In this way the Queen marveled at all the oaths being sworn.

The Red Knight, who was very eager to win the Queen's honor said: "I will challenge the Knight of the Tomb, and if I defeat him will tell you the secret that we all want to know." This was a boastful oath, said many, for none had been able to defeat the Knight of the Tomb, let alone return to speak about it without being sorely wounded or afflicted.

Though the Red Knight was unmoved and, on the next day, he set out through the forest after the Knight of the Tomb. He went deep into the forest and, after three days of travel without food or water, came to a clear and cool spring next to a meadow. He let his horse graze and drank the water from the spring. He rested on an oak tree, for he hadn't rested since he left the Queen's castle.

While he slept he had a vision of a marvelous castle somewhere in the wood nearby. There was a huge celebration going on, and all the people in the hall were so joyful that he had never seen such happy people. The hall was large and spacious and he saw a lady that was so beautiful he had never seen one like her. She had long blonde hair and a shining red gold crown, bejeweled with many emeralds and rubies, around the gleaming circlet. She wore exquisite garments of the finest, emerald green silk embroidered with gold lining and lined with vair fur on the inside. A great fire roared in the hall next to a long wooden table. On the table a great feast took place, and there was everything from pressed fawn to wild boar and spiced wine available in abundance. The people all danced and went caroling through the night. Seated in a golden throne at the end of the hall he saw a man; he thought he could recognize him but, the harder he tried to focus on him his vision was blurry. Then, suddenly, he awoke back in the forest, amazed at what he had seen.

He was hungry so he went through the forest, searching for game. He killed a deer and brought back a big haunch to eat. He pressed all the blood out between two stones and, when it was dry as can be, took an array of spices from his trusty pouch and seasoned it well, rubbing the spices in. Know that a good knight never went on an adventure without his spice pouch, and he was always willing in able to press the blood out of the deer between to stones, eating him raw. This was a long custom practiced for those who lacked fire or other comforts!

When he had eaten his fill and washed it down with the cool spring water, he saddled his horse and donned his arms again. Alas, the Red Knight was fully ready for combat. Just before he began to ride a light came from the heavens and directed him down a path he hadn't

239

seen before; it was as if someone was trying to give him a message. Eager to get going, he galloped off down this path. It wasn't longer before he arrived at the stone tomb where the Knight of the Tomb awaited challengers.

When he arrived at the tomb he found a stone pillar with an ivory horn on it. He gave this a blow so that the blaring sound reverberated through the forest. Not long after, Taules came out from the tomb. He saw the gleaming red knight and said: "What ever do you want? I was just about to have lunch." The Red Knight said: "It can wait, for I challenge you, in the name of the Holy Spirit, to tell me why you stay here without leaving!" The Knight of the Tomb roared with laughter and responded: "I won't give up my secret willingly. Therefore, I challenge you to combat! If you are made of metal and can win, than maybe I'll tell you." The Red Knight explained that he had sworn to the Queen under oath he would challenge him. The Red Knight was much younger and eager to prove himself. He loved a lady in court very dearly, and hoped that, if he won against the Taules, he could win enough honor to ask for her hand in marriage. So the two knights separated on a level field that opened up several bow shot lengths. Which would win, the bachelor or the settled man of marriage?

The two horses careened forward faster than hawks when they set their eyes on prey. The clash of arms was wild and sounded like thunder. The fairy watched from the invisible tower in amazement, observing: "I dare say, I don't think a challenger has ever had so much zeal and prowess. My love may be in trouble!" The two knights struck each other violently, splintering their lances to bits. Little did they know one another's true identities, for they never would have delivered such violent blows if they did. Both knights took a violent tumble to the earth. The Red Knight shattered his lance on his shield while Taules's lance struck the Red Knight in the chest but didn't break through the hauberk, fortunately! The Red Knight was quite stunned when he fell and had almost ruptured his wind pipe. Taules got up quickly and recollected that he had never been thrown from the saddle since he had begun challenging knights at the tomb.

240

Eventually the Red Knight got back up and a vicious sword fight began. The two knights attacked one another with such strength and might that they seemed the two greatest knights on all the earth. Sparks flew and hauberks rings, mail hoods and shield bits littered the grass as the blows became mortal. Then Taules hammered the knight to the ground with a fearless blow that was so powerful that the Red Knight went hurling to the ground. He got back up almost immediately and returned a blow that cut into the flesh of his shoulder. Wounded, Taules became incensed and started hacking away with perilous speed. The Red Knight defended himself valiantly and returned as many blows as he received. Eventually, both knights were covered in blood and exhausted from the toil.

Taules wondered who he was fighting, for if he knew the man he would surely stop the battle and invite him to the invisible castle, telling all: "I'm curious, for you have fought quite valiantly. No knight has struggled with me this long. Tell me, what is your name and where do you come from?" The Red Knight replied: "They call me the Red Knight, for obvious reasons." He looked at his armor, which was flaring red. "Though my real name is Tarquin, and I come from the castle of Corbenic. My father was Gallafur, and I am a knight of Jesus Christ. Who are you?"

When Taules heard this he was amazed. He kneeled before the knight and turned his sword over to him immediately. "Alas, are you really Tarquin? My father, Olifer, was Gallafur's brother and the ruler of Cornwall until he died gazing at the Yelping Beast, whose neck shimmers so many magical colors. Do you know about the grail? For I hear the disciples of Christ live in Corbenic. No matter, we are cousins. It would be shameful to fight you."

The two cousins were reconciled and embraced one another so fervently. The joy didn't stop there. The fairy saw what was going on and realized that she should make the castle visible. She did something or other and suddenly the magnificent castle appeared to Tarquin so that he could see the massive structure looming over the tiny tomb. Tarquin was shocked at this and said: "Is that where you live?" He smiled and replied: "Well, cousin, you

241

may know all the secrets, since you are family. My wife is a fairy of the forest, and she created this castle for us to live in. That is why I remain here and will for my whole life, challenging passersby." Then the Red Knight recalled his vision the night before, and suddenly realized that the great hall he saw was in the invisible castle where his cousin lived.

They entered the castle and had a sumptuous feast prepared for them. The servants took off their armor and applied ointment to their many wounds. The horse's were taken away and stabled; they were given good hay and oats. That evening Tarquin got to meet his cousin's wife, who he knew nothing about. Taules also had two little boys he sired, both strong and good natured. The night was a very joyous one and, because he was so delighted, he stayed at the invisible castle for two whole weeks. When he realized the Queen would worry and think he had died on the quest, he decided to return from whence he came.

Tarquin took leave of his cousin and the faery, returning to the castle from which he set out with the brave vow to conquer the Knight of the Tomb and learn his fate. He returned the court and told about how he was in love with a fairy who lived with him in splendor at the invisible castle. He described the castle in great detail too. This was a marvel, and everyone that heard it was completely astonished. A group of knights left the court the next day to search for the castle, but, no matter how many came to the tomb, the fairy made it completely invisible so that no one could find it. Indeed, Tarquin had done what he set out to do.

The Queen said: "You have achieved a task I though impossible. Since it is so, ask of me what you will and I will grant it." Tarquin kneeled to her and humbly replied: "My lady, if you would give me the love of a lady in your services I will ask for nothing more." The Queen, delighted that he had a lover, replied: "Ask and, if she is willing, she is yours along with my lands in the North for you to be Lord over!" The Queen was very generous. In this way the two lovers were married and, by the power of the Holy Spirit, given land to rule over and a great many followers who were also good christians.

# 30 TROUBLE ON MOUNT DOLOROUS

Listeners, gladly I will now share with you a story that brought strife to knights but one man, the very pillar of chivalry, was so able to thwart wickedness and evil that he set right the wrongs that many had failed to achieve before him. There are those that fall and lay on the ground groveling. Yet a true knight rises from the dust and claims victory over evil while praying fervently to the Lord for guidance and deliverance. Perceval was that knight.

Let me tell you, a knight carries a sword with two edges. With the first edge of his sword he administers justice on earth by freeing those poor of spirit and impoverished; he also carries on this edge of the sword equity and mercy with a willingness to forgive those who anger him. With the second edge of his blade he protects Holy Church and God from sinners and those who commit treason. Thus, with each edge the knight rightly protects with justice and God at his right and left sides.

Now let us learn about something completely different. You may recall that Merlin built a marvelous pillar on top of Mount Dolorous. This pillar was constructed with his power of enchantment and is an incredible wonder for it reaches the clouds, its summit not viewable to the human eye. The pillar is almost a half mile long and is the same width as it is length. Surrounding the pillar stood fifteen crosses. Five were white as sweet briar, another five red as a rose and the last five a rich, royal blue. On the north quadrant of the pillar there is a very beautiful golden ring that a traveler may use to tether his horse. Though it has an inscription that reads: "ONLY TETHER YOUR HORSE IF YOU ARE THE BEST AND MOST VIRTUOUS KNIGHT IN ALL THE LANDS. BE SURE TO STAY AWAY FROM THESE ADVENTURES FOR ALL WHO CAME HERE MEET WITH SUFFERING."

Such was the custom set forth by Merlin that no knight could tether his horse to the pillar unless he was the best in all the lands; both in spirit and strength. This was done by Merlin so that King Arthur could learn who should be most honored. And in this way many knights came to that place to try their skill but failed. Every knight who went there met shame and went mad on the adventure. Mount Dolorous was a place full of enchantment, deceit and treachery. Evil spirits loomed overhead and they possessed knights who, in their pride, attempted to achieve the adventure.

So it happened that, one fair summer day, Sagremor and Gawain rode to the top of Mount Dolorous to test their prowess. Sagremor had a gold shield with a red griffin on it while Gawain carried a red shield with three blue lions on it; such were the escutcheons that each knight carried among these noble knights. It was true that, concerning worldly affairs, these two knights were the best of the court, excepting Lancelot. Yet the Mount Dolorous adventure required a knight of a different caliber, who was both strong and of virtue. For the evil spirits were not defeated by human might alone, it required a strong faith in God. It was the Holy Spirit that created a well fortified mind to conquer the evil spirits of the forest, that would dement, curse or deceive the knights on the mount.

But let us learn more about these well adorned knights from Arthurs court, who enjoyed much wealth. The crest of Gawain's helm had feathers from a peacock that blew in the wind while the ribands were of the purest red; those ribands went all the way to the tale of his horse. He had a mighty gascon steed, and a silver saddle that had the finest embroidery work one could imagine. His helm was bejeweled with the fines rubies and his hauberk glimmered in the sun. So did Sagremor carry fine apparel himself. Though, in all sincerity, a knight is not best judged by the garments he wears, but rather by his deeds.

In this way the two proud knights rode to the top of the mount, very eager to have an adventure. I can tell you that they were sure to get one. They crossed themselves in amazement when they saw the massive crosses that loomed over them. Each one was over ninety feet tall. No amount of human craft could have placed them there. Then they were even more astonished by the massive pillar at the center of the peak, which went so far into the air it seemed a bird couldn't fly over it. The golden ring at the base of the pillar was made of the purest red gold and was a fine ring to tether a horse to.

When they approached the ring on the pillar they met with grief, even after reading the inscription they still, to their misfortune, wished to continue. Gawain tethered his horse on the ring and called out: "Is anyone there? See how I have tethered my horse without any conflict?" When he spoke both of them were bewildered by a demon who, when he saw the horse tethered, flew from the forest. A great storm arose and torrents of wind came in gusts, knocking the knight's to their feet. Black smoke wiped around them as a voice called out: "What have you done? You think you can tether your horse here? By order of the one who banished me, no man can until the most virtuous knight in the world comes."

The demon had the name of Anemi and he was the very devil; he most enjoyed tormenting the knights on the mount. So Anemi possessed them and turned the most joyful companions to bitter enemies. He said to them: "Both of you will suffer for your transgression here." So Anemi covered them with black smoke and they cried out in anguish. They suddenly became confounded.

Gawain said: "Foul Sagremor, if it wasn't for you we would be safe. It was because you aren't honorable enough that the demon wished to punish us." Sagremor rebuked him: "You are the proud one who wanted to come here. I only came cause your Uncle made me so that you would go off and die." In this way the evil spirit got the best of them and they began cursing each other.

Friends became enemies and, because they were so possessed a viscous combat ensued. They galloped up and down the mount shouting at one another and hurling spears at one another. Sagremor bled when a lance thrust grazed his left side, leaving a horrific wound that cut to the ribs. Then he charged at Gawain, thrusting his lance into his chest, knocking him from the saddle. In the midst of the storm and rain they drew their swords and struck at one another mightily. Gawain thrust his sword into Sagremor but he blocked it with his shield. Then Sagremor hammered him to the ground with a blow over his head. Gawain returned the favor, hitting him on the head so hard that he tumbled to the ground, stunned. His helm

245

flew off his head and he feared he would die, leaving his head so unprotected.

In this way they hacked and hewed at one another, getting very bloody. Anemi, for that was the demon's name, rejoiced: "I love possessing knights to hate one another and do such violent deeds. Soon one will kill the other and, stained by mortal sin, I will take him away with the help of a host of demons who will whisk him into the air. Then his soul will be mine!"

While this terrible battle occurred on the mount, let us return to King Arthur's court for a moment. The ladies at court, when they heard Gawain and Sagremor were going to the mount, were very worried. Two ladies in particular, who were very fond of these knights, asked leave of the Queen: "They are going to their death, I'm quite sure of it, unless we can save them. Let us go after them to make sure that nothing dangerous happens!" The Queen, realizing they were wise in many matters, gave them leave. She reported to King Arthur what the girls thought and this made Arthur very pensive. He groaned and refused to dine that night because he was sorry worried sick about his nephew. "Hopefully Sagremor can keep him out of trouble, but I greatly fear the enchantments of Mount Dolorous will prove too much for them." So the two ladies set out in a hurry, hoping to save their lovers.

They had followed the path to Mount Dolorous until they arrived at a clump of trees near a spring. When they got off their horses to rest, they suddenly heard a violent storm arise seemingly out of nowhere. Then they heard the two knights shouting violently at one another, and the clash of metal and steel on shields made the ladies tremble. Wherever Sagremor and Gawain were, the storm followed over their heads. That storm was nowhere else all throughout the land but over their heads; now it rained on both the knight's and the ladies. They were all in such a pitiful plight with no remedy!

The ladies went out from the spring and saw, just nearby, the two knights fighting so violently. They began to weep bitterly. It was clear that they had already become enemies and were set upon killing one another. Gawain's eyes were ablaze and black smoke came out all around him. He bellowed and roared like a beast, delivering the most terrible blows you could imagine. It was no light jest or game, these knights meant to kill. Sagremor defended himself for dear life and his strength began to wain. The two ladies watched in horror as the knights hacked and hewed. Blood was everywhere for their hauberks were now useless as they had been hacked to bits. Their many wounds gushed forth and blood ran all over the grass.

By now the two ladies, entranced by the powerful demon, began arguing amongst themselves. "It is your fault, you let them have leave from the Queen without stopping it! You could have made them stay if you wished it. You wanted them to die!" Then the two ladies, in a most uncourtly fashion, began hitting and scratching each other with their fists and nails. It was a terrible sight, and the whole group seemed to have created such a thunderous din that it could be heard throughout the forest. It was chaos! All they could do was call out to the Lord for help, but they were too drunk on demon enchantment to call out to the omnipotent one.

Fortunately, Perceval, the one who we spoke about earlier who was the very flower of chivalry, could clearly hear all these loud lamentations. Desiring to save the ladies who seemingly wailed and walloped simultaneously, he spurred his horse in that direction. Perceval, being the flower of chivalry, never left a maiden in distress.

Perceval saw the ladies and said: "I could hear your cries, what would you ask of me? I will help you in anyway I can." The ladies were too enrapt in their own fight to respond. Though a nearby woodsman, who had witnessed it all, yelled out: "These ladies are from King Arthur's court and that is Sagremor and Gawain. They are possessed by the demon, and mean to kill each other if you don't do something quick!" When Perceval realized that it was Gawain and Sagremor who were fighting he was deeply incensed.

Perceval spurred his into the thick of the combat. He used the chest of his horse to knock down Gawain who went tumbling down, quite exhausted. Then he jumped from his horse and wrestled Sagremor to the ground, keeping him in a head lock until he willingly surrendered. He bound them both as they cursed him in tongues that were the devils; for they were wildly possessed and knew not what they said. Just as the divine and incorporeal light can enter a corporeal body, so can the wicked enter in, if they are invited. So, fair reader, take care that you cleanse yourself often, and prayer to the Lord for deliverance. But, let's get back to the story. Perceval saw his two friends on the ground, their eyes as black as the inside of a tomb and their heads spinning, and he knew just what to do. He took out a relic which he carried on his saddle. It was no ordinary relic that you find everyday, but the very cloth that Jesus used to wipe his face before getting crucified. How did Perceval the Welshman come upon such a treasure? I will tell you.

Foremost, Perceval was a true man of God. That is why, in the midst of his many adventures, he ventured to the gates of heaven. It wasn't his time to go into the kingdom, but he wallowed about the outside and looked in curiously. He saw the beautifully wrought iron gates of white and even gazed on the golden steps and heard the trumpets of heaven blaring off in the distance. He saw the gatekeeper, who was a man dressed in white with a long flowing beard down to his knees. He had a spear in his right hand and seemed very agile for his age. His eyes were ablaze like fire balls and he was surrounded by white light.

The gatekeeper pitied him because he could only gaze in wonder from the outside. As much as it was a gift and treasure to behold, he was just a passing pilgrim. That man, in all his grace, gave Perceval something to take with him, something that could help him in the future: "Take this, it will save your fiends in a great time of need." That is how Perceval came upon the cloth that Jesus used to wipe his face when he carried his cross. This cloth had the power to heal any afflictions and confound the devil. Indeed, it had already cured countless lepers and blind men when it was once given to Josephus.

Perceval was well reminded of all this when he thought about how best to save his two friends. First he separated the two ladies and put the cloth in their hands. When they touched it they ceased to fight and wept for their sins. Then he bid them take the cloth to Gawain and

248

Sagremor. The two ladies put that holy cloth upon their faces and they were instantly cured. The power of the Lord was such that, he who asked, was cured. In this way did Perceval confound the will of the devil and amend the situation. The two worthy knights rejoiced at being saved and the ladies also wept for joy. They went to embrace their lovers and took them back to the castle with gladdened hearts. While the two valiant knights were free there was still more yet to happen on the mount. In this way we leave Sagremor and Gawain, who were restored to sanity by the good graces of the most holy knight Perceval.

Perceval continued on to the top of the mount and tethered his horse to the ring of gold. When he did this a beautiful maiden came from a leafy bower on the ridge. She was very beautiful and Perceval's heart leapt when he beheld her. She wore a white chaplet of roses that covered her blonde tresses that were long and would have gone all the way to her waist if she hadn't put them in beautiful, crisp braids. She had the finest silk dress that was blue and it was embroidered with rich red samite. Her body was slender and comely. I will say no more about it as not to tempt the senses for she was the type that would destroy a good man of reason! Nearby there was a bower to protect from the sun's gaze and that is where she had come from; she invited Perceval over to this place and he gladly followed her. S

When they reached the bower the lady showed the remarkable treasures she held in her hands. In her left hand she had a coronet that was decorated with golden lilies and precious stones. Around the inside there were scenes depicting the history of the Grail, starting with its journey with Joseph from the Holy Land and also there was the miraculous feeding of his five thousand with bread from the heavens. It also depicted Perceval in the house of the fisher king. In her right hand she carried a coat woven with silken flowers and embroidered with little green birds that seemed to be singing harmoniously with the wind and coming alive through the fabric. These gifts were joyfully bestowed upon Perceval, who was the best knight in the land. He graciously accepted them but could not help to ask there meaning.

The lady told him: "I will gladly tell you all I know. This coronet was made when the Holy Grail came to Britain. It is a gift from the fisher king who sent me here. Since he keeps the Grail safely at his castle it is right that he would give you such a worthy gift, since you are the one that seeks it plainly and will one day be its protector. Since you are holy, chaste and virtuous it is most befitting. The coat is a wonder made by the ladies of the forest. Some say they are fairies but truly they have learned much from Arthur's sister Morgan. They have the power to do wondrous magic and this garment has many powers. Know that, while you wear this coat you are invulnerable to attacks and spells; also, you will have the power to be invisible if you wish it."

After telling him all he wished to hear, the lady, who was too beautiful to describe with words, asked for his love. Though Perceval told her: "If I commit that to you it would be a great sin. For my love is for God alone as I adventure into the forest and seek the Grail. If I fall into folly I will surely lose the Grail along with the great mysteries of the kingdom of heaven. It grieves me to leave you, for you are very beautiful and I would do just about anything but grant you my love. For the sins of the flesh are fatal to the soul."

The lady was angered by this response but could do nothing about it. Before leaving him she gave him one other gift. "Fair Perceval, since you are so virtuous and chaste I have little doubt you will discover the mysteries of the Grail. Therefore, since I know much of these wonders, take this ring." She pulled out a ring made of stone with a green emerald set in it. She gracefully slipped it onto his finger where it, to his wonder, fit perfectly. "Wearing this will guide you to the Grail and the mysteries you seek. Pray to God that he may guide you there safely! All enchantments will be dispelled to he who holds this ring."

Perceval was amazed by such a wonderful gift. He was sure to thank the lady for her kindness and generosity. In this fashion the great Perceval went on to achieve the mystery of the Grail along with two other knights who were equal in prowess, virtue and might. Sir Bors and Galahad were the other two who were holy and willing enough to accomplish the great the mystery of the grail. Know that these three knights achieved the Grail and restored the lands to their former glory. For all the lands were wasted until that mystery was revealed.

Even after the holy grail was found those who followed the way of the flesh withered and died in the midst of a horrible civil war. It was made so by God that there were two types of adventures: worldly adventures of the flesh and holy ones of the spirit. Galahad, Bors and Perceval were both mighty knight's of prowess and holy ones full of virtue. So it was that they accomplished both deeds of prowess and those of virtue, in winning the most holy grail. Though they brought it away from the land, and, seeing the world wrought by sin, they had no choice but to take the grail away to the holy land. For the grail saved those who believed, it let the others die. Despite the marvels they saw when the Holy Ghost came to Arthur during Pentecost (they saw the flaming tongues of the holy spirit and the trinity, they were even quenched of their hunger and thirst through the presence of the most holy grail), despite the quests Galahad achieved that no other could (when he cooled the flames at the burning tomb of Simeon and bore the shield of Tholamer), despite seeing the way of the spirit as the only true way to life, they continued to live in sin which, alas, brought the whole kingdom destruction!

Even Lancelot, the mightiest knight of the world, saw the grail procession and the chapel where it was worshipped. If he had turned from sin then he could have been given all he desired, but he continued in adultery! That was a great shame, that was a misdeed that God saw plainly, even though he is ever merciful and forgiving.

Therefore, fair reader, repent, and you too may experience the presence of the grail and understand its mystery! The grail wasn't brought into worldly affairs any more than worldly affairs were brought to the grail. To each is his own quest to discover the path to enlightenment and, thereby, attain the mysteries. That is why the path to heaven is narrow and only followed by the few, where the path to hell is wide and broad, more like a highway, followed by

251

the multitudes. Be on your guard, and hope that you too can achieve the most holy grail!

If the picture is more clear we can now return to the deeds of the marvelous knight Perceval. As I said, he was capable of many miracles. When he returned from the mount he went to court and ventured to sit in the perilous seat. The perilous seat was put there by Merlin and I will tell you what it was. It was an empty seat at the Round Table that was forbidden to be sat in by anyone; any knight who sat in it was engulfed in flames and a black pit that went straight to hell. At the feast of All Saints, when the dining hall thronged with proud knights and the wine flowed, many stubborn warriors vowed to sit in that seat, come what may. In fact, six were so bold as to test the perilous seat. Arthur pleaded them to do otherwise but each one, when they sat in the seat, vanished into a black hole that appeared beneath it while being engulfed in flames. After this had happened, a voice called out: "You will not see those knights again until they are redeemed by the most holy knight in all the land. Only then will those transgressors be redeemed. Until then, make sure no one sits in the seat!" Everyone witnessed this marvel and feared the Lord greatly because of it.

Yet one knight could sit in it: the one who was most worthy in all the land. That one had truly earned the right to sit in it. Many months passed since that tragic feast day where those six knights had perished. Though, when Perceval returned to the court, he, like the other knights, was certain that he would sit in the perilous seat. Arthur was horrified that one of his favorite knights wished to throw his life away. He begged him against it, imploring him with riches and lands. Though the good Perceval replied to the King: "You offer me riches and lands, but these are just more worries. All I ask that you bestow is the grace of God." The King responded: "Good knight, I'm afraid you ask for something I cannot give." Then Perceval smiled and gently walked over to the perilous seat which so many feared. Everyone cringed as they saw him so calmly sit in the seat.

They were astonished when Perceval sat in the seat and, rather than being scorched in flames, bright light came down from above and filled through the windows of the great, wide hall. This miraculous light shined on Perceval's face, making him radiant. His face was covered in a ball of holy fire and flames shot forth from him in every direction. It was so bright than many dare not look at him for they were very afraid of his presence. Then the marble floor surrounding the seat crumbled while the seat, with Perceval in it, remained suspended in the air. From the dark pit emerged those six knights who were sorely repenting. They climbed up from the pit in a ladder and many rejoiced to see them again. So it was by Perceval's holiness that those six were raised from the dead. These knights were thus forgiven for their trespasses and redeemed.

# PART 2: 1 THE MAIDEN OF THE FORD

In the Kingdom of Logres so many marvelous adventures happened that it is hard to find the right place to start. So it happened that there was once a powerful lord who had a great deal of land. His name was Barfluer. He ruled well and judiciously. His castle was well situated on a hill top overlooking the farm land and meadow. It was a well fortified keep complete with a deep moat and ramparts. As a result of his good nature and generosity he was very rich and powerful.

The King and his subjects sat down to a great feast on the day of Pentecost; suffice it to say such a splendid feast was never seen. The maidens were all exquisitely dressed and took to caroling and dancing. The knights were equally noble in looks and deeds. Some spent the day before the feast jousting and showing off with great deeds of prowess. A good many lances were splintered and sword strokes were delivered leaving the field full of broken mail hood rings, ventails, helms and shattered shields.At the time there was a custom in the land that everyone waited to dine until something marvelous happened; that is, a great adventure was awaited! For this was well before the adventures of the most holy grail by almost a century. Yet he carried that custom up until the time of King Arthur who was known as the King of Adventures.

So it was that, on this night, while the court was preparing for dinner, a beautiful maiden entered the hall. When she entered, the whole court stood still for they were astonished at her great beauty. She wore a blue silk dress and her hair was as red as blood. She seemed in distress and before she could speak a knight in black armor came in behind her. He took her and put her on his horse so that she screamed. The men all realized that she was being kidnapped in the court. Before she left the hall she said: "How could I be kidnapped in the court of Barfluer? He does not avenge me? Grief and shame should come to all his knights for they failed a maiden in distress."

She asked for the king and went to him, saying: "Fair king, if you will save me from this knight I will show you a series of adventures that you will not forget for all your life." The king was enticed by this and assented. So he mounted and followed the maiden despite his counselors who advised against it. One of the king's men said: "King, beware! For this maiden has treachery on her lips." The king refused to acknowledge that he was in peril. For he thought it right to care for a maiden, especially one in distress. Indeed, it was concluded that there was no better reason to fight than to defend the honor of a lady, especially one that was so wrongfully shamed in the court!

The maiden set out from Barfluer's castle with the black knight who had her over his horse's neck. They rode for many hours until the night turned to dawn. The king had not eaten and was still very hungry but continued in pursuit of them. At last he caught up with them at a ford at the edge of the woods. They were both tall and strong knights; Barfluer yelled out: "Stop there, you who has shamed me in the court by kidnapping a helpless maiden! You know it is the custom of these lands that no maiden is wrongfully shamed and that a good knight must always save a lady that is in danger. Prepare yourself for battle, make sure your shield is on your neck, your girdle fastened, and you lance tilted, for I will give you a rough time of it!"

The Black Knight responded: "If you think you can take me down your in for a surprise. Let my pennon do the talking, for it will soon be leveled into your shoulder!" He set the maiden down and spurred his swift charger into combat. The two knights collided fiercely so that the horses were completely dazed. The Black Knight put his lance into Barfluer's shield and it splintered completely. Barfluer struck a might blow through the hauberk, forcing the Black Knight to the ground in a heap.

The Black Knight had a terrible gash in his left side and he bled quite a lot. Barfluer saw he was wounded so he drew his sword and charged at him like a mad man. The Black Knight got up and defended himself. Sword strokes drew blood on either side so that both knights were wounded in at least ten places. The blood flowed all over. They were weary and King Barfluer said: "You are a strong knight but you have dishonored my court by taking a maiden who was under my protection. Yield her over and I will grant you leave." The Black Knight replied: "She

255

has done treachery to me and will do the same to you. Do not help this maiden! I will not be shamed by her or you!"

When the knight failed to surrender Barfluer delivered a might blow on his head that went crashing through the helm and into the flesh. His helmet flew into the bushes and blood poured down his face so that he couldn't see. When this happened he struck blindly at Barfluer who dealt another blow that clove his arm from his shoulder, straight through the bone. The knight was screaming in anguish and fell in a swoon to the ground. Barfluer threatened to take his head from him before he said: "Though it is a great shame I will now yield to you, King Barfluer. My name is Ordain and I am a Saxon from the North. I have traveled here to take this maiden and mock you. Truly she is a noble lady of your lineage but I wished to shame her at your court." Then the knight, who was in very poor condition, died. The king was glad that he had been avenged though felt pity for the man who had been so heavily wounded.

After the battle the maiden rejoiced and told him that she would take him to her castle nearby. For they had travelled so far into the woods that her castle was closer than his own. He gave the lady the Black Knight's horse and they rode swiftly on until they reached a magnificent castle on a hill overlooking the sea. No greater castle was ever seen. It was also full of magic for, little did the King know that the woman he was with was a fairy capable of enchantments. This castle was invisible and only seen by those whom the lady wished it to be seen. When they were on the road the drawbridge was lowered; they entered a courtyard where a company of servants helped the knight dismount. They unarmed him and cared for the horse splendidly so that he lacked nothing. Then they gave Barfluer a scarlet mantle that was splendidly embroidered with gold patterns. When they entered the fortress the maiden had prepared a room for Barfluer where he was healed by the best physicians of the time. He spent a month there before being fully healed from his battle wounds.

When Barfluer was better he explored the astonishing palace. The door to the main hall was crafted out of ivory. It had beautiful spiral carvings in it. Then, in the great hall, there was a gilded table of copper. Each pedestal was massive and extraordinary to gaze upon. Surrounding the table was a series of tall chairs of gold; surely one of those chairs was the very perilous seat that Merlin had prophesied about! No doubt, the chairs were marvelous; each one was inlaid with gems and seemed to be a throne for a king. The hall was adequate to house the emperor Alexander.

Indeed, Barfluer was beginning to think he was not in the world because this place was so lavish. He thought to himself: "My life has suddenly became a marvelous pink cloud. I don't imagine myself leaving here, for my every desire is attended to with such care and grace that I see no reason. All the cares of the world, alas, lead only to folly and dismay. For my work is so insignificant, let the multitudes decide whats best and suffer for their folly. I will remain here in bliss!"

Then a large company of fifty damsels came into the hall with exquisite accoutrements and gowns of bright colors; they all wore garlands of flowers on their heads and welcomed King Barfluer; they sat around the table and served each other the most exquisite dishes of venison, boar, and fish with all kinds of exotic spices. On the table were many golden chalices and silver grails; the lady of the castle took care to pour out plenty of wine for the guest.

Among the beautiful maidens he found much pleasure. The Queen said to him: "All hail Barfluer, may his reign be long and joyful. Your whole life has been laden with care and turmoil; take time to find peace in your heart. My company of ladies, for this is the very fairy castle of ladies, will treat you well. For you are the one who gave birth to the splendid custom that protects all women from vile men who seek to do wickedness to them." With this silver tongued words the King was so enamored that he thought of little else but his own pleasure. They treated him so well that he quite forgot his people and land. All of the people in the hall were very happy to have such a King in their midst. Everyday he awoke to servants who attended to his every need. Sometimes he would go hunting, other times he would remain in the castle playing games,

257

dancing or caroling. Everyday was a great source of pleasure. In just this way Barfluer forgot of his duties and
stayed with the maiden and her people for many nights.

After a while, however, the King worried for his
people and kingdom. It was time to return to his people,
he considered. So he came to the dinner hall and said: "It
has been some time now since I left my people behind.
While this has been the most marvelous of adventures it is
time for me to return to my duties." When the king had
said this the ladies were all very grieved. The Queen, who
was distraught, told him: "Fair king, if you choose to leave
us I must tell you that you will meet your death." Barfluer
was unsure what the maiden meant by this and disregarded
it, insisting that it was time for him to leave.

The next morning he rose early and, after hearing
mass, donned his armor-which was quite dusty- and
mounted his horse who had grown old. He bid the ladies
farewell and was shocked to see them all lamenting so
harshly; not one of them wasn't filled with tears. He left
that place and rode all the way to the ford where he had
slain the Black Knight. All the maidens followed after him,
begging him not to leave. Though, with great ignorance, he
bid them farewell and continued on his journey.

When he had crossed the ford the ladies following
him suddenly vanished, as did the castle in the distance
where he had taken so much pleasure. This was shocking
to the King and then a great marvel happened.

He met a squire on the other side of the bridge
and saluted him, saying: "Tell me where to find my castle,
for I am Lord Barfluer who rules these lands." The squire
was very confused at this and said: "My lord, Barfluer has
been dead some two hundred years. It is a very distant rela-
tive of his that now rules these lands."

Alas, how grief stricken was the King when
Barfluer heard it had been over two hundred years since he
left that castle of pleasure! Suddenly he was overwhelmed
with a strange feeling in his body; as if the realization that
he was over two hundred years old suddenly caught up
with him. The reality was that the Queen's magic could no
longer protect his body after he crossed the ford. So, al-

most instantly, his body began to decay and crumble like an old stone statue.

The squire watched in horror as Barfluer's body and horse fell into pieces and the flesh turned to dust. When the king lay dead before the squire, he wept bitterly. He tried to gather up the remains but they were just globs of dirt. He managed to find the skull and Barfluer's sword in the heap and he brought it back to the castle. He brought these items back to the King of the land, who was a great grand nephew of his, who was astonished to see the very bejeweled hilt that the great King Barfluer had worn into battle. This amazed all the wise men of the courts, who had often told of how the King had disappeared mysteriously after following a maiden from the hall. Oh wickedly he was deceived! They buried the skull in the temple beneath the altar.

The remains were interred in a splendid tomb made just for Barfluer, it was made of stone and inlaid with much gold. On his tomb an inscription read: "HERE LIES BARFLUER, THE KING WHO TOOK A PER-ILOUS ADVENTURE FOR THE LOVE OF A MAID-EN". That is why it is now a custom in that land that no king take an adventure from a maiden until they understand the maiden's true intentions. It was only much later, through the tale being passed down, that everyone realized the Black Knight had lied, even in the grips of death, about the true nature of the maiden that Barfluer avenged. Though it is known that Barfluer, because of his virtue in protecting the damsel, had his soul in heaven among the saints of this world.

# 2 LEWR AND THE CAVE OF BANISH-MENT

The adventures of Lewr were some of the most magical that were to come in the kingdom of Logres. Lewr was an extremely noble fighter who had slain many Saxons in his day. If you haven't heard the Saxon's had fast become the greatest enemy of the Britons at this time. For they came over in large fleets of ships with many warriors; they were pagans seeking to destroy the Christian Britons.

Lewr was incredibly brave and often went to seek adventure alone, to the dismay of the court who highly valued his life. Lewr loved to ride into the forest in search of adventure. It was by chance that while riding he came upon a hedged rose garden. Behind it there was a stone wall and closed off portico. Large rounded towers stood at each end of the wall. It was seemingly a castle that had undergone many assaults. The gates were black iron and half torn apart; the place was eery and quite abandoned. Even the moat was dried up and the drawbridge splintered.

Also, it seemed like there was little joy from the inhabitants in the village nearby for the land was totally barren. The farm land was all rotted and decayed. From the wall a watchmen poked his head when Lewr rode his charger up to the gate. Lewr demanded entry: "A knight of the Round Table wishes to see this gate opened. Can you provide lodging?" The watchman snarled and rejoined: "No fair knight may enter here without losing his life. If you wish to seek your death I invite you in. Otherwise, begone from these forests and ne'er return!" Lewr was not startled by this in the least and demanded entry a second time. The gates were hardly functional so, without permission, Lewr rode in unopposed. The dusky hour was silent but for the crow on top of a pine tree who ominously watched the courtyard which Lewr entered. It was cold and the wind was biting for it was only the month of March.

Inside the stronghold was a courtyard littered with arms and bones of dead men. Lewr entered and the gate , which seemed to have been broken, immediately locked behind him. When he sought the watchman he had completely vanished. So Lewr tied up his horse and entered the keep. He climbed the steps and, sensing danger, drew his sword from its scabbard. The door to the keep was left open. The inside of the keep was not lit but for a single torch from the outside which he took in with him. Lewr advanced into the blackened hall. Around each corner he expected foes.

At the center of the keep there was an abandoned table. Goblets were knocked over and chairs in disarray. As could be seen the long table was once the center stage of carousing for the nobles of that castle. It was a mighty hall with high vaulted ceilings. Behind the table there was an iron throne positioned on a raised platform. The throne was not empty but a dead corpse sat in it. He seemed to have been dead for weeks as the flesh from the left side of his face was eaten through by maggots and worms. The cold wind blew through the hall as Lewr gazed at the dead man. He was slouched on his throne in death. His right-hand grasped a golden scepter. A large worm exited from his head where the skin had been devoured.

Behind the throne a small side door was open. Lewr entered it to find an alleyway which led into a secret cave. Lewr advanced into the crevice upon a narrow pass. Lewr feared no enemy. He crossed himself on the brow and prepared for the worst. When he neared the end of the trail  he could hear weeping. Below him there was a man who screamed and wailed. When Lewr approached his armor hit upon the rocks and startled the man, for he ceased to wail and scurried off at the sound of the approach. When Lewr reached the bottom of the cave he saw a luminescent pond with a cot nearby it. All around the cave was strange writing and demonic symbols that had been drawn by someone. When Lewr could not find the man he ascended to the main hall. When he re-entered the room he found the iron throne where the dead corpse had been resting empty. The body of the lord was gone, this astonished him as he rightly wondered, where had it gone?

Suddenly, from behind Lewr, a swift running enemy hurled toward him. He was quicker than a leopard and yelled treacherously. Alas, it was the corpse from the throne come to life! He wielded the golden scepter and delivered a blow on Lewr's shield that knocked him to the ground. His power was that of ten men as he hewed many strokes at Lewr with the scepter. His attacks had completely destroyed Lewr's shield and he bled greatly beneath his hauberk for he had been hit on the shoulder.

When his enemy had proven his might, Lewr went on the offensive. He thrust his sword into the dead corpse but it did very little, for he was already dead! Each stroke against him was as if Lewr had been striking at sand for this man lacked the feeling of pain. He was not an earthly creature but demonic. Then the demon vanished and could be heard laughing at the other end of the keep. Lewr was frightened and began to leave the place but was immediately stopped by his enemy who, suddenly reappearing in front of him, gave him a mighty blow on the head that made blood run down his face. He fell on his back and spurted blood from his mouth.

He was in great agony and thought that he would be killed. Suddenly the whole keep became bright with light. The demon screamed because he was in extreme agony when the light shined throughout the hall. Then Lewr opened his eyes to see Regnar, his trusted companion. Now Regnar was an enchanter who knew a lot about evil spirits. He was also a great holy man who could vanquish any evil spirit back to hell. Regnar shouted to him: "You have roused a demonic beast. Stand up, my lord, and get out of this place!" Regnar used his magic to cast fire upon the beast which cowered in the corner of the hall The beast's flesh began to burn in agony by the light exuding from Regnar's hands. He fell to his knees and withered up.

Lewr kneeled before Regnar, praising him for saving his life. Then he questioned him as to the origins of this place. Regnar replied: "Some things in this forest are meant to be unseen. Some rocks are never meant to be turned over to discover the serpents that make their homes beneath them. Is the greatest depth of the ocean charted? The crows told me of the danger you were in. I'm glad I came in time to save you. This lord was once powerful and mighty. He had a daughter who was more beautiful than any damsel. But the neighboring barons grew jealous of his might and wished for his daughter's hand in marriage, for she was very beautiful. This man refused to give her up for he wished to give her to another king. One night the barons plotted to kidnap his daughter. After a marvelous banquet in this very place the whole castle was in a deep sleep. The wine-drunk men were asleep when the baron's plotted their treason. When she awoke at the hands of her abductors she let out a terrible scream. Her father awoke and armed himself but it was too late. The men summoned by the baron were forty in number. They slaughtered everyone in the castle who was unarmed. This treacherous act has created this demon who has killed everyone who has entered here since as vengeance for the evil the baron's had done. It is called the cave of banishment because it is a custom in some towns here to take prisoners who committed treason to this place so that the evil spirit can punish them."

Lewr was astonished when he heard all of this. The tale of the forgotten lord grieved him because he was unjustly slaughtered in the night by jealous enemies. However, Lewr rejoiced at being saved. When he returned to the city he summoned all the people for a great feast. The halls were decorated with garlands and flowers. Large groups of nobles gathered in the hall and a sumptuous feast was prepared. Maidens met new lovers and talked together. Shouts and carousing filled the city with joy. Everyone was dancing and there was no lord more generous than Lewr. For he gave of himself and his money freely. Then everyone sat down to hear the tale of Lewr's adventure and it was duly recorded by the clerks there.

During the feast foreign knights from other countries came. They gathered together outside the hall and subsequently challenged Lewr's retinue to jousting. "Let us hold a great tournament and the winner can be given my daughter in marriage, since she is the very pearl of Logres!" A splendid tournament was prepared and all the knights were eager to win for the foreign king's daughter was more beautiful than any lady they had ever set eyes on. Her very presence made knights out of cowards. Heralds sounded the horns and the knights gathered, brandishing their swords for competition. Maidens came in large companies to watch from the castle walls the great feats of prowess. Each knight was enlivened by the amorous looks of the ladies.

Thus a great tournament ensued where lances splintered and a thunderous din of combat was heard. Knight's were wounded and unhorsed in great numbers. Gwallag the stout-hearted, one of the knights of the court who was extremely valiant, went into combat with ferocity. He felled four knights before breaking his lance and falling to the ground. Iowry, another knight of noble stock, was such a skilled rider that he unhorsed ten knights before resuming battle on foot with his sword. They didn't have any fear but road to the thickest press, wrestling men to the ground if needed. Lewr disguised himself by painting his shield black so no one would recognize him, for good or ill. Then he put his shield on his neck and lowered his lance, taking off in a full gallop. He rode against the neighboring king's men with such grace and form that none could unhorse him. He unhorsed twenty knights that day. All the heralds, maidens and people marveled at his prowess and declared he was the best fighter.

When the horn blew and supper was prepared the foreign lords all swore that Lewr should be awarded the prize of the tournament. Though he was disguised and, being full of meekness and humility, rode off into the woods without claiming the prize. They continued on with the feast, honoring the mysterious knight of the black shield who had won the tournament and the hand of the foreign king's daughter. Lewr returned in the courtyard after the feasting. The foreign king offered his daughter to him, as was the agreement of the tournament, but he replied: "Alas, I can't take her, though she is very beautiful. I have sworn an oath and, by God, I shall take no woman as my own because of it." The king was very grieved for he thought Lewr a most noble knight.

When Lewr entered the hall and removed his helm the lady was struck by his beauty. The king's daughter was truly struck in the heart a fatal wound, for she fell deeply in love. "I could jump from a tower and die for this love! There is no other man I have ever seen who I desire more.

I love him and dream about him in anguish as a monk does a nun as he kisses his pillow at night!" She pleaded to her servant. This servant was an older lady who was well capable of magic and enchantment. When she heard that her lady loved Lewr she took to cleverly getting him to love her back.

When all had retired to bed the servant went to Lewr's chamber. Lewr was still awake and, when he saw the woman, he said: "What brings you here at this hour?" The lady said: "You have greatly wronged the king's daughter, for you won the tournament and refuse to take her hand in marriage. I ask that, as recompense, you wear this ring the lady has given you so that you may always remember this shameful act." Yet when Lewr put the ring on his finger he instantly became enchanted. He was so enamored with the girl that he stupidly wondered to her room that very evening: "I am so sorry for going against her wishes. I clearly see now that this was a great wrong. How may I make amends with the lady?" The servant said: "Don't tell it to me, but go to her yourself and apologize!"

Lewr entered the girl's chamber and begged her forgiveness. She was eager to take him to bed and she easily did so for the enchantment was very strong. It wasn't until morning when Lewr, rubbing his hands in joy, accidentally slid the ring from his hand. Only then did he realize he had been betrayed. Rather than marrying the girl he set out into the forest, mad with grief. Know that they had conceived a child that day and he was to become a great knight that would be known throughout the land. It is that sometimes the Lord graces us with great gifts; it was clear he took pity on the knight who had sworn to be a virgin for all time, even though the wiles of enchantment had subverted his will so wickedly.

# 3 THE NOBLE BEDIVUE

In King Arthur's time there lived a noble knight named Bedivue who was cup bearer to the king and a good knight of the table round. He was lord over an entire fiefdom and had received much honor for his prowess. At Chesterfield, a vicious assault between the Saxon's and Arthur's knights, he was the most achieved warrior and slew hundreds of the enemy warriors. He avenged the British people upon the Saxon hordes and was remembered for all time for it. It is because of this that King Arthur gave him the royal cup that was worth more than an entire castle. It was one of the best possessions that Arthur had; it had a magical enchantment on it so that it would provide any drink the bearer desired.

Not only was Bedivue a mighty warrior but also a man of great learning. Bedivue was also virtuous and chaste. Bedivue was famous for jousting, they even called him the "King of Jousters". He could unhorse ten or twenty knights without fail and prove his prowess in a single day. He was feared and maidens all sought his love. Though it was a custom of his that he would never kill a knight who asked for mercy.

Bedivue carried a white shield with a blue swan on it. His lance had a blue pennon and his armor was white. He wore a scarlet sash on his arm that was his lady's. King Arthur relied heavily on Bedivue in those days. I will not tell of the many battles in which he fought for the king because it would take up many volumes and I do not have the space for it. Suffice it to say that in battle he smote his foes on the left and right hand with ease because he was so well trained in arms. He never entered into a fight unless the cause was just. Most remarkable was his exploit in the Northern kingdom to save the maidens who were in great peril by a group of giants. There was never a greater man who would risk all to save a maiden in danger. He went after those giants in the hills and, blowing an ivory horn, challenged them to battle. They swung terribly large clubs at him but he dashed the clubs against the rocks and cut open the giant's bellies for however terrible they were he was more skilled with the sword than any. When he killed all the giants in the northlands he brought the head of the giant king back to Lord Arthur and gave the lands to him; this was concluded with great celebrations.

After the many conflicts where Bedivue achieved renown he took to court life. One day a hermit brought to Bedivue a golden locket. "This locket comes from our ancestors. It was brought from the promised land and given to a virgin maiden. That same maiden was renowned throughout the land for her works towards God. Then she died and buried this locket in the ground. You are the most virtuous knight and should rightly have it. So virtuous are you that you will benefit greatly from it. Your prowess will grow by wearing this locket. It will give you immeasurable strength and will blind your enemies in battle for it is full of the divine light. Wear it always, and may God keep you!" Bedivue thanked the hermit for his gift. So gracious was Bedivue that he kept him for the night and provided him with a bountiful feast. Though the hermit, humble as he was, declined the meal, drank only water and slept on the stone floor at court.

Bedivue took the locket and wore it proudly. It shined so bright when revealed that no enemy could stand before him without being blinded. At receiving this divine gift he beamed with confidence. In that time there was an adventure known as the Chapel Perilous. No knight had gone there and returned to tell of it. So Bedivue set out to accomplish it. He asked leave of the king and said: "When I became a knight you promised you would grant me a boon. Now I ask of you such a thing. I must take this quest to the Chapel Perilous for your honor and my own. If I can defeat whatever evil that is there I may bring honor to you." The King was saddened because he thought that Bedivue would surely die from such a journey. He begged him to stay but he refused. Eventually he gave him leave but much to his displeasure. For he had promised to grant Bedivue whatever he wished. It is hard to keep a good knight at the court because he gets bored very easily, hoping to achieve further feats of prowess he is aching to go! Thus he entered the dark forest and proceeded to the Chapel Perilous. Bedivue feared little and rightly sought to purify the Chapel that was full of wickedness and evil spirits; he even took that locket with him that would, by the grace of God, be an effective defense against demons.

One day, after hearing mass, he set out towards the place. As he entered the woods a maiden approached him. "Turn back, for if you proceed towards the Chapel Perilous you will surely be slain! My brother was taken from this world in the same way. His pride to accomplish such a task was too much." Yet Bedivue was not the type to be scared off by a warning. He promised to avenge the maiden's brother and continued on the path.

At last he came to a path that led to a meadow. On top of a hill there was a pine tree. Perched against the tree were three lances, upside down. Bedivue took one of the lances, which was stout and sharp, and approached the chapel. It was small and made of stone. Yet the place was teeming with evil for there were demons who inhabited it. When he entered it the wooden door and windows rattled and the earth quaked. A great storm arose in the sky and all kinds of tormenting voices yelled out: "Leave here now, terrible things are coming your way!"

Alas, he became locked inside when the door slammed shut. Then darkness filled the room so he could not see a foot in front of him. Now, underneath the chapel, a great many tombs were lain from the time of the Saracen invaders. These men had been buried but not by the christian right. They were controlled by wicked evil spirits and the bodies rose from the dead to attack him.

Blinded, he took out the locket so that the whole room was filled with the light of Christ. Then he saw that the dead skeletons were coming from the tombs beneath the chapel. They attacked him and struck many blows as there were over thirty of them. Bedivue threw the lance he had so that it went right through the chest of one of them, hurling him to the ground. Then he took out his blade and delivered mighty blows so that he cleft arms, heads and entire bodies apart. The battle was fierce and the skeletons fought wickedly, hoping to dishonor the knight.

Yet there was no better fighter than Bedivue, who slew all thirty of them. Every one of the enemy was killed by his magnificent swordsmanship. Then, below the floor, a lion and a leopard emerged. The two were ferocious and charged towards Bedivue. When he saw them he showed those demons the locket. They hissed and growled as the most villainous beasts that they were. They could not touch him when he wore the locket and the light burned them. So Bedivue came after them with his sword and slew them. He delivered a stroke on the lion's neck and took its head. He did the same to the leopard. They howled and were defenseless because his sword was directed by God. Then he prayed fervently for having slain all the evil spirits in the Chapel Perilous.

People who had followed after Bedivue to see if he would achieve the quest rejoiced when they saw him exit the Chapel alive. Great rejoicing began and word was spread throughout the land. They called him the mighty dragon for he defeated the most evil beasts of the land who had plagued the Chapel. Bedivue took the head of the lion and leopard with him, attaching it to his saddle for all those to see.

He returned to the city in the midst of celebration and a great many followers. On his way the same maiden who had lost her brother saw him returning along the road and embraced him for avenging her brother. He entered Camlan with a band of rejoicing people. He was welcomed by Arthur and his court with the greatest honor. After recounting all that had happened the court was truly astonished and recorded his good deed. Bedivue was known throughout the kingdom of Logres as both the giant slayer and purifier of the Chapel Perilous.

After remaining at court for some time he met with another adventure. One day he set out with some fellow knights to hunt. They left before dawn as they were eager to come upon the best game. After arming, they released the hounds and galloped from the keep. They blew their horns and the dogs took off barking. Bedivue had the best hounds in the kingdom. The hounds rustled up every part of the forest causing all kinds of disturbances. Between the thickets Bedivue caught his eyes on a white hart of marvelous beauty. His hounds chased it deep into the woods. Bedivue galloped for so long that he became lost in the forest. Then he found a trail beside a fountain.

At the fountain there was a squire. Bedivue kindly asked the man: "Have you seen a white hart come this way?" The squire told : "I am he! By your looks you must be a king. I will gladly take you to my lord for lodging." Bedivue did not understand how a man could turn into a hart. Nevertheless he was grateful for the company for he was weary from travel. So the two set off together.

Bedivue followed the squire into the mountains where they walked under a waterfall and into a cave. The tunnel of the cave was lit by torchlight. Once on the other side they met with an open valley. In that valley there was a magnificent castle between the rocks. Never had Bedivue seen so remarkable a fortress nor could he explain how he had arrived there. The stone walls seemed to have emeralds in them as they sparkled when he passed by. The setting sun made the sky purple and the flag atop the tower blew proudly in the wind.

He followed the squire and entered into a glorious hall where there were servants with large plates of food. There were drinking vats, golden goblets and many merry people. Couples danced and made cheer to the music played there. The harp and minstrels brought joy to everyone's hearts. There were many strong warriors there who enjoyed themselves.

Then the squire led Bedivue into a separate room where a group of twelve noble knights, who were sober and had flowing white beards, sat down at a large round table. Each of them had the strength of a giant and were very wise. You could tell by their age and broad shoulders! They were the mightiest knights he had ever set his eyes on. When they were all seated a man approached the table with a golden chalice in his hands. Each drank from the chalice and was fulfilled. It was later known that this was a magical chalice that provided whatever the bearer desired if he was virtuous enough to accept it.

As they were graced by this chalice in such a way one of the men from the hall outside asked for admittance. He was refused but came up to the only empty chair anyway. He was drunk and not aware of the mortal sin he had committed by sitting in the chair. As he sat in the empty chair it swallowed him and his body burst into flames. No one has seen that man since and that is why no one enters that room unless rightly admitted. That hall was sacred and only the most virtuous were allowed into the room.

Moreover, Bedivue could not understand how when he drank from the chalice all of his desires and longings were fulfilled. He was astonished by the power of the chalice. He asked the men what it was and they said that it was the Holy Grail. He had never heard of such a thing but swore that he would discover what it was. All of the men there lived entirely on what the Grail provided. After eating and marveling at those in the hall, Bedivue found his way to a room where servants took him to bed.

In the middle of the night he awoke to a shining light that entered his room. It was as if the sun had arisen early. Curious, he left from his bed and followed the light. He came before a closed door at the end of the hall. Then he heard voices in prayer. When he opened the door he saw that the light came from a golden altar. Several beautiful maidens were praying before it and were startled when he entered the room. The altar filled the whole room and had four golden pillars on each corner. Beneath the altar were a series of candles. At the top of the altar was the symbol of the golden trinket that matched the same trinket Bedivue wore. He marveled at this for some time. Bedivue became stupefied at the sight of it. He fell to his knees in tears. He could not utter a word but showed unto the virtuous ladies the locket he wore. He then fell in a swoon to the floor and slept a deep sleep.

He awoke in the morning, fully armed, beneath an oak tree on a grassy hill. There was no more room with an altar, nor any castle before him. He sought after his palfrey and found it by an apple tree close by. Confused, Bedivue leapt unto his horse and made his way from the area. Not before long he came to an open plain where a large band of thirty warriors made a trail of dust. Bedivue rode after those warriors with haste. When he reached them he inquired: "Have you seen a magnificent castle with a band of virgin ladies inside worshiping an altar?" One of the men who seemed to be the leader replied: "We have seen them. We destroyed every stone of that castle and took the wealth for our kin. We captured the ladies and brought them into slavery. We defiled the altar and sold it in the market."

When Bedivue heard these words he grew red with anger. So furious was he that he beheaded the one who spoke without any further words. When the others saw this they charged in a fury but he lopped off their heads, arms, legs and bodies. He assailed the men on both the right and left side. His horse was swift and the enemy became blinded by the power of the locket. After he killed ten of them the others started to flee. Still, he chased after them without mercy. In this way he killed every member of that band except one. The prisoner pleaded for mercy when Bedivue told him: "You have defiled a sacred altar and brought dishonor to the most virtuous ladies that ever were. Before I slay you right now you will tell me where I can recover what you have taken!" So the prisoner told him where to go. Bedivue set off and left the prisoner in the field. He was covered in the blood of his companions and trembling.

Raining fury and vengeance on the vile thieves Bedivue ventured into the forest after them. Bedivue traveled for two days without food and he grew weary. Though he refused to rest until he could have his vengeance. There was no food to be had. The ladies were abducted and the land was cursed because of it. The plants and trees in the forest were withered in the middle of May. The wasted lands brought sickness to the people for they could not reap any food. Many village-folk were dead from starvation. The wells, where their had been many, were now all dried up. People in that land had gone to the wells for sustenance for centuries and, when the evil warriors captured the maidens who guarded the altar the wells dried up. Now the whole land was a complete waste land!

Bedivue finally made it to a cowherds house by the road. There was a hermit there too and Bedivue asked him how to cure the land of the wasted state it was in. So the hermit told him: "You must find those who hold the virgins captive. It was by their worship upon the altar that the land maintained its prosperity. Now that they are gone the land will become an utter wasteland until they are saved. You must slay the heathens who took them and de-

272

filed the altar. Fill their blood in vats and spread it across the soil. Then take the rest of it and fill the dried up rivers. Then will the wasteland be restored and renewed. A great rain will fall and bring new life." The hermit was very good to Bedivue and fed him what little he had. Bedivue confessed to him that he had not always lived on the right path but swore to avenge the fair maidens.

Saying farewell to the hermit Bedivue ventured further into the forest after the heathens. It is then that the knight met a raven by the road. The bird flew south and Bedivue pursued it. The bird brought him to a hidden encampment near a lake. It is there that he found what he was seeking. The men had a camp by the road. They had the virgins on carts being humiliated. Their clothes were torn and they were all but naked upon the carts being chastised. The men made jokes at them and had begun to violate them wickedly.

Bedivue grew enraged at the sight. Never before was he so wroth. He charged at them with the fury of a boar. Bedivue took his charger to the center of the encampment and when it whinnied everyone looked at him. He leaned on his lance and said: "Stop this and put back those chaste women. I will take vengeance on you so arm yourselves for I will never fight men unarmed because it is a great shame to do so." When the encampment heard Bedivue's bellowing voice and saw his proud visage they cowered in fear. Many took to flight at the sight of him. A great multitude of men congregated against him. They numbered one hundred.

The bold Bedivue crossed himself upon the brow and hurled upon them with the strength of a lion. He thrust his lance into the thickest press and it went clean through a man's body. He took it out and then aimed it at another one's neck. It plunged into the neck and blood went everywhere. Then he drove it through a mens stomach and it broke inside. So he drew his blade, which was sharp and bejeweled, from his scabbard and began assailing the men on all sides.

He slew thirty of them with his sword. No one could defend against his mighty blows that came down like hammers on an anvil. He lopped of heads and limbs with

273

ease making those wicked men look like fools. Then Bedivue's horse was pierced by spear. When they killed his horse Bedivue continued the onslaught afoot. He hacked and hewed them down for their armor was light and he was fully armed. They were no match for his prowess in arms for he was a knight errant.

They feared him greatly for he gave mercy to none of them. He did not fear their numbers but continuously slew them. With his sword he splattered brains and intestines to the earth. By nightfall all the one hundred were dead and Bedivue was covered in their blood, his eyes full of rage like a lion. He had some wounds and needed rest. The maidens, who had watched the battle from the carts, came to him and tended his wounds. One of them had a most holy ointment, which had been used to wash Christ's feet at one time. She applied it and he was quickly healed of all his wounds.

Then the maidens praised him: "Fair and worthy knight you have saved the land with your strength and bravery. Glory is to you who has protected the realm from becoming a wasteland." So Bedivue followed the maidens to a pavilion where the altar was resting. They sanctified it and prayed. They took the blood of the one hundred and placed it into a cauldron. Then Bedivue and the fifty virgins filled vats with the blood. They scattered it on the soil and filled the rivers with it. After this they grew very tired and slept in the pavilion next to the altar. That night it rained heavily and Bedivue had a vision.

A brown eagle circled the skies in search of prey. Before long he caught sight of a mouse and dived for it. When the mouse was caught it pleaded for its life. The eagle asked it: "Little mouse, I am hungry. What could you offer me in place of your life?" The shrewd mouse answered: "Take instead the berries that grow near my home. It is said that if you eat of them you will never hunger again." The mouse showed them to the eagle and he was delighted. "I thank you mouse for you have taken my desire for food." The presumptuous eagle began to eat of the vine where the berries grew. It wasn't long before he died, for the crafty mouse had led the eagle to berries that were poisoned.

The next day a snake approached the same mouse. Just as it began to clench its jaws upon him he pleaded for his life: "Fair snake, before you devour me learn of the immortality I can offer you!" The snake held back his venomous teeth and listened: "Not far from here, outside the forest, is an ancient fountain. If you drink of it you will live for three hundred years. Please let me live and I will take you to it!" The snake allowed the pardon but still planned to eat the mouse once he led him to the fount of immortality.

They reached the fountain which stood in an open plain where no trees grew. The mouse then told the snake: "There in the distance of this open space lays the fountain of immortality. Drink of it and you will live forever. You must follow the path outside the cover of trees to drink of it. I will never go near it for fear of its power." The snake, arrogant and proud, ventured out of the forest coverage towards the fountain. The trek was long and during this time a great many eagles encircled the skies above. It was easy for them to spot the snake as he drew towards the fountain in the open space. The snake was so blinded by his lust for immortality that he did not recognize the grave danger he was in. One eagle came down upon him and devoured him, for it was hungry.

When Bedivue awoke he recounted the vision. The maidens heard about it, from start to finish, and laughed. They interpreted it thus: "You are the mouse who has beguiled your enemies by throwing the one upon the other. So have you found ways to establish your prowess and bring vengeance on your enemies in a just manner. Likewise, your victory over enemies for all time will establish a covenant between us." The maidens all praised him. In the light of the morning they saw that the lands had been restored to prosperity. The fields were lush and green again. The rivers were flowing. People harvested wheat and were overjoyed at the lands restoration. Bedivue returned the maidens to a castle nearby where they were to live out the rest of their days.

Bedivue, having completed his quest, stayed with the virgins. He made a vow to protect them at the castle and establish a legacy in the land. The altar was taken to his magnificent castle to be praised eternally. It was so sacred that they deemed it essential that knights band together to protect it from invaders for all time. For when the altar was secure the wells of the land were no longer dried up and the people could draw from them once again. The manna that came from those wells was directly related to the state of the altar and the worshiping of the virgins.

Thus Bedivue and his whole lineage swore to protect the maidens and the altar from evil. They created a covenant and became the Order of the Maidens to protect the lands prosperity. So did all those knights who protected the maidens after Bedivue swear oaths of chastity and were men of the utmost virtue. King Arthur praised Bedivue until the end of time for he had felt the land return to abundance when the evil one hundred were slain and their blood sacrificed. That altar stayed in the Kingdom of Logres for many years. It was only later that, when the nobles turned to sin and avarice, this altar was moved to the holy land by the most noble Galahad, Perceval and Bors.

It was returned to the promise land where it eventually went back up to heaven. Those maidens were buried with it, along with Perceval's sister who was the holiest of them all. That lady, whom is spoken of in the french book, is said to have given life to a leprous woman with her blood. When God saw that she had so selflessly given herself away he reigned terror on the leprous woman and all her people so that they were all killed and the castle was raised to the ground. For Perceval's sister was most holy. That is why her death was avenged on that whole city so that it was raised in flames and turned to ashes. Similarly did the treacherous Vortigern perish by flames in his fortress because St. Gildus prayed for it; for he had let the Saxons enter the lands and refused to give the kingdom to its rightful heir.

# 4 THE RAVEN KNIGHT

Hear now of a tale that emerged from an adventure at this time. There was a beautiful lady who was much given to the art of enchantment who lived in the forest alone. Her name was Gwen. She was a marvel to look at and the most beautiful maiden there was. It was no wonder the most powerful magician in the land loved her. She lived by a lake in a magical mansion that was built for her by this magician. The mansion had the quality that it would only appear to those whom she wished it to be revealed to. The magician loved the maiden dearly for she was more beautiful than any creature. Yet she betrayed him by imprisoning him in a stone cave with the magic he had taught her.

When this happened the whole kingdom lamented because the magician was an important counselor to the king. I will speak no more of this occurrence as it is recounted in the old french book. For the magician was named Merlin and Sir Bedivue was the last to talk to him before the quest for the Holy Grail began. After Merlin had been unjustly interred through wicked magic the lady rejoiced because she was free of his love.

One day, a knight was in the area looking for adventure. He was greeted by this very maiden. He saw her face and, noticing her beauty, became enchanted. The fires of lust grew heavy in him at the sight of her. The knight asked her if she needed company. She told him that she was in distress and required help.

Here is what she said: "Fair knight, since the magician that created my home has been imprisoned I have had many torments from the beast in the lake. This monster is frightening. He has eight eyes and huge claws. His feet are like a lion, his head like a serpent and his body is like a bull. His neck turns many colors and enamors the beholder so that he can attack you more easily. Moreover, he is full of lust and has tried to assault me. I have been unable to keep my maidenhood! I must confess that I trapped the magician because I did not want to be defiled by him, however gracious he was. Though now, without his protection, I am continuously defiled by the beast of the

277

lake. If you are noble and courteous you will avenge me for the one who has taken my virginity did it unlawfully."

The knight was taken back by the lady's words. She was right to have wanted to protect herself. The knight was of the court of King Arthur and was sworn by oath to help a lady in need. He felt torment at the vision of her being defiled by a monster. The knight agreed to save her but related that he would under no circumstance tell her his name until after the monster was dead. The lady agreed and took him to the invisible castle which graciously appeared before him.

When the mansion was revealed to the Raven knight he marveled for some time. The inside was spacious and luxurious. The hall was composed of white marble and many bronze statues encircled the hall. The table cloth and gowns the servants wore were of the finest silk and of many colors. The stone walls were inlaid with emeralds that shined brightly.

At the center of the hall was a long table with a cauldron on top of it. Food was readily available from the cauldron at any time because it had magical properties. A company of ladies sat around the cauldron praying and this seemed to produce the food. In this way the cauldron held the food that the recipient most desired. There was a river that flowed through the main hall that had water that could cure of any illness if one only drank it. It was full of minerals and made the water a bright purple. The river led outside to a waterfall where the maiden often drank and bathed. The water kept her in her youth though she had lived there for almost a hundred years.

The raven knight sat down to eat and talked of many things with the lady. They grew tired and slept in a royal bed that was most elegantly adorned with every kind of soft fur. In the morning, the knight armed himself. He said prayers and crossed himself for he was preparing to undertake a most perilous journey. The knight was very tall and handsome. His long black hair was smooth. His armor was heavy and gold. His shield was black with three yellow ravens on it. He was known as the Raven because of his shield and arms. It was also heard that he could turn himself into a raven and fly to different places at will. Many

278

feared him because he was so powerful and unable to be defeated in combat. When he armed he asked leave of the damsel. Before leaving he made a request that if he should be victorious that she grant him whatever he wished. "I will gladly give you what you most desire, provided I can give it without dishonor."

The raven knight leapt unto his charger and went to the shore of the lake to await the monster. He sat there for some time before seeing the cruel beast rear its ugly head from the water. He then called out so that it would know that it was being challenged. "Come here, foul one! I will take your life for defiling this good lady!" The beast laughed and snarled as it arose from the murky lake. It had many boils and scars on its massive body. It was a slime-green color. It had over fifty arms that were incredibly long as they came out from his body. His arms carried sharp talons that cut like razor blades. His mouth was huge for it was a very gluttonous beast. Its teeth were many and sharp.

The beast exited the depths of the lake at the sight of the challenger. It showed off it's gleaming neck that had an array of colors on it which shimmered in the sunlight. The Raven knew of this enchantment and covered his eyes at the sight of the colors; for if he was given to looking he would surely have died. The beast opened its jaws and struck the raven knight in the leg so that he fell to the ground and bleed a great deal.

The second time the beast came for him he dodged out of the way. Then he struck one of his arms completely off with his sword. The beast swooned in anguish and the blood spurted everywhere. The beast then picked him up from the ground and attempted to eat him whole, licking his lips. His mouth was larger than the man's body so it would not have been difficult.

Yet the good knight was clever and resisted with his shield as he came against the monster's teeth. When he had successfully defended himself he saw the beast's tongue coming for him. This was no ordinary tongue but it was covered with boils and hideous swells. The stench from his breath was terrible and ghastly. The Raven cut the gluttonous beast's tongue with his sword so that it fell completely off. The monster was in great pain at this.

279

When it felt that it had lost its tongue it immediately dropped him. He was now on the offensive and charged at it.

It was distracted and so he brought his sword into it's scaly side. He saw that the scaly armor was impenetrable so he got beneath it and thrust his sword all the way to the hilt into the beast's belly. Then he ran across the length of the body opening the entire belly. The cut was over eight feet in length. The beast's intestines fell on top of the knight so that he was completely immersed in them. That vile beast groaned, became unconscious and slowly died.

The Raven rejoiced, though covered completely in his enemy's intestines. He bathed himself and returned to the maiden. He told her his name was Loren and he was a prince from the castle of Durden. The lady was very grateful for being avenged. She swore to be his lady and love him always. Though Loren was a noble and courteous knight. Hear what he told the lady: "Fair lady, you are very beautiful but I will not take you with me. You said you would do as I request and here is what I ask of you: return to the magician that made this mansion for you. He loves you dearly. Free him from the imprisonment you have made for him and take him as your lover for all time."

The maiden accepted the task and immediately freed the magician, despite her quarrels about it. Thus the two lived together in the invisible castle for many years in great happiness. Loren returned to his kingdom and recounted the tales to a scribe who set it in writing. Thus ends the tale of Loren, otherwise known as the Raven.

# 5 THE WOUNDED KNIGHT

Here a tale is recounted about a knight who was grievously wounded during battle. This knight fought for King Arthur against the Saxons and participated in the fighting where it was worst: upon what they call today slaughter bridge. That river ran red and many foes and friends alike were slain there. The Britons drove the enemy back in flight that day but many were killed in the effort. A great many fairies from the forests went about healing the wounded men. They were under enchantment to use their craft to make the knights and wounded warriors better. They took them to their castle in the forest where a great multitude of men sat in the hall, lamenting their abysmal fate and gaping at their wounds. Nearby the battlefield there was an isolated area in the mountains where the fairies lived. The drawbridge was lowered and all the wounded were welcomed. Some were carried on carts or biers while the more fortunate walked in on their own. Many wounded lay stricken with their death wound throughout the stone halls. Limbs were struck from bodies, and blood flowed copiously unto the cold stone floor. There were not enough beds so that men sat in the hall, dying in the arms of helpless maidens who were full of tears.

So many suffered that there were thousands left in the field, dying of their wounds without treatment. This had been the bloodiest battle beyond reckoning. Both sides started with over one hundred thousand men. So many were wounded and had little hope for life.

Yet the magic in England was a great marvel. Many that came to the castle were healed because of it. Near the castle where the wounded resided there were large fruit trees. Upon these trees were a great many juicy apples. The apples were picked and placed into a vat. Blades grinder the apples and squeezed out juice into a cauldron beneath the tree. This cauldron had boiled water that heated the juice and made it into an unguent paste. The fairies took this paste and brought it to the wounded.

There were three thousand who lay wounded in great peril; all of those who drank this mystical liquid were healed almost instantly. This was a marvelous feat and to this day the region is known as the healing orchard. At night the warriors who were tormented by their wounds heard the fairies playing harps and accordions in the meadow outside the castle. This entranced them as they dozed off, finding themselves healed by morning.

After great tumult there is always everlasting peace. Slowly Arthur's army grew in strength and they returned to court. Subsequently, as more wounded filed in, the tree would grow more of the apples seemingly overnight and they would go into the vats. Several men helped the fairies with the paste and brought it to the castle, applying it liberally on wounds.

One knight sat on the stony floor in great anguish. He had been a very valiant knight who had killed several hundred of the enemy with his battle axe alone. When one of the Saxon princes saw that he was hurting his forces he grew vengeful and full of anger. The prince and his brother plotted to attack him at the same time. In the thick of the battle he had received a horrible blow to the head that had all but killed him. When he lay on the ground, unhorsed and stunned, he realized that his skull had been opened at the top and his brains were exposed. He could not speak but felt that he would surely die.

Though feeling terrible pain the men brought forth the healing ointment for him. It wasn't long before he was healed. The knight had been healed but was completely shocked. He didn't know if he was dead or otherwise. He remembered not his name or what had happened to him. When he came to his senses he ran from the castle into the forest where he tore off his clothes, running around like a mad man. His squire pursued him in hopes of recovering his health to little avail.

The knight spent many days in the forest eating raw flesh and nuts. He did this for some time before a miraculous thing happened. He found a group of people in the forest playing games, caroling and dancing. There was so much merry making and it pleased him greatly. They seemed to be enraptured and so he joined them in the dance. Though when he joined them he became imprisoned in a trance.

His squire, who had loyally followed him for many weeks, tried to take him away from them but they all just kept dancing to their hearts' content. Convinced that all efforts were hopeless, the squire finally left his knight. It was clear these men and women were forced into revelry by some spell or otherwise. For good magic could heal all of Arthur's army but bad magic could imprison the best knight's of all!

Then a lady among the company in the forest asked the knight to sit on the throne at the center of the camp. A beautiful iron throne was there upon a dais. The wounded knight willingly agreed and, when this was done, the carousing stopped and everyone was immediately restored to sanity. The knight, now finding himself completely naked, sought to cover himself for he had been brought to his senses at that very moment. Whatever enchantment that had been upon him was removed when he sat in the throng.

The ladies and men of the party were incredibly grateful for him for they could not find anyone to stop the spell that they were in for a very long time. The lady said: "Alas, we've been saved, for we were forced to do this for one hundred years until a knight virtuous enough could free us." Their was rejoicing among all the party. They begged him to remain their ruler but he refused, yet he would have made a great king if he chose it.

The knight then set out towards the castle where he had been healed of his wounds. Fortunately he had returned to sanity so he was welcomed joyfully by the men who had sought after him.

Then he retired to the meadow and sat by a lake in the sun. Sticking out of the water was an arm and in it was the most beautiful sword he had ever seen. The sword was completely bejeweled with red rubies at the hilt. The blade was sharp and had gold letters written on it: "HE WHO TAKES THIS BLADE WILL ACCOMPLISH AN EXTRAORDINARY ADVENTURE." The knight was aghast because he could not believe such a phenomenon. Being a strong youth he set out into the river that came up

283

to his shoulders. He took the sword from the arm which immediately receded back into the water. When he returned to the shore he saw that the sword had many inlaid emeralds and was very beautiful to look at. On the other side of the pommel another inscription wrote: "THIS SWORD WAS BUILT IN THE FLAMES OF AVALON." Astonished by the markings, the knight found it clear that this sword was no ordinary sword. Moreover, he was very eager to test the blade's strength.

Suddenly the lake, castle and all his fellows disappeared. He found himself on a road in a forest far away. At this place there were a number of hostile men and giants. The knight rode towards them and demanded them to leave the place in peace. The giants were large and brutish. They immediately became enraged at this remark and threw large stones at the knight. One of them yelled out: "This is our land and the British King has no sway here. Welcome to the wild marshes where you will meet your death!" He used his shield to defend himself and dodged the stones with great agility. Then a host of wild men charged at him. There were over twenty of them in the camp. Yet the wounded knight, who was now fully healed, gave a great battle cry and ran into battle more fierce than a wild boar. He knew that he could kill this wild band and restore the northlands to the Scottish king.

He took the sword from Avalon and plunged it into bodes, covering it in red blood to the hilt. He hacked and hewed with such might that he made a great pile of limbs before him. Even the giants couldn't kill him despite their mighty clubs and big bodies. He did not fear being outnumbered because of the strength he felt from the sword and his own prowess.

He delivered a blow on a giant's head that opened the skull to the brain, and in this way he was rightly avenged. Moreover, the blade cut through heavy armor with ease. Its power was astounding. Arms, legs, heads and entire bodies were cleft with it's blows. After the entire twenty men and beasts were dead, he rejoiced at the victory. He was a very powerful knight and in that whole battle he remained mounted without any wounds.

284

The knight journeyed beyond this camp and found a fountain. He approached it and found that it was connected to seven different streams that drew water from it. Each stream extended from the stone fount and at each head was an intricately carved face. The knight marveled at the beauty of the sculpture and was very thirsty. He sat down near it and drank from each of the different areas. This water surely had magical properties for he grew more vigorous than he had been before. A loud voice then shouted out: "This river is a testament of the seven great kings who will restore Britain to glory. They descend from the most holy Joseph who came to these lands with the Holy Grail. Know that the land will be restored through a most virtuous knight who is soon coming to King Arthur's court!" The knight was astonished and swore to report this to Arthur when he returned.

After he had quenched his thirst he saw a white crane nearby. The crane spoke plain english, which was a surprise to him. He asked a favor of him as the most courteous knight who ever lived. "Well, pretty bird, if it is within my power and does not give me shame I will do it." The crane asked him to return the sword because it was meant for another who was soon to return to life after being dead many years.

The knight agreed to this for he felt the blade was far to powerful anyhow. It is known that this knight returned the sword out of goodwill and because of this he was known as the most courteous knight of all time. For he could have kept it and led a viscous rebellion against the King but refused to do this for his love of chivalry. He was awarded by holy men many great riches for returning the relic to the hand he had found it in when he returned to the South lands.

Know that the crane was preparing the sword for the return of Arthur many years later. Many of us humbly await his second coming where he will return Britain to its former glory and bring peace to the lands again! So ends the tale of the wounded knight who was strangely healed, became mad, was restored and discovered the sword known only to the most marvelous king in history. Know that after this many called him Menlyas the courteous.

Later it is told that this sword was returned to King Arthur when he came back from Avalon with his sister Morgan Le Fay. He returned to Logres to defeat the perilous enemies who tormented his people. He bore a shield with a cross on it and avenged his people through many bloody battles. He restored christianity to the lands and made everyone joyful again. In this way the Kingdom of Logres was returned to Arthur and God: may God's grace always be upon the land of Britain and may it receive his abundant gifts and blessings by the power of the Holy Spirit!

# 6 PERDER AND IOLA

Now the story tells of two knights who were cousins and saw many marvels together. It was by good fortune that they both lived during the time of King Arthur. They were known as Perder and Iola and they came from the distant lands of Brittany. Among their line were great kings. They had descended from King Bans of Benoic and Lancelot was their cousin. They came to Logres to accomplish a number of adventures which made them known throughout the kingdom.

They were courteous men and never displeased ladies in distress. In this way they were the very flowers of chivalry. When jousting they proved their skill of arms. The two cousins were ferocious in battle. Perder wore marvelous white armor and his shield was red with a white lion on it. Whenever he entered the lists everyone feared the white lion. Iola wore the same white armor but with a white shield and a red lion on it. The two knights were handsome and agreeable in demeanor and body so they were marvelous to gaze at, especially amongst ladies who hoped the winners of the tournament would deign to give them their love!

They attended many tournaments and often carried off the prize unless Lancelot was there. Perder could strike with his lance with more accuracy than any other. He unhorsed many foes, making the tumble to the ground in a heap! Iola was very quick on his horse in such a way that no one was such a good rider. After gaining much renown and prowess in King Arthur's lands they ventured into the forest for other adventures. Arthur begged them to stay but they took leave and were granted that boon.

When they left the city and rode around the coastline looking for adventure. It wasn't long before the two cousins came across a ship. "It seems this ship has come from out of nowhere. Though if it is an enchantment than it must be leading us somewhere to achieve glory. Let us set sail and accomplish whatever task it asks of us." Said the one. They entered the ship and it immediately departed. On the sail there were gold letters that said: "He who comes on this ship must conquer the Wild Marches, which are full of evil and wicked customs." On that ship were cots and enough provisions to last them the month. After many nights' journey the two cousins reached a distant island. The ship anchored all on its own and they exited the ship onto a sandy shore. After riding a little they found a windy path through the forest that took them to a fork in the road. One path went to the left and the other the right. The cross at the ford read: "Beware to enter the right path for only the knight who is clean from all sin will survive its adventure." This was a challenge and both the cousins said that they were eager to take the right path. For these two knights were both very virtuous and good christians.

After some hours without any encounter they came across a band of men. They were greeted and asked where they could find shelter. The group of men were five in number. They were tall, hairy and large in stature. They were wild men and one could tell by their ragged clothes they were living in the woods. Iola and Perder were very courteous knights. Yet the wild man were irritated by the whole encounter and told them that, since they were knights seeking adventure, they must flee before nightfall. "It is a custom of this land that all knights who come here are attacked at night; none has come here and survived." When questioned further the group of men jeered at them and fled into the forest. It wasn't long before the darkness made the two cousins uneasy.

By nightfall the cousins had taken refuge on the high ground overlooking the forest. The full moon kept the forest well lit so that they could see the wild-men in the forest below. Although something about them had changed. At night these were not ordinary men but they changed shape into beasts. Alas, they were terrible wer-wolves! The cousins were astonished to see such a thing and, never having disarmed that night, they mounted, grabbing a lance in one hand and placing their shields about their necks. The beasts charged up the hill, snarling and eager to draw blood from the valiant warriors. They rode quick and seemed like sprinting bears as they hurled into the galloping horses coming down the hill. The knights spurred their chargers and went into battle fear-lessly.

Perder plunged his lance into the chest of one of the beasts so that it splintered, leaving the tip inside his body. Then Perder was knocked from his horse by another one that he hadn't seen. It flew through the air and brought his horse to the ground, devouring it. Even though he had tumbled to the ground in a heap he quickly arose and drew his sword from its scabbard. Perder consequently delivered a blow of such might that he sliced the head off of it. Then another came upon him and he wrestled with it. For it tackled him to the ground so that he tumbled, fortunately he trusty hauberk protected him from claw and teeth. While the two wrestled one another Perder received a mighty blow on his head that made his blood spurt from his mouth and nose.

Perder was in great danger as the beast took him on the ground and began clawing through his helm and hauberk. After much battle Perder used his shield to bash the beast to the ground; then he grabbed his blade from the grass and thrust it into the beast's shoulder. The wound proved fatal as it fell to the ground, whimpering. Then Perder chopped off its head.

Meanwhile, Iola was lost on the other side of the wood in a terrible battle. He was beset by two werewolves that leapt for him. The first he struck with his lance so that it ran straight into his neck and through the other side. When the lance broke in two, he drew his blade and delivered a mighty blow on the other beast. It clove his arm off from the shoulder blade through the bone and out the other side. When he saw his cousin wrestling the beast he came to his aid.

One of the wolves who was wounded by Iola's lance took the shape of a man again. Iola said: "Strange creature, you have sought violence and brought this upon yourself. Tell us now what has caused you to become a beast?" The wolf man spoke as he coughed up blood: "I have given my life to protect the enchanted forest. We, like you, were once out here seeking adventure as good knights do. Then we met a beautiful damsel in the forest. She lured us to her castle. She gave us food, women and many riches that made us content. It was not long before we grew to trust her so much that we forgot our desire for adventure.

One night she took us to the garden and had us pick the most beautiful roses in the garden. We brought them back to the hall she had prepared for us. Yet, when we put the roses on the table the scent began to poison us. Those roses had an enchantment on them and with this she put a terrible curse on us. When we arose in the morning we took the form of beasts. That is why they call me the Beast of the Rose. She said that we must search the forest for good knights to capture and bring to her. We have imprisoned many in the same way. Please save my friends, some of them are still imprisoned by the damsel!"

The cousins then swore to avenge the helpless knights who had been cursed by a terrible damsel. After speaking the creature lost consciousness and died. They buried the poor beast along with his fellows. A stone inscription suddenly appeared where they buried them: "HERE RESTS THE BEAST OF THE ROSE AND HIS COMPANIONS WHO WERE ENCHANTED BY AN EVIL MAIDEN AND SLAIN BY THE TWO VALIANT COUSINS: IOLA AND PERDER."

When they had mourned the dead men enough the two cousins followed the path until they reached the maiden's castle. They were quickly greeted by the beautiful damsel who was eager to allure them. She came from the drawbridge with a large company of maidens. They were dressed in scarlet and fine ermine furs. Yet she did not know that her demons had been killed and that the cousin's were aware of her treachery. Indeed, her false deceit had been practiced unjustly for too long.

She brought a stout and grumpy dwarf along with her who took to riding a mule; he had a rod in his hand and wickedly struck the beast as it hobbled along. She also brought an assembly with her. A minstrel played the harp very well; this tune was enchanting, as was no surprise to the knights that she attempted to beguile them so. In this way they were welcomed with great rejoicing and were offered rest from their long journey. The dwarf along with a number of servants disarmed the knights and took their horses away, as was the custom of the castle.

After fighting with the beasts in the forest the two cousins were weary but they tried not to show it for they still feared for their lives. They entered a large banquet hall where they were given sumptuous feast with all kinds of entertainment. Everything imaginable was provided for them and they were greatly pleased.

Then Perder whispered to his cousin: "Dear Iola, if I didn't know this damsel's mischief I would gladly spend my final days here. It is no wonder the Beast of the Rose, who was so valiant, was easily beguiled. Such revelry I have not seen before. This is a joyous occasion and everything is provided for." In this way the entertainment continued so that the two knights felt completely content. The merry making continued into the late hours well after everyone had eaten the many courses.

Then the lady led the two knights to the garden. She showed them the roses and asked them each to take the one that struck them to be the most beautiful. "This is a wonderful game to play for the roses can later be given to the maiden you so choose among the many in my castle." Each rose was sweet and budding, even though it was February! Some were red, others pink and white.

Perder was flushed with wine and began to gaze in wonder at the roses. He had forgotten the maiden's treachery in the midst of the entertainment and was eager to pick one. Just before he did so, however, Iola came to his senses. For he saw the dwarf from across the garden carrying his shield. On the lower part of his shield there was a cross. When he saw the cross he remembered his Lord Jesus Christ who had died for the sins of man; then he recalled the treachery the beast had told him about, and especially the tragedy of the cursed rose. The sight of the cross broke the enchantment and he became conscious of how much danger they were in.

He then spoke: "I have never dared to strike a woman but you must perish from this earth for your wickedness! Swear to give up this evil custom and cease your enchantments or I will kill you. This treacherous witchcraft must cease!" The damsel turned very wicked and suddenly all the beauty she had left her; for her appearance was all a wicked enchantment. She called for her guards. "Slay these knights who refuse to take a rose of they're choosing, get them out of here!" Before anyone could do anything Iola ripped her head off with his bare hands. This was to the amazement and shock of the spectators at court, who all fled in terror.

Then the cousins chased down the hobbling dwarf, grabbed their arms and quickly donned them. They guarded each other valiantly, back to back, in the hall. A large company of men came after them but they were to difficult to assail. Iola plunged his blade into so many warriors that it was red all the way to the hilt. He himself was covered in the blood of the warriors that he killed. They stormed the castle, room by room, until about fifty men were slain.

After seeing the garden and hall filled with dead men, many fled to the keep in fear. The two knights were not content until they broke the door to the keep and killed those who had fled. When they had defeated the soldiers in the keep they found the damsel's dwarf. He was terribly scared and swore to surrender. Perder said to him: "Tell us where the prisoners are." So the dwarf showed them to where the damsel had kept all her prisoners. The chamber was dark. In it there was over one hundred prisoners. They were terribly thin and nearing death. The dwarf opened the gate and they were freed. It was by the grace and courtesy of the two cousins that their was much rejoicing to be had. The men all stayed at the castle until they were fully healed. In such a way the knights feasted and rejoiced.

After the death of that vile damsel, Perder and Iola were known throughout the land for they had freed a good many knights from that land of enchantment. It was such that the damsel had put their shields in her hall, so there was so many shields hung from the wall of the knights she held captive. In the midst of the rejoicing the freed prisoners went about removing their shields from the wall and taking back their arms, which was a great honor. Yet the cousins were still eager to explore the land for they did not think the Wild Marches had been purged of all wickedness. So they traveled down a dirt path from the maiden's castle in search of more adventure. That is why, in the time of King Arthur, it was called the era of adventure.

After four days of traveling they encountered a river. Near it, a mad man sat in deep contemplation. They saw from is unkept hair and nakedness that he was mad. Taking pity on the man, Iola asked: "Sir, what brings you to these parts and how may you be helped?" The wild man, clearly startled by their presence, fled towards the opposite side of the river. He jumped eight feet across the rapid waters. His strength to have completely cleared the ford was quite remarkable. The cousins were amazed by this feat and were sure he was a miracle worker. When safely across the river the mad man proclaimed: "Gentle knights, this river has been made by my hands. Drink from it and you will find eternal strength to protect you on your journey. This water represents the blood of your ancestors who died protecting these lands from enemies." The two cousins pleaded that the man tell them his name. It was known that mad men of the forest were often prophets or magicians. He refused to tell them anymore. Yet he did another feat that was astonishing. He quickly changed shape into a white hart. The cousin's were aghast. They spurred their horses in pursuit but the animal was much too fast and they found no way to get across the river.

So they did as the man had commanded and drank heartily from the river; soon they felt its powerful effects felt. The water had a special enchantment on it that made them see their ancestors before them. The spirits loomed above their heads in the sky and graciously saluted them. The spirits addressed them and told them they were their ancestors, Their was much embracing and joy at the reunion. Old warriors with long flowing beards and mighty arms smiled and gave one another counsel. They knew of the future and told of the past with delight. The knights learned that their adventures would bring eternal glory both on earth and in heaven. Suddenly the ancestors vanished and they were transported from that place. They didn't know what had happened other than that they felt a great winged beast propelling them forward faster than any horse could ride. When they dozed off in the midst of the activity they found themselves in a far different country when they awoke.

They set off from the river and rode for some time without any adventure. Then, by afternoon, they spotted bright pavilions in the distance. It was there that they met with a large group of knights beginning a tournament. All the knights prepared to joust and began hurling at each other, splintering lances. Cheers from the crowd began and heralds started acclaiming noble feats as men fell from their horses and blood was drawn. Then sword strokes began and a mighty din arose as the unhorsed knights began combat for their honor and lady love.

King Arthur was there and he resided over the tournament; He was very pleased to see the two valiant knights, Iola and Perder. They recounted their adventures but most of the host already knew of their accomplishments for the word had spread since they released the prisoners: "Don't you know it has been many months since the Beast of the Rose was defeated?" They were confused, for it seemed only a few days before to them. Though they were enchanted with magic!

So in this way a great tournament began. King Arthur offered, as a prize for the tournament, one of his castles in the Northlands. So the jousters cheered from all sides and even more knights came every hour to enter into the lists. Iola and Perder set out against a number of other knights. These two were unmatched in the tourney and they dealt more vicious blows so that all the heralds acclaimed them as the mightiest knight's there.

They wounded all their opponents, unhorsing them so that they came crashing to the ground. Fortunately they did not kill anyone for their blows were treacherous and death dealing. After jousting the knights took out their swords. A whole twenty knights set upon the cousins to avenge the shame brought upon them during the joust.

Yet, even outnumbered in this way, the two cousins were unfailing in combat. They wounded their opponents who greatly outnumbered them. The sword fight continued for hours and the two cousins became weary. The opponents realized that if they continued the battle they would receive nothing but shame since they so greatly outnumbered the two cousins. Therefore, bloody with many wounds, they retired and the tournament ceased. Since Perder and Iola knocked all their opponents from the saddle with ease and fought so well with the sword they won the award that day.

King Arthur rejoiced and gave them his castle in the Northlands because they were able to win the tournament. He would have rather given such a large reward to no others. At the feast the cousins recounted their many adventures in detail, leaving nothing out. King Arthur marveled at it all and had the missing prophet searched for. Yet they never found him. They say that he was not of this world because he could change shape so easily. Even so, after the tournament his voice was heard throughout the valley: "Iola and Perder have the power of their ancestors and cannot be defeated." Everyone was astonished to hear the voice of a man that could not be found.

The next day, as the knights continued to feast and rejoice, another wondrous marvel occurred. Many credit the mad man who had spoken to the people there with it. Suddenly the earth quaked and different river emerged outside the pavilions where they were eating.

This startled everyone so that screaming and yelling was heard throughout the valley. When the river emerged the water gushed from the soil and earth. At this time that same prophet said: "Drink to your heart's delight so that you may be at peace." The entire company ventured outside, amazed at the newly formed river. They eagerly drank from the river hoping to acquire as much strength as the cousins had. Though they became very sleepy afterwards. The whole company ceased the festival and took a long rest. It was not until mid afternoon the next day that Iola and Perder awoke. When they came to, they found that none of the company remained. They were in the barren Wild Marches again! The pavilions were gone and so were all the people.

They came to a castle where a wicked King lived. Rather than welcoming them he shunned them because they were from King Arthur's court. They were at the gatehouse, calling to the man: "We ask for lodging, can you give it?" The keeper replied: "As long as you aren't knights of King Arthur, for we of the Wild Marches oppose him and all his knights." Then Iola responded: "That is a wicked custom. We challenge you or anyone who denies to pay King Arthur homage!" Greatly incensed, the two cousins waited outside for a response. Amongst loud deliberation the drawbridge lowered and ten angry knights came out to meet them. They were donned in black arms and one of them, who was the king and led the pack, called out: "King Arthur has no sway here. We will fight you. If I win I will take your heads and send them to your Lord. If you win I will swear to pay homage to the King and go to him as a prisoner." This was agreed upon and so a combat began.

Perder took out a strong ash wood lance and unhorsed the first three knights, one after another. Then Iola jousted and took down two more. The last five knights, who were amazed, assailed them on all sides at once. This was very shameful for no knight deserved to be attacked by multiple enemies if all those in combat were considered honorable. So a skirmish ensued. Perder broke his lance as he drove it through the shield and hauberk of a knight. It stuck fast in his belly and tore apart the man's insides. He fell over his horses rump and crashed to the ground in a heap. Then he drew his sword and struck a might blow that hit a knight on the head so hard it went through helm, skull and brain straight down to the shoulders. His upper portion split in two and all the insides could be seen plainly.

Iola rode straight for the king and spurred his steed towards him. They crashed into each other. Both horses fell for they bucked head to head. Each knight flew from his saddle and their lances shattered. They rose and struck one another with swords, dealing heavy blows. They hacked and hewed so that shields were shattered and hauberks were no longer worth any protection. Then the sword strokes cut open flesh. Each knight had terrible wounds and bled profusely. Finally, Iola struck the king on his head so that his helm went flying and blood streamed down over his face. He was quite shocked by the blow and blindly flailed his sword in the air. Then Iola tackled him to the ground and threatened to behead him. The king was not responsive so he waited until he came to his senses.

Then he threatened to behead him a second time and the king said: "I'll surrender and, as agreed, go to King Arthur as his prisoner." Iola responded: "And you are to tell him how wickedly you spoke to us and that you had refused to be gracious to anyone from his court." The king humbly replied: "Whatever you ask I will do it." When the king surrendered the others followed suit, even though there were only a few remaining.

In this way Iola and Perder put an entire castle under Arthur's subjection. They refused to stay any longer at that place but received fresh horses and left. They got back on the road and were angered to find that the mad man had cast a spell on them, for they were now very far from King Arthur's court again. Suddenly they heard a voice: "You have defeated the evil of the Wild Marches, so rejoice and be merry!" Then a storm arose that raised such a din they were quite helpless. They pulled off the road and hid under their shields. When they fell asleep they were picked up by a great winged beast and carried to the lands of King Arthur. Know that this was the doing of the mad man, who always played with them. Though he assured them that, because they defeated the Beast of the Rose and freed the prisoners, the Wild Marches would now come under King Arthur's rule.

When they returned to Camlan they gave an account of everything that had happened. King Arthur was shocked because he had thought the cousins were lost forever. Yet, since they were still alive, they were given the castle in the Northlands by declaration of King Arthur. Perder and Iola lived out their days serving King Arthur in that region. They managed to slay many barbarians in the Northland when the invasions arose. They also had many churches built and converted the pagans there to true Christians. The tale here tells no more about these two noble knights.

# 7 THE TOURNAMENT FOR THE MAIDEN

In the furthest regions of the mountains, closer to modern day Scotland, there was a city of people who lived without the bother of so many others. It was a fine castle and well situated in the mountains, so secluded that it wasn't easily found. Nearby the castle there was a large lake. The inhabitants got all they need from the lake and the surrounding forest. They fished from there and also hunted game. There was an abundance of deer and boar making the people merry. The Queen of that land gave birth to a single daughter. Oh, how that birth was a curse for it brought that lovely little place under the world's judgmental gaze. The Queen's little girl was more beautiful than any lady in all the world, which quickly turned their peaceful home into a zoo of suitors and knights of prowess jousting in tournaments that could be seen from the castle wall. Indeed, all the knight's in the world were drunk with lust for her.

It was the fairness of her face, the smoothness of her skin, the perfection of her breasts and the way she laughed. Her cheeks were rosy red and skin fair white. Her hair was the color of a broom, blonde and smooth as silk. Her body was perfectly proportioned and her skin as soft as a peach. Her lips and smile would make the coldest man melt with pleasure and burn with lust. She had the beauty that men start wars over; my Lord, isn't beauty really a terrible curse making the world rife with jealousy and violence? Nobles came from all over to see her and win her love. Those knights who traveled for her had only heard rumors of her beauty. When they met her they suddenly realized that she was beyond any cry of the imagination.

So it was settled that she would have to be married off, but how could they do this when their were so many suitors? So they devised a way of finding the best suitor. There was an island in the moat before the castle wall. Any knight who wished to have her love had to remain on that island for sixty days, defeating all those who challenged him. If he stayed for sixty days, without being defeated, then he could have the maiden as his wife.

298

So the knights lined up, making oaths upon relics that they would take on the perilous quest. Indeed, there were so many of them that they went about unhorsing one another round the calendar. It went on for many years like this. Some knights could endure as many as three days before being unhorsed by some new challenger.

The suitors eventually grew angry for they realized that it couldn't be accomplished so easily. They gathered together and took counsel on what best to do. One said: "We keep waisting all our efforts. We will never have her hand for there are too many that want her. I suggest we hold an extravagant tournament and, whoever is the best at the tournament can have her hand, provided she is willing." Many knights agreed that, after much deliberation, it made sense to hold a tournament. Among the group of suitors was the might King of Denmark, the King of Brittany, the King of Ireland and many other valiant noblemen.

So the next morning the inhabitants of the castle awoke to find a large company of servants and squires bustling about, clearing the field and setting up stands for the tournament. Many spectators gathered to that place, killing off the animals in the forest and drinking the spring dry. Indeed, so many people came from all over to see the splendid tournament that the place was overrun and over peopled to the point where you couldn't find a moment of peace and quiet!

Now I should tell you the beautiful damsel had a name and it was Rhonywan. They say her mother and father came by the union of the King Arthur and a river goddess, who lived in those parts as a worshipped deity before Christ came to the earth. The River Spirit was more beautiful than any in Logres and was found in the Northlands by Arthur. Arthur would hide the fact that, when he conquered the North, he came across this marvel. He came to the river and saw her as she bathed. Now Arthur had just accomplished his campaign in which he subdued the picts in the Northland and he was weary from battle. Being victorious, he came to the river to wash the blood from his body and face. For he had slain so many that he was covered in blood and even had some wounds of his own.

When he reached the river and saw the beautiful maiden, he knew that there was none more beautiful as her. She was weeping and lamenting bitterly and Arthur felt a good deal of pity. King Arthur, distressed, asked her: "Why do you weep, fair one?" The lady responded: "For I am forced to remain here washing by the river until a man of prowess takes me away. There is no greater torment for I am lonely and the water is cold." When Arthur heard this he, recognizing her great beauty, took her away with him. They conceived two children. One of which was later killed by the Giant Lohian and the other married off to a powerful baron at the castle in the mountain. It was a quiet subject that she had truly descended from Arthur. Now you realize why Arthur established the custom that a damsel in distress should always receive help from a knight of his court; and that the very flower of chivalry always did right by ladies. This is the story of how Rhonywan's parents gave birth to her and why she was so beautiful to behold.

Now, back to the tournament. The knights all fought openly on the field. The King of Ireland was very mighty and he unhorsed the multitudes with his unfurling pennon of green that fluttered in the wind so proudly. Lances splintered in every direction as the knight's jousted ceaselessly. Mail hauberks were torn about the shoulder arm and waist and littered all over the field along with splintered and shattered shields. The King of Ireland, bearing a checkered green and white shield, seemed to come off best, another knight, with a blue and white checkered shield, unhorsed him with a mighty blow to the chest. His lance thrust made his enemy far worse off due to the swiftness of his charger. This made the King of Ireland, quite bashful about it later, mortified at being un-horsed in such a way.

Alas, what a great fortune to have unhorsed the one that the heralds praised so highly! The blue knight stormed the field and raised a mighty din. He advanced into the thickest press and dealt wounds on both his left and right side. Blood gushed out from his fearful enemies that sorely

300

repented ever having challenged him. He had no other man that could challenge him, for he was far too mighty and fierce. Just then, from the forest, a red knight who had a red and white checkered shield spurred into battle, creating a terrible storm. In his wake, a multitude of unhorsed knights cried out in bitter anguish.

He spurred towards the blue knight, jealous that he was getting all the acclaim. They hurled towards each other and collided upon one another so hotly that they were both unhorsed in the tumult. They got up, though the red knight had the worst of it, and drew their swords. The red knight ran at him and delivered such a forceful blow on the helm that he split it apart to the ground. Then the blue knight returned the favor, knocking him over with a blow to the shoulder that cut through the mail hauberk. The red knight was stunned and fell to the ground. The blue knight ran over, tore off his helm and made him surrender then and there. Which he gladly did, for he had enough!

The heralds blew the horns to mark the end of the tournament, for it grew dark and all the knights were exhausted along with their horses. The heralds all proclaimed: "Hail the blue knight, mighty champion of the tournament." Afterwards, they held a marvelous feast in the castle and all proclaimed the deeds of the good blue knight. Although, to their dismay, the blue knight had left the field after the heralds blew the horn and no one could find him anywhere. The Queen was dismayed and blamed the heralds for letting him get away. "Alas, he's gone, how can we retrieve my true lover who has won the tournament?"

Meanwhile, the blue knight was off at a nearby hermitage, tending his wounds and lamenting his fate: "I may have achieved many good deeds today but I am so love struck that I don't know what to do! How can the maiden love me if she hasn't even seen me? What if she turns me down? I can't go back there, for they will tear me apart. I wouldn't know what to say and I can't bear the jealous looks of the older knights too!" In this way, the love struck knight pondered what to do. He was deeply dismayed, for he could fight so well but knew not how to speak to a lady. What a bind that was!

Meanwhile, at the castle, the King's all held counsel about what best to do since their champion was missing: "Well, since we can't seem to find the blue knight. I suggest we arrange another tournament so that he has no choice but to return. Even if he is disguised, i'm sure the lady will recognize him by his feats of prowess. Then, just before the tournament ends, we will seize him and force him back with us. He will have no choice but to marry the maiden!" The lady, who greatly desired to see the blue knight again, came up with a cunning plan: "When I recognize him, I'll have him offer me a rose. When he brings it to me, have ten knights surround him so he can't get away." They all thought this a very cunning plan and made merry for the rest of the night, giving no further thought to it.

At first light the next day, preparations were made for a second tournament. The heralds made their horns blare throughout the region, signaling all knights in want of honor to be summoned for another tourney. The blue knight, who wasn't far off, caught wind of this and promised he would prove himself again: "If my lady see's me fighting a second time then maybe she will realize how much I truly love her!" He painted his shield half yellow and half black so that no one would recognize him.

Thus all things were in order and, on a bright summer morning, the second tournament began with a clash and thunder of arms. The knights were all arranged and many late comers, who had missed the first tournament, arrived from foreign lands to try their lance with the many good knights there. The tourney was a marvel to watch. Thousands of ladies, damsels and maidens watched from the stands and castle wall in excitement as the knights clashed into one another, creating a thunderous din and splintering lances left and right. The loud sounds of combat and the acclaim of the heralds went on the whole morning and well into the afternoon. Shields were cracked and many good knights were unhorsed in the midst of the excitement.

The tournament went on for some time in this way and the lady of the castle who was to be wed grew anxious: "It doesn't seem that the blue knight has come to the tournament, our plans are ruined!" Lo, she had spoken too soon, for hear how a great marvel occurred.

Just then, she saw a knight on a swift charger, fully armed, idly watching near the stands. His shield was split down the middle: half black and half yellow. Yet, he had no lance to joust with. When she saw the knight so idle she bid her friend to take him a lance and said: "Whatever is this idle knight standing around for, have him take this lance and put it to good use!"

Then the lady carried the lance over and said to the knight: "The princess bids you good day and wishes you to take this lance and put it to good use, for she hates seeing anyone so idle!" When he realized that the one he loved had wished him to fight, he awakened from his reflections immediately and, taking the lance, spurred off to battle. He bore five knights from their horses in a swift display of arms that was hardly more than a miracle. The lady, when she saw this, thought that she recognized the way he jousted. "Is it possible that this is my beloved blue knight?"

The knight continued to fight so valiantly that he immediately won all the acclaim from the heralds. He eventually shattered his lance but didn't give up there. He continued to fight with his sword, dealing mighty blows all around until all the knights surrendered to him. He knocked down the King of Ireland with a mighty lance thrust that sent him hurling to the ground. Another knight in green tried to unhorse him but ended up getting thrown from the saddle so violently that he caught a handful of dust in his mouth and broke his arm.

After so much combat the blue knight took a moment to rest his horse and himself near the stands. He passed the time gazing intently on the lovely damsel, hoping he had caught her eye with his feats of prowess. He was very right to think so, for she then purposefully did something to show her love. She took the wimple from her head and, pretending she dropped it, flung it from the stands down to the knight. When he saw this, he delicately lifted up the wimple, offering it in return. Yet the maiden said: "Oh, it was just an accident that I dropped it. Well, maybe you can wear it, as a sign of my love in respect to your deeds today."

Rather than taking this as a joke, he was filled with love and he adorned the wimple on his head proudly, leaving his shattered helmet on the ground. When the maiden saw his handsome face she was stunned: he looked as handsome as he was strong.

Meanwhile, the red knight, who had been getting all the acclaim until are friend had arrived, grew very jealous. He saw the blue knight so distracted and hoped to come upon him in surprise. He spurred his stead into a full charge and tilted his lance. He was just about to bore the distracted knight to the ground when he turned his gaze and realized that the red knight was upon him. He quickly spurred after him, forgetting that he had a wimple on his head, and collided with the knight, dealing him such a terrible blow that he fell over the rump of his horse and into the hard dirt.

Everyone burst out laughing as they saw the knight with the wimple defeat the jealous red knight, who now had cheeks as red as his armor for he was very embarrassed. The blue knight was less than content with this; he got off his saddle and ripped off the red knight's helm, demanding he surrender. He did so, for he was utterly defeated.

When the lady of the house realized he was the very same knight that she loved, she went about capturing him. She sent for her messenger and bid her tell the knight: "if he wished to win her love he must bring her a fine red rose as a gift." When this message was delivered, the blue knight was filled with excitement, and set off in a hurry towards to woods to find a rose. He came across a rose bush in the midst of some brambles and plucked the finest red rose you could imagine.

He swiftly spurred on towards the stands where the lady sat along with the nobles of the country. He went up the steps and kneeled before the lady. Then he nervously uttered: "My lady, I desire nothing more than your love. Take this rose as a testament to that." Just then, the ten armed knights surrounded him and ardently refused to let him run off as he did the last time. Then, as he was stuck there, the heralds blew the trumpets to sound the tournaments end. Alas, the blue knight was trapped! He had truly won all the acclaim too.

When the tournament finished and everyone was walking back to the castle for the feast, the lady took the blue knight aside. They were all exhausted form battle but he was so elated by love that he had never felt more joy in his heart. The lady looked up at him and softly said: "Are you the one that was here yesterday carrying blue arms?" He was very embarrassed by all the people around but managed to nod in assent. The heralds all marveled and yelled out: "Here is the winner of the tournament, the blue knight!" Horns went blaring when they had identified the victor of the tournament for both days.

He later confided that his name was Gautimer, and he was King of Scotland. Everybody was amazed that she was to be wed to a knight of such a noble line. In this way the winner of the tournament was given his prize, which was the most beautiful maiden in all the land. He had earned this through the prowess of his remarkable feats in the tournament! When her father passed away they became king and queen of that whole land.

# 8 KING ARTHUR'S DREAM

King Arthur campaigned for many years against the Saxons. In his twelve battles he was able to accomplish more than any Welsh king had done before. Before the battle of Badan Hill upon Slaughter Bridge there was a peculiar vision that the king had which I will tell of. It is known that Badan Hill was a massive battle that took place between the Saxon and Welsh forces. Before the battle Arthur spent his day with his counselors, who advised him in various ways. Though nothing created certitude in him more than the vision he had in his pavilion on the battle-field the night before. After many hours of deliberation he grew tired and took a nap. Then he had the vision that proved to be a determining factor in the battle.

Arthur envisioned a great bear who was ferocious. It was hairy and had large claws for striking. It had red eyes and frothed at the mouth for want of blood. The bear emerged from the skies and seemed to be suspended in the air. It was full of rage and ran towards a dragon who was laying down in a field. The dragon was near a fountain encircled by three rings of fire. The bear had a terribly vengeful desire to strike the dragon. So he ran at full speed through the rings of fire and tackled the beast. The dragon fought him for many hours. At the last he struck the bear in the gut so that his intestines spread out on the floor. Yet the dragon had lost so much blood from the teeth and claws of the bear so that he too also fell to the ground in anguish. After groveling on the ground the dragon rested beside the fountain in the grips of death.

Yet a man came out from the forest and attended to his wounds. He brought the wounded dragon water from the fountain. This water was able to heal the dragon fully. Yet shortly thereafter another dragon came to that same place to drink from the fountain. When he did so he grew very strong and fierce. This dragon was a good deal younger than the first one. To test his strength he entered into combat with the older dragon. In this way both the dragons were slain by one another. Know that the older dragon was white and the other red.

After Arthur had witnessed this he realized he was sitting on top of a great big wheel. From the top of the wheel he could see the whole Kingdom of Logres that he was lord over. It was a marvelous sight and he could see all across the open lands, every bit of it was under his lordship. Alas, what a glorious kingdom it was. Yet, slowly but surely, this wheel turned in such a way that he went from the very top of it to the very bottom. When the wheel began to descend to the bottom Arthur began to grieve. As he approached the lower area he found himself in the throws of hell. Demons snarled and snakes hissed at him. The valleys that were green became dark and desolate. Indeed, he had no happiness in what he saw. Worms and maggots ate at his skin. Then he was taken from the wheel and thrown into a chamber. Fires roared around him and he lay inside of a dark dungeon. Arthur weeped at this for he had descended from the most glorious place to a place of shame. Thus he burned in the terrible fires of hell. Indeed, he had very little comfort with so much tribulation. Then a voice shouted out to him: "Arthur, you have been removed from your seat of glory because of a mortal sin that you committed. Your kingdom will lay in ruin because of this sin. Pray to god that you may be restored to your original position and, if he is truly merciful, he will grant it."

After this he awoke from the vision, he was astonished and wondered what it all meant. Truly, fortune is a fickle thing. Those who rise to a seat of power and go so high that they cannot be seen by others eventually fall. All the great empires of the world have fallen in a similar way by their own folly. They beat others down and those, learning the tricks of the victor, do the same to them until they rise to power, defeating those that beat them. This happens over and over all over the place in many different contexts. Eventually, the great will fall, and the good men will die. Just the same, the worst of sinners can rise to glory and became spotless through noble deeds and repentance.

When Arthur awoke he marveled at his vision. Then he recounted it to his counselors who were overcome with curiosity. Unable to decipher its meaning they summoned

Merlin who was the wisest of wise men. He heard about this vision and told them all: "The death of the bear, representative of the Saxons, will bring peace to the Welsh kingdom temporarily. The Saxon invaders will be repelled by the dragon who is Arthur. Yet, another dragon, who is younger in years will bring a worse tragedy, yet he will come to fruition, being the same blood as Arthur, by a great mortal sin. For Arthur's son Mordred, the red dragon, will betray his own father commencing the greatest civil war that ever occurred. When this happens the kingdom of Logres will be destroyed. The, when the forces of Briton are killed in this great civil war, the Saxons will invade a second time and no one will be there to defend it." What Merlin said was no surprise for he later told it to his scribe Blaise before it happened. It is also recounted in full detail in the old French book.

Merlin went on: "The two will fight fiercely, like the two dragons, and, in the tumult, slay one another. Unless it can be prevented by counsel this will plummet the kingdom of Logres into great despair. No more adventures will be had because of it. Just as you saw the wheel of fortune turning from prosperity to despair so will the kingdom be destroyed by this conflict." Then he looked directly at Arthur and took him aside privately, saying: "The mortal sin that you committed must be confessed. When you slept with your sister and had Mordred know that you created a demon that did not obey God's command. I ask you now, as a Christian, to confess of this before it is too late."

It is known that, when Arthur defeated the Saxons, he went on to conquer Gaul and even defeat the Emperor Claudius. For Claudius had brought men to the kingdom of Logres to demand tribute from Arthur and he roared with laughter, demanding tribute from them in return. When Arthur demanded tribute from the Romans just as the Romans demanded tribute from him, a great battle ensued. When he sent the messengers of Rome back to the city empty handed they were very angered by it. Rome summoned the pagan powers of the East to do battle against Arthur. Arthur summoned all of the men of his kingdom. Knights from Ireland, Wales, Denmark, Gaul and other places united against Rome. In this battle Claudius was defeated decisively. The good Norman poet Wace speaks of this in great detail, so I will only briefly touch upon the subject.

# 9 ARTHUR AND THE GIANT

King Arthur had a great host of knights to combat the Romans. When the twelve arrived to deliver him the decree of Claudius there was a great feast at Camelot. Arthur had united all of the isles and many men worshiped him because of his generosity. That is why when Claudius demanded tribute the counselors told Arthur to rebuke them. So Arthur spoke gladly to them that he had a right to tribute from them more than they did him.

When Arthur brought his host together to march on Claudius it was a remarkable sight. The two great armies gathered and were spread out through the valley so that a great field, two leagues long and wide was completely filled with soldiers. The valley was completely full of pavilions. All of them with armed knights who had sworn fealty to Arthur. Men from Denmark, Scotland, Ireland, Finland, Germany and Gaul all rallied together for his sake. Since Arthur had conquered these lands and held many fiefs which he granted generously to lords of the land none would dare to oppose his sovereignty.

I won't tell of the battle, but, as mentioned before, Arthur utterly destroyed Claudius and was rightly claimed emperor, though he was never coronated for lack of a better word, for he had a most pressing matter to deal with in Britain.

However, when Arthur left Britain and ported in France to gather more men from that region. He appointed his son Mordred to be in charge of his lands, declaring to all the barons: "Do as he says, as he will rule in my stead until I return." In this way he set off with his fleet and army, arriving in port quickly after for the winds were in his favor.

Arthur was much elated that he had such a strong host of men to oppose the emperor, whose pride he would dearly pay for. Know that Arthur was truly a good Christian and that he carried on his shield the cross of Jesus Christ to protect him from all evil. He did this because his ancestors had taught him of the new law early on and that the Lord would give him strength in battle if he truly believed.

Indeed, Josephus, who first came to Briton by the very call of God, was the one to bring the holy grail to Britain, teaching those thereafter, by its miracles, that God was good to those who believed. Since then his line honored Christ through the generations. King Crudel, the wicked pagan, was destroyed utterly by King Mordred, who called upon Christ to save Josephus. When this happened, the marvel of the grail was housed in Corbenic to the delight of all the Britains.

In this way Arthur and his force made it to Brittany to a small town called Benyeoc. Arthur walked through the town and couldn't help but notice the despair of the people there. For every person there was forlorn and mourning grievously as if a great tragedy had occurred. Arthur found a beggar on the street and asked him why everyone there mourned and, the poor man sat up and replied: "Blessed be your sovereign lordship over our people for you are truly king. The town is distraught over a great tragedy. In the castle near here our lord's daughter was praised for her beauty and benevolence. Know that she made all of our hearts sing for joy as she was very sweet and generous. Not two days ago a terrible giant came to our village and kidnapped her. He was bigger than ten knights and had vicious red eyes. Wild with rage, he ran into the castle, killing many soldiers and kidnapping the lady. We have not seen her and many believe she is dead because of that cruel giant who came here."

Arthur was filled with pity by this story and also for the poor man who told it. He went to give him a gold coin but then, suddenly, the poor man vanished. He was amazed by this and then called out: "Don't give that poor man anything. For the bowl he had for begging was wrought of the finest gold and worth a fortune!" At this, the King said no more, and carried on to the hall to grieve bitterly with the Lord therein over the case of his abducted daughter.

Truly, when Arthur heard about abduction he was completely filled with grief. They went to the hall and met with the lord, who was so distraught over the circumstance that he could barely speak.

Arthur gathered his counselors and thought about the best action to take. Arthur said: "Alas, let me go after him and kill him with my own blade!" Many of the counselors tried to dissuade him from this so as not to risk his own life. Though he was adamant. "Do you have any faith? I have faith in the Lord and know that he will give me the strength to kill this giant, and it will bring courage to all the valiant knights who followed me here."

In this way Arthur went to the Lord of Benyeoc, whose name was Mardu, and told him: "It grieves me to hear of your daughter's abduction. Know that, whether she lives or is dead, I will avenge you, bringing back the very head of that beast who took her!" Mardu, who sat in the hall so downcast and sorrowful, could do very little but cry as Arthur spoke to him. He was full of grief at the thought of his daughter. Nonetheless he mustered up the courage to bid him farewell and was very honored to have the king go after her.

At first light the next day Arthur donned his armor and set off into the mountains where the giant was known to live. He brought his cupbearer Bedivue with him but refused to bring along anyone else, despite many requests and conditions.

The army waited in port and, when they heard Arthur was going to slay the giant who everyone feared in that land, they rejoiced at having such a brave leader. It was after a day of travel that Arthur arrived at the mountain where the giant lived. They found a winding steep path that led to where he slept. Know that they could see a large fire burning on the very top of the hill. Arthur kneeled before the path and prayed to God for deliverance. He crossed himself on the brow and began the ascent to the top of the hill. He bid Bedivue await his command at the bottom of the hill, coming up only if he needed the help.

When he reached the top he heard the shrieking of a woman. When he went closer he could see a beautiful maiden that was bound by her hands and feet. She was tied to iron bars before the roaring fire. It was clear that the giant was planning to place her in the fire to cook her in the flames. Arthur became sick with pity when he saw all this. Her clothes were completely rent and she had many

312

wounds. Her eyes were full of fear as she gazed at the fire helplessly. She was quite bewildered, being abducted and all that. When she saw Arthur she yelled out: "Save me from this beast who has plans to roast me tonight in the flames you see here!"

When the lady yelled out the giant heard it too clearly. He was on the other side of the mountain in his cave, picking at some animal bones as an appetizer. His footsteps sounded like thunder and he breathed heavily, being such a beast he was disgusting to look at. His teeth were few and rotted. His red eyes sank into his skull. He had no hair on him but had a massive head. He picked up a cudgel laying by the tent near the fire and, looking at the lady near the fire, licked his lips with hunger. "I'm looking forward to roasting this maiden, but first I'll have my way with her. Royal blood is very yummy; it is the baby fawn of all meats!" Arthur was not in the least bit amused by this, and he wished nothing more than to behead that foul creature so that it was dead forever.

Arthur made the sign of the cross a second time, for that was his true light and guiding force, and ran towards the giant with his sword drawn from its scabbard. The giant was surprised at the sight of a knight who was brave enough to fight him. He ran towards the king and struck him such a blow that he tumbled down the side of the hill. That cudgel was mighty and would have killed any other instantly, but Arthur held his ground.

When Arthur felt the strength of the blow he was sorely bruised but got up and ran towards him a second time. Just as the evil of sin may knock a knight down it is the only the bravest who rise again renewed and eager for battle. In this way did Arthur rise and keep from despair. The giant assailed him and hurled the cudgel over his head a second time. The force of it came crashing down but Arthur moved out of the way just in time. The cudgel smashed the ground and went several feet deep so that he had a hard time removing it from the whole it went in.

This was a perfect opportunity for Arthur, who took his steel blade and slashed at the giant, ripping upon his tendons and gut. The giant let his cudgel be and tried to tackle Arthur, but he dodged it again, this time sticking

313

his sword into the giant's stomach all the way to the hilt. The blade went through him and out the other side. The giant opened his eyes wide and let out a loud howl, he was really hurt! The giant was quite shocked for he had just received his death wound. He fell over and the blood spurted out from his wounds, creating a puddle of red. Arthur, bemused, took his blade and chopped the giant's head off.

He carried the head and the maiden down the hill, until Bedivue saw him. He was very pleased, seeing his master with his hands full. "My lord, do you need a hand?" He replied: "I may need a few, but this giant surely will be missing his body for eternity in hell." Bedivue had brought an extra horse so she mounted and all three road back to Benyeoc.

Know that Mardu was the happiest man on earth when he saw his beautiful daughter returned to him. The giant's head was attached to the sharp point of a lance head and paraded through the ranks of the army who celebrated the prowess of their king. When Claudius and his army heard this story they were struck with terror at the thought of Arthur, the giant slayer. Later, the people of Benyeoc rejoiced and had the giant's head hung in the hall for everyone to remember the honor Arthur had brought them. So ends the tale of Arthur and the giant. Know that Arthur left that place and continued on to defeat the emperor Claudius in a series of valiantly fought pitched battles.

# ABOUT THE AUTHOR

Ian Cleary graduated from Santa Clara University in 2016 with a degree in English. Since then he has enjoyed studying the Arthurian literary genre. Before graduating from college he was able to spend time abroad in Oxford, Costa Rica and Vermont. In these places he was able to develop his understanding for various cultures and develop his writing. Ian currently lives in Northern California and is attending university to receive his Masters in teaching.

53127404R00194

Made in the USA
San Bernardino, CA
06 September 2017